HAWTHORN ACADEMY

DISORDER

DISORDER

book one

KATIE LOWRIE

Author's Note

This is the second edition of Disorder.
The story itself is mainly unchanged, but nearly every sentence has
been reworked.
There are new chapters and a new timeline.

I hope you enjoy! I really have put a lot of my heart into this book.

For any content warnings you may need, please head to my website.

P.S. A quick heads up: the vocabulary, grammar, and spelling of
Disorder is written in British English.

TO THE CITY
FARMLAND
TRAIN STATION
HOSPITAL
SUPERMARKET
MARKET
THE DIVIDE
HOLLOWDALE ESTATE
HOLLOWDALE HIGH
To LAKELAND
Beurre

Hawthorn Academy
Hawthorn Hills
Cafe
Road to Prison
Police
Henrick Manor

DISORDER

noun -
a lack of order; disarray; confusion
a deviation from the normal system or order

verb -
to upset the order of; disarrange; muddle
to disturb the health or mind of

Prologue

LOOKING INTO HIS COLD EYES, I could see the true depth of his hate. Could see the contempt he felt towards me, and the disgust on his features only confirmed it.

I knew things had taken a turn for the worse.

That the boy standing across from me was no longer the one I had got to know. No longer the one I thought meant something to me.

Cold. Detached.

His eyes, normally a startling bright blue, had turned a dark indigo filled with anger and loathing.

I could see the exact moment the mist descended. The exact moment his emotions flipped.

A bone-deep shiver ran through me, and it wasn't because of the cold chill in the air.

I wasn't sure what else I could do. Where else I could run. A place where he wouldn't find me again.

Trapped. Alone.

The worst part? I'd been blind to my situation and had walked willingly to my fate.

I was the reason I was here. Every decision, every thought,

every moment had led me to the spot I was rooted to, and there was nobody else to blame.

'W-why are you doing this?'

My whisper carried. The high ceiling and the echo of the swimming pool meant he heard me clearly.

Something must have happened to have caused his change. No part of me could accept that this had been coming for longer. No part of me *would* accept it.

The slow smile spreading across his features broke my heart. Shattered it into tiny pieces that clattered to the floor, spilled for all to see.

'You don't belong here, Skylar.' He smirked. 'You never did.'

I crumbled. Tears pricked my eyes, and I tried my hardest to stop them from falling. The second a tear fell, I knew everything would become real. That he truly was looking at me like I was worthless.

I should have known better.

I should have never fallen for the beast, and I most definitely should have never thought of myself as the beauty.

Fairy tales were just that for a reason. Real life was never as satisfying, and there certainly wasn't much truth in happily ever after.

One

EVEN THE BIRDS outside knew the day was different from any other. They'd been outside my bedroom window, incessantly chirping for three hours and, fuck me, I wanted to hurt them.

My first day at Hawthorn Academy, and if I was being completely honest with myself, I was absolutely bricking it. My stomach formed into knots from the moment I woke up and still hadn't untangled itself.

Being a loner, I'd always been, well, alone. I found friends overrated. Or maybe just the idea of friends. But I wasn't always like that. Growing up, I had a couple of friends who lived on the same estate as me. We were mostly friends because we had circumstances in common, rather than personality things. One of the girls, Remi, was a few years younger than me but always acted older, so we never noticed the age difference. Well, until she started befriending the popular girls at school, but that was a whole other story.

The town of Beurre was divided into a rich side and a poor side. Two guesses as to what side I belonged to.

The Hollowdale estate where I lived was where those with less money resided. And most of the time, it didn't bother me.

Some people weren't born into money, and that was just how it went. No point in being bitter about it. It was how it was, and I could either fight against it or let it defeat me.

Already, in my sixteen short years of living, I'd found out that in this life all I could rely upon was myself.

God, even my family was a total waste of space. Well, I say family, but really it was just my mum, Cora. I didn't know my dad. He disappeared when I was young. At first, I wished he'd show up on the doorstep and whisk me away to his palace, but he never did. Not that he had a palace. Or maybe he did. Not like I'd know. Whenever I asked about him, Mum would clam up. Which, if you knew my mum, that was the complete opposite of her usual M.O.

'Skylar! Skylar! Get down here at once!' Mum shouted from the kitchen and if I didn't make an appearance downstairs within minutes, she'd send Andy up to get me. Something I definitely didn't want to happen.

Andy was my mum's new, totally useless, husband. He had no job, no money, and absolutely no manners. From the moment I first met him, he gave me an icky feeling. He'd never outright been inappropriate with me, but some of his lewd comments and the way he looked at me made me super uncomfortable. My skin crawled at the way he perused me from head to toe, his beady eyes bugging out of his skull.

'I'll be down in a minute, Mum. Just getting dressed,' I hollered back, hoping she'd hear me and give me a moment. I wouldn't put it past her or Andy to disrespect my privacy and just barge into my bedroom without invitation if given the chance. Mum was always bursting into my bubble without permission, but so far Andy hadn't actually stepped across the threshold of my bedroom. Sometimes, though, I could sense his presence outside my closed door while I changed. A shadow lingering underneath the doorframe. A creak of the floorboards.

I rushed around my room and threw on a vest top and joggers at lightning speed and hot-footed it down the stairs as fast as I could. It was my final day with them, and I wasn't risking shit.

With my head down, I turned the corner into the kitchen without looking where I was going. Stupid of me really, because I nearly walked straight into Andy's chest.

'Shit, sorry!' I said, looking up to see his crooked brown teeth lurking above me, a wicked smile set on his features.

Goosebumps covered my entire body in seconds, and yet, I couldn't look away from his searing gaze. I gulped, willing my reaction to his closeness to go unnoticed. It would only give him a thrill if he knew how uncomfortable he made me, and I refused to give him that satisfaction.

'You should watch where you're going, Sky. You never know who could be around the next corner,' Andy said with a wink. As if he hadn't just lingered in my personal space for longer than needed, he turned around and walked further into the kitchen to sit by my mum, almost making me believe I'd imagined the entire thing.

'Oh, there you are, Skylar! Did you get the shopping I wanted?' Mum asked, her tone one of exasperation.

My eyes went to where she was sitting and I repressed a laugh at her appearance. No point antagonising her over breakfast.

Cora looked old and haggard. Her blonde hair resembled straw, coarse and dry, and it looked to me like she'd taken her makeup tips from the local clown, Bingo, who performed at all the kids' parties. Or I assumed he did. I'd never been lucky enough to have one, and it wasn't like I got invited to many parties growing up. I only knew him because he lived around the corner, offering out pencils instead of candy when the local kids went trick or treating.

Honestly, Mum had looked that way for years. Tired and old. Even though she was only in her thirties.

I tried to find it in myself to have love for her, but I struggled. It always made me feel super shitty, though, as everybody should love their mum, right? It made me wonder if there was something wrong with me, if it was all my fault we never developed a bond. But then I remembered she was a huge narcissist, so that probably had something to do with it.

'Course I did,' I replied with a sigh. 'I put it in the hallway last night when I got home.' I gestured towards the hall, where the carrier bags were in the exact same place I left them the night before. The bags she would've walked past to get to the kitchen and actively chose to ignore.

During the summer holidays, I worked in the local supermarket, so most nights Mum would send me a long list of items she needed me to get for her so I could use my staff discount to make it cheaper. Not that it mattered to her how much the shopping cost, seeing as she had never once paid me for anything I had brought for her.

'Cheers, love. Remind me again why you can't shop for us anymore?' she asked, her over-plucked eyebrow rising slowly. Every time she asked me a question, it was with a tone of disbelief. Like I was going out of my way to be awkward on purpose.

'I've told you so many times, Mum. I'm starting at Hawthorn Academy today. The big elite boarding school on the hill. We definitely spoke about it...' I tapered off mid-sentence when I noticed that neither Mum nor Andy was paying me any attention. The two of them were staring at her phone, probably at some crappy selling page post that was selling a used sofa for pennies. A sofa so cheap because really it belonged in the nearest skip.

'Yeah, yeah, Sky. I remember,' she said, but when she looked up from her phone, her face told me otherwise. Honestly, the woman was constantly attached to that thing like it was another limb. Around a year ago she was adamant that she'd never trade in her trusty Nokia as she "couldn't handle technology like that." Then Andy came along, and voilá, the woman had a brand-new shiny toy she loved more than she loved me.

'What did I even just say, Mum?' I sighed, knowing I'd lost them both. Not that I really had them to begin with. Although sometimes in my head I fooled myself that I was important to her. Being her only child and all.

'School on the hill, Sky. Honestly, I'm just trying to watch this video Leslie sent me and you keep ruining it.'

So, yeah, there she is, ladies and gentlemen. The woman who birthed me.

Leslie was her best friend and just as boring and desperate as her. A match made in heaven if you asked me. The two of them were in constant contact. Pretty sure they even told each other when they were going to the toilet, they were just that close.

'Well, guess I'll be going upstairs to get ready and check my packing.' I looked around the kitchen of the house I'd lived in my whole life, and I knew I wouldn't miss it one bit. The memories weren't exactly horrific or anything, but they weren't particularly stellar either. It was just another place I hated. Another place I was more than ready to escape from.

Mum wasn't abusive. She never laid a finger on me or even threatened to. But she didn't care about me. Not one bit. And as fucked up as it sounded, I couldn't decide what I thought was worse. Because at least if she raised her voice at me, she cared a small iota, right?

I'd always been at the bottom of her list of things to give a shit about. Even our menagerie of pets had always come before me, including the time we had two ferrets named Bert and Ernie. Even when Ernie had nearly bit her finger off, she cooed at him and told him she forgave him.

She hadn't yet forgiven me for the time I ate the last chocolate bar ten years ago.

I was used to it.

I got up from the table, and I could feel Andy's beady gaze regarding me, a thoughtful expression on his face, and I could tell that whatever he was thinking about hurt. I wished I knew the thoughts running through his mind and why he seemed to be aiming them at me.

The fact the man was thinking that hard, in my direction no less, was a major red flag. My mind screamed *"DANGER!"* Yeah, he'd always been a creep, but I'd never felt scared of him before.

But like all moments, the moment passed, and I was left wondering whether I'd imagined it entirely.

BY LUNCHTIME, I was changed into something a little more presentable, counting down the minutes until the car arrived. I'd checked and triple-checked my packing and the list of items the Academy required me to bring. Actually, I'd been checking every day for the last two weeks. Nothing could mess up my opportunity, and I didn't want to arrive and realise I'd forgotten something important.

When I received the letter of acceptance, I was a little startled at first. It arrived at the beginning of the summer break, with no postmark. The letter itself was strange, to put it mildly, and even though it had been over a month since I'd received it, I still reread it every now and again to make sure I wasn't reading it wrong. Not that I could read it wrong, but more in the sense that I may have got the intention wrong.

Dear Miss Skylar Crescent,

It is my pleasure to inform you that you are the recipient of Hawthorn Academy's newly established annual scholarship fund for the next two years. There were many worthy candidates, but after looking through your application thoroughly, we believe you are a perfect fit for our fine establishment.

Enclosed is a list of items you will need to bring and a list of those the Academy will provide.

We look forward to seeing you on the first day of term, September 4th, and hope you are pleased about this news.

Yours sincerely,
Ms Winifred Hawthorn, Headmistress

The list of items I had to provide contained obvious items you'd expect to find on a boarding school list, such as toiletries. Then there were some that were a tad more unusual. For example, new lingerie with tags still attached, in one of the school colours. Seeing as the main school colour was a dark bottle green, it was pretty hard to do. Only the fanciest boutique in town had what I was looking for, and I only managed to save up enough the week before. The money I made working wasn't enough to buy expensive, luxury shit. It was barely enough to buy non-expensive shit. Before, my small underwear collection came from the local supermarket. I wasn't sure I wanted to know why my lingerie was of importance to them. I had tried to do some research into the scholarship and the school itself, but my online searches yielded little result. It was like the school was one big secret. All I could find was your generic bullshit about the school, its benefactors, and famous alumni. As if that was enough for anybody to go on.

The whole scenario was strange as fuck because I didn't recall even applying for a scholarship at Hawthorn Academy. When I emailed Ms Hawthorn to ensure that I was the correct recipient, I received a very curt email response that made it clear how stupid she found my enquiry to be. According to her, the name and address being correct on the invitation was confirmation enough it had gone to the correct person. Which made sense to a degree. They knew my full name and address, after all. The scholarship was "newly established," so maybe a teacher at Hollowdale put me forward for it without me knowing.

Guess the scholarship being new explained why I couldn't find much information online about it. Plus, I was so desperate to leave this place that I saw it as a blessing. One of those divine intervention moments where your life changed all because of one letter. One moment in time. One person. Even if I should look more into it, I knew I wasn't going to. The hope the scholarship provided me was enough for me to overlook all the weird shit attached to it.

The list of items the school was providing contained the usual suspects, like pens, paper, that kind of thing, and ones I found very hard to believe. They were providing the school uniform itself, which was fair as uniforms could be pricey, especially ones with fancy blazers. The school was providing me with a laptop and a mobile phone to access the school internet system and complete my assignments. The website didn't have any pricing listed, but from the list of school provided items, I knew it must be a fortune.

Then there was the downright bizarre. The school would provide health check-ups and any protection deemed necessary. What the fuck did that even mean? And why was it of importance to the academy? Then again, rich people had never made much sense to me.

Reading the list once more as I paced my room, I paused when a large thud sounded outside in the hallway. My stomach dropped, and dread filled my gut. I tried to ignore it and continued to read, but there was a feeling gnawing at me. Something telling me that the sound was something to worry about. My bedroom door pushed open, the creak it always made giving it away, and I turned around to find Andy standing at the edge of the threshold, smirking at me.

'Off to your fancy school today, ain't ya?' he asked, his words slurred. The smell of stale beer instantly surrounded me, entered my nose, and clung to my skin. Just one of the many things I looked forward to not having to deal with at Hawthorn.

'Yeah...' I tailed off as he took a step closer to me, entering my personal bubble. I stumbled backwards, the backs of my legs hitting the side of my bed, while trying to smile as if nothing was wrong.

'Guess I won't be eyeing up your young, curvy body for much longer. Pity. You really are quite stunning when you try, Skylar.'

I held back a gag, not wanting to give him the satisfaction. Knowing Andy, he probably thought of his words as a compliment, as something I should be thankful for.

He took another step towards me until he was close enough for me to see the broken capillaries on his nose. All red and irritated, his problem with alcohol on full display for anybody to see.

On his final step, he stumbled and fell forwards. Or at least at first I thought that was what had happened, but when he grabbed me and pulled me tight against him, I knew the stumble was filled with purpose.

His body pressed flush up against mine, the hardness in his joggers causing vomit to rise in my mouth. My heart, and my head, knew this was what he intended to do when he entered my room. A last-ditch attempt to grab me before I left. All those looks over the years culminating in that moment.

His closeness suffocated me. My heart started to beat so fast, I thought it would become visible through my clothes. Fear and anxiety mixed together to create a crescendo of beats.

'M-my mum will wonder where you are,' I said, my stutter showing my surprise. It was rare my stutter came out anymore, especially at home. When I was younger, it was a lot worse, but once my nursery helped with arranging therapy, things had improved. It still lingered under the surface, never fully gone, only showing itself in times of fear or when I was overly anxious. Overthinking too much about everything.

I didn't even attempt to pull the *"I'll tell Mum"* card with Andy as I knew she wouldn't listen anyway. Or even care. She'd believe him over me any day of the week. She always did.

'Oh, but, Sky, that's where you're wrong,' Andy said, confirming my thoughts. 'I told your mum I was coming up here to talk to ya. You're going to meet a load of fancy wankers at this fancy school, so I told her I'd warn you about them. She doesn't suspect a thing.' The slur of his words made his cockney accent thicker than usual, and it made my skin crawl all the more.

He was telling the truth, too. I could see it in his evil, brown eyes. He'd obviously seen his opportunity and pounced on it, knowing I would leave and wouldn't tell anyone about it.

The smell of stale alcohol lingering on his breath invaded my senses. Revolting, rotting, and putrid. Just like him. His face loomed closer to mine, his eyes making his intentions clear. I tried to turn my face, to look away or shout out, but his hands clamped to my cheeks, keeping my face in place. He kissed me, shoving his tongue deep in my mouth and moving it around violently with no mercy. His tongue slithered around, slimy against mine, and I could taste the beer he'd consumed all morning. Without thinking, I raised my knee into his crotch, causing him to stumble backwards, losing his balance. It felt empowering to hurt him, even if only a little.

The knee to the balls seemed to bring Andy to his senses, grimacing through the pain. He shook his head at me in disappointment.

'You'll pay for that, Skylar, just you wait,' he spat ominously and stormed out of my room.

All I could do was stand still in shock, thinking of all the ways I could rake my tongue to get him off of me. To get the lingering taste of stale beer out of my mouth and out of my brain, forever.

THE LONG, sleek, *expensive* black car arrived at noon.

The driver, a tall, dark-haired man with dark sunglasses on, even though it wasn't overly sunny, handed me a Non-Disclosure Agreement the moment I opened the front door. No greeting. No how do you do? Just a piece of paper thrust into my hands with a fancy-looking fountain pen.

'Er,' I said, looking down at the paper in my hands. 'Thanks?'

'Sign the form please, miss.'

'Okay...' I trailed off before joking, 'I'm not signing my life away, am I?'

'If you could please sign the form please, miss, then we can be on our way.'

'Okay, sure. But *why* am I signing the form?'

'I'm not at liberty to say more until you sign the form.'

I rolled my eyes and read the agreement as thoroughly as I could in the short time I had, then signed on the dotted line.

Pretty sure I hadn't just signed over my firstborn.

Well, fifty percent sure at least.

'Thank you,' he said, taking back the pen and signed form. 'The car is ready for you, Miss Crescent. I'm able to answer any questions you may have on the journey, but I must insist that we leave right this instant.' His voice was a low, tense tone that brooked no argument. I beamed at him, hoping he'd soften at my winning smile, but I barely got a lip twitch back. *Tough crowd.*

'Do I have time to say goodbye to my family?' I asked. The words came out very reluctant. I knew I *should* go and say goodbye to Mum and Andy, even if it mattered to neither of them. If anything, I wanted to make my leaving official.

See you later, wankers. And all that jazz.

'Be quick please, miss. We're on a tight schedule and must

be at the Academy for the welcome briefing from Ms Hawthorn at two.'

I nodded at the driver and dashed to the kitchen where I once again found my mum and Andy looking at something fascinating on her phone. Andy acted like what happened upstairs hadn't taken place, and trust me, I wouldn't be the one to remind him.

'The car's here,' I told them. 'I don't know when I'll be home next.'

'That's lovely, sweetheart. Have fun,' Mum said, still looking down at her phone. The only discernible movement came from her hand, which moved quickly, in something that sort of resembled a wave. And I use the term sort of loosely.

You wouldn't have known that her only child was leaving, would you?

Oh fuck it, why did I even bother anymore?

I knew why, though, even if I didn't want to admit it. There was a small part, buried deep down inside of me, that still wished to be loved by its mother. Still wanted to feel wanted. Loved.

And I hated that part of me. That weakness.

I stormed back to the front door, angered at myself for letting my mother's shitty actions affect me again. Taking in a deep breath, I filled my lungs with the cool, fresh September air, and made my way towards the fancy car idling on the street. Towards my new life.

Once inside, the driver handed me an information pack.

'You should have a good read of that, miss,' he mumbled, turning back to the front and arranging his rear-view mirror. 'Tells you all you need to know. I'll answer your questions if I can.'

'Th-thanks.'

Flipping through the pack, nothing looked too out of the ordinary. At first glance, I saw a map of the school and my class schedule. You know. Normal introductory school things. But as I kept flicking through, the last few pages made me pause. It was a social calendar of sorts, with galas and parties listed. But it wasn't on an official school letterhead. It looked haphazard and hastily drawn up. I wondered how it had got in my pack.

I'd never been one to socialise often. It wasn't like I'd attended many parties, and galas in general sounded intimidating to me. My whole life I'd suffered from terrible anxiety. I struggled to even make phone calls to takeaways on the odd occasion I could afford one.

Finally, the car moved away from the only home I'd ever known. I had to remind myself to breathe. In through the nose, out through the mouth. Or wait, was it the other way around?

As I watched my childhood home fade away out of the back window, I smiled. Onwards and upwards to a better life.

Two

HAWTHORN ACADEMY LOOMED at the top of the hill in the wealthy area of town aptly named Hawthorn Hills. It had always seemed elusive to me. I never thought I'd have the chance to find out what happened at the top, but apparently somebody else had a different plan for me.

The car ascended at a snail's speed, so slow that I hyper-ventilated. Well, maybe that was a bit dramatic. My breathing increased, and my skin prickled with sweat.

The more I worried, the more my anxiety grew as we got closer to the top. Like a thick fog, ready to cloud my vision and leave me sightless.

The nerves overtook me so much that I couldn't even form questions for the driver. When I got in the car, I had so many swirling around in my brain, yet the moment I got inside, they all disappeared. Ran away from me and deserted me in my time of need.

As the car slowly travelled up, block-shaped buildings came into view on the right-hand side of the road and when I looked out the other window, large sports fields were directly in front of me. Being somebody who detested sports, I didn't know much about the school's athletic accolades. Hollowdale, my old school, prided itself on being a sports college. Which translated to a lot of sports, even if you didn't want to take part. I hoped it was different here.

In the far background, there was a long line of trees as far as the eye could see. They moved with the wind, swaying to and fro in a unified frenzy. Red berries covered them, creating an eerie view as they swayed in the wind. The branches seemingly taking on a life of their own. They were pretty, too, in their own way. But mostly eerie.

Questions began to form in my mind the further up the hill we went. Questions I couldn't exactly ask the driver, even if my tongue wanted to speak. Things like: What if I made no friends? Or what if I couldn't keep up academically? Some of the kids would've attended since they were eleven, not to forget that they were very rich, and I had no doubt they had the best private tutors if they were struggling. For all I knew, they could be fluent in frigging Latin!

And I supposed if they were, they'd understand the school motto without having to look it up on an internet search the way I had.

Yep. The school had a motto. A motto that loomed above the car on a sign upon entering the Academy grounds. An idea I always thought was lifted from a movie or a gothic text.

Large and sinister. Welcoming me.

Warning me.

Audentes fortuna iuvat.
Dulce periculum.

Literally translated to English:

Fortune favours the bold.
Danger is sweet.

So yep, that was that.

AFTER THE CAR finally pulled up to the front of the main building, I realised just how big the school really was. Even what I'd seen from the car didn't fully convey the sheer size of the place. How many buildings there really were.

I had always known it was large, but it turned out that what you could see from the bottom of the hill was only the tip of the iceberg. The hill, and the many trees, had hidden so much. I wondered just what else was being hidden in plain sight. Hidden from the town below.

On the front of the main building, a stone gargoyle sat above each corner of the large dark wooden double doors. A shiver ran down my spine at the gothic vibe I got from the building. It was all little turrets and spikes, gargoyles and stained-glass windows. Very picturesque. Very creepy.

The gargoyles' beady eyes looked down on all who entered. Shit, even their sheer presence was menacing and foreboding. A chill crept up my spine, the cold seeping into my bones. *Think happy thoughts. Think happy thoughts.*

Ha. Listen to me. I sounded like a badly written gothic novel. Nothing worse than sounding like *Wuthering Heights*. And trust me, I never wanted to sound like that shit show. It happened to be my least favourite of the classics and that was saying something. Give me *The Old Curiosity Shop* any day.

'We're here, miss,' the driver said, turning around in his seat to look me in the eye. My spider sense was telling me there was so much he wished he could say to me but wouldn't dare to. Or couldn't. Or maybe he merely didn't know where to start because I'd sat in the back of the car acting like a fucking mute even after he told me he'd answer what he could if I asked.

'Thank you. Do I need to grab my bags or...?' I trailed off, uncertain and insecure. It was one of the things I hated most about myself. My inner voice could be strong and feisty; my actual voice, not so much.

'I'll take them and somebody will deliver them to your room after inspection,' he said with a broad smile. He got out of the car and came to open my door for me, giving me my first taste of what it must feel like to have money. Or how I assumed it would feel. Did chauffeurs actually exist outside of fiction?

Taking a giant step, both physically and mentally, I got out of the car. The fresh, brisk September air outside hit me right in the face and I nearly stumbled at the sheer force of it. Great. If I didn't die of embarrassment through existing, maybe I would when I fell over in front of everybody due to the *wind*.

Righting myself to get my balance back, I rubbed my hands down the front of the pinafore dress I chose to wear. It was the nicest thing in my closet, and even though it was thrifted, you couldn't tell.

The main building in front of me beckoned, and I walked towards it, sensing that was where I should go next. A group of four bleached-blonde girls nearby in my peripheral clustered together in a pack. All talking at once, giggling really, and all looking at me. Self-doubt hit me, and shame rose in my cheeks, colouring them in an instant. Their actions, and my reaction to those actions, instantly pissed me off. Why was I letting them get to me already? They had no idea about me, and I knew nothing of them, either.

The only thing I could determine was that they were a similar height and build to each other. You know the "popular" type: slim and petite.

Must be about my age, too.

Wonderful.

Every Academy story I'd read had a grand staircase leading into the school where, usually, the female main character would glance up and see a group of scary, hot guys giving her an ominous look from the top.

I noticed the stairs, but there were no hot guys staring down at me from the top.

Go figure.

No, instead when I looked up, all I could see was a stern-looking woman impatiently waiting for somebody. Pretty sure that *somebody* was me.

I made my way towards her, trying to keep calm and act as if I wasn't about to shit myself any moment. I wasn't wearing a watch, but it hadn't been long since I arrived, so I wasn't quite late yet. I hoped.

'Hello, I'm Skylar Crescent,' I said, holding out my hand to her. I knew instantly that she wouldn't take it, though. A look of impatience mingled with disgust twisted her features, reminding me of a fairy-tale hag of sorts.

'Yes, hello there, Miss Crescent. I'm Ms Hawthorn. Headmistress here at Hawthorn Academy,' she said, her nose upturned and her voice serious.

Everything about this woman was grey. Her eyes, her hair —even the colour of her skin. Maybe she didn't get out much.

'I'm here to welcome you to our fine institution. You are the only recipient of the scholarship fund this year. There is one other recipient of the fund in the year above, who will be along shortly to give you the tour.' The irritation emanated off her in waves, and I swallowed, choosing not to speak and annoying her more.

I smiled, hoping she'd notice and not think I was some uncouth heathen. The look she gave me back told me that my smile wasn't helping matters. If anything, it was making it worse.

'Here she comes now,' Ms Hawthorn said, focused on something over to my left. 'I'm sure you and Miss Luck will get along just fine.'

Just fine didn't exactly sound like a ringing endorsement, did it?

Then she turned around and walked away without so much as a "goodbye." Leaving me there, alone, as I awaited the arrival of somebody called Miss Luck. What were the odds that she lived up to her name and was a lucky person?

As the girl got closer, she wriggled her fingers, and I warmed towards her in an instant. The first thing I noticed about her was her long, dark auburn hair as it swished back and forth in the wind as she walked. At five-foot-five, I'd always been the same height as most other girls my age, but I could already tell that with her, I'd feel like a giant. An inviting enough smile with straight, shiny teeth—too perfect, almost. Little laugh lines lived on either side of her mouth. She was curvy in all the right places and it suited her. I bet she got a lot of attention from the boys here.

'Hey! You must be Skylar, right?' she asked, looking closely at my face, taking it all in. I nodded in response, too nervous to talk just yet. She smiled and said, 'I'm Clover. Yes, I am aware of just how wank my name is. My parents apparently decided from birth that I deserved to be ridiculed.'

She rolled her eyes, and I wasn't sure how to respond. Did I laugh and agree? Did I nod my head, hoping that was the correct response?

'... what do you think?' She watched me expectantly, yet I had no clue how the question started. I'd been off in my own world as usual. I stared blankly back. Way to look like a brain-dead zombie.

Great first impression, Sky.

'I am so s-sorry. I sort of spaced out back there. W-what do I think about what?' I asked, nerves jumbling around in my stomach so bad, I thought I might vomit on the spot. My stutter had started already and I could feel the blush rising on my cheeks. I knew how much I judged people on first impressions, and I felt like I'd messed this one up for myself completely.

'No problem.' Clover laughed and my anxiety wondered whether she was laughing with me, or *at* me. Who fucking knew? 'I was asking if you wanted to see your room first or the rest of the school?'

'I'd love the tour, thank you,' I said quietly. We made eye contact and smiled, the warm feeling returning to my gut. I didn't want to be one of those girls who automatically believed they'd found a new best friend due to a shared look and circumstance, but I thought that maybe I could become friends with the girl. Not straight away, but sometime in the future at least.

'THAT'S THE POOL BUILDING, but I'd avoid going there unless totally necessary,' Clover told me, pointing at a large red brick building on our left. It didn't look like any pool building I'd ever seen. It wasn't sleek and modern like the one at my old school. It was old-fashioned, and the colour made it seem out of place, but the architecture was in line with the rest of the buildings.

So far, Clover had shown me the buildings that held the classrooms and inside the large main building where the cafeteria and admin offices were. Not that I would call it a cafeteria. It was more like a fancy dining room than anything else.

The school was a lot bigger than I expected, and, even armed with my map, I knew I was going to get terribly lost. Ever since I was young and went on a camping field trip with the school, I'd known I had an awful sense of direction. God forbid if somebody ever handed me a compass and a direction to head in because I would never find my way.

'Why should I avoid the pool?' I asked, the curiosity getting the better of me. It was the first time she'd commented on a building and, call me intrigued, I needed to know why.

'Oh, well, that's where...' Clover stopped herself mid-sentence and scoffed. 'Talk of the devils.'

I turned my head to look in the same direction as her and nearly swallowed my tongue. Three guys were exiting the pool building together, and I shit you not, they looked like gods among men. They were unlike any other teenager I'd ever seen before. Each of them had wet hair and looked good enough to devour. I had to stop myself from drooling on the spot. The three of them were beyond gorgeous. All tall, tanned, and as rugged as a teenage boy could be.

'W-who are they?' I asked, my stutter rearing its ugly head. But I couldn't help it. The sheer sight of them had caught me off guard. Had caused my heart rate to spike and my body to break out into all over shivers.

'The one with blonde hair and blue eyes is Leo Hawthorn, the oldest of the three, and trust me, he likes to wield the fact that he's a Hawthorn like a weapon. He's in my year.'

She sighed, rolling her eyes, and I thought that maybe there was more to it. I stayed silent, waiting for her to continue, but she stopped talking about him and moved on to the guy standing beside him.

'The one with red hair and a cheeky grin is Griffin, but everybody calls him Griff. He's in your year. I'd be careful with that one if I were you.'

I nodded absentmindedly. Obviously, I was wondering why I should be careful with Griff, but then he caught my eye and focused his cheeky grin in my direction. I had to stop my mouth from opening of its own accord. He winked, and I averted my gaze fast. *Be careful with that one.*

'Last but not least is Oliver Brandon—only call him Ollie if he tells you to, and even then, I probably still wouldn't. He's also in your year and is one of the most sought-after bachelors at this school.' She fake gagged, and if I wasn't sure about there being history between her and those three, then her gesture had all but confirmed it. 'Be careful you don't end up in his eye line. All the girls here would fight for even a speck of his attention. Believe me, you'd do best to stay away from all three of them.'

Clover's eyes locked with mine and somehow managed to convey every emotion at once. Like I could see into her soul and know the seriousness of her words. It was overwhelming, to say the least.

Oliver was by far the hottest guy of the three. My ovaries were screaming just looking at him. He had that whole chiselled jaw thing going on. You know, imagine the character Charles Brandon in the early seasons of *The Tudors*. That was who Oliver reminded me of. He also had something that was uniquely his own, though. Something I couldn't quite put my finger on. He noticed Griff looking over in our direction and turned his head to see what the fuss was about.

Our gazes collided. I gasped at the sheer intensity of it. Like Leo, he had blue eyes, but his hair was the colour of hazelnut. That perfect shade of light brown that looked good enough to eat.

Jesus, Sky, get a grip.

'Is that a bad thing then?' I asked. Clover looked at me perplexed and I added, 'The fact that the other girls want him?' I felt so naïve. At my previous school, I minded my business. I had never needed to know the inner workings of a group of girls before or how they operated.

'Oh, honey. It's a very, very bad thing.' Clover looked at me with sympathetic eyes. I noticed that they were the same shade of green as our uniform, but I didn't want to compliment her on how unique they were in case she thought I was being mean. She'd been nice to me for the few hours I'd known her, and I *definitely* did not want to screw up what could become my first friendship at my new school.

At that moment, I could have sworn that the air around us began to change, and no, it wasn't because the wind had picked up. Well, the wind *had* picked up, but that wasn't why.

No.

It was all because the boys were heading towards us.

Shit.

Clover stood next to me, staring at them as they got closer, then rolled her eyes, her irritation at their existence clear.

I froze. What was I meant to do? Was I even meant to do anything at all?

Should I introduce myself? Stay silent?

Too many variables ran through my head and I could feel the slow simmering burn of a panic attack building. Wires were short-circuiting up there, frazzling. My anxiety always got worse around new people and new situations, and no matter how much I prepped myself during the summer, that feeling hadn't gone away. Black slowly crept in around the edges of what I saw, my vision a pinprick, still fixated on the three boys coming closer. My breathing was so fast, yet I wasn't taking any air into my lungs. The tightness hurt.

My sight cleared to all three of them standing in front of me. Tall, imposing, and dramatic.

Griff glanced at me, his gaze amused, yet assessing. Leo, the rather gorgeous blond one, looked bored by the whole situation. But it was Oliver I focused on. He looked at me with pity shining in his blue eyes, his lips curved up at the edges in a sympathetic smile. Or was it sinister?

I hated not being able to read people that well. It was

something I always struggled with. If somebody had a good poker face, then I would never win in life.

'Everything okay here?' Oliver asked, looking at Clover, but we all knew he was talking to me. Or maybe *about* me.

'Sure is. This is the new girl, Skylar. Sky, I already told you who these three are. If you know what's good for you, you'll take whatever they say with a pinch of salt.'

'No need to be like that, Clo. We're all friends here. An introduction is the proper way.' He turned to me with a grin wide on his face. 'I'm Griffin. Call me Griff.'

'Hello,' I mumbled, a small smile playing on my lips at his cheery attitude.

'Don't be fooled by that smile, Sky,' Clover warned, crossing her arms on her chest.

'I'm sure Sky can make up her own mind, can't you?' Griff asked, looking at me. He smiled wide again, and I realised the grin must be his trademark look. He definitely had to know how endearing it was. All straight white teeth and dimples.

'I g-guess,' I said. My breathing sounded like I'd been in a boxing ring for all twelve rounds. That, along with my stutter, I was certain I was making a fool of myself.

'Oh cute, did you hear that, Ollie? She stutters,' Leo said, looking around himself as if he would rather be anywhere else. His tone was filled with derision and clearly he was over the entire situation and wanted it to be finished as soon as possible. He made no eye contact with either me or Clover, preferring to look at the group of four girls who'd laughed at me earlier in the day.

'So she does,' Oliver said, his voice like honey. Sticky and sweet. 'Sky, was it? Nice to meet you. Welcome to Hawthorn Academy. Clover here will make the school rules clear for you, I'm sure. Wouldn't want you to forget any now, would we?'

Oliver smirked in Clo's direction, and something private passed between them. Something I wasn't yet privy to. Maybe never would be.

'Come on, lads,' Oliver said, elbowing Griff in the ribs. 'Let's leave the girls to it.'

The three of them turned and walked away in unison. No more words said. A well-oiled machine, practised and polished to perfection.

I looked at Clover, and her face had gone as red as her hair.

'Those boys will be the death of me, I swear it. Every time I'm near them, I just get so blood-boiling mad! Don't listen to them, seriously. The three of them think they rule this school because their families are rich.'

I laughed. Clover seemed genuine, and I hoped I hadn't blown it by acting a little tongue-tied when the boys came over. Making a friend at Hawthorn was vital if I was going to survive. I'd never been around this many rich kids before, and I hadn't grown up with money. I assumed that if Clover was here on scholarship too, then she understood how I felt. Overwhelmed.

It had only been half a day, and already I needed to process a lot.

'What did they mean by rules?' I asked as Clover led us towards another building.

'Oh, didn't you read through your welcome pack? Duh'— she hit her head playfully—'of course you didn't! Let's go to our room and I'll tell you all about it. I can show you the Hive too. To be honest, it's probably best we talk about all this in private anyway.' Clover's words and tone were light as a feather, but I could feel the heaviness of her statement living beneath the surface.

'Our room?' I asked. It was the part of her sentence that I'd homed in on, happy to hear that I wouldn't be living alone in a strange place.

'Yeah. As the only two scholarship students here, we're sharing a room as our funds only cover the basic necessities or some kind of crap like that. Didn't really listen, to be honest.'

'My letter said that the scholarship fund was newly established?' I asked. 'But you're clearly not new this year?'

'What makes you say that?'

'You seem super familiar with everyone,' I pointed out. 'You knew the guys and that.'

'Oh, well, yeah. I started last year.' She pouted her lips and looked away before returning her face to mine with a large smile. 'Got to know the douchebags pretty quick.'

'Fair,' I said, her explanation making sense. Even if she started last year, that was still pretty new for an establishment that had been around for over one hundred years. 'I'm glad we get to share a room. I was worried I'd be alone and isolate myself away.'

'I'm sure you'll be thankful we're sharing in due course.'

Clover's cryptic answer did nothing for my anxiety, but I attempted a smile, anyway.

Pretty sure it came out as more of a grimace.

Three

OUR ROOM WAS LARGER than my one at home, that was for sure. It may even be bigger than the living room, too.

Most likely one of the largest rooms I'd ever been in, to tell the truth.

It made me wonder how large the other rooms were, and just how expensive they were, if Clover and I needed to share due to budgeting.

On each side of the room, there was a double bed pushed up against the wall, with some space in between for a rug and some bedside cabinets. It was obvious which side of the room belonged to Clover as she had covered the pinboards with pictures and newspaper cuttings. One of the pictures was of Clover and two people I assumed were her parents. They had the same hair colour as her. Plus, their eyes were the same unusual green hue.

'Do your parents miss you?' I asked, pointing at the photograph.

Clover's smile faded and soured.

'They hate that I'm here,' she admitted, twisting a strand of hair around her finger. 'But they also know it's for the best.'

She shrugged and I said no more. I may not always be able to read facial expressions, but I also liked to think I knew when to stop talking.

My eyes went back to taking in everything in the room. There was a little kitchenette in a small space in front of my bed and an en-suite bathroom to the right of the kitchen area. It was more than I hoped for. In my head, I had some awful visions of having to share a bathroom with every girl on the floor and having my clothes stolen—or worse.

The light cream colour of the walls went perfectly with the black furnishings dotted around the room. I loved it. It resembled how I always wanted my bedroom at home to look but never quite achieved. Happiness filled me. I would be living here for the next two years. It was a whole lot better than I imagined it would be. Lying in bed at night, thinking of the academy, I always found it hard to envision it. Whenever I thought about how things would go, it had taken on a mythical quality in my mind. Dreamlike and hazy.

Clover flopped down on her bed and sighed extra loud. If the walls were thin between our room and the one next to it, they definitely heard her. Our room was the last one at the end of a corridor, so the bathroom wall was joined to another one, and I supposed the wall behind the built-in wardrobe that took up the wall space at the end of Clo's bed.

I wanted to ask why she'd sighed so deep, but I felt self-conscious about it. I kicked myself for feeling that way. It was stupid, really. At no point during our tour did she give me the impression she'd be judgemental like that, but guess there was no way to know for sure. Like a fish out of water, I hovered. I didn't know the rules and I felt completely out of my comfort zone.

Luckily for me, Clover broke the silence first.

'You can call me Clo, by the way. I know it sounded super shitty and sarcastic coming from Griff, but that's the nickname I answer to.'

I nodded, thankful she'd told me, because I was already thinking of her as Clo in my head, anyway.

'It's the only nickname I can get away with, really. Nobody wants Ver to be their nickname, I can tell you that. The bitches always shortened it to Over, which was highly original as you can imagine.'

Her tone of voice and her open face really were comforting and a smile broke out across my face. Feeling welcomed here in such a short period of time was more than I could've hoped for. Warmth spread through me and my feet were grounded to the floor, settled and ready to tackle the journey ahead.

'Over,' I said with a laugh. It always amused me the wit of kids and bitches. 'Back at your old school?'

'Right. My old school...' Clover's eyes shifted around the room, no longer looking at me or trying to catch my eye. 'And here, too. Guess it's not that original after all.'

I nodded. Lucky for me, my name couldn't be shortened to anything like that. And shortening it to Sky wasn't exactly going to win them points in the bullying stakes. Not that I'd been bullied at Hollowdale. Just... ignored.

'I need to fill you in on some things, Sky. Things here at Hawthorn, I mean. The girls who go here are twats nearly all the time. Leo and I were friendly when we were younger, and the girls here didn't like that one bit.' Clover looked out the window, her tone softening when she spoke again. 'They call themselves *The Set*.'

She rolled her eyes so hard, I thought they were going to leave her face.

'*The Set*? Original.' I laughed, trying to ease the tension that had seeped into the room. I could taste it. This urgency that hadn't been there before. I knew Clover wanted to tell me more. My brain urged her to tell me more.

'Yeah. There are four of them and they are the biggest bitches I've ever met. I don't use that term lightly. Their names all begin with the same letter like some knock-off *Heathers* shit.'

'So, who are they? What do they do?'

'Well, they can be any age, but it's usually reserved for the upper two years. And when the older two graduate, there are two new members all primed, ready to take their place. It's an old tradition. Passed down through years and years of snobby people who send their children here. Kind of a birthright thing?'

'Right...' I said, wrapping my mind around it.

'So, you have Olivia and Odette. They're in my year. Then there's Ophelia and Oralie. They're in your year and have only been members for a year. They take it all very seriously. Most of the time, they use their words to keep people in check. They've escalated to *pranks* in the past, though, and believe me when I say that there's nothing harmless about *those*.' Clover's eyes met mine from across the room. 'Read the rules, Sky. I know it sounded like Oliver was making fun when he mentioned the rules, but they really do exist.'

'Where can I find them?' I asked. I couldn't recall seeing them when I flipped through the welcome pack in the car, but I wasn't exactly looking for them either. 'Are they in the pack I got?'

'Of sorts,' Clover replied, getting up a screen on her phone to show me. 'This is Hive. An app the school designed to keep students aware of news, etcetera. Now, it's controlled by *The Set* and—'

I stopped her mid-sentence and asked, 'Let me guess, there's a boy version.'

'Bingo!' Clo said with a laugh. 'And of course it's the three boys I introduced you to earlier.'

'Of course.'

'But let me make one thing clear. The boys will never refer to themselves that way, so probably best not to say it to their faces. It's more something the Os and the rest of the students say, okay?'

'Okay… Is there a fourth I didn't meet?'

'Nope. They decided they didn't like anybody else enough. And with Leo's dad owning the place, not like anybody could say shit against them.'

'So what name do they go by?' I asked, feeling silly. It was a valid question, though in the alternative world I'd found myself in. In the bully academy books I read—and loved—they always had a group name, but, fuck me, it didn't make me feel less stupid.

I fully expected Clover to tell me they were the *Kings* or the *Princes*. Something obvious and stereotypical. There had been a group at my old school that referred to themselves as the *Rebels*, but that wasn't because of money or tradition or anything like that. No. They were just kids with big egos from the poor side of town.

'They call them *The Sect*.'

I could see that Clover was trying her hardest to keep her face semi-straight.

'Apparently, those names have been in place ever since the school opened in 1850. This school has always had some kind of self-opposed royalty. So fucking sad.'

Clover couldn't keep her laughter in any longer. Tears started streaking down her face, a level of hysteria plain to see.

At first, it kind of unnerved me. It wasn't *that* funny. But as with all hysteria, I got swept up in its midst.

Obviously, I did what everybody else did when watching a laughter meltdown unfold. I laughed too.

The hardest I'd laughed in a long time. Maybe the hardest ever.

That kind of infectious laughter that made no sense to anybody else, that when you tried to stop, you'd catch one another's eye and start up again.

And it was at that moment, lungs burning in protest, that I felt a genuine connection to Clover. That maybe I would survive my time here with her as an ally. Maybe one day even as a true friend.

We were both here on somebody else's money, trying to get by and doing our best to better ourselves.

My whole life nobody thought I would amount to much. Everybody I knew believed I would work in a supermarket forever, wasting away.

We would see about that.

THE EVENING PASSED, and as it progressed, I found myself falling for Clover. Not romantically. But in that way girls did when they wanted to be friends with somebody and wanted them to love them and befriend them in return. A major girl crush.

'So,' I said around the cheese roll Clover had made for our dinner, 'tell me more about *The Set* and *The Sect*.'

'Well, what d'you wanna know?' she replied, swallowing her bite of food before wiping the back of her hand on her mouth. I smiled at her lack of manners, knowing we were going to get along more and more by the minute.

'The history of it all, I suppose? Must'a started somewhere.'

'Right'—she nodded—'okay. So the school was founded in 1850 by Robert Hawthorn and introduced the groups to keep students in line, but their roles changed over the years, I guess. A scholarship fund was first introduced in the 1950s, and they were used as a way to keep the younger students and any scholarship recipients in line. There hasn't been a scholarship since the early noughties, though.'

'Why's that?'

'No clue. Nobody really talks about it. But we're the first since then. They're used to create order and stop anybody from rising too high above their station in life.'

I rolled my eyes at that as Clover made bunny fingers, clearly as unimpressed as me. The thing was, though, I also fully believed that was why they did it. Rich people definitely had different priorities in life. That was the conclusion I'd come to.

For the last two years of my life, I'd often wondered about how I would afford to keep food in the house or rent paid on time, and then there were these fuckers worried about some eleven to sixteen-year-olds dating somebody in a different pay bracket. Madness.

I glanced at my class schedule while I finished eating. Most of the lessons were in typical subjects like English Literature. Then there were subjects I hadn't ever thought I'd be able to study, such as Philosophy and Ethics. Luckily, because I didn't join at age eleven, the school didn't expect me to study Latin. *Of course they all know frigging Latin.* The language I studied at my old school, French, was listed instead.

'Want me to show you the rules on Hive?' Clover asked,

finishing her roll and rubbing her hands together to get rid of any crumbs. She picked up her phone and went back on the app she'd briefly shown me earlier. It was a bright garish yellow with a bee emoji in the top left-hand corner. 'You'll have your own personal log in on your phone. I'll set it up for you. So, you click the bee for the menu to drop down.'

I nodded, watching as she navigated the app. The menu listed her class schedule, test results, and some other things I would need to know. Then she clicked on the section of the menu that said *Other*.

Wording instantly appeared on the page in an elegant script I could barely read.

'Can we get this up on a laptop?' I asked, squinting at the phone in Clo's hand. 'I can barely read it.'

The school had provided me with a phone, laptop, and other necessary supplies like they had said they would, so it made sense to make the most of them. It was strange to own something as expensive as the phone and laptop the school provided, but I wasn't complaining. My mum may have the newest iPhone, but I had been holding on to my trusty Blackberry for years, praying it wouldn't die on me. The phone was so old, they didn't even make it anymore! It's not like I had needed a phone to talk with friends, anyway.

We loaded up the laptop and while we waited, I asked, 'Surely none of these rules are that hard to follow?'

'It's not that they're hard to follow per se. It's more of just what each rule means in actuality.'

Rules of Hawthorn Academy:
As decided by The Sect and The Set.
All students must adhere or face the dire consequences.

I looked at Clover and asked, 'What does it mean by "face the dire consequences"? Sounds like something that would happen in a bad made-for-TV movie.'

I laughed.

She did not.

If anything, her face got even more serious as she said, 'Seriously, Sky, I don't want to be *that* person, but I mean this. You do not want to find out. Do not give them any reason to look at you. They all saw you today and the Os definitely know that the boys spoke to you. Do us both a favour and just stay away.'

'I promise, Clo, I'll try.' Her seriousness put a chill inside of me. We had been joking all day about the other kids that go here and about rich people in general. At no point had she sounded so sombre.

My eyes went back to the page to read the rules.

Rule One: DO NOT approach *The Sect* or *The Set* without being summoned first.

Rule Two: DO NOT look at the above-mentioned groups unless deemed necessary.

Rule Three: DO NOT bring shame upon your family or this fine institution.

Rule Four: NEVER date someone above your class without asking for permission.

Rule Five: NEVER turn down the invitation of somebody from *The Sect* or *The Set*.

We will punish anybody failing to adhere to the above as we see fit.

I got colder after reading each rule. Technically, I had already broken one of them without even meaning to. I had looked at the girls laughing at me, and I had *definitely* looked at the boys before they came over to us. I wondered what they meant by "deemed necessary." How could you know whether to look at them? Who even determined what was necessary or not? Maybe I just ignored them unless they talked to me and looked at me first. That seemed the best bet.

'Clo, what is the punishment for breaking these rules?' I wondered whether it could be as serious as it seemed. Surely not? The students here were aged between eleven and eighteen. Could the punishment really be that severe? The faculty must know about them if these groups have existed for as long as the school itself.

'Well, it totally depends on what rule you break and who you've pissed off. The boys play dirtier than the girls. Remember that. Girls will be blatant and in your face. Boys, they'll ruin your life without you even knowing they lifted a finger.'

'How comforting,' I said in a dry tone. I could feel it in my bones, though, that she wasn't making any of it up. Clover really believed what she was saying. I wasn't saying that it wasn't true, but *c'mon*, maybe it was a slight exaggeration.

'I'm not exaggerating, Sky,' Clo said, her eyes cutting into mine.

Well, there went that theory.

Clo didn't notice my distracted look and continued talking, 'I've heard stories that would make you run far from here. A couple of years ago, somebody upset *The Sect*, and it was horrible. I'm not sure what they did, and I doubt they did anything to justify what happened to them, but they ended up in the hospital. They tried to take their own life. It was dark.'

I gulped.

The air became thick, and suddenly, I found it hard to

breathe. I felt like I had earlier, when the boys had approached me. My vision started to fade, black around the edges once again. I couldn't place why my body was betraying me. Why a panic attack had started at Clo's words. Maybe it was from the seriousness of her tone.

Either way, the last thing I remembered was staring hard at Clover and trying to communicate just how trapped I was feeling in my own body.

Then nothing.

Four

I OPENED MY EYES, expecting to see Clover's scared green ones looking back at me.

That was not what I saw.

At all.

Bright blue piercing eyes were looking down at me instead. I couldn't place them at first, but there was one thing I knew.

You know when you could tell something just by looking into somebody's eyes?

Well, I could tell that these eyes held secrets. Lots of them.

'Hey there, are you okay?' the owner of the eyes asked. I blinked, trying to adjust to my new surroundings. The azure eyes belonged to Oliver, and I was staring into their light.

Wait, am I already breaking rule number whatever?

I hoped not. He looked into my eyes first, not the other way around.

'I-I'm fine, I think.' *Man, I wish my stutter would just piss off.* Although really, I should cut myself some slack. I had passed out and awoken somewhere unfamiliar. 'Where am I?' I asked. I couldn't see around him to figure out where I was.

'You're in the school's hospital wing,' he answered, and all that was occupying my mind was that I really was in an academy novel now. Complete with a wing for ill people.

Wait. An entire wing dedicated to ill students didn't bode well, did it?

'How? What happened?' I had no recollection of the events leading up to that moment, like, at all.

'You passed out. I was about to knock when Clover burst through the door, saying something about how you were acting strange and blacked out,' he said, gazing at me intently. 'So I carried you here, to the hospital wing.'

I nodded. In theory, his story made sense. The last thing I remembered was Clover looking at me funny. I had no idea why he would be outside my room, though. Surely he hadn't been coming to seek *me* out. When we first met earlier that day, he made it clear I was beneath him. Somebody not worth his time.

'T-thanks, I appreciate it. You really didn't have to. Sometimes I get anxiety attacks and feel faint,' I told him, hoping he'd leave now that I'd woken up. Then it hit me. 'Where's Clover? Did she not come with us?'

'Clover's outside the room. I said I'd let her in once you were awake,' he said, his eyes shining with humour.

What a beautiful boy, I thought. I shook my head and laughed out loud.

'A beautiful boy?' he asked, chuckling.

Realising my error, I stopped laughing abruptly. Oliver's lips twitched, but he stopped himself from laughing any more than he already had. I couldn't believe I said that out loud. That I put those words out into the universe where he could hear them. No doubt he thought I had a few screws loose.

'I'm beautiful? Really? You don't think I'm sexy?' The amused look on his face, mixed with the teasing in his tone, made me want to shrivel up and disappear. Looking closely into his eyes, I could see a hint of something else lingering in his gaze. A kind of heat that made me feel a certain way. I imagined how dominant he'd be in private, and I could feel my cheeks going red. No matter what I did, my cheeks always showed my emotions, which caused me some awkward situations in the past.

'I—' I started talking, attempting to prevent him from looking so intently at my cheeks.

He cut me off. 'I'm joking, Sky. I'm glad you've noticed me,' he said, seeming genuinely perplexed, shaking his head, as if he couldn't quite believe somebody like me would think so highly of his looks. Which, let's be honest, was the biggest load of bullshit acting that I'd seen in a while. Maybe ever.

'Everybody notices you, I'm sure. Ever considered that they're too scared to look at you? You know, because of all those rules on Hive?' The moment the words left me, I wished I'd kept my mouth closed. Of all the things I could have said, I had to say something about the rules. About the fact that he and his friends thought they were untouchable. What was wrong with me?

'Maybe you should remember that fear is good. Being scared can ensure you live. That you don't make life-threatening mistakes. Ever considered that, Little One?'

The second those words left his lips, Oliver left the room, taking the heat with him. His words—fuck, the entire conversation—had made me feel frozen inside. Was that a warning or a threat?

Not long after Oliver walked out, Clover entered, curious.

'So… What did he say?' she demanded the moment she came into view.

'Nothing much.'

'Nothing much?' she asked, disappointed. 'Why don't I believe you?'

'No idea.' I shrugged, staying tight-lipped. I hadn't even had time to process what happened myself. Not that much *had* happened, but still. Clover meant well—I assumed. Not like I knew the girl well enough yet to truly know her motivations.

Although, a kinship of sorts was building between us, and one day I could see us being the best of friends.

Still, I was wary. I didn't want to give her all my trust and then have it thrown back in my face in the future. I had no idea who I could truly trust, and I wouldn't be stupid and make that big of a decision on my first day.

The sour-faced, miserable-looking nurse approached and Clover stopped the words that were about to leave her lips.

You know when people's lips looked as if they'd been sucking on a sour gobstopper for hours? All pursed and puckered. Well, that was the face on the nurse.

'Can I leave and go back to my room?' I asked her. I really didn't need to be there. My vision had returned to normal and I no longer felt faint.

'You'll leave when I have permission from Master Hawthorn,' she replied, her voice as dull and lifeless as the rest of her. My mind instantly went to Leo, and I wondered why he had anything to do with me getting out of here. My eyes found Clover, questioning, hoping she'd have an answer for me.

Clover just shrugged, though. Maybe it was the way things went at Hawthorn.

I wanted to leave and get settled in my bed and prepared,

both physically and mentally, for the next morning. There was to be a huge assembly for the entire school first thing, and attendance was mandatory.

I was already nervous enough, but after my stunt that evening, there would be rumours flying around about the "New Girl" and the reason why she ended up in the hospital wing with Oliver by her side, of all people.

After another hour or so, the sour nurse finally relented. She must have heard from Leo. Or realised that it was absolutely bloody ridiculous to keep me there on the whims of a seventeen-year-old boy. Either way, midnight had long passed and my eyes could barely stay open. The entire day felt like a clusterfuck of emotions. So much had happened in such a short period, yet I'd only been on school grounds for eight hours. Eight hours that felt a hell of a lot longer.

Clover stayed with me the whole time, keeping the conversation flowing. She kept it light and surface level, which I was extremely thankful for, even if I didn't respond to half of what she said.

ON OUR WAY back to our room, Clover tried to help me figure out where on the property we were. She'd pointed out the hospital wing on her tour, but it wasn't somewhere I thought I needed to become acquainted with, so I'd failed to pay much attention. Apparently, we were now on the second floor walkway that led to the Admin building.

'Are we near the pool house?' I asked, trying to recall the map of the school in my mind. Pretty sure we were on the west side of the campus. 'A—'

'Shh,' Clover whispered, bringing her finger to her lips. 'Be quiet a second.'

She stopped on the spot, and I halted too.

'Can you hear that?'

My ears strained, listening for any sound other than our breathing, but if I was being honest, I couldn't hear a thing.

'What is it?' I hushed out, keeping my voice as low as I could.

'I'm not sure. But it sounded like noises coming from down the hall,' Clover said, nodding in the direction we were headed.

We continued up the corridor on silent feet, listening out for any more noises.

A low moan reached us, and that was when I saw *them*.

Two figures were up ahead, standing so close to one another, they were almost one. I couldn't make out anything but their body shapes. No faces or features.

I put my finger on my lips and gestured to Clo to follow me as I once more tiptoed up the hall, towards the couple.

Like the saying goes, curiosity killed the cat. And often, I acted like the cat. It was as if a compulsion took over me and I had to know what was happening. I knew I should have just continued on my way and gone to bed. *Obviously, I should have done that.* But nope. Instead, I crept closer.

Leo Hawthorn stood beside one of the O girls Clover had told me all about, but I wasn't sure which one. The two of them were definitely kissing—potentially more. Heavy breathing filled the air, and it became obvious they hadn't noticed us.

A gasp came from behind me, but when I turned my head to glance back at Clover, I saw her back as she ran away. She had left me there without an explanation. No words. Nothing.

What the fuck?

Clover's gasp echoed through the hall and the two of them stopped making out to stare at me. The dim lighting of the hallway made it hard to see much, but it was light enough to make out facial expressions. The girl was pissed.

Great.

'What are you doing here, New Girl? Can't you see we're busy?' she spat. The girl had long, ice blonde hair. Perfectly straight, reaching all the way down to her waist. It swished with every word she spoke.

'I-I-I...' I couldn't speak. My tongue became heavy and felt like it was glued to the roof of my mouth. My vision blurred around the edges and moisture slowly covered my body in a thin sheen of sweat. I hated myself at that moment. I hated how weak I felt.

'I-I-I...' she mocked, looking me dead in the eyes. 'Leo, can you hear this shit?'

Her laughter rang out, reaching every corner, as she turned back to face Leo once more.

'Leave her alone, Odette,' Leo snapped. He looked at me, his eyes taking in the full length of my body. He didn't look interested in me. He didn't look disgusted either, though. He was just... looking.

'You're seriously going to take her side?' Odette seethed. 'Honestly, Leo, she's a poor, ugly nobody. Probably riddled with disease, too. She doesn't deserve to even be here.'

Her beautiful features morphed into something evil. Something almost otherworldly, the light hitting her at an angle that only made her look more sinister.

'Get off me,' Leo growled, shoving her from him with such force that she nearly fell over. Luckily, she caught herself in time. 'Go back to your room, Odette. I don't want to see you again tonight.'

'What?' she roared, even more pissed than she was before. 'Are you being serious? Le—'

'Get out!' he said, cutting her off before she could plead her case. 'Leave!'

Odette huffed and turned to storm away. Not before delivering her parting shot to me, though.

'You better watch your back, New Girl. Oh, the things we could do to you.' Her words reminded me of a Seuss poem. Odette continued to laugh like a villain in a second-rate horror film as she disappeared around the corner and out of our view.

Leo watched her go, his expression unchanging. He didn't smile or show that he wanted to exchange pleasantries.

'Ignore her,' he said, nodding down the corridor in the direction Odette stormed off. 'She's a bitch.'

He moved to face me, a blank expression covering his face.

I wasn't panicked before, but the moment he faced me, my heart rate shot up. All I could focus on, all I could think about, was the fact I had broken their stupid rules and would have to face the consequences. Clover made it clear those rules were to be taken seriously.

'O-oh, it's okay. I'm sorry I'm looking at you,' I said.

'Well, you don't seem to be looking away even now that you've realised,' he said, his tone bored, but his eyes lit up, giving away his amusement. My cheeks flushed, his bored low grumble sounding so sensual in the dimly lit corridor. I watched his lips move, but the words weren't computing. My brain was mush, complete goo, as I tried to look away. Tried to control my embarrassment.

'...If you are, come and tell me. Or Oliver,' he said, the smirk fully established on his face. 'He'll want you to tell him about anything the girls do to you.'

'I don't have permission to come talk to you without being

summoned first,' I joked, tongue in cheek. An attempt at a joke at least. Not sure if it landed the way I hoped. Leo's face didn't change.

'I'm giving you permission now, aren't I?' He cocked his head, no longer looking as disinterested. 'Don't disappoint me, New Girl.'

'Thanks, I guess...' I mumbled, my sentence trailing off at the end, no idea what else to do or say. I found Leo intimidating. At over six feet tall, he seemed like a giant compared to my five-foot-five—although he made me feel even shorter than that. *Or maybe he just makes me feel small?*

'No problem. I'll see you around,' he said, all of his teeth showing. Sinister, almost. A threat.

Leo's strides were filled with purpose as he walked away. He didn't look back at me once. I did hear a chuckle come from him, though, before he was completely out of my eye line.

I walked back to my room, thinking back over what the fuck had just happened. I would definitely be giving Clover a piece of my mind.

Or maybe I would give her a piece of my mind in my own head.

I didn't want our friendship on the rocks before it ever had the chance to take off.

It took me a while to struggle back to my room. On more than one occasion, I couldn't figure out where the heck I was in the school. I couldn't catch my bearings and kept coming across dead ends and wrong turns.

I hoped dead ends and wrong turns wouldn't become a common occurrence. But knowing my luck, they for sure would be.

Five

THE ASSEMBLY for the entire school was taking place in the large auditorium located in the main building. Once inside the hall, the enormity of the room took my breath away. The ceiling was so high, it reminded me of a cathedral. The stained glass windows probably helped that.

On the wall opposite the entrance, there was a large rectangle stained glass window, the beauty of it shining throughout the entire room. The morning sun coming through created the most beautiful colours on the grey stone floor.

Nobody seemed to pay attention to me or Clover on the surface, but the surrounding whispers sounded like angry bees, buzzing away; the stares as sharp as daggers when we weren't looking. After the run-in with Leo and Odette last night, I didn't want to draw any more negative attention to myself. My gut was sure the girls were already plotting something for me. Something sinister.

'So.' Clover halted once we reached the seating area and said, 'I have to go sit with my year in the last row.' She rolled her eyes, making it clear how unimpressed she was.

'Where do I sit?' I asked her, looking around, not seeing any signs or anything. Guess it was a situation where people just *knew* what to do. Something I wouldn't know being the new girl.

'The last two rows of the stands are for my year, and the two rows before that are for year twelve. Sit in any seat but try to get a seat on the aisle. Means you can make a quick getaway when it's over,' she said as she gave me a slight shove towards the steps and I made my way towards the rows she'd pointed out. I took a seat near the end of the row, leaving the last seat of the row empty. Nobody liked the dickhead who didn't move all the way down a row and expected newcomers to climb over them.

Clover was sitting a few rows behind me, next to Leo of all people, and I could hear the two of them grumbling at one another. No idea what words were being spoken, but it didn't sound friendly, that was for sure.

After a few minutes, I sensed a body dropping into the seat next to me.

'I hope you don't mind me sitting here.'

I groaned inwardly. I recognised that voice. Oliver's voice. Looking at him only confirmed it.

'Sure,' I said with a sigh, knowing that there was nothing I could say or do to change it. A very small part of me didn't want to change it—but I'd keep that to myself. 'Of course I d-don't.'

One day soon, I hoped I could come across as a normal teenage girl and not some tongue-tied loser. Alas, today was not that day.

'Thanks. I feel like we haven't formally introduced ourselves. I'm Oliver Brandon,' he said and held out his hand for me to shake. I sat frozen, uncertain. Had he forgotten yesterday? Or had our conversation in the hospital wing been a part of my imagination? Pretty certain we were introduced yesterday and had multiple run-ins. *Right?*

'I'm Skylar Crescent,' I said as he moved his hand and placed it in mine. What happened next startled me. I shit you not. An electrical current travelled up my arm, starting in my fingertips until it reverberated through my shoulder. Shocked, I darted my hand away. A smug smile covered Oliver's face, the speed of my action amusing him.

'I know who you are,' he said, the condescending tone not lost on me. After a beat, he said, 'Leo told me about last night.'

'He d-did?' I asked, puzzled as to what he meant. Or what part he'd told him about. He'd been there for half of it.

'Leo mentioned he told you to come to me if any of *The Set* bothers you. He said you were worried about punishment for not following the rules, so I wanted to clear it up with you.' His eyes glinted with excitement when speaking of punishment, but the glint disappeared as fast as it came.

'T-thank you. I really appreciate it.' I'd been doing so well in controlling my stammer, but this guy was so hot, he was melting my brain a little. Up close, I could see his blue eyes had flecks of silver running through them. His lips were full, and I really wanted to take a bite out of them. I could feel my face heating. My thoughts were clear on my face for all to see, my pale complexion giving it away. And my thoughts were heading to a really dirty place. Having his hand hold mine even for the briefest moment had me imagining where else he could use his hands.

Get a grip, Skylar.

'You're really cute when you stammer, you know. Makes me wonder how much I could make you stammer with my dick deep inside you.' The casual way in which he spoke made me choke on air. It was so left field, but now those images filled my imagination to the point I couldn't see anything else—the hall no longer registering.

'Err...' I was at a loss for words. I raised my eyebrows, not sure about the correct response. I'd never found myself in a similar scenario before.

I was so lost in Oliver's suggestive look, I didn't notice that Ms Hawthorn had walked to the centre of the stage at the front of the hall.

'Silence, everybody,' she called out, her tone assertive, echoing throughout the hall. Her gaze covered the entire room and with her words, every single student went quiet. A pin could have dropped and everybody would hear. 'Welcome to a new year here at Hawthorn Academy. We have a new scholarship student joining us this year by the name of Skylar Crescent. I hope that everybody will make her feel at home.'

I shrank in my seat, hunching my shoulders to try to make myself as small as possible. I hadn't expected her to namedrop me like that. The way she said it made it sound like a threat, paranoia playing within the deep recesses of my brain.

Oliver nudged me with his elbow and smiled widely. I thought his smirk was sexy as fuck, but wow, his smile was even better than his smirk.

'So, New Girl Skylar, how can I make you feel at home here?' he asked, having come closer to me, entering my space. His words whispered over my ear and made me tingle from head to toe. Goosebumps covered my arms, and I tried to focus on whatever Ms Hawthorn was saying—but I was failing miserably.

Even just sitting next to Oliver made me nervous, and I counted down the minutes, hoping this torture would be over soon.

'Enjoy the first week, students,' Ms Hawthorn said, ending

her speech—a speech I'd heard none of. *Hope it wasn't important.*

People moved in their seats and stood to leave.

Thank fuck it was finally over.

But before I could leave in silence, Oliver put a hand on my arm to hold me in place.

'How about you join me tonight for dinner at my table?' he asked, and on noticing my reluctance, he added, 'Bring Clover, too.'

'O-okay,' I said, a rabbit in the headlights. No other words would come to mind. And with that one word, I sealed my fate.

AFTER I AGREED to sit with him at dinner, Oliver didn't utter another word. Just left the hall, leaving me standing there a little shaken up. I had no idea what to expect. Clover and I had eaten breakfast in our room as we'd overslept, and last night I'd missed dinner in the dining hall while lying in a hospital bed and had to make do with some sandwiches the nurse begrudgingly handed out.

Clover met me after the assembly ended and when I asked her what she and Leo had been discussing, her face turned sour.

'Leo's the biggest prick I know.' She pursed her lips together, saying no more on the subject.

Duly noted.

While walking down the corridor to my first lesson here at the academy, I remembered what I agreed to during that brief conversation with Oliver in the assembly.

Here goes nothing.

'Clo,' I mumbled, taking in a big breath to prepare for my next words. Or maybe I was preparing for her reaction to said words. 'Oliver's asked if I'll sit at his table tonight for dinner. He said you can join us if you want to. I may have agreed...' I trailed off when I saw her face. Her green eyes narrowed and her lips puckered, acid dripping from her features.

Clover looked at me like she personally wanted to deliver my death.

She stopped in the middle of the corridor, some poor kid bumping into her back and running off when she glared at him.

'I'm sorry, but what did you just say?' Her voice was ice. 'I thought I just heard you say that you'd agreed to sit with *The Sect* for dinner? But that can't be possible because there is no way you're that fucking stupid. Right?'

I squirmed. I knew she wouldn't take it well, but to drop the F-bomb that early in the day meant she was even madder than I expected.

'I-I must be?' I asked, looking everywhere; anywhere that wasn't Clover.

'Skylar Crescent, didn't I say yesterday to stay away from those boys? Did you not listen to anything I said?' She was shaking her head and giving me a pitying look. I felt embarrassed. I *had* listened to everything she told me, but when Oliver was asking me to join them, I just couldn't stop myself.

'I promise I did, Clo. It is one of the rules, though, and...' I was still looking around and trailed off when I saw Griffin approaching us, waving exaggeratedly at me. So exaggerated that he hit a girl so hard, she stumbled. Even that couldn't stop Griff's cheeky grin, planted firmly on his face, and I couldn't help but smile back at him.

'Yo, girls, what's happening?' he asked loudly and pulled me into an awkward hug that I hadn't seen coming as he trapped my hands between us. He buried his nose into the nape of my neck. 'Damn, New Girl, you smell like girlfriend material.'

He let me out of the hug and all I could do was gape at him. I mean, seriously, did that line ever work on anybody?

'Just ignore him, Sky. The boy doesn't know when to stop.' Clover's bemused face made me smile. Griff seemed to have that effect on people. I always wondered if people who came across as easy-going were actually hiding something darker underneath the surface. Something they wanted to keep hidden so badly that they'd joke about anything, act the fool, so nobody would look deeper.

'A-and what does girlfriend m-material smell like?' I asked, holding back a laugh. My smile stayed firmly in place, though. I felt so much more at ease with him than I did with Oliver or Leo. Within moments of being near him, a warmth entered me and filled me with a sense of joy.

'You,' he whispered, his hand caressing my face. He seemed super proud of his comeback.

I laughed for real then, letting it bark out of me, my smile manic.

'Oh, ha-ha, Griff,' Clover said, her voice anything but amused. 'You are such a wind-up. Leave my girl Sky here alone. She's already sitting at your table for dinner, after all.'

She crossed her arms over her chest, making it clear once again that she thought I'd made a poor decision.

'New Girl, you are in for a treat! Please sit next to me, pretty please,' he said, ignoring Clo's negativity as his eyes met mine and his pleading tone made me laugh a little. I had no romantic attraction to him, but he really was a force. He even batted his eyelids at me, his long eyelashes fluttering with the motion.

Words failed me, but I gave a small nod of the head, agreeing with his request. He pumped his fist in the air and shouted, 'Score!'

The few students left mingling in the hall all turned to stare at the commotion that was Griffin Cooper, and their eyes widened when they realised he was conversing with me. I wondered if he was acting out of character. I also wondered how many of them would've been punished—or already had been—for doing the same thing.

Griff looped his arm through mine, and then Clo's, to walk us to my first class of the day, History. I didn't ask how he knew where I was meant to be. Seemed like a waste of breath, as I knew he probably wouldn't tell me, anyway.

'Here you are, my fair lady,' Griff said, sweeping his arm towards the classroom door and lowering himself into a bow. 'Learning awaits.'

I shook my head and waved bye to him and Clover, who was biting her bottom lip, a mixture of amusement and anger dancing on her face.

The moment I entered the classroom, I spotted a few empty desks. I chose one in the back row and took my school laptop from my bag.

A velvety voice entered my ear.

'Fancy seeing you here.'

Oliver.

'Yes, f-fancy seeing me in class at the school we both attend,' I snapped. My words came out a lot more snarky than I intended, but there was just something about that boy that really put me on edge. One of my flaws was that when my anxiety couldn't handle a situation, it turned me into the biggest brat known to man. *This* was one of those times.

'Whoa,' he said, raising his hands, palms facing forward. 'Slow your horses, New Girl. I meant it in jest. You know, after we sat together for assembly, I didn't realise I'd be seeing you in my first class, that's all. I would have walked you here had I known.'

'Yes, well, Griff walked me here, so no sweat,' I said, looking around the classroom instead of directly at him. Whether I liked it or not, the boy made me sweat.

Oliver visibly bristled at the fact Griff walked me to class, and I felt a little smug about it. He threw himself into the empty seat beside me and I rolled my eyes.

'*Griff* walked you here?' he asked. I couldn't decide if it was the sheer fact that Griff had done something nice for me pissed him off the most. Or the fact he hadn't thought of it himself first.

'Yep. He wants me to sit next to him tonight at dinner, too. Seemed super chuffed to know I was joining you.' Internally, I laughed. On the outside, I remained cool as a cucumber. I just couldn't help myself. Riling up the devil was my idea of fun, clearly.

'You'll do no such thing,' he growled.

Still refusing to look at Oliver, I glanced around the room some more, taking it all in. Everything looked a little different from the classrooms I was used to back at my old school. The technology here surpassed anything they had at Hollowdale High.

At each desk, a student sat with their school issued laptop. A SMART board linked up to a computer took up the majority of the far wall. Honestly, at my old school the teachers were still using dry-erase boards as the school had spent all of their funding on the science labs and the sports programmes.

'I'm sure I read in the rules somewhere that us mere p-peasants can't turn down the invitation of somebody from *The Sect*. Griff asked me to sit with him and I said yes. Pretty simple if you think about it, Oliver.' I shrugged.

I knew I was holding out on a technicality, but fuck him. Sure, it was Oliver who asked me to dinner in the first place, so he probably intended for me to sit with him. But I hated the attitude and bullshit of it all. Yeah, I'd accepted his invitation. But I never specified who I would sit with, and he never speci-fied I had to sit with *him*.

The moment I referred to them as *The Sect*, though, Oliver's face soured. His lips formed into a point, and his eyes darkened.

'Call me Ollie,' he said, his nostrils flaring, his tone deadly.

The teacher arrived, and Oliver said no more.

I remembered what Clover told me: nobody called him Ollie unless he told them they could.

The teacher started the lesson, and I ignored *Oliver* for the rest of the lesson. There was no way I would bow down to him. We weren't friends.

The lesson itself was about the art of warfare.

How fitting.

THE REST of the day flew by and I had made it to the last period without making a total fool of myself, which was a real plus in my eyes.

In every class there was at least one member of *The Set* or

The Sect. Oliver was in my History class. Griff was in my Philosophy and Ethics class. The two O girls, Oralie and Ophelia, were in English.

It was time for French, the last lesson of the day, and I sighed deeply as I slumped into an empty seat in the back row. In every class, I had taken a seat in the back to stay out of the limelight a little. I'd already heard people whispering about Oliver sitting with me in assembly and him inviting me to dinner. The rumour mill at Hawthorn was similar to my old schools'—filled with half-truths and blatant lies.

I walked into the room and my eyes snapped to the blue ones staring at me from the back row.

Oliver was sitting with Oralie and Ophelia on either side of him, smirking at me. The only available seat in the room was the one next to Oralie, and although I didn't want to sit next to her, I knew they had thrown down the gauntlet so to speak.

I slumped into the chair at the same time a high-pitched voice whined, 'Oh, Ollie. Don't you think you should tell *that* girl not to sit there? She doesn't deserve to sit with us.' Her hand was running up and down his arm, her fingers grazing his skin in a casual way that was completely at odds with the strained look on her face.

'She's a nobody. Did you hear that she interrupted Ode while she was with Leo last night? Bet she's one of those freaks who enjoys watching others get it on.' Oralie joined in.

Ode?

What kind of a shit nickname was *Ode*?

A giggle bubbled out of me—I couldn't help myself. My eyes went to where Oliver was sitting, wanting to see his reaction to the lies Oralie was spouting. His eyes lit up, a dark glint flashing through them before disappearing without a trace. *Is he a voyeur?*

I tried my hardest not to roll my eyes. I *really* did. But some reactions just happen involuntarily.

'Lay off her, girls. I've invited Sky to sit with us at dinner tonight,' he said, his tone harsh.

My heart thudded in my chest. With *us*?

Stupid old me hadn't fully realised that eating dinner with the boys would also mean eating dinner with the girls, too. No wonder Clover had been ready to kill me for accepting the invitation. After what happened the night before and over the course of the morning, it had become clear that Clo was definitely keeping things from me.

I tuned my ears back into the conversation.

'But whyyyyy?' Ophelia's whine reminded me of the whine of a four-year-old meeting Santa at a local mall. One who wanted all the toys but left with none.

I scoffed at her theatrics. Something I was already learning here at Hawthorn was that rich girls were another breed. My old school may have sat dead centre of the 'divide' between the poor side of the town and wealthier side, but nobody acted the way these girls did.

Unfortunately for me, Ophelia heard me.

'What are you scoffing at, you swine?' she spat. *Literally.* Her spit landed right in front of Oliver, drawing my eyes' focus.

I laughed. *Swine?* Was she for real?

'I said, leave her alone, Ophelia!' Oliver raised his voice so loud that the entire class stopped their conversations and turned to face us. Slumping even further down in my chair, I tried to make myself as small and invisible as I could. 'Move now, Oralie. I'm not playing around.'

I was still slowly sinking in my chair as Oliver sat down into the one Oralie had sharply vacated.

'I'm sorry about her,' he said, leaning in to whisper in my

ear, his breath causing a chill to run down my spine. 'About both of them, actually.'

I nodded. I just knew I would stutter if I replied to him. My brave behaviour towards him was a thing of the past.

The teacher entered the classroom and assessed the room, his eyes narrowing when they landed on a certain someone.

'Master Brandon,' he called out, his voice deep and booming. 'What are you doing in here?'

'Thought I'd learn some French, sir,' Oliver said, the smirk firm on his face. So sure of himself and filled with an almost egotistical swagger.

'Get out, or I will report you to Ms Hawthorn,' he said, his rotund face turning a shade of red that reminded me of a dark wine that was very popular at the supermarket I worked at.

The more red his face got, the more I genuinely worried he would have an attack of some sort, being both *very* short and *very* large. Nobody else seemed worried about him.

'We both know that isn't exactly a threat, sir,' Oliver said but stood and left the classroom anyway, winking in my direction before disappearing from view.

I rolled my eyes and chuckled lightly, even though he could no longer see me. He had some gall. I'd give him that.

The rest of the lesson passed in a blur. All I could think about was the fact that Oliver wasn't matching up to any of my preconceived ideas about him. Clover had told me to stay away. The rules I'd read on the Hive also made me believe I should steer well clear of him.

But Oliver wasn't acting the way I thought he would. Each new encounter led me to further question my judgement. He'd been a dick yesterday when we first met, then there was the whole hospital wing fiasco. Plus, I still didn't know why he'd been about to knock on my door. He was a flirt in assembly, and every time I recalled that whole stutter/dick line, I flushed the deepest red. Then he was sticking up for me against these girls he'd known for years. None of it added up.

When the last bell of the day rang, I still hadn't figured any of it out. I spotted Clover waiting for me outside in the hallway and I rushed out of the door as quick as I could, grabbing her arm when I passed her, and ran towards our room with her dragging along behind.

'Sky, what the hell's got into you? Why are we moving so fast?'

'I'll explain when we get back to our room. Just hurry!' I pulled her the entire way back, then, once inside, I slammed the door behind us and locked it. I didn't want anyone "accidentally" entering. Or anybody overhearing, either.

Clover sat down on her bed, and I sat on mine, facing her. Trying to catch my breath, I put my hand out to halt any words Clover might speak. Our sprint through the school had once again reminded me I was super unfit. Raking my hands through my hair, I sighed.

'Clo. I think I'm in trouble,' I said, urgency in my tone.

'What do you mean, *in trouble*?' she asked, confused.

'Well, you know how you basically implied that I should avoid the pool building and the boys who occupy it?'

'Yes...' Her eyebrows rose, climbing up her forehead. I was being cryptic, and fancy, to try and quell my nerves at talking to her about it.

'And you know how I agreed to sit with them for dinner tonight?'

'Yes...'

I could hear her getting impatient with me, so I decided to blurt it out, 'Well... I think I'm developing a major crush on

Ollie.' I said it super fast, hoping that would make it easier. Like ripping off a Band-Aid or a waxing strip.

Clover gasped when I used his nickname.

'He's been so nice to me today, standing up against the O girls for me. Plus, he may have made a comment this morning about wanting to hear if I stutter with his dick deep inside me.' By the end of the sentence, I was whispering and my face must have been redder than a fire engine. I covered my face with my hands, trying to hide it from her.

Clover's expression turned to one of pity as she made the sign of the cross.

'Oh, honey, no.' Shaking her head, she said, 'You can't feel like that about him. Trust me when I say that he's not a good guy. I know he was there last night and was nice to you today, but I promise you, Sky, he has an agenda. It may not be obvious right now, but he definitely has one. Those boys do nothing without some kind of endgame. Even Griff can be a prick when he feels like it.'

'I know, I know. I don't *want* to feel this way!'

'Maybe we should just eat dinner here, get something delivered to the school gates? I'm just going to put this out into the universe so that when shit comes back to bite you, I can say I told you so, okay?'

I nodded.

Clo looked at me imploringly and said, 'Sky, you know deep down that he's playing you. Or that he has some kind of motive.'

'No. I don't know that for definite. We're going to go eat dinner with them, Clo. I'm not having people talk shit about me on my first full day. Plus, I'm pretty sure the rules say you can't turn down an invitation from them, right?'

'Right,' she said, reluctantly agreeing with me.

Six

THE CAFETERIA, if you could even call it that, resembled a fine dining restaurant rather than any school dining hall I'd ever been in. The sheer size of it was overwhelming. I half expected Oliver and the others to be sitting at some kind of large top table like royalty, but instead they were occupying the large circular table in the very centre of the room. Knights of the Round Table, much?

Clover and I made our way to the table and sat in the two empty seats; me beside Griff like he had requested, with Oliver sitting on my other side. Clover had to sit between Leo and Olivia, and trust me, her face made it clear how pissed at me she was for putting her in that position. With a wince and a shrug, I looked back at her, trying to send my apology telepathically.

Once we sat down, servers flooded over to take our orders, like rain beetles at the first sight of water droplets. I'd never felt so out of place. I glanced at the menu in front of me, but none of it computed. On my way in, I'd spotted a kid eating *snails* as if it were a regular dinner you'd find at any school. Yeah. Any school for the extremely wealthy.

The O girls were doing nothing to hide their feelings about

me and Clo sitting with them. They were beyond livid. All four of them kept looking at me and then each other, then Clover, then the boys. It went on for a full five minutes and nobody spoke.

It was awkward as fuck.

'S-so how was everybody's day?' I asked, trying to break the tension seeping into the atmosphere and tainting the air. The moment the words left me, I hoped my chair would dissolve into the tiled floor.

'That stutter is honestly the cutest thing,' Griff said with an overdramatic sigh. 'Don't you agree, Ollie? Damn, Sky. I'm hard just hearing it.' I realised it was his signature grin planted firm on his face, his dimples pressed in and his teeth on show.

Well, *that* broke the tension.

'Oh, shut up, dickhead,' Clover said, trying to contain her laughter. 'Do you think before you speak or does it just come out unbidden?'

'My sweet lucky Clover, has anybody told you you look hot when you're acting all fierce? Don't you agree, Leo?' Griff asked, his eyebrows waggling in Leo's direction, teasing in a way only a true friend could.

'Hmph.' Leo was too busy looking at Odette while she stared back to give Griff a proper answer. I thought I saw her hand moving underneath the table in a suspicious rhythm and my face heated at the implication.

Surely not?

One thing was certain. Rich people acted weird.

'Don't mind him, he knows the truth,' said Griff, nodding. 'My day was perfect. I got my dick sucked in the caretaker's cupboard earlier and I'm hoping I'll get a repeat later.'

I gulped and averted my gaze. I was so out of my league here.

It sounded like a cliché, but I was a virgin. A rather non-experienced virgin at that. My whole life I'd never spent time around people who talked like this; so open and honest with no regard to who could hear them. No care in the world.

'Nobody needs to hear about you getting your dick sucked, Griff. Don't worry, though. I'm sure Oralie will repeat the favour for you for her dessert,' Clover said, her smile dripping poison, giving Oralie a look of pure condescension.

'As if!' Oralie sputtered. 'I wouldn't go near *that* even if you paid me.'

I rolled my eyes, a small giggle leaving my lips, and when I looked to my right, I found myself staring directly into Oliver's azure blue ones. They had a glint of menace, but he covered it up pretty fast and then they just looked bland.

'Nobody would pay for your mouth. More like you'd have to pay them,' Clover smarted back at her.

'I could kiss you, my lady luck!' Griff looked in his element, rubbing his hands together with glee. He reminded me of a bad cartoon villain, and I couldn't help but laugh. He raised his hand in my direction and I gave him a high-five in response. Who was I to turn down the calling of the high-five?

Griff didn't seem so bad. Out of the group at the table, he seemed the most chill one. The one you could have a laugh with. But then Clover's warning from yesterday came back to me, and I had to wonder just what Griff kept hidden.

Finally, the food arrived, and the mood around the table improved by a margin. Other than the odd spurts of banter between Griff and Clover, nobody else said much, though. Food silenced everything and everyone.

Leo and Odette were still touching one another intimately, and I reckoned Clover had considered stabbing him with her steak knife multiple times.

Griff grinned wide and acted like everything happening around the table amused him—it probably did. The O girls were whispering about something the rest of the table weren't privy to. Both Clover's and my names popped up multiple times, so chances were it was something about us.

Then there was Oliver, who had put his hand on my thigh during the main course and was yet to remove it. Both of us were silent, caught up in the moment. His fingers moved in a slow circle, drawing a swirling pattern on my bare skin from where my skirt had risen, his hand touching my bare leg.

Other than the leg touching, he'd made no effort to interact with me. He hadn't spoken to me once. Or to anybody at the table, come to think of it.

I couldn't tell you what I'd expected, but I *had* at least expected him to converse with me a little. You know, acknowledge my presence with words and not just his hand that was wandering higher up my thigh with each second.

'W-what are you doing?' I whispered as low as I could, turning to face him, not wanting the rest of the table to hear me.

He leaned into me, pressing his mouth flush to my ear. His breath warm as it skated across my skin, causing shivers to erupt all over.

'Don't try and tell me you aren't enjoying it. I can feel the goosebumps. Feel the excitement. You like this just as much as I do.'

'Like what?'

'That we haven't said one word to each other, yet I'm touching you, anyway. Taking what I want.'

I gasped as his hand went higher, touching the outer edge of my underwear, teasing me. Clover raised her eyebrow at me, a silent question. I shook my head at her, hoping I didn't look as flustered as I felt. And boy, did I feel flustered. Oliver spoke the truth. I *was* enjoying this. It felt so naughty and forbidden that he hadn't said a word but pushed my boundaries, regardless.

'You're beautiful. You know that, right?' His tongue briefly grazed my ear before he leaned back in his seat.

Fuck. I was a goner.

The spell between us broke when Griff started shouting while flailing his arms around, 'Yo! Did anybody even hear what I said?'

'Yes. The entire room heard you, Griff,' Clover deadpanned. 'Even Ms Hawthorn in her office three corridors away must have heard you.'

'What shit you chatting now, wanker?' asked Leo as he turned to face the table, looking at everybody in turn. Come to think of it, I couldn't think of a time yet where Leo hadn't seemed bored. But then it hit me. He hadn't seemed bored last night when I'd bumped into him and Odette tangled up in one another's webs. He had been the complete opposite, in fact. His eyes were amused then, and his face had given him away for just a moment.

Like he had a secret only he knew about.

AFTER DINNER ENDED, the girls stormed off as a pack.

Leo wasn't far behind, as he disappeared the second we left the hall, not telling anybody where he was dashing off to. He left without saying a word to anyone.

Oliver whispered that he would see me tomorrow and then also vanished down the corridor, heading in the direction of the pool building. *The Sect* were a part of the school swim team and were the reason the school had so many accolades—probably helped fuel a little of their popularity, too. Leo had a swimmer's body, but if you looked at the other two, I would've sworn they played football or maybe even rugby. Some kind of contact sport, at least.

Griff was the only one who stuck around, and like a gentleman, he walked us back to our room and hugged us both good night, winking before he left. I was softening towards him. He was charming, and he seemed so laid back compared to the other two.

Once settled on my bed, I grabbed my phone to aimlessly scroll through *Hive*. Maybe look at some extra-curricular activities or clubs I could join. Make my time at school even more worthwhile.

'Sky. What the hell was happening during dinner?' Clover pounced the second she got comfortable on her bed, her question shooting from her like she'd been holding it in the whole walk back. 'Don't even think about saying nothing because I swear to you, I am not that dumb.'

'Nothing,' I said, brushing it off, even though my blush probably gave me away that I was bullshitting. 'Seriously.'

She narrowed her eyes, not believing me for a second, and the pressure emanating from her made me feel I needed to say more. I caved, the ice queen look gutting me in the heart. Plus, I didn't want my only friend pissed off at me. Not like I'd had other people fighting over me today trying to become my friend.

'Okay, fine! Oliver may or may not have been touching my leg.'

'I bet he was,' she seethed. 'Be careful, Sky. I don't know why the three of them are acting nice to you.'

I looked at her questioningly. She'd seemed friendly enough with Griff on the walk back and throughout dinner.

'Okay, the two of them,' she clarified, amending her previous statement. We both knew that Leo wasn't acting anything towards me except disinterested.

'Talking of being careful, *Clo*. What exactly did Leo say to you this morning in assembly?'

'Nothing.' She averted her gaze, opened her laptop, and started tapping away at something.

'I'm asking nicely.' I fluttered my eyelashes at her, hoping she'd take pity on me and spill her guts. I could sense that she wanted to talk about it but was scared of something too. Maybe her need to get it out in the open would win out.

'I promise that one day I'll tell you everything, Sky, but today is not that day.'

After I'd read a few posts on Hive and was getting comfortable, I sensed fidgeting on the other side of the room that drew my attention.

'Sky...' Clover looked unsure, words sitting on the tip of her tongue.

'Yeah?'

'Have you ever been in love?'

In the short time I'd known her, I hadn't seen Clover look this shy or self-conscious. She was a badass, and she knew it. But this was a completely new side to her. I scoffed, wanting to make her feel less self-conscious about her question.

'Nope,' I replied, shaking my head. 'I've never even had a boyfriend.'

'Oh... Right.'

'Have you?'

'Have I what?'

'Ever been in love?'

'I thought I was once. But now I realise it was just how it looked in the light of day.' She lay back down on her bed, facing the ceiling. 'Skylar. I think you and I are going to be friends for a long time. Maybe even for life. Something's just clicked, you know?'

'I feel the exact same way,' I replied, my smile taking over my face. It was nice to have a friend.

I wasn't lying, either. Something in my heart knew I'd found a soulmate in Clover. Ride or die. After so many years of being a loner, it felt good to have somebody in my corner. One who wouldn't judge me for the stupid decisions I was no doubt about to make.

Trust me, I knew I would eventually throw caution to the wind in order to find out just what Oliver wanted with me.

There was something drawing me in. Pulling me to him. Two magnets, locked together, the reaction they experienced once they'd found their mate.

Seven

THE NEXT MORNING, I was thrilled I didn't wake up late. That mainly had to do with the fact that Clover had thrown a croissant at my head. She'd woken up early and gone down to grab us some breakfast, but when she tried to wake me, I didn't listen to her shouts—hence the croissant. It seemed like breakfast was more casual than the fine affair dinner had been last night. There was no assembly, either, which was a total plus.

The wind whistled through the trees in the distance, and when I looked out our window, I could see across the campus to the trees that lined the edge of the hill. A chill ran down my spine.

My first lesson of the day was History, a class I knew Oliver was also in, and it filled my stomach with nerves, my anxiety creeping up a notch with every action I took to get ready for my day. A small part of me wanted him to sit with me and give me attention. *Stupid Skylar.*

'Remember,' Clo called from her side of the room, throwing her blazer on. 'Keep to yourself today, Sky. I know you didn't have a bad day yesterday, but trust me when I say that these bitches are probably just trying to lull you into a false sense of security.'

'By bitches you mean the O girls?' I asked her, certain I knew the answer but wanting to hear it leave her lips, mainly to see if it riled her up.

'Of course,' she said as her face flushed. I laughed and when she saw my face, she realised I had been joking. Clover's shoulders deflated as she relaxed a little. 'You got me for a moment there. I genuinely believed you didn't know who I meant.'

'Oh, come off it, Clo. I'm not that dense.' I stopped and quickly added, 'Right?'

'Well...' Clo's smile grew super wide after a few seconds, 'No, you're not.'

'Phew.'

OLIVER DID SIT NEXT to me in History class and I tried my hardest the entire time to pay attention to Miss Woodland and not to anything he tried to whisper to me. And believe me, he was trying to whisper a *lot* of things. *Dirty things.*

Okay, maybe they weren't that dirty. They were phrases like, *I wish I could kiss you all over, see if you taste as good as you smell.* Or there was, *One day soon I'm going to bend you over this desk and fuck you from behind.*

Okay. Maybe it was hard to ignore.

His words were filthy as fuck and all I could do was think about the salacious images he painted in my mind with his words. I had no idea what war the teacher was telling us about.

The only war I knew was the one going on between my head and, well, not my heart, that was for sure.

By the time the class ended, I was the colour of a fire engine and I think I may have even foamed at the mouth a little... which really wasn't a good look. I think Oliver also believed I'd turned into a mindless zombie from the way his eyebrow twitched in my direction. I just couldn't wrap my head around it, though. I used to think I could see through bullshit—I'd always seen through my mum and Andy—but with Oliver, I just couldn't figure him out. Was he genuine? Was he interested in me? Or was I a target for some kind of game I didn't know I was playing? I sighed, making a mental note to myself to talk to Clover and find out more about him and the others.

'What're you thinking about?' he asked as we left the classroom and I moved towards my English class. The halls were abuzz with students, but when they saw Oliver coming, they cleared a path for us, like it was second nature to them.

'W-what?' I hadn't fully heard him, too lost in my head.

'What're you thinking about?' he repeated.

'Oh... Things.'

Great answer, Sky.

'By chance do those things have anything to do with what I said in class?'

'N-no,' I sputtered. 'You just caught me off guard, that's all.'

'Sure I did.' His tone was filled with amusement. 'I'm also sure the reason your face is bright red has nothing to do with me either.'

I took a glance to my left, to find him looking so smug, so sure of himself. I knew I had to knock his ego a little, but I wasn't experienced in this kind of psychological warfare. I found it hard enough to not get distracted by his eyes, or his chiselled jawline. Or the way his blazer strained across his broad shoulders. Even just looking at him, I felt myself getting hot. Then the perfect insult hit me.

'Oh, believe me. I was imagining your words...'

Oliver's face lit up, his eyes glinted with mischief, but then I delivered the blow.

Putting emphasis on the first word, I said, '*But* I replaced the thought of you with Griff.'

Take that, I thought, feeling good about myself for the first time in an interaction with him. Every other time we had spoken, I hadn't been thinking fully, totally flustered at the situation.

Oliver didn't seem to find my words funny, though. Instantly his eyes darkened in anger to an indigo instead of their usual light sky blue colour. He grabbed my upper arm tight, stopping me from walking further.

'What did you just say to me?' he rasped. His eyes were hard, with no trace of humour left in them—or on his face for that matter. I'd made him mad, and a small part of me was happy about it. Served him right.

'I was f-fantasising about Griff,' I said. The stutter didn't help me sound certain, but by the look on his face, Oliver only registered the words and not my awkward, stutter-filled delivery.

'Griff?' he questioned, his face growing darker somehow. The pressure from his hand got tighter with each word he spoke. 'You're going to regret saying that, New Girl,' he spat. A tiny fleck of it landed on my cheek, and I tried to stay calm. Letting go of my arm, he turned around and stormed off, leaving me alone in the now empty, silent corridor. I rubbed the top of my arm, trying to soothe the ache, knowing he'd probably left a bruise. *Dickhead.*

There wasn't enough time to stand and think about it as I needed to get to my lesson. My feet moved down the corridor, as I kept my head down low, and I silently slipped into my English classroom, hoping that somehow I had become invisible in the last hour. An empty seat in the back row beckoned me.

Not long after I'd sat down and got comfortable in my chair, Oralie and Ophelia entered the classroom together, staring at me once they spotted me in the back. Instantly they started whispering to each other. I rolled my eyes at their behaviour—even though I knew I shouldn't. I knew I was playing with fire, but I couldn't help myself. I had a gut feeling that the girls definitely took the rules more seriously than the guys did, and I shouldn't be pushing my luck—especially on the second day of term.

'Eurgh, Lia, why on earth is the New Girl looking at us?' Oralie asked, raising her voice to ensure I heard her. That the entire classroom heard her.

'I have no idea, but she better stop right now if she knows what's best for her,' Ophelia answered, looking way too happy for somebody delivering a threat.

'Bitch, don't you remember the rules? I *do not* deem it necessary for you to be looking at us right now,' Oralie snapped at me. 'And trust me, little girl, I will punish you.'

I sank further down into my chair. Inside, I told myself not to listen to her words. They sounded like a budget movie villain's lines that weren't overly thought out. And I knew there was nothing she could really do that would hurt me mentally.

But let's be honest—she *could* do a lot to hurt me *physically*. Teenagers can be cruel, and bullying was rife back in my old school. And from just a couple of days at Hawthorn, I could tell rich girls played even dirtier than those I grew up with.

I watched as Miss Morrison, our English teacher, swept into the room and started playing "Wuthering Heights" by Kate Bush through the whiteboard speakers, and I swear I died inside even more. The song was undoubtedly a tune, but it could only mean one thing; we were about to read *Wuthering Heights*, and I couldn't think of anything worse. The façade of the main building had already reminded me of it. I didn't need to be studying it too. Every teenage fiction book I'd read had some kind of sick fascination with the love story of Cathy and Heathcliff, but honestly, they were both toxic as fuck to one another and she died halfway through the book, so they weren't ever together anyway. Definitely not my idea of a love story.

Miss Morrison announced our new topic for the term, gothic literature, and lazily said, 'Solo reading for the next hour, please. Start the book and highlight any passages of note.'

I opened the book and began reading, hating every second of it. A rustling of pages and students shuffling in their seats filled the room. At least solo reading meant I didn't have to talk to anybody.

Oralie and Ophelia spent the first hour of the double period talking about me and trying to encourage others to do the same. The words, "scum," "slut," and "bitch" were whispered across the room, reaching me every couple of minutes. They were slowly building an audience, too. The girl at the desk next to me kept staring at me before leaning in and murmuring to me that I'd really fucked up by angering *The Set*.

At first, it didn't affect me. They were just trying to make themselves feel better about the fact that Oliver seemed to have taken an interest in me. But after the first hour, it sank in and as the dark cloud of their words hit other students, I could feel myself breathing slower. It was like that first night in my bedroom again. The world blurred at the edges and I didn't dare talk as I knew I would be a stuttering mess, making no sense. The room spun. My vision faltered. In my mind, the chair underneath me melted.

I can't black out here.

The girls would never let me live it down and I had heard nobody talking about my visit to the hospital wing the night before, so maybe Oliver and Leo had kept that tidbit quiet.

Or I just hadn't heard that particular nugget of gossip yet.

An hour of solo reading passed.

Miss Morrison had realised that maybe the class wasn't actually reading the book in their heads and were actually more focused on aiming nasty words and soggy spit wads at me. How original.

'Ophelia, dear,' Miss Morrison called out, surveying the classroom. 'Could you read aloud from the beginning of chapter three?'

'Of course, miss, it'd be my pleasure,' Ophelia said, her tone sickly sweet. Like butter wouldn't melt. Nausea rose in my stomach, and a slight huffing noise left me. What a little kiss arse.

Ophelia started to read out loud, and I followed along in my copy, but after a few pages, she stopped.

'Miss,' she said after a small pause. 'I feel like we should let somebody else read now. I don't want to bore people with my voice.' She tittered, or at least that was the only word I could think of to describe the noise she'd made. All girlish and fake. 'How about we let Skylar read now? She *is* new and I wouldn't want her to feel excluded. She's a Hawthorn girl now, after all.'

Well, fuck me. It was obvious to me that Ophelia knew exactly what she was doing, although I honestly wasn't sure whether the teacher knew that Ophelia was being a bitch to me or whether she genuinely believed she was trying to "help" me. What help would it really be for me to read out loud to a class of pupils I'd barely met?

'Oh, what a lovely, inclusive idea, dear. Skylar, please stand and read to us starting from page thirty-six,' Miss Morrison said, her gaze finding mine. Her smile was encouraging enough and her kind blue eyes looked open and honest.

I knew there was no way out of this. The fact I had to stand made it even worse. All eyes were on me. Even though I was at the back of the classroom, every pupil had turned to face me, their gazes taking me in from head to toe. I prayed I wouldn't stutter my way through it. I wasn't ready just yet for that kind of humiliation, thank you very much. I definitely didn't want to draw even more attention to myself than what had already been thrust upon me by eating dinner with *The Sect* last night.

I stood and raised my book, to read of course, but also to use as a shield so I didn't have to see the entire class looking at me. You would think they'd be looking at their own copies in order to follow along and make notes or some shit—but apparently watching the New Girl flounder was more exciting. Which, yeah, in their position, I would agree. Seeing me falter would be more interesting compared to *Wuthering Heights*.

'"If the little f-fiend had got in at the window, she p-probably would have s-strangled me!"' Aware of my slow pace, I tried to read faster, but the faster I read, the more mistakes I made.

Not like it mattered. The entire class erupted in laughter the second I stuttered over the first word and didn't stop from then onwards. I could hear them repeating my mistakes, emphasising every stutter and trip-up. Every error reverberating through the room, until I couldn't see the words in front of my face any more from the tears blurring my vision.

'Not the w-w-window,' Oralie mocked, nudging Ophelia in the side with her elbow.

I knew miss could hear them, could see them making rude gestures at me, but she never once told them to stop. She'd turned a blind eye to proceedings, sitting at her desk and drinking her coffee with no care. She wasn't going to put a stop to any of it. I was on my own.

Of course, Ophelia and Oralie were jeering the loudest. The whispers surrounded me.

"She should go hide in her room. Nobody wants her here."

"She should go slit her wrists. Not like anybody would miss her."

"She's so ugly, only a blind man would fuck her."

It took everything in me not to let the tears gathering in my eyes fall.

'You can take over reading now, Wesley,' Miss Morrison said, aiming her words at a boy sitting in the row ahead of me. 'Thank you, Skylar.'

I slumped down into my seat, thankful for the reprieve, and kept my head down as I listened to Wesley pick up where I left off.

Finally, the class neared its end, and all I wanted to do was get out of there as quickly as I could and disappear deep into the library where nobody would think to look for me. Thankfully, it was lunch next, followed by a free period, and I was so ready to become invisible.

I looked up as Miss Morrison wrapped up the lesson and I saw Oliver standing in the doorway, leaning against the doorframe in that way popular, hot guys seemed to do *really* well. I shrank even further into my seat. I had no idea how long he'd been standing there, but I reckoned he saw at least some of what Ophelia and Oralie had started. His facial expression gave nothing away, though, and for all I knew, he could be standing there waiting for the girls to go to lunch with him. We hadn't exactly left things on great terms earlier. My arm still smarted from the way he'd gripped it so tight.

The class filed out of the room and I stood slowly, wondering if he would walk away with Ophelia and Oralie when they passed him. I had to admit that I felt a little smug when he paid them no attention at all. I waited until every single student had left the room and Oliver still stood there. He was definitely waiting for me.

'H-how long were you standing there?' I asked.

I vowed one day I would talk to him with no stutter, but once again, it was not that day.

'Long enough,' he said. His clipped answer and tone told me all I needed to know. He'd witnessed what the class had done to me—what they'd been saying to me. He knew how they had all been laughing at me.

'R-right,' I mumbled. 'Well, I'll see you later.' In an attempt to rush around him, I darted right, but he caught my arm before I could get away. I grimaced. It was the exact same part of my arm he'd grabbed in the corridor earlier. Why was he so interested in me, especially after I pissed him off earlier in the day? The dark, twisted look on his face told me he knew how much his tight grip hurt me. Yet he didn't care either way.

He tightened his hold.

'Where d'you think you're going?' he asked or demanded.

'To the l-library.'

'It's lunch time,' he said. 'What are you doing about food? Gotta eat, right?'

'I was going to grab something on my way.'

'I'll join you. I have a free period after lunch, too,' he said, finally loosening his grip around my arm. Oliver's lips rose at the corners, a semi-smile of sorts. One filled with warning.

I nodded, resigned to my fate, and let him drag me along beside him.

It wasn't until a lot later that I realised I'd never told him I had a free period after lunch.

Eight

HEADING STRAIGHT FOR THE LIBRARY, I tried to ignore the imposing figure next to me, but he was hard not to take notice of. I kept trying to walk faster, but with every two strides I took, he only needed one, so there was no way I was going to out-walk him—or outrun him, if I ever needed to.

I also couldn't help but notice how handsome he was. He really had that whole *I'm a good-looking guy and I know it* vibe going on. Oliver was hot, and I'd be lying if I said I couldn't see why all the girls here were hoping to one day "land him." I'd literally heard some girl use that phrase and it still made me die thinking about it.

We headed across the school grounds because even though you'd expect the English classrooms to be near the library, they were actually the furthest away. Ignoring Oliver was difficult when he kept entering my personal bubble.

A quick stop in the hall for lunch and the two of us stayed silent. The tension in the air was palpable, and all I wanted to do was get away. Everybody stared at us, the whispers growing louder each second. In no time at all—that felt like a heck of a lot of time—we got to the front of the line and grabbed some sandwiches and put them in a to-go bag.

Leaving the hall with our lunch, Oliver asked me, 'You going to tell me what happened back there?'

'Back where?' I asked, pretending I didn't understand the question. Oblivious to the end.

'Pretend you don't know what I'm talking about all you want, New Girl,' Oliver said, shrugging. 'Not like I'm going to give up.'

'I-it was nothing.' I hoped he'd leave my blatant lie alone. It was only my second day, and I didn't want to have the wrath of *The Set* fall on me so soon. It had already started in English and I prayed I wouldn't have to endure that in every class I shared with them. It would make my time here at Hawthorn a lot harder than it needed to be.

'That wasn't nothing, Sky. You were shaking and on the verge of tears when I got there.'

'Seriously, *Oliver*, it was nothing.' I stressed his name, hoping he would take me at my word as I didn't want to rehash any of what had happened to him, of all people. I picked up my pace, but he matched me step for step.

'Thought I told you to call me Ollie?' he asked, his irritation at my refusal clear.

'You did. But I decided not to,' I told him, not completely certain where this badass-ness was coming from. Well, as badass as I could be with my stutter.

'And why is that, New Girl?' he asked, his tone dark.

'Because we're not friends,' I told him. I wasn't sure how he would react, but ever since he'd told me to call him by his nick-name, I just couldn't bring myself to. Not even in my head. I'd slipped when talking to Clo one time, but since then, I'd been careful. It was a slippery slope.

Oliver didn't answer.

After what felt like a lifetime but was in actuality probably only a few minutes, we finally made it to the library.

For me, the library gave away the school's age. Large, old, and daunting, it looked to be one of the oldest buildings, and fuck was it impressive. Clover had briefly taken me here during her tour, but we hadn't focused on it for too long. At that point, it wasn't like she'd known how much I loved books.

But I did. I loved reading, and I loved seeing all these books together, just waiting for somebody to pick them up and find the wonder that lived inside their pages. I used to spend all my time at the local library in town—when I wasn't working at the supermarket or at school. It had been my respite when things were hard at home. When things became too much for me to handle. Books were always there, and within the pages of books, I'd found many friends and worlds I would've done anything to visit—I still would if given the chance.

Being older now, I was more likely to read romance books that you wouldn't find in your local library—but I still visited all the same. It was one place I could truly find peace.

Sadly, being in this library with Oliver meant I probably wouldn't get much peace. I knew he hadn't finished asking his questions. He was biding his time. Waiting it out. Then he would pounce, like a beast from the shadows.

I found a table at the very back of the library to sit at, dumping my lunch and my bag filled with my books and laptop down with a thud.

Oliver placed his food and bag down gently and took a seat, meaning I had no choice but to sit next to him.

Well, that was what I told myself, anyway, and I was sticking to it.

We sat next to one another in silence for five minutes—a fucking long time to sit with anybody in uncomfortable silence, believe me. Part of me felt excited, but the majority of me just felt irritated that he was interrupting my peace and not even saying anything.

The silence was obviously affecting Oliver too, as he turned to face me and asked once again, 'What happened in class, Sky?'

'I told you, nothing important.'

'I saw the end. The girls were picking on you. I thought Leo told you to come to me if you had any trouble with them?'

I stayed quiet. Yeah, Leo had said that to me, but I hadn't believed him. I thought he'd been lying or, I don't know, trying to make me feel better or something. I felt stupid saying that out loud, though. I felt stupid saying mostly everything out loud, especially when I stuttered like a little bitch. Plus, it wasn't like I'd had much chance to tell Oliver prior to him asking.

Oliver's face darkened, his eyebrows furrowing, and his mouth as straight as I'd ever seen it. He resembled the Oliver I'd seen leaving the pool house on the day I arrived. When Clover had warned me about them. Shit, had that only been two days ago? I must try to remember that the girl I'd formed a bond with here—make that the only person I'd connected with —made it very clear that I should stay away from *The Sect*. Obviously that included present company. Rule number five could kiss my ass. If he invited me to dinner again, I would refuse.

'Sky, I won't repeat myself. Come to me or Leo or, fuck, even Griff if you need to, okay? Just let us know what's going on and we can sort it.'

'O-okay.'

'Please tell me what happened,' he said. The sincerity in his tone and the pleading look in his eyes made me finally cave.

Also, the fact that he had actually said please to me made my heart warm a little.

'I-it was nothing. Oralie and Ophelia thought it would be funny to have me read aloud,' I admitted with a sigh. 'And my stutter definitely makes reading in class hard.'

'They're just mean, rich girls, Sky. I'll talk to them.'

'Please don't,' I whispered. The last thing I needed Oliver to do was talk to them and make them want to hurt me even more than they already did. I wanted to fly under the radar, not become a beacon.

'Fine. But I swear to God, Skylar, if you do not tell me about them in the future, I will spank you so hard, you won't forget again.'

I choked on the bite of sandwich I'd thought it was safe to take.

Oliver had a habit of slipping these dark, flirtatious sentences into conversation and expected me to take them, no questions asked. I blushed at him, which only seemed to make him more smug.

'Y-you wouldn't.' My words sounded a lot more confident than I felt.

'Oh, you'd be surprised at just what I would do to you, New Girl.' His tone was dark and delicious, causing a shiver to run down my spine. 'Ever since I first saw you, I've wanted to get under that skin of yours and see the true you. Figure out exactly what makes you tick.'

His blue eyes stared into mine and it felt to me as if he wanted to see into my soul. *Which was absurd, right?* We'd only known each other for a few days and it wasn't like we'd had any in-depth convos in that time or anything. When I first saw him, the connection between us had sparked to life, but I definitely only felt attraction—not obsession. Oliver seemed the type to obsess over small things. Guess I was one of those *things.*

'I d-don't know why. I'm not important,' I said. My voice quavered, and my true opinion of myself bled through my words. I could feel them in the atmosphere, threatening to choke me with embarrassment. Man, I was pathetic and chances were at this rate anyway, that Oliver would notice pretty soon just how much of a loser I truly was.

'Don't say that,' he said, his tone harsh and abrupt. It surprised me. Fucking *shocked* me, actually. I thought that maybe he'd just agree with me or something. His eyes stared into mine, imploring. 'You are important.'

We both fell silent after that.

We finished our lunch and both started on our homework. It was quite nice to work side by side in silence. Every now and again, I found my gaze wandering in his direction. He really filled the school uniform out nicely. His broad chest and wide shoulders looked so good in his white shirt, and even though he was wearing a bottle green blazer, he was really making it work for him. You know that saying, *"wear clothes and don't let the clothes wear you"*? That sprang to mind whenever I looked at Oliver. And I appreciated it—appreciated him.

But the silence couldn't last forever.

Oliver turned to face me, and the look on his face told me he really didn't want to say the words about to leave his mouth, but he was going to say them anyway.

He sighed and whispered, 'Sky, why don't you think you're important?'

I closed my eyes and did that whole *I wish the ground would swallow me whole* thing, but it didn't work. When I opened them, his face was even closer than it had been, and his eyes were staring into mine. Attempting, but failing, to unravel all of my secrets.

'I never have,' I admitted, realising I needed to give him a little more. 'I guess I never had many friends or family there to t-tell me otherwise. Believe it or not, Oliver, I've always been a bit of a loner.'

I hated focusing on my lack of friends and the fact that my family didn't give a shit about me. My mum may be the worst, but she kept a roof over my head to an extent and she never abandoned me. Even if sometimes I thought my life would have been better if she had.

My dad, on the other hand, I'd never met. He split from my mum when I was a few months old and nobody ever really talked about him much. I knew he existed once upon a time and that he and my mum came from totally different upbringings and backgrounds, but that was all I knew.

Having no friends was another thing entirely. After we hit secondary school, I had nothing in common with the girls I'd grown up around. Especially Remi. The girls were interested in boys and makeup and having the newest clothes and all that kind of material rubbish. I just wanted to read and escape into the book world. I had no time for boys, and makeup and clothes were luxuries I couldn't afford. Before Andy came along, I was lucky if my mum even remembered to fill the fridge with edible items.

Oliver speaking brought me out of my dark thoughts.

'Believe it or not, New Girl, I *can* believe that.' He was laughing—at me or with me, I wasn't completely certain. 'But now you don't have to be. You've made friends with Clover, right?'

I nodded. 'Yeah, she's great.'

'And you're now a part of the inner circle too, what with us inviting you to hang out and all.'

I looked away, the bookshelves suddenly seeming more enticing to me than his mesmerising blue eyes. I could hear an underlying threat hidden underneath his kind words. Why did I get the impression that being a part of the inner circle was the last thing I should want?

'I g-guess.'

'Did you mean what you said earlier?' he asked, changing direction. Confusing me.

He changed the topic so fast, I almost got whiplash turning abruptly to face him once more.

'About w-what exactly?'

'Did you mean what you said about Griff? Imagining him doing the things I whispered to you.' He leaned closer, his words whispered against my ear, and I shivered at the slight touch of his lips.

'No.' I shook my head, both in response to him, but also as an attempt to clear the fog my mind seemed to have clinging to it. 'I just said those things to make you m-mad.'

'Would you believe me if I said it worked?'

'You deserved it, Oliver.'

'*Please*, call me Ollie,' he said, almost pleading with me, and I couldn't help myself from smiling with satisfaction. There wasn't much I could do to piss him off, yet calling him by his full name seemed to work as a treat. I highly doubted that many people ignored him when he gave a direct order, let alone when he asked politely.

'I'll think about it. But I still don't think we're friends.'

I needed to create some distance between the two of us. I could still feel his whisper in my ear. His lips had grazed my cheek and the featherlight touch of it lingered.

The effect he had on me irritated me. Why was I letting him get to me so much?

Aggravated, I stood abruptly, the chair nearly falling to the floor from the shove I gave it. I don't know what it was about Ollie that riled me up so much, but I did know one thing. I couldn't sit there across from him pretending to study any longer.

I had to get away.

Shoulders tense, I spun away from his smirk and stomped off. My mind was buzzing with thoughts just as my body buzzed with restrained emotions, trapping me in my own little world. I wandered deeper into the library, absently headed toward the part I knew no one visited. It would be nice and quiet. Just what I needed.

I quickly found my way to the non-fiction section of the library. No other students were around, and I sighed in relief when I made it to a dead-end. My shoulders rose and lowered again with the motion. It was a deep sigh. I needed to find a history book to complete an assignment, and I didn't want anyone stepping inside my personal bubble.

One time, back when I worked at the supermarket, I'd had an anxiety attack because somebody had come too close to me when I was stocking a shelf. They'd reached across me, innocently enough, yet my heart had stopped and my vision had wavered. How humiliating.

It wasn't until I stopped beside some shelves loaded with thick hardbacks that I sensed someone at my back. I realised immediately it wasn't just anyone who'd followed me back here.

I was just about to turn around when a hard body pressed up against my back. An arm came up on either side of me, caging me in, stopping me from going anywhere.

'Running away, New Girl?'

His words whispered against my neck.

'Leave me alone,' I growled, whipping around to face him, but he moved his hand in order to hold my neck firmly in place.

The only thing I could hear in the silence was our breathing. I swore the people around could hear my breathing throughout the entire library.

Oliver started placing small kisses up and down my neck. I moaned in a mix of frustration and arousal. His hardness pressed into my back and all I could think about was how he must look naked.

He grabbed me by the waist, hard, and flipped me around so we were facing one another.

'God, you don't realise just how fucking sexy you are, Skylar.'

He was *seriously* in my bubble now, those hard muscles tempting me from beneath his shirt. With him so close, I had to tilt my head back to look up at his irritatingly smug face. Eurgh, why did all the hot guys have to be such gorgeous dickheads?

I hated the way my body responded to Ollie, making me fight what seemed to be a natural pull toward him. It would have been so much easier to give in, but I was not about to give him that kind of power over me.

'Tell me to leave then,' he whispered, leaning in even closer, my body lighting on fire at his closeness.

Breathless, I couldn't find the words to tell him to go.

Ollie's grin grew, taking me in with his gaze in a way that made my knees feel weak.

'That's what I thought.' His smile turned sinister. 'You secretly like me being close to you, don't you, New Girl?' His voice dropped in volume as he leaned in closer and took a subtle sniff of my perfume.

I didn't move, staring at him warily, feeling lost in this new situation.

But he was right. There was a part of me that didn't want to run from him anymore.

Then his lips touched mine, devouring them. The action was almost violent. The way he forced my mouth open—the way he used his tongue against mine. All of it. *Pure violence.*

The kiss was anything but sweet and I could feel his hard length pressing up against me, which only made me want it elsewhere. My hormones were racing through the roof and I tried to focus on what was happening, to stay in the moment.

I stopped fighting him, stunned.

Ollie was *kissing* me? Ugh, why did I like it so much? Why did he have to be such a surprisingly good kisser?

I had no strength to push him away. Feeling helpless, I warily allowed him to kiss me, secretly relishing in the way he devoured me like he'd been starving himself for weeks and I was a meal delivered to him by the gods.

One of Oliver's hands was in my hair, gripping it tightly; the other hand squeezed my nipple through my bra. The pain mixed with the pleasure and I moaned even louder. I was so turned on, I couldn't think straight. The way he was making me feel was unlike any way I'd ever felt before. I was riding high, enjoying his attention.

'Fuck,' he groaned.

He stopped the kiss abruptly.

He moved away from me, creating a gap between our bodies. His expression dark, his emotions shutting off in front of me.

'You want to be right here, pressed between me and the

bookshelf,' he continued, just as my shoulder blades hit the shelf behind me from the way I was still leaning back from the gap he'd created between us. Yet, my feet wouldn't move. My body wouldn't escape. My attention was riveted on Ollie as his face came too close to mine... again.

'As for me,' he continued talking, 'I want a little more than just this.' He growled, low in his throat, causing my heart to beat twice as fast. 'I'd like to have you a little more pliant. Less resistant. I want to feel you melt against me.'

Once more, his arm darted out and slipped behind my back and pulled me to him, throwing me off-balance. As I fought to gain control of myself, he pressed his lips to mine in a softer but still demanding kiss.

I felt hot by the time his lips broke from mine, pulling back just enough to let us both breathe. Before I could truly recover, he pressed me back against the bookshelf with one arm, the other roaming down my side as his gaze locked with mine.

'Very good, New Girl,' he breathed. 'But now I want more. I want this'—he squeezed my arse hard, nearly bruising it before moving his hand back up, skirting across my hip on its way toward my left breast—'and I want these. I want you to moan as I leave bite marks all over your body. As I draw your nipples into tight, needy little buds.'

His face lowered from mine, giving me a sense of relief that lasted for only a second as I felt his breath on my neck instead. A moment later, he bit my neck, sending another rush of heat through me.

Oh, I hated it. But damn, did it feel so good.

As he nipped at my neck harshly enough to likely leave marks, his hand moved to my nipple, pinching and pulling at it. My resolve to not make a sound wavered as he worked me over, and my hands gripped the bookshelf at the back of my thighs hard as I fought to control myself.

'I've never had sex in a public place like this before,' Ollie muttered against my jaw just below my ear, his hand once more travelling further south. 'What do you think? Could you handle my cock if I stripped you down right now?'

A small squeak left me when his hand went under my skirt, and his fingers curled against my clit, my body shuddering as the need for release skyrocketed. I felt his grin against my throat as he slipped my panties to the side, touching me directly in a way I liked far too much. A way nobody else had before.

As his fingers worked expertly on me inside and out, I wiggled and even let out a few whimpers, but I was too hungry for more to pay it much mind. At least, until he pulled away from me suddenly, leaving the air feeling too cold and empty in his absence.

My fingers involuntarily touched my lips in a daze. I looked around and luckily found myself alone still.

I felt like I was living in my very own twisted tale; left in a library, the feared monster gone, my heart slightly thawing.

As he left, I could only watch him with a swirl of emotions I was pissed at him for leaving me with.

What a dick.

Nine

PHILOSOPHY AND ETHICS was the class I was looking forward to the most. It hadn't been offered back at Hollowdale High. It was yet another advantage the scholarship to Hawthorn could give me. I had to remember that. I couldn't forget that my end goal was to graduate from here with the best grades I could get in order to apply to the best universities. There was no way I was going to waste the opportunity. No matter what happened with deliciously dark boys who pinned me up against library book stacks and then said nothing before they left.

My mind wandered to the way Ollie looked before he stormed away from me. *Tormented.* Out of control.

Griff strode into the classroom, looking like he had no care in the world, which when I thought about it, he probably didn't. Ever since meeting him, I'd never once seen him take anything seriously. He constantly cracked jokes and made everybody around him smile. Or groan—in a heartfelt way.

He fell into the chair on my right, looking at me questioningly.

'Well, well, well, New Girl. What have we here?' His wide smile covered his face. 'You look a little... flushed.'

I wanted to smack him and hide from him simultaneously. I decided not to respond, mostly because I had no idea what to say. I was still processing what had happened with me and Ollie in the library.

Shit.

I was thinking of him as Ollie.

It was official. *I was fucked.*

Griff couldn't see the turmoil going on in my mind, though, as he continued talking and said, 'So, Sky. Would you say the History section or the Science Fiction section is better for hookups? I'm asking for a friend.'

I rolled my eyes at him, trying my hardest not to smile but feeling my lips twitch, anyway. He sure was persistent, though, got to give him that.

'New Girl, I'm messing with you. I give zero shits about you hooking up amongst the library shelves. Actually, I'm sort of cheesed off that I hadn't thought to try it before.'

'C-cheesed off?' I giggled. Then quickly put my hand over my mouth, but the damage was already done.

'Was that a giggle I just heard, New Girl? Damn. I did *not* have you down as a giggler,' he teased, unleashing a bright smile in my direction, and I swear to you, I was almost blinded by his teeth. 'Now you've made me wonder how your giggle would sound with me doing all sorts of naughty shit to you.'

'What is it with you guys and w-wondering how I'll sound when you're inside me?' I asked, definitely raising my voice too loud, but I couldn't help it. First Ollie with my stutter and now Griff with my giggle. These boys were going to be the death of me.

'I'm just messing with you, Sky. We're friends and I just know we're going to be *best* friends. Nothing more,' he said, his eyes matching the sincerity of his words. He had called me by my name, for starters. 'Ollie, I can't vouch for. He definitely wants to know how you'd sound around his dick,' Griff added as an afterthought.

Then I made a noise that I couldn't even find the word for. It was like a mix between a guffaw and a chortle. I covered my mouth again. I needed to try harder to keep a hold of myself.

'I'm sure he doesn't,' I sputtered, whilst trying to stop myself from laughing more. I just couldn't understand it. Even though Ollie *had* just kissed me in the library—a little more than kissed me—I couldn't compute in my mind that he actually *wanted* me.

I was a game to him. Nothing more.

'I'm serious,' Griff said. 'That boy wants you bad. Even threatened me after what you said to him this morning about fantasising about me. Super handy for the ego, love. I knew you wanted a piece of the Griff-man.'

'Please never refer to yourself as the "Griff-man" ever again,' I said. I couldn't stop my laughter now that it was coming full force. A tear escaped from my eye, trailing down my face until I could taste the salt of it on my lips.

'New Girl,' he said, his tone surprised. 'Your stutters disappeared.'

'Oh.' I shook my head in confusion. I hadn't even realised it. The only other person I'd been able to talk to here without a stutter was Clover. She was the *only* person I felt comfortable around, full stop. But there was something about Griff that eased my anxiety. I think it had something to do with the fact that he didn't seem to take anything too seriously. He was full of jokes and had made me smile more than anybody else here. 'I guess your bullshit has made me realise there's no reason to be nervous around you.'

'Should I take that as an insult, New Girl? 'Cause I gotta say, that doesn't sound too flattering.'

'No. You should actually be super happy about it. Means I like you.'

'Well, then!' He slapped his hand to his knee, and I giggled again at his enthusiasm. He smiled, teeth on show, and said, 'You should've just said that.'

I smiled back as the teacher, Mr Sommers, entered the classroom. He was a towering beanpole of a man. Sort of reminded me of the tall one from *Fantastic Mr Fox* by Roald Dahl—one of my favourite stories growing up. Roald Dahl's stories had always fascinated me. For a child with no father and a shit mother, his stories had shown me that there were many children out there suffering at the hands of stupid adults.

In all honesty, I barely paid any attention to the lesson, even though I'd been so excited about it. My mind was still stuck in the library. My time with Ollie replaying in my head on a constant loop. A sick perversion that wouldn't leave me, and every single time, the scene progressed further. Or I did something different, evolving the fantasy into something *more*.

Frustration and stupidity at my actions hit me in a gust of thoughts. I knew Ollie wasn't actually interested in me and that this was surely some big game to them all. The fact that Griff had known what happened when we'd got to class meant that *somebody* had already told him. My money was on Ollie, as nobody else had been there.

And if Ollie had passed it on that fast, then it surely meant nothing to him at all.

I needed to forget it happened. *Easier said than done.*

AFTER CLASSES HAD ENDED for the day, I made it back to Clo's and my dorm room in record time.

I desperately needed to talk to Clover, to get her opinion on everything that had happened. It felt like so much had changed since I saw her that morning. Chances were she'd just roll her eyes and tell me I was making a huge mistake by getting involved with any of them in any capacity. Regardless, I wanted to hear it from her lips, anyway. I needed talking down from the ledge I seemed to have found myself teetering on.

Entering our room, I could see Clover sitting on her bed, engrossed in something on her laptop screen. She looked up at me and instantly said, 'Spill.'

'Spill what?' I asked, shaking my head in wonder at how she could tell I had gossip after only looking at me for a second. Was my face that much of a dead giveaway?

'Spill whatever it is you wanna tell me. You look fit to burst. Plus, you made it across campus super fast. I wasn't expecting you back for at least another ten minutes.'

'I can walk fast when I want to.' I shrugged, trying to calm down the thoughts racing through my head. Even I could hear the defensiveness in my tone, though. 'We're not all lucky to have a free period at the end of the day.'

'Just tell me, Sky, and we can sort whatever it is.'

'So...' I took a deep breath. 'I may have kissed Ollie earlier.'

I threw myself onto my bed in a super dramatic fashion, the mattress screaming in protest. I covered my ears, knowing that a squeal was about to come out of Clover's mouth.

In three... two... one...

'You WHAT?' Clover asked, her voice shrill and so loud, I wondered if anybody lingering in the corridor could hear her.

'Well, actually. He kissed me. In the library.'

'With his tongue?' Clover said and started laughing, and I wasn't positive, but I reckoned she was trying to make some kind of *Cluedo* reference. You know, the board game with Miss Scarlett and the rope. A board game of tact, if you knew how.

'Yeah, with his tongue,' I replied, a smile playing on my lips. Even just talking about it caused a visual to materialise in my mind. I could still feel Ollie's lips on mine and his chest pressed up against me. His fingers sliding against me. Touching my bare thigh. Chills covered my arms and I rubbed them to ease the ache.

'Wait a minute!' Clover gasped. 'You're fucking calling him Ollie now, too? Oh hell no, Sky, what on earth are you thinking?'

'Pretty sure I wasn't really thinking.' I pondered for a moment and added, 'Actually, I *was* thinking, but they weren't exactly PG thoughts.'

'You definitely weren't thinking, Skylar. This is going to blow up in your face. You know that, right?' she asked, her face exasperated.

'It might not,' I said, petulant as a child.

'Oh, baby girl, it definitely will,' Clover said and looked at me with pity.

'What makes you so sure?' I asked her, mostly because I wanted to believe that things could work out for me. The way Ollie kissed me was so different from what I'd had before. He kissed me with passion, with no restraint, and by God, the boy could do things with his tongue—and hands.

'I just know, Sky. I know these boys. I've known them forever and not once has Ollie ever taken an interest in any girl.

Not being funny, but you're on scholarship here. Did you not read the rules?'

'Course I did. We read them together and scoffed over them, remember?' I asked rhetorically.

'Right. So you'll have remembered rule four. The one that says about dating above your class. And you can bet that you and Ollie dating is something they wouldn't be okay with.'

It surprised me that Clover knew the rules by heart, numbers and all.

'But surely he doesn't have to ask for permission? If he upholds the rules, then surely he can break them? What's the use of being in a position of power if you can't do shit-all to do what you want?'

'Sort of not the point, Sky. The point is, I find all of this highly suspish,' Clover said, her eyebrows knitted together.

'So, w-what, you don't think Ollie could actually fancy me?' I asked, my lip quivering slightly, a little upset by her statement. I didn't want to be that girl, but her words had hit me in my already rather low self-esteem.

'No, sweetie, I don't mean that,' Clover said, throwing a compassionate look my way. My mattress depressed as she sat down beside me and pulled me into a one-armed hug. 'I just mean that it seems funky to me, that's all. On tour day, the boys definitely saw you as a new toy to play with, and now we're meant to just believe that Griff is your friend and that Ollie wants you? I'm sorry, but I don't—I can't.'

'No, I know. I get it. I do. You know them better than I do, after all.' I hugged her back, so glad that I had her on my side. 'I just need to think about all of this logically. Not get caught up in what happened in the past to others. Who knows, it may have meant nothing to him and I'm getting all worked up for no reason.'

'I mean this for your sake. I hope he isn't toying with you. But yeah, girl, keep your guard up just in case it is all bullshit.'

'You're right.'

We dropped the conversation, and Clover moved on to telling me about her day that was totally uneventful compared to mine.

I tuned her out, making encouraging conversation noises every now and again when she needed it, and instead thought of the events of the day. *Fuck me.* I'd known that I fancied Ollie. Who wouldn't, after all? But I also hadn't expected him to do that, and as much as I talked a good-ish game with Clover, I was in way over my head. I didn't want to get my hopes up, but I knew I would, anyway. No matter how much I didn't want to. No matter how much I shouldn't.

'Wait, Sky,' Clo said, breaking her stream of words about what something said during class. 'I heard something about what happened in English.'

'Oh…' I sighed and asked, 'What exactly did you hear?'

'That those absolute bitches picked on you, forced the teacher to pick you to read out loud, and took the piss out of your stutter.'

'Yep. Pretty much sums it all up,' I mumbled as moisture filled my eyes. I'd been trying so hard all day to forget about what had happened. About how it had made me feel. Small. Helpless. An outcast. I knew that if I put too much energy into thinking about it, I would bawl my eyes out all night and not stop. Something I really didn't want to do. I hated crying and was always more likely to cry when angry than when I felt sad. Yeah, messed up, I know, but I'd been that way ever since I was a kid.

'I know this is going to sound so fucking stupid, Sky, but

you really need to ignore the O girls. Or at least try and rise above it all. I've been there, and it's shit.'

'Thanks, I think?'

Although Clo's words weren't the best or the most uplifting, they were the truth—her truth. I appreciated that she was trying to help me. I still didn't know the full story of Clover's past, and I could sense that it wasn't the time to ask her about it, but I was aware that shit had gone down in her past between her and *them*. And that one day she would tell me all.

All I could do was try and survive my time at Hawthorn. I mean, it had only been in one class and it hadn't been too bad. I just needed to grow a thicker skin. *Or grow a new, stronger backbone.*

I planned to ignore *The Set* while I tried my best to put the kiss with Ollie behind me. I had to try.

For my sanity.

Ten

THE REST of the school week passed without much to report.

Well, actually, I'm totally bullshitting.

It wasn't completely without drama.

The Set announced on the third day of school—the day after Ollie kissed me in the library—both in the hallway and on the Hive, that I was persona non grata to them and that nobody should enjoy my company or make me feel welcome. What that meant exactly, fuck knows. All I knew was that the rest of the student body helped them in their tirade against me.

Clover declared it all to be bullshit the second Odette announced it and made it obvious that she would stick by me, regardless.

"They're just twats, Sky. Definitely not going to let them decide who I can and can't be friends with. I've got your back."

There was one aspect of it all the O girls couldn't have predicted, though, and that was the fact that both Ollie and Griff ignored *them* now. They sat with me in every class that we shared, and the four of us had taken to sitting with each other at breakfast, lunch, and dinner. I told them they didn't need to, especially as Leo had chosen not to leave the girls and still sat with them. I didn't want either of them to feel as if they were choosing me over one of their longest friends—and over school tradition. From what little they'd told me, I gathered the three of them had been friends since birth. Well, something like that, anyway.

When I mentioned to them they didn't need to choose me, I got two similar, but also completely different, answers.

Griff declared, *'There's nothing those little bitches can do to make me side with them. Gosh, New Girl, what do you take me for? A total dickhead? I'm* on *your side, Sky.'*

I'd smiled and hugged him when he said that to me. He was slowly growing to be one of my favourite people, not that there were many people fighting for that spot.

When I asked Ollie, he said, *'I'm in the best place for me right now. I'm* by *your side, Sky.'*

I noticed the "right now" in Ollie's response, but honestly, I couldn't really expect more than that from him. Not like we meant anything to one another. Yeah, there was everything that took place in the library that one time, but nothing had happened, or been said, since. Not one thing said between us about it since. Not the kiss and not the fact he'd left me in the library, alone. Even the flirting and whispered dick lines had died down to nothing.

It made me question every interaction we'd had together. Had I made it all up in my mind? Did he not want to talk about it with me? Or was it meant to add an aura of mystery? *Fuck if I knew.*

I tuned into the conversation happening around me.

'So then I said, you telling me you don't want my d in your v?' Griff laughed. 'Apparently, that was not the right thing to say *at all*. She went and got her brother and told him what I'd said. He was a big motherfucker too.' He was in the middle of telling some story about a girl he tried to pull at a school party a few years back. His stories always made us all laugh. Sometimes with him, and sometimes *at* him.

'Serves you right!' Clover laughed and I could tell she was enjoying the story, even if her expression showed disbelief. Griff had a way of telling a story that gripped you entirely, holding you by the balls until the very last sentence. Even when he wasn't coming across in the best light, you still wanted to give him a hug and keep him safe. Sometimes, the boy was too much of a cheeky dickhead for his own good.

'It doesn't serve me right at all. I didn't even say anything offensive to her!'

'Pretty sure she got offended when you offered to show her your dick, mate,' Ollie said, joining the conversation. A smirk covered his face, amused at Griff's antics.

The four of us were sitting together in the restaurant-like dining hall, waiting for our food to arrive, and I could sense the eyes of *The Set* on us. Leo, however, paid no attention to his surroundings. He looked so bored, and as if he believed he was completely above the hierarchy bullshit the girls were trying to drag the entire school down into. Whether he agreed with them or not, he still chose to sit with them over us. I didn't know him well enough to be upset about it, but none of it made sense to me. Leo was the one who told me to come to him if the girls picked on me. So, why he would now choose them and ignore me, confused me.

Ultimately, though, Leo didn't owe me anything.

'Nah, that wasn't it at all,' said Griff as he shook his head at Ollie's words. 'I technically never offered to show her my dick. Just offered to put it inside her.'

'Bit of a technicality, mate,' Ollie joked at the same time as Clover.

''Cause that's so much better,' she said, wiping tears from her eyes, the story too much for her. It didn't take me long to realise that a lot of Griff's stories revolved around some kind of sexual situation; or something he'd said or done to some girl or another.

'W-well, I'm sure she felt blessed for you to even offer,' I said, joining in with their banter.

'See, Skylar gets it,' Griff said, putting his arm around me, pulling me close. He did this often. Made me feel cared for and happy. 'She's my new favourite. The two of you can piss right off.'

We all reacted to his words at the same time. Clover hit him from his other side. Ollie rolled his eyes, while also looking slightly bemused. I giggled, quickly putting my hand across my mouth in an attempt to stifle the noise.

'Definitely my favourite. Are you sure I can't hear that giggle in a more intimate setting?' Griff let me go and made a love heart with his hands, batting his long, fair eyelashes at me. Pretty sure he waggled his eyebrows, too.

'Oh, stop.' I hit him on the head with a laugh. The whole thing felt good, though. Like I had become a part of something. A part of a real friendship group, with people who laughed together and enjoyed each other's company.

But when will the other shoe drop?

NEARING the end of my second week, I had just got comfortable in my seat next to Griff in Philosophy class when an announcement came over the school speakers.

Would Miss Crescent please make her way to Ms Hawthorn's office. I repeat, Miss Crescent for Ms Hawthorn's office immediately. Thank you.

All eyes in the class turned to me in the back row as I desperately wished to make myself invisible. Luckily for me, the worst of the bullies weren't in the class with me, but there were still some horrible, shitty people in the room.

'Ummm,' said Griff, making the noise a five-year-old did when another kid was in trouble. I jabbed my elbow into his rib. 'Oof, no need to hurt precious cargo, New Girl.'

'Off you go then, Miss Crescent.' Ms Wella smiled at me, her eyes crinkled and kind, and I packed up my table as swiftly as I could. I wondered what it was Ms Hawthorn wanted to talk to me about. I hadn't seen or heard of her since the assembly on the first morning of term. It was as if she was a ghost that had vanished into the ether.

The campus was empty as I made my way across, what with most of the pupils in class and those that weren't in class holed up in the library or the common room. The closer I got to the administration offices, the quieter it became.

I'd become accustomed to the strange school layout, so it didn't take me any time at all to get around anymore. No more getting lost in the corridors, or making wrong turns.

When I reached Ms Hawthorn's office, I knocked on the dark wood door and waited.

'Enter.' Her voice came out muffled through the thick door.

I walked into the room and took in my surroundings. The room was quite large, with dark wood panelling and an enormous fireplace on the left-hand side. Ms Hawthorn's table was directly in front of me, with her seat facing the door and a large black ornate empty chair sitting empty across from her. It looked a lot fancier than any office I'd seen in my old school; but let's be honest, my old school wasn't for the obscenely rich—not entirely. The kids—and the parents—there were lucky if they could afford to pay the bills and buy food. Or at least half of them were.

'Take a seat, Miss Crescent.' Her tone of voice was cold; seemed she hadn't changed her opinion of me in the two weeks I'd been a student here. Her eyes were still focused on her desk, not having raised them to even glance at me.

I took the empty seat in front of her desk, and for at least a minute the two of us existed in silence, as I waited for her to finish reading the paperwork I could only assume was important. She'd called me here, after all. No like I wanted to be in here.

After what felt like an eternity, she finally looked up at me and frowned.

'How are things going for you here at the academy, Miss Crescent?'

'Err, f-fine, thanks, Ms Hawthorn,' I said, wringing my hands together under the table. A habit of mine that would make Lady Macbeth proud.

'I take it you've settled in well to your classes and made some friends?' Her shrewd grey eyes could only be described as looking into my soul. There was something off about this lady, something that made me feel strange deep down, but I couldn't place a finger on what it was that had me feeling so out of sorts.

'Yes, thank you,' I replied, eyeing her warily. 'Clover has been a good friend to me. So has Griff.'

At that, her face soured like she was sucking on a lemon. It made the wrinkles around her mouth even more prominent, even more grotesque.

'Yes, I've heard that Master Cooper has been paying very close attention to you.' Her eyes were intense and focused on mine. A slight flicker of her eyelids had discomfort rushing through me. 'Please remember, Miss Crescent, that we expect you to be on your best behaviour while you are a student at this establishment. I've been hearing some unsavoury things about you.'

Unsavoury? What on earth?

I'd barely done anything wrong since I started. Nothing I could recall, at least.

Confused by her words, the heat of her gaze burning, I maintained eye contact with her, knowing that if I broke it, she would think even less of me than she already seemed to.

'Yes, Ms,' I said in response, trying to sound polite. I didn't want to get on her nasty side, but it seemed as though I may already be there.

'You may return to class. I'll be talking to you soon,' she said in a final, ominous sort of way.

Clearly dismissed, I stood up from my seat.

What a waste of my time.

Ms Hawthorn had already returned to her paperwork and clearly wanted me gone. It made no sense to me why she'd wanted to see me in the first place. Her questions weren't overly important and it wasn't like she'd said anything that couldn't wait. Maybe she just wanted to warn me again about my behaviour. *Odd.*

Leaving the room, I closed the door softly behind me and turned to face the corridor.

'SHIT!' I physically startled, jumping an inch off the stone floor. Ollie stood outside the door leaning on the wall on the opposite side of the hall, a smirk planted on his face. The epitome of cool, calm, and collected.

Oh. And amused.

'Sorry, I didn't mean to scare you,' he said, looking contrite. Or at least, I thought it was a look of contrition. It was always hard to tell whether somebody was being true or if they were genuinely sorry.

'That's okay. What are you d-doing here?'

'I heard the announcement on the Tannoy. Wanted to see what the old bat wanted with you.' He gestured towards the door I'd just closed.

'Oh, well, t-thanks. I guess?'

'So, what did she want?' he asked, looking all sorts of handsome. The dark brown of his hair caught the light, and he brushed it out of his face, messing it up.

He looked so good, my mind was thinking of licking him instead of paying attention to the question he'd just asked.

'Errr...' I trailed off. I'd lost all my brain cells in the last twenty seconds. Ollie's blue eyes were so clear, like the ocean on a summer's day. I could easily get lost in them and never come back up for air.

'You okay?' he asked, looking like he wanted to laugh at me but was reining it in. The wide smile on his face was a rare sight—even his teeth were showing.

'I'm fine.' I smiled back, pushing my hair behind my ears. I tried to stay still and not fidget, but nerves filled me. My stomach a swarm of butterflies and anxiety. It was the first time we'd been alone together since the library. Since the kiss. Since... more.

'So,' he continued, assessing me. 'Are you going to tell me what that cow wanted?'

'She just wanted to know how I was g-getting on. Friends

and things.' I shrugged, not sure what else to say. The conversation wasn't exactly in-depth, and there really wasn't much else to elaborate on.

'And what exactly did you tell her?'

'I told her I'd made friends in Clover and Griff.' Our eyes locked together, and his smile dimmed a little, a crease forming at the edge of each eye.

'Are we not friends then, Little One?' he questioned, one side of his mouth tilting upward.

'I don't know,' I whispered, deciding to go with honesty.

It was the most honest I'd been in a while. I didn't know if I would class him as a friend. I'd started to think that maybe we could be friends, but then he went and left me cold and alone in the library like a piece of trash on the side of the road.

'Well, guess I'll just have to do something to change your mind.'

'L-like what?'

'L-like this,' Ollie said, mimicking my stutter. He pushed me against the wall and kissed me.

The kiss was so different from the one he gave me in the library. The kiss was gentle. Sweet. A soft brushing together of lips. His hands softly cupped my face, revering me, like a precious gem; unlike last time when they had roamed all over me.

The kiss ended not long after it started. It was as if we both came to our senses together and remembered we were in the school corridor, out in the open, outside Ms Hawthorn's office.

'What was that for?' I stuttered. I took a step away from him, needing some space. It was rare that I let people into my personal bubble, and even though I wanted Ollie—I *really* wanted Ollie—I also needed to keep my head about me. I couldn't let his chiselled jaw and beautiful eyes pull me in.

'I just needed to do that,' he said, his smile once again wide and carefree. 'I'll see you later.'

He left me standing there, alone once more. But at the end of the corridor, he turned and shouted back to me, 'There's a party. Friday night in the woods. Be there.'

He knew I couldn't turn down that invitation. Not without having *The Set* come after me even harder than they already were, and believe me, they'd started coming for me pretty hard. Every class I shared with them, they had turned all the other students against me.

So far, they had attempted nothing physical. It'd all been words, or mean looks, or gestures across the dining hall, or a classroom. But I knew it was only a matter of time until they escalated.

Bullies and bitches usually do.

Eleven

FRIDAY NIGHT ARRIVED, and we were getting ready to go out. I didn't own many clothes suitable for a party, but luckily Clover had a few pieces I could borrow and although we weren't the same size, we could get away with sharing some items.

'Are we even allowed to party in the woods?' I asked Clo after Ollie invited me to the party in the corridor by Hawthorn's office.

'Technically... No. But none of the faculty ever pays any notice to what the rich kids get up to. After all, the generosity of the school benefactors pays their salaries. Benefactors who are the parents of the shitty rich kid students that go here. The only way they'd get involved is if something bad happened.' Clover's eyes went out of focus for a split second. 'Well, you'd think so anyway,' she muttered, almost too quiet for me to hear.

'Sorry?' I asked, hoping she'd clarify her mutter, but Clover didn't take the bait.

'Oh, nothing. Just me mumbling to myself as usual,' she said, adding an odd 'ha' at the end to sell it as a quirk of hers, but I'd honestly never heard her talking to herself. Of course, that wasn't to say that she didn't when I wasn't around. I did it frequently.

'So, will you come with me?'
'Come with you where?'
'To the party of course.'
'Well, I'm not going to let you make a tit of yourself alone, am I?'

So yeah, Clover had sort of—not really, but kind of—agreed to come to the party with me. Mostly I reckoned she agreed to come because she didn't trust Ollie and wanted to keep an eye on me.

The whole school was buzzing about it. It had been the main conversation topic in the dining hall over last week—I'd also heard a few mentions of it while sitting in class, too.

'Are you sure we need to go tonight? Wouldn't you rather we stay in and just eat pizza?' Clover almost pleaded with me. I understood her qualms. Even shared them. But Ollie *had* asked me to attend, and I couldn't break the rule.

Just one week ago some girl looked at Odette wrong, and the next thing everyone knew, she was suspended for some nonsensical reason.

'You don't need to come with me if you're really against it, Clo,' I said, looking at her across our room. She was sitting on her bed, still in her uniform, procrastinating from getting ready. 'But I would love to have you there with me. You *know* I can't bail.'

'I *know* that and *that* is the only reason I'm coming with you,' Clover said. She pouted, jutting her bottom lip out slightly, and widened her eyes at me.

'Don't give me that look, Clo.' I laughed at her childlike tactics. 'It's making me want to give in and give you your way. But I can't, and if I'm being a little honest here, I don't want to.'

I'd tried to come to terms with the fact that a large part of me really wanted to go tonight. I'd also tried to tell Clover multiple times that I wanted to go in a way that wouldn't cause conflict between us, but I still hadn't found the right words. Clover and I may have grown to be pretty good friends pretty fast, but it had still only been a couple of weeks and I didn't want to rock the boat.

Already dressed and ready to go, I waited on Clover to get ready too. We'd decided that I should wear something a mix between casual and sexy. We went with high-waisted dark denim jeans, a white Bardot crop top, and white plimsolls. My light silvery-purple hair was styled in loose waves that came down just past my shoulders. Before coming here, I'd never made much of an effort with my appearance—except my hair. My hair was something I'd always changed. Changing my hair colour and style always made me feel better when my anxiety became overwhelming. It was something I could do for myself, too; no friends or trips outside of the house needed. Minimal cost if you got the home box dyes.

Clover dressed herself in black skinny jeans, a band shirt, and black Converse. Her auburn hair was tied up in a high ponytail, with two wisps of her fringe hanging down on either side. She looked like a rocker chick, with her eyeliner super thick around her green eyes, making them stand out.

'You look hot!' I raised my eyebrows up and down at her. She chucked a pillow at me.

'Stop it, I look ite.' She waved me off, a small flush on her cheeks. 'You, however, look mighty fine. The boys won't know what to do with themselves.'

Clover grabbed both our phones, putting hers in her pocket before passing mine to me.

'By boys I meant Ollie and Griff, if you weren't sure.'

'You know Leo will totally be into how you look right now,' I replied. I wanted so bad to know more about her history with

Leo, and I was sort of hoping that Clover would drink enough tonight for her tongue to loosen to get the goods. Loose lips sink ships, and all that.

'I give zero shits about what Leo thinks,' she said. The bite in her tone shut me up. 'Let's go.'

I opened our door and nearly went head first into a very hard, very muscular chest.

My eyes tracked upward, and I found myself looking into Griff's eyes. I'd never noticed before, but his eyes made me think of a meadow on a summer's day. They were that truly rare colour; blue edges with a green centre. He looked debonair, or in less fancy terms, really fucking hot.

'Whoa. Be careful, Sky,' Griff said. His smile was super wide, the dimples in his cheeks pressed in, his eyes shining bright with amusement. 'You might run into somebody who doesn't want to let you go.'

'Oh, ha-ha.' I faked laughter, smiling back at him. 'Who would that be?'

His expression changed. Like day to night in a millisecond. His eyes darkened, and I worried I'd said the wrong thing.

'There are beasts lurking around every corner, New Girl. Remember that,' he said, his tone one of warning.

'Okay.' I was too stunned to say more.

I looked around us. There was nobody in the halls, and I assumed that was because of the party. From what I'd gathered from Clo, pretty much everybody went. Even the younger years would try and sneak out from their heavily guarded dorms to join in.

Nobody wanted to miss a party.

THE OUTSKIRTS of the woods were only around a five-minute walk from campus, but the clearing holding the party was another fifteen minutes' walk away.

'I didn't realise the surrounding land was this big,' I said after we'd been walking in silence for some time. I would've said anything, just so we weren't quiet anymore. The whistle of the wind through the leaves was disconcerting, to say the least.

'Well, yeah. The school's on the hill too, remember? So all the land up here belongs to the Hawthorn family,' Clover replied.

'I totally forgot Leo's family owned this place. Suppose he's related to Ms Hawthorn?' I asked. I'd never made the connection before.

'Sadly, yes. His aunt,' Griff said, looking at me. 'But nobody ever acknowledges it. Best not to bring it up with him.'

'Pft, yeah, like I even talk to Leo, anyway. He's taken his side,' I said.

He had, after all, hadn't he? He may have told me that first night I could come to him, but absolutely none of his actions afterward had backed up his claim.

'Of course he has because he's a massive cumstain who should really just piss off,' Clover said, her eyebrows furrowing, her dislike of Leo oozing from every pore.

'A massive cumstain?' I sputtered, laughing at her, raising my eyebrows. She was always so serious but also so comical when it came to talk of Leo. Even when she didn't mean to be. Like how young children acted on a playground with the people they fancied. Pick on them, call them names, all to disguise the fact you like them.

'You know what I mean!' Clo said, joining in the laughter, which stopped abruptly when we came to the dimly lit clearing. Tiny lanterns placed in the trees were giving off little light, creating a seedy effect.

The bass of the music thumped and vibrated through the soles of my shoes as it made its way up my legs, and there were bodies everywhere. Some stood on what looked like a makeshift dance floor, grinding on one another. Others dotted around, standing in friendship groups; talking, playing drinking games or hooking up. It was all happening around us and I felt overwhelmed. I'd never been to a party like this before—I'd never had friends in school that would invite me to anything like this. The popular kids at my old school all went to the field on a Friday night, but I never did. It wasn't my scene—plus, I had to work.

I spotted Ollie across the clearing, standing with Leo, but when he saw we'd arrived, he left Leo's side and came straight over to us.

'You're finally here,' he said, relieved, his eyes taking me in from head to toe. 'You look beautiful.' He kissed my cheek in greeting and then said a quick hello to Clover and Griff. 'Fancy a drink?'

'P-please,' I said, nodding at him. I watched as he headed over to a table set up with bottles of booze covering it, all different types and strengths. I hoped that Ollie didn't get me anything too strong. I'd never been much of a drinker and was so worried that I'd end up drinking too much and embarrass myself. Clover and I ate a big dinner, though, so we wouldn't be drinking on an empty stomach.

'Remember the motto, Sky.' Clover grabbed my attention

from Ollie and shook my shoulder. 'Beer before liquor, never sicker.'

'Liquor before beer, in the clear,' we said together, ending the fun phrase Clo had taught me earlier.

I took the drink Ollie offered me on his return and took a tentative sip. The taste of cranberry and vodka hit me. It wasn't overly strong, and it tasted all right, so I continued to sip at it.

'Is this your first party then, New Girl?' he asked.

'Y-yeah. Is it that obvious?' I was worried I'd embarrassed myself already, but even for me that was a bit ridiculous.

'You look nervous,' he said, reaching his hand out to touch my cheek before it slowly trailed down my neck. The touch was soft, sensual, and full of warmth. Light. My breath hitched, my stomach fluttered, and I felt nauseous all at once. All I could think in that moment was I hoped I didn't look as much of a fucking lemon as I thought I did. My face must've stuck in a confused expression because Ollie looked at me and raised his brow in question.

'You okay, Sky?' His eyes rose and his lips formed slowly into a smirk.

I wanted nothing more than for him to kiss me properly, but it wasn't the right time for that.

'O-of course. I'm solid,' I replied, trying to put an airiness into my voice. *Solid? When the fuck have I ever said that before? Ground, swallow me whole.*

'Glad to hear it,' he said, brushing his lips on my cheek in another subtle kiss. I didn't know how to react—he'd never shown me affection in public before, and I didn't want to get too excited in case it meant fuck all to him.

Ollie sauntered to stand behind me, wrapping his arms around my shoulders as he leant his head on top of mine. I was the perfect height for him to do it comfortably. Bewildered by his actions, I had no idea of how to react to any of this.

The whispers of *The Sect* followed me around, and I knew Ollie could be having me on. Playing a cruel joke on me.

I needed to keep my wits about me and not give into him so easily. But damn, his face made that hard to do.

I felt so new to this shit. I had entered a world with multiple rules that I knew fuck all about, and I wasn't sure how to cope with it all without losing myself.

A FEW DRINKS into the evening, I started to feel the effects, to the point where I started seeing two of Ollie. And they were both hot. Even my stutter had taken a leave of absence for the night. *Loose lips sink ships indeed.*

'Want to dance?' Ollie asked, sneaking up behind me as I was sitting on the floor playing *Never Have I Ever* with Griff and Clover. He began rubbing my shoulders, kneading out the knots there.

I looked back and up at him, a wide smile on my lips unbidden, as if I couldn't help being happy in his presence. He moved his hands, so that one was now directly in front of my face, offering to help me stand. I took it, and the force of the pull had me hurtling into him at a faster speed than I expected.

'Whoa, be careful there, little lady. Maybe you should slow down on the drinks,' he said, a caring look in his eyes. I laughed, giddy.

'I'm okay, big boy.' The words left my lips before my mind caught up with them, but the moment it did, I froze, a slow flush creeping onto my cheeks.

Was I at the point of slurring my words? I couldn't be sure. They all sounded perfectly fine to me.

Ollie laughed at me. 'Big boy? I'll prove just how *big* I am one day.' His promised words made my face heat further. He had me running hot and cold all the time, so much, it made me worried I'd get chilblains.

'Come dance,' he demanded. People filled the dance floor, bodies thrummed to the beat, and more couples than not reenacted the opening credits from *Dirty Dancing*, or they were full-on making out with no care about who could see them.

Ollie held me close, and we swayed together.

'We can't slow dance to this,' I told him quietly. The music was upbeat, and it was awkward to step from side to side to it. I'd never been much of a dancer. Rhythm did *not* come naturally to me.

'We can make it whatever we want it to be,' he whispered, his fingers playing with the waistband of my jeans.

'Oh, we can, can we?' I sassed, raising my eyebrows at how casual he was. His fingers continued playing with the top of my jeans before fumbling with the button at the front. 'What on earth are you doing?'

'I know you want me to touch you. You've been giving off signals ever since we first met that you want me,' Ollie said, his hands still travelling around my hip bones, tickling me.

'You seem very sure of yourself. Maybe even a little *too* sure.'

'You're talking a big game, Sky. Let's see if you can walk the walk.' His eyes were wide as his face came closer to mine, leaning down into my bubble.

Lips touched mine. Fingers still reaching, trying to breach my underwear and make their way to the place I wanted them most. To the place he'd touched in the library that day.

That day we'd never spoken of since.

'Can we move into the shadows?' I asked, stopping his hand from moving further, intertwining our fingers.

He didn't say a word in response, but I led him away from the spot on the dance floor and we headed further into the trees. Far enough away that we couldn't be seen, but close enough that we could still feel the bass, the thrum of energy in the air.

Hidden away from the others, I felt bold. My veins on fire, and my mind brave enough to take what it wanted.

I initiated the next contact between us.

Grabbing his face between my hands and pulling it down to my level, I kissed him, as if my life was dependent upon it. Beneath my lips, I felt the moment Ollie snapped—the moment he became an active participant. His soft lips pushed against mine, a small nip of his teeth on my bottom lip sending my mind into overdrive. My hands moved to his chest, roaming, his pecs hard underneath my fingertips, and his abs even harder.

With force, Ollie pushed me into a tree, using his strength to pin me there. Trapped. At his mercy. His hands moved down to my thighs, pushing them, causing my legs to fall apart in a wider stance so he could step between them.

His dick pressed into my right thigh, and all I wanted to do was touch him. My hand moved towards the top of his jeans, but he stopped me by raising my hand to his mouth and biting down on it, hard. *Fuck.* The heady mix of the alcohol and his touch meant I was turned the fuck on. I could feel my wetness, and every move he made, every touch, only made me wetter.

The jean button that had caused him an issue earlier was undone in a flash. The zip came down, fingers now making their way down, down, and into my lace underwear, leaving a trail of heat in every place they touched. My skin on fire, the burn worth it.

Ollie plunged a finger inside of me, hard, and I gasped at the sudden invasion. There had been no build-up. No teasing. Yet I was ready for him, my warmth welcoming him in.

'Your moans are so fucking sexy,' Ollie whispered. His mouth on my ear and his whispers caused goosebumps to rise along my arms.

'Don't stop,' I said, my breath coming out faster.

His finger started moving, building in speed, and when I thought I could take no more, he added another finger.

'You're killing me,' he moaned. 'One day, Sky, I swear, you *will* stutter around my dick.'

My orgasm was building, threatening to push me over the edge, climbing with each stroke of his thumb on my clit, and each time his fingers moved inside of me, it got stronger. I wasn't a stranger to orgasms—I knew how to get myself there —and although it was completely different having Ollie touch me, the sensations inside of me remained the same.

When Ollie bit my bottom lip, his sharp teeth causing blood to rise up and spot on my lip, he added a third finger and my climax hit me in full force. It was like I'd been climbing until there was nowhere else to go. Lightheaded and dazed, I looked into Ollie's burning gaze.

'So fucking hot,' he whispered, almost too quiet for me to hear. My pulse was loud in my ears, drumming away, and I couldn't hear much else, lost in the sensations.

I sighed contentedly. A chill ran up my arms, and the cold became more obvious than it had a moment ago. It crept back in slowly now that I was coming down from the high my body had been on. My mouth felt dry; the aftertaste of blood still coating my tongue. That metallic tang overtaking everything.

Ollie stepped away from me, creating distance between us, and raked his hand through his hair that looked slightly gold in the moonlight. *What a rogue.*

'I'll go get us another drink,' he said and walked away, back towards the clearing where the party was still raging on as if we hadn't slipped away. The two of us weren't missed, that was for sure.

Waiting for him, I lost track of time.

He returned after five minutes, maybe? He had a cup in each hand, both filled with red-purple liquid. Passing me one, he said, 'Here you go, Little One.'

I took the cup, thankful, and gulped down the cranberry juice and vodka concoction inside. The orgasm he'd given me was still moving through my body like little shock waves. Little ripples of emotions I didn't want to face yet, so I drank it all. It was the strongest drink I'd had all night, but also rather sweet tasting—something I could focus on. Ground myself with.

'You'll feel better soon,' he said, breathless, hugging me close once again.

The hug was warm and comforting. I'd never been much of a hugger and I rarely instigated contact with people first. Ollie's arms were no longer bare, but instead were covered by a soft black leather jacket. He must've had it stashed out here somewhere, knowing how cold it would get. I wished I'd thought to do the same thing. An off-the-shoulder crop top was *not* the perfect September attire, especially when on the top of a cold, windy hill in England.

'I know,' I replied, my voice whisper-soft, muffled by his hard chest. 'You're here after all. Nothing bad can happen to me now.'

The last thing I remembered was Ollie's face gazing at me

intently. The moonlight hitting one side of his face, almost like a mask, making his features look sinister. Dark.

A hard glint formed in his eyes and they looked darker than they normally were.

Then everything went black.

Twelve

SHIT.

My head was banging. A cacophony of drums played inside my skull, pounding away. Like a truck had hit it, or even maybe a brick repeatedly smashed down onto my skull. Alongside the headache from hell, my mouth was dry, scratched, and tasted foul. *What on earth happened last night?*

It was probably the worst I'd felt in my entire life, and I wasn't even exaggerating—much.

I needed water and some paracetamol stat.

My eyes fluttered open, and I tried to get my bearings without drawing too much attention to myself. I had no idea where the fuck I was, and with little memory of how I got there, it could be anywhere. The room looked familiar in that way dorm rooms do, but it was one I hadn't seen before.

Beads of sweat rose up on my arms, and an all-body chill rushed through me. My anxiety always got worse when unexpected things happened; things outside of my routine or the norm.

This is one hundred percent outside of the norm.

The scent of tobacco and vanilla was strong in the air, and slowly, as my mind caught up to my nose, I realised where I knew that specific smell from. It had been invading my personal bubble ever since school started, no matter that I'd tried to avoid it.

I startled when a door opened nearby.

Looking around again, I noticed the room had an en-suite attached and only one bed. It was a suite more than a room, at least double the size of the one I shared with Clo.

And then there in the doorway of the bathroom stood Ollie.

In a towel.

Looking fine as fuck.

Oh, fucking hell.

Of course it was Ollie's room I was in. Which meant I was lying in Ollie's bed. Ollie's very large super king-sized bed that could definitely have fit an Ollie-shaped body next to my smaller one. The pillow next to me had a head-shaped indent. I had slept next to Ollie. The guy who fingered me up against a tree last night before everything went black.

My cheeks were aflame as I took a quick inventory of my clothes and noticed that I was still wearing my underwear—and nothing else.

Double shit.

Double fuck.

Double everything.

I decided I wouldn't be the one to break the silence and tried to pretend I was still asleep, wrapping myself up in the duvet, all warm and cosy. Like I hadn't noticed where I was. Like I hadn't seen him two seconds ago standing in only a towel, with water droplets still making their way down his abs. His very fine abs.

'I know you're awake, Sky.'

'H-how do you know that?' I asked, keeping my eyes

squeezed closed. I wanted to still have some form of deni-
ability.

'I've been beside you all night and your breathing's different when you're asleep,' he replied, his smile reminding me of Griff's. Cheeky and all-knowing.

'Surely, you slept too? How can you be so sure?'

'I didn't exactly sleep, New Girl. Had to stay awake and watch you. Be responsible. You know, make sure you didn't choke on your own vomit and all that good shit,' he said, a smile playing at the corner of his lips.

'What?' I sputtered.

'You don't remember much from last night, do you?' he asked me, but I was pretty sure it was rhetorical, so I chose not to answer. 'Someone drugged you last night.'

He didn't sugarcoat it. Didn't slowly build up to it. Nope. Not Ollie. He just threw the words out there, with no thought to how they would sound. It was almost careless and unfeeling.

'I was what?' I raised my voice at him, my displeasure bleeding into every syllable. Thinking I'd got drunk and not understanding my limits had been bad enough, but to hear that someone drugged me, in such a casual manner, flabber-gasted me—so much so, I thought of the word flabbergasted.

'Somebody spiked your drink. You must've accepted one that the girls had tampered with or put yours down at some point,' he told me as if it was the only explanation, no question about it.

'But I didn't,' I said, looking at him head-on for the first time since I woke. 'It was in my hand at all times.'

I knew I didn't let go of it, and I knew I hadn't taken a drink from a stranger. It was something I was super conscious of after reading one too many horror stories online about girls who were date raped.

'I only took drinks from Clover, Griff, or you.'

'You must have done, Sky. There's no shame in it.'

'Ollie, I swear to you I didn't!'

'Well, somehow your drink *was* messed with and I offered to bring you up here and look after you. The faculty's less likely to be monitoring this hall, especially on a Friday night.'

I rolled my eyes, then regretted it two point five seconds later as it made my head pound even more. I believed him about the faculty not monitoring these halls as closely, though. Bet they were paid a fair amount not to. Not that Clover and I had seen them often, but every now and again we would see a caretaker or hall monitor outside our room, making sure that nothing was amiss.

Ollie didn't believe me. I could tell I'd disappointed him in a way that didn't quite make sense to me yet. None of this was making sense to me. All I knew was that I hadn't been careless with my drink like Ollie was implying, yet there was no way to prove it.

Ollie sat on the edge of the bed, facing me, still wrapped in only a towel.

'I need to let Clover know where I am.'

'She knows where you are, New Girl. It took all four of us to get you back here last night,' he said with a lazy smirk.

'The f-four of you?' I asked, puzzled.

'Me, Griff, Clover, and Leo.'

'Oh, right.'

'There was no way I could've done it by myself. You weren't able to control your limbs, and you kept telling me how you wished I *had* found out what your stutter sounds like with my dick inside you.'

You know when you could feel a blush on your face, but you had no idea how to stop it from happening? I covered my burning face with the duvet in shame, even though I had no way of knowing whether he was telling the truth. For all I knew, he could be teasing me on purpose to embarrass me.

'I've never mentioned it before, but you are really quite cute sometimes, Sky.' He chuckled. Even his chuckle sounded X-rated to me.

'Are you trying to make me feel worse?' I shrieked. 'What time is it?'

'Ten. We missed breakfast but, lucky for you, I got Griff to deliver some to us before the buffet closed.'

'Don't really f-feel like eating.' I swallowed hard again, trying to get the lump out of my throat that seemed to have taken root there. 'A drink would be g-great, though.'

Ollie instantly got up and moved to the kitchenette area on the left-hand side of the room, then came back with a glass of water in his outstretched hand. I took it and chugged it down in one go. He instantly took the empty glass from me and refilled it.

I grabbed it, and while taking small sips, I regarded him.

'Thank you. For looking after me, I mean. Not for accusing me of being irresponsible.'

Ollie's eyes warmed. I could swim in the blue of his eyes.

'I'm not a *total* dick, Sky. I wouldn't have left you like that.' He came to lie down beside me, keeping on top of the cover, leaving a small distance between us. 'And we *will* find out who did this to you.'

'Surely there are only four suspects?' It made total sense to me that *The Set* did this, right? I knew I had made no friends outside of Clo and Griff, but drugging somebody was a step further than mean comments during class.

'You think the O girls did this?' he asked, his eyebrow arching. I'd never heard him call them that before. Come to think of it, he'd never really referred to them as anything at all. Even though they'd been the topic of conversation more than once recently, he never said their names. Ollie had never said more than a few words about their actions, choosing to stay silent about their cruelty towards me.

'Who else would?' I asked, feeling like we were going around in circles.

Slowly, the two of us gravitated towards one another on the bed. His breath felt warm on my face, his eyes staring into mine.

'They've m-made it clear that they hate me.'

'Seems bold, even for them,' he said, dismissing me, but he softened the blow of his words by tucking a piece of my hair behind my ear.

'Does it? I heard from Clover that somebody died last year?' I asked, curious, even though I knew I was pushing my luck with him. Not like he was gonna tell me the truth.

'That's nothing for you to worry about,' he said, dismissing me once again. I was about to prod him more, try and get more details from him, but his face told me not to bother. His chiselled jaw was clenched tight, a slight tick of his eye.

I didn't even want to examine what it meant about me, but my God, he looked even hotter when he was angry. I'd always found that in books and films, I was more attracted to the *bad boys*. Those characters who acted like total dickheads, but you couldn't help but want them, anyway. Not that I'd actually met any guy like that before coming to Hawthorn.

'Whatever happened last year has nothing to do with what's happening now. I can promise you that.'

'Yeah?' I asked, my tone unsure.

'Skylar, I swear to you, this is all because the girls are feeling threatened by you. You're beautiful, funny, and everything they wish they could be. You've caught my eye and Griff loves you. Even Leo's got a soft spot for you.'

He was full of shit. That wasn't how it was at all. Yeah, I was friendly with Griff, and Ollie *acted* interested in me, but that could just be because he wanted in my pants. The part about Leo was a stretch, though. The boy barely looked my way, and if he did, I assumed it was only because I was usually sitting next to Clover.

'You're s-such a liar.' I giggled, not believing him.

'Either way, those girls are bitches. Don't let them get to you, no matter what, okay? They're not worth it.' He reached out to trail his finger up and down my arm, causing goosebumps to rise in the places his fingers grazed.

'Bitches with power. The other kids follow them.'

'I'll see what I can do,' he said. His ominous tone gave me pause. I thought he'd already been trying to see what he could do, but maybe the fact that someone drugged me had made him realise this was more serious than some kids taking the piss out of a girl's stutter and family background.

The rest of the day, the two of us stayed in Ollie's room until dinner—in silence, mostly. We watched films and just lay next to one another, not touching, but comfortable in one another's company.

I didn't want to imagine how badly last night could have gone if he hadn't rescued me—hadn't looked after me. He may be a self-entitled dick, but last night, he'd been my saviour.

Okay, yeah, a bit dramatic, Sky.

But still, I couldn't overlook that, no matter how much I probably *should*.

Thirteen

THE THIRD WEEK of term started the same as the two before it, but as the days went by, things kept getting worse and worse.

It all began when Oralie and Ophelia cornered me in the girls' toilets on Tuesday. I'd gone in there to use the facilities, but when I exited the stall, the two of them were standing by the sinks, waiting for me.

'Look who it is, Lee. The trashy, charity tramp,' Ophelia said. Her face was one of disgust with her over-enhanced top lip curled upward, her eyes narrowed into slits.

'Eurgh. What are you looking at, slut?' Oralie asked, equally livid, her face scrunched up.

'I'm just looking ahead?' My words came out as a question when I wanted to sound assertive.

Even though the two of them had been making English class unbearable and were encouraging everybody to pick on me throughout the school day, I usually had either Clover, Ollie, or Griff with me. People would only say so much in front of the guys and nobody had taken anything beyond words yet, but I could feel it brewing. I knew *The Set* wouldn't stop at just slander, and I knew the time would come when things would escalate.

Seems today is that day.

'Nobody wants you here, skank,' Ophelia said as Oralie nodded beside her. They were standing together, a united front; one with her hands on her hips and the other with her arms crossed across her inflated chest.

'I'm here on scholarship. I didn't even choose to be here,' I said. They knew that, too. I still wasn't sure if I preferred it at Hawthorn over my old school. The only two parts that were a win were my friendship with Clover and the fact I didn't have to live with my mum and Andy anymore. Who, funnily enough, I hadn't heard from since I left. I'd always known they didn't give a shit about me, but it was nice to have it confirmed with their silence.

'We can tell,' Oralie said, looking super smug. 'That you're poor, I mean.'

'You're such a little bitch. I thought at first you were putting the stutter on to get attention, but now it's clear that you're actually a scared, pathetic pussy.'

The two of them advanced towards me in tandem. I would've been impressed if I wasn't so alarmed at the look of menace on their faces.

'Maybe we need to teach you a lesson.'

As soon as Ophelia said those words, Oralie pounced faster than a tiger and grabbed both of my arms and held them behind my back, gripping them tightly in place. Not wanting to waste a golden opportunity, Ophelia punched me in the middle of my face, catching me on the nose, causing blood to gush out.

Shit.

That hurt. A lot.

I couldn't give them the satisfaction of letting them know just how much. Still, Ophelia kept hitting me. Punching me. In the face, the arm, the stomach. Anywhere she could. I fell to the floor, no longer able to hold myself upright, but the two of them proceeded to kick me instead. My stomach was tender, and I knew this was going to bruise like a bitch.

The punching and kicking continued. My vision had blurred after a couple of minutes, my anxiety peaking once again. I *was* getting beat on by two bitches, after all, and neither of them was holding back. All of their anger and frustration aimed at me.

In the distance, I could hear muffled shouting, the noise getting louder by the minute. Getting closer to where we were.

Lucky for me, the girls heard the shouts and realised they were pushing their luck. That they would be discovered soon. Somebody was bound to enter the room. They blinked, looking down at me, taking stock of the situation they'd found themselves in, shocked they'd gone as far as they had.

'Shit,' Ophelia said and hit Oralie on the shoulder. 'This isn't over, charity trash.' Her spit hit my lip, yet I didn't wipe it away. I had a lot more to worry about at this point—like the intense pain in my side and the blood drying on my face.

With one last kick, they hurried out of the room, leaving me sprawled out on the floor, unable to move.

The door didn't fully close behind them as somebody pushed it open, catching it with their foot before it slammed.

'What the fuck?' Clover screamed, her gaze finding me on the floor. Tears filled my eyes at the sight of her. I wanted to tell her what had happened, but the last kick winded me and I was struggling to catch my breath. Clo popped her head outside the door. 'Shit, guys! She's in here!'

Her yell caused both Ollie and Griff to storm into the room, their fury coming off of them in waves.

'Who did this, New Girl?' Griff asked with an urgency that was new for him.

My eyes trailed upwards to glance at Griff, and the look on his face was so unlike the expression he usually wore. There was no hint of a cheeky smile or any dimples, and I didn't want to be Ophelia or Oralie when he caught up with them.

'Leo needs to put them on a fucking leash,' Ollie said, spit spraying from his mouth. He looked so mad. Like a beast, ready to rip the heads off of those responsible for my despair. Even I could admit I was slightly scared of him at that moment. I'd never seen this dark of an expression on his face before, and I was so glad he didn't aim it at me. Ollie looked at Griff. 'Go find Leo and tell him about this.'

Griff was leaning over me, and Clover was hovering nearby, feeling out of place. When neither of them moved to follow Ollie's instructions, he roared. 'Now!'

Griff stood, leaving the room, but not before he kissed my cheek and whispered some words in my ear. 'We're gonna kick their butts, New Girl.'

Hands helped me into a sitting position, and after a time my breathing returned to normal. Blood was dried on my face, but at least my nose had stopped bleeding, and other than feeling a little swollen when I prodded it, I didn't think it was broken like I'd first feared.

'How are you feeling?' Clover asked. Or more demanded.

I understood it, though. I'd probably be acting the same way if she were in my position. I would hate not knowing whether they hurt her more than the eye could see.

'Sore,' I groaned, gripping my side, trying to alleviate some of the pain there. Lifting my shirt, I could see the bruises already forming. Swirls of pink and red bloomed under my skin. The repeated kicks to my side and stomach were going to leave their mark for a while. 'I wasn't able to s-stop them. Held my arms back.'

'Shh. Let's get you to our room,' Clo whispered.

'No. She'll come back to my room where I can keep an eye on her,' Ollie ordered.

'You've done enough!' Clover spat out. If a look could kill, then Ollie would be dead with the way Clover was looking at him. 'This is *all* your fault.'

'And how do you gather that?' he asked in a clipped tone.

'After the party Friday, after they'd *drugged* Skylar, you knew the girls would escalate.'

'I suggest you stop right there, Clover. Just because you're Sky's best friend doesn't mean I'll let you talk to a member of *The Sect* like that,' Ollie said, his lips forming into a sneer.

Clover's hands clenched at her sides, and I thought I'd have to prevent her from clocking him one. The two of them had been wary of each other before today, but I never thought they'd actually come to blows. Especially over something as stupid as my safety.

'Guys, stop!' I pleaded. 'I just want to g-get off the bath-room floor.'

Clover rushed to help me up, and I used her body to hold myself up. I felt like Quasimodo, all hunched over and standing awkwardly.

'Come on,' Clo said to me, keeping a firm grip on my arm.

The hallway was clear of students when we exited, which was the first bit of luck I'd had all day. No bells had rung while I was in there—not that I heard—but a new period must have started.

Slowly, we made our way across campus with me limping

beside Clover. Ollie on the other side of me, staying close just in case I needed him. It surprised me he hadn't demanded that Clover move, but I thought maybe the two of them were trying to be civil just so I would get back to my room and rest.

After what felt like years, we finally made it back to my room. Clearly, by being the one to steer me, she'd got her way and got to decide what room I went to. I just wanted to get into a bed—any bed.

'Do you want to shower?' Clo asked, and I nodded in response. I wanted to wash, but if I was being honest, a shower didn't sound overly appealing. What I really wanted was a long soak in the bath. I was a bath girl through and through, and I would never understand the appeal of showers. Standing up would never seem relaxing to me.

'I could help with that,' Ollie said, without a trace of joking or flirting in his voice. No ulterior motive. I would've been annoyed if Ollie had used a sleazy tone, but luckily for his balls, he sounded like he genuinely wanted to help me. A large part of me wanted him to help—he had the strength to hold me up —but an even larger part of me wasn't ready for that. It was next level shit.

Fuck, the two of us hadn't even spoken about any of the shit we'd done together. And if I was being honest, I'd never been naked in front of a guy, and it was okay to admit to yourself that you weren't at that stage yet mentally.

'I'll do it,' Clover snapped at him. I attempted a shrug, but the movement hurt me too much. I hoped my face conveyed my emotions to let him know I wasn't mad at him, but that I wanted Clo to help me. The narrowing of his eyes told me that maybe my intention had got lost in translation.

Like a lot of things when it comes to Oliver Brandon.

THE SHOWER HELPED me feel slightly more human and once he tucked me into my bed, Ollie left after saying he had some errands to run. I wasn't even going to guess at what those were. Griff arrived shortly after and hugged me so tight, I thought my ribs would bruise alongside everything else.

'Honestly, New Girl, you cannot be going anywhere alone anytime soon. Those girls aren't messing around,' he said in greeting.

'Well, hello to you too!' I said, laughing at his no-nonsense tone. 'You already come with me most places.'

'I mean it, Sky,' he said, sitting down at the bottom of my bed, making sure not to touch me. The use of my name sent a chill down my spine. It wasn't like Griff. 'Until we've sorted this shit out with them, you're not to be alone.'

'Ay, ay, Captain!' I said with a mock salute. 'Did you go speak to them?'

'I hope you kicked their asses, Griff. I don't care if they've got vaginas,' Clo piped up from her spot on her bed, looking so fierce that if I were *The Set*, I'd be terrified. She was *not* playing around.

'Classy, Clo,' Griff said, his smile cheeky, but I also noticed he deflected the question asked. 'So, whores, what are we going to watch tonight?'

'Whores?' I asked, sputtering. The boy was something else. My mouth moved into a lopsided smile at him.

'Is that not what the girls say? Want me to call you sisters or girlies?'

'No!' Clover and I both yelled, shaking our heads at him in amusement.

'Let's pick a film, girlies,' Griff said, defying us as he got up Netflix and started flicking through the options. His watch list killed me. It had some of my favourite films on it and I smiled, wondering if Griff had them on there because he liked them or in order to have a quick "Netflix and chill" film on hand.

'*To all the boys*?' I asked the room and got a resounding 'YES!' from Clover and a, 'Oh, I love a bit of Peter Kavinsky,' from Griff.

'Let's do this,' I said, getting more comfortable in my bed, pulling the duvet up to my chin. Griff settled beside me while making sure he didn't touch my side or hurt me further.

Having friends was such a novelty to me, but if the warm and fuzzy feeling growing in my gut as we ate takeaway pizza and watched films was what it felt like, then I never wanted this feeling to go away.

Fourteen

HEALING after the O girls beat me up was a bitch. It was a couple of days before I was able to get up and walk without wincing at each step. The first few days, the door of my room was constantly revolving. Clover, Griff, and Ollie barely left me alone and one of them was always by my side. Even when I would've rather been left alone.

It took me a week to return to classes, and even then, I still dawdled everywhere. My sides were bruised, but mentally I was okay—and that was what mattered to me. I wasn't going to miss out on my classes because of some stuck-up snooty bitches who thought they had the right to harm me. I couldn't miss any more classes without my grades suffering and Ms Hawthorn forcing me to come into her office to discuss the terms of my scholarship was not something I wanted to do right now. It wasn't something I wanted to do *ever*.

Six weeks later and things were slowly returning to normal. No students were looking at my face with sneering smiles anymore now the bruises had faded—or at least none that I could see. Sure, they were having a field day of murmurs behind my back, though.

'Kant's a bit of an unfortunate name, isn't it,' Griff said, and

I nodded, only half listening to whatever it was he was wittering on about. The boy didn't stop talking, and I wondered how he managed to fill his lungs with enough air to keep up his constant stream of babbles.

The two of us had just left our Ethics class and were heading towards the dining hall to grab some lunch. That was one thing I could say about Hawthorn: the food was to die for. Everything from the pastries at breakfast, to the rich pasta dishes at dinner. Even the pizza they sometimes had on the menu was elevated above anything I'd ever tasted before. No thick, greasy, cheese pizza for such a fine establishment.

Griff continued prattling on, and I kept nodding at what I thought were the right moments. The occasional hum seemed to satisfy him. It was in the middle of one of those nods that I bumped into somebody. *Leo*, in fact. And by *bumped* I meant I literally walked straight into him, colliding with a loud thump.

'S-sorry.' Like any Brit that bumped into another person, my first instinct was to apologise profusely. After the third 'sorry' he took pity on me.

'That's okay, Stutter,' he said, his mouth tilting up on one side, the amusement dripping off him. His hair was brushed to one side and I found myself wanting to run my fingers through it to see if it was as soft as it looked. *Down, Sky.*

I blinked at him, processing his words. *Great.* I'd got a cute nickname from Leo. At least it was better than trailer, charity trash, which the O girls were lovingly calling me every time they saw me.

I brushed my hands where we made impact, then realised what I was doing and stopped straight away, resting my hands on his chest near his heart.

'I should really w-watch where I'm going.'

'Must have distracted her with my manliness,' Griff said,

his words catching me off-guard. I snorted loudly with laughter, covering my mouth with my hand.

'And she snorts too.' Leo's face became even more amused. 'Stutter, if you ever want to ditch that tool you're currently attached to, I'm available.' His bored tone didn't match his words or the expression on his face in the slightest. He sounded as if he didn't give a fuck about any of it, which only made me wonder more about him.

'If Ollie fucks it up, which, let's be honest, could happen soon, then I'm definitely the next in line. Right, Sky?' Griff asked, his signature grin in place.

'Sure, Griff,' I said to placate him, tapping his shoulder before I pulled at his arm to get him to continue walking with me. Away from Leo's inquisitive gaze.

Leo's tone may be wary, but his eyes were anything but. He was looking for something, and I couldn't quite figure out what.

My bump into Leo wasn't the last time I ran into him during the week. I bumped into him again a couple of days later, but sadly, I wasn't with Griff.

Nope. I was with Clover—the girl who hated Leo's guts more than anyone else at school.

Plus, Leo was *not* alone.

The two of us had just left dinner and were making our way back to our dorm when Clo suggested we go a different way. To mix it up a bit.

Going our usual route typically meant we ran into Odette and the other O girls, or people who were only too happy to prove their loyalty to *The Set* and call me names. Some people barged into me, trying to knock me into other people in the hall or into walls.

So I agreed to go a new route.

And that was how Clover and I found ourselves in the hallway that attached the pool house to the hospital wing. We avoided the pool house as a rule, mostly because that was where you could find Leo, Ollie, and Griff when they weren't bugging us. If they weren't with us or in class, then they were at the pool. The three of them were on the swim team and were apparently fantastic to watch, winning the school all kinds of trophies and shit. I was low-key excited to watch a meet. Mainly because I wanted to see those three in speedos. *Sue me.*

The corridor was dimly lit in comparison to the rest of the school. Griff had told me it was because these buildings were some of the oldest and they hadn't installed as many light fittings or some shit like that. The school board had kept it that way too in order to keep the original building's authenticity. And they'd succeeded. It looked exactly how you'd expect it to look. All brick walls, high vaulted arch ceilings, and wooden flooring.

Our conversation topic: the upcoming Parents' Day that Hawthorn threw once a year. The one day where every student could invite their parents to come visit, and then be thankful that they left at the end of it. A day for the parents to meet the teachers and see how their kids were doing. Find out if they were engaging in any extracurricular activities. Find out exactly what they were doing with their twenty thousand a year plus education.

'I'm not asking mine to come.' Clover shook her head as if the thought of her parents coming was too much for her to cope with.

'How come?' I knew little about her parents—not once since we became friends had she mentioned them.

'I don't want to subject them to it. Fuck, Sky, I don't want to subject myself to it either.'

'I get you. I've not invited Mum and Andy either. I'm already the butt of enough jokes. I don't need the two biggest jokes in my life coming here and making things ten times worse.'

And they would make things worse. It was the curse of Andy and Cora. It was what they did no matter the situation.

The thought of them sharing air space with the likes of Ollie and Griff made me shudder. I knew they were my friends, sort of, and that they liked me for me, or at least I assumed they did, but still. Everybody already knew I came here because of the scholarship. Inviting Mum here would only highlight just how little money I came from. It was for the best that they never set foot on Hawthorn grounds.

'Can you hear that?' Clover looked at me, making a shushing motion with her finger, even though she'd just asked me a question. I shook my head. I couldn't hear anything outside of our footsteps. We hadn't passed another student.

Then I heard it. The smooching and smacking sounds of two lips going at it got closer, and eventually we could see the couple up ahead.

Of course. It just *had* to be Leo and Odette. *Again.*

At least Clover didn't instantly run off and leave me standing alone like last time. She continued walking and when we got close enough for them to hear us, Clover coughed while actually covering up a word.

'Skank.'

I wanted to laugh, but the fake cough didn't cover her

chosen word at all, so instead I stayed silent. No need to provoke the beast.

The two of them stopped what they were doing. Odette, using reflexes I didn't expect her to possess, reached out and grabbed Clover's arm, gripping tight.

'If you've got something to say, *Over*, I suggest you share it with the class.'

'Get off her! You're hurting her.' I didn't even think before I acted. I just grabbed Odette's hand and yanked it away from Clover as hard as I could. There was no way she was gonna put her hands on my best friend without me getting involved.

She let go, a scowl on her face aimed at me. I'd caught Odette off-guard.

Fuck. I'd caught myself off-guard.

I was certain she had something to do with Ophelia and Oralie attacking me in the toilets, but there was no proof of that. Even though *The Set* didn't have an actual leader, everybody knew Odette classed herself as the one in charge. Probably because she was the one hooking up with Leo, the oldest member of *The Sect*.

'Get your fucking pauper hands off me!' Odette shrieked, looking at Leo. 'Are you not going to say anything?'

Leo stayed silent, raising an eyebrow at her, the slight quirk of his top lip letting us into his mind.

'Really, Leo?' Odette demanded, stomping her foot. 'Again?'

'Stop, Stutter, stop,' Leo said, uninterested, mocking her. He wanted me to stop as much as he wanted to be involved. But that didn't stop Clover from looking over at me, betrayal plain in her features. It was clear she thought I was closer to Leo than I'd let on. The fact he'd made a *cute* nickname for me didn't help my case. I raised my eyebrows at him in warning, but he only smirked in return.

'Are you for fucking real, Leo Hawthorn?' Clover asked, disbelief in her voice.

'What's the matter, Red? Jealous of your new friend?' Leo asked, his tone having lost the disinterest he constantly exuded. It was like he'd come to life. His eyes were sparkling with malice, the darkness simmering just under the surface, wanting to be let free. Leo calling her Red told me more than he'd probably meant to.

One day soon, I would make sure Clover told me more about their history. She'd been disguising just how well they knew one another, and any time I asked, she clammed up, refusing to tell me anything.

'I'd never be jealous of this Barbie. I hope you get chlamydia or worse. Maybe if I'm lucky, your dick will drop off and save the rest of the female population. Oh, wait. They're already safe. The size of your dick won't do them any damage.'

With that, Clover walked off. Stomping down the corridor, without once turning around, away from the bomb she'd just unleashed. Odette was foaming at the mouth, her eyes narrowed on Clover's retreating back.

'Go on, Stutter. Better make sure Red doesn't go find a blade and come back for more,' Leo said, dismissing me, his attention once again returning to Odette, trying to calm her down.

I walked off slowly, trying to make sense of what I just witnessed.

One thing I knew: Leo was playing some kind of game, and I had a feeling it could be a long one.

FOR THE REST of the night, Clover wouldn't talk to me more than to tell me she was going for a shower and then putting on her headphones and getting some essays done. I found the last part highly suspicious, though, as Clover's classes were practical subjects with barely any writing attached, like food tech. If she wanted to block me out, then I'd let her. She wanted to stop me from asking her any probing questions.

I'd respect her wishes for now, but I was getting sick of her trying to block me out. Friendship went both ways, or so I thought, and I'd definitely been a lot more open and forthcoming with her than she ever had with me. I'd told her things about my life before Hawthorn. My lack of friends, my relationship with my mum. I'd even told her about Andy's advances on the day I left. Yet all I'd got from her was that her family fell on hard times a couple of years ago.

That was it. *In six weeks.*

I knew some people found it hard to open up, hard to talk about the deep shit, but I thought I'd made it clear that I was her friend regardless of what had happened. I wouldn't judge her, and it sucked that she thought I might.

I put my headphones in my ears and pulled up Netflix, chose one of my favourite films and pressed play. I barely got through the opening credits before I got a text from an unknown number.

Only Clo, Griff, and Ollie had this number.

STUTTER. KEEP AN EYE ON RED FOR ME. LET ME KNOW IF THE

Confused by the entire message, I tried to make sense of it in my mind. Leo had my number and had used it to message me... about Clover?

I looked over at Clover and wondered whether I should bother her. Maybe she'd be able to shed some light on why Leo texted me about keeping an eye on her. But knowing Clo, she'd just fob me off again, and I wasn't in the mood to disagree with her.

I texted back one word.

OKAY.

That should be enough. I saved his number under the name Thorn, as in thorn in my side, amusing myself. After all, Clo was saved as Lady Luck and Griff was saved as Hercules —*don't ask.*

I'd debated for some time about what to save Ollie as.

Before the party in the woods, it had been *Ollie,* then after the whole drugging and rescue thing, it had been *Hero,* but that didn't fit him either. After the girls beat me up in the toilets, and he was the most angry I'd ever seen him, I changed it to *Beast.* Mostly because I knew that deep down, lurking under the surface, he could be the worst kind of monster that existed.

And I needed to keep my wits about me around him.

Fifteen

PARENTS' Day was a big deal at Hawthorn Academy. It was a way for the faculty to prove to the rich parents that they were spending their hard-earned cash well and that, if they felt so inclined, they could always donate more—the school would always highly appreciate it.

It was also the event that led into the October break, meaning that some of the students would return home afterward with their parents. I could sense the excitement, so palpable in the corridors, it was close to overwhelming, the atmosphere almost feverish.

'Do we even need to attend if our parents aren't coming?' I asked Clover. All I really wanted to do was spend the day in our room, gorging on sweets and lusting after Ryan Gosling.

'Yep. It's a part of the required social calendar, the one on Hive. You got a copy on your first day, right?' Clover groaned. 'Have to look like they're treating us charity cases well, after all. No preferential treatment here at Hawthorn.'

'True. So do all the parents attend?' I asked, curious.

'If you're asking if Ollie's and Leo's parents are coming, then yeah, they'll be here,' Clo said, only partially answering my question.

'What about Griff's?'

'Oh, er... No,' Clover mumbled, her eyes shifting around the room. It looked like she wanted to say more but had bitten her own tongue to stop herself. Unlike the other things she wasn't telling me, I could understand this one better. Whatever it was wasn't hers to tell, and I could respect Clover for that.

'Fair enough. I'm just glad my mum knows nothing about today.'

And I meant every word. Thank fuck Cora was none the wiser.

THE MAIN HALL had been transformed from its usual plain area into a fete of sorts. An event like that would be better outside, but the weather in England in October could be a little unpredictable, to put it mildly, so I understood why they were holding it indoors instead.

Everywhere I looked, there were tables set up with teachers stood behind them and each department had its own table. Then there was a long table filled with refreshments along the left-hand wall—a bar of sorts. In the centre of the room were the tables we usually ate our dinner from, all arranged with name cards for each student and their parents. *How fun.* A formal situation.

'Thought there'd be more tables,' I mentioned to Clo, looking around the room. 'Bit of a surprise.'

'A lot of the kids are related. Or like mine, their parents aren't coming.'

Huh. Made sense, I guessed. Rich people *were* popping out children in hopes of business and world domination, yet didn't actually *care* about their children for any other reason.

Guess they weren't much different from my parents—although mine definitely didn't have me for world domination.

The two of us began wandering around the room, taking in the parents and kids who were already there.

'I wonder whose parents they are. Must be one of the younger years,' Clo muttered beside me, looking at a tall, thin couple dressed in expensive fabrics standing by the entrance.

'Huh?'

'The couple that just entered... I've never seen them before. Just odd. Thought I knew everyone.' Clo shrugged and I turned my attention back to the band setting up on the stage. 'Oh wow. Now that's a funky outfit.'

I turned to see the person she was talking about and my heart melted. Fully melted, and the pieces puddled together on the floor in a big wet mess. *Shit.*

'Darling!' my mum called across the hall. 'Oh, how lovely you look!'

Of course she was trying to put on her *posh* accent, which, if anything, just made her sound even more common. She even put an emphasis in the middle of the word lovely, and I cringed so hard, I thought it would never stop.

Andy, the slimy toad, stood beside her, and I realised they'd attempted to dress up for the occasion. By that, I meant they'd brushed their hair and worn clothes without stains. Clothes that were obviously cheap that definitely didn't fit in with the surroundings. Mum had even put on a large red fascinator that clashed terribly with her orange V-neck top, and I was pretty sure my shame levels couldn't go any higher.

'Fuck. What are they doing here?' I asked, bewildered.

'That's your *mum*?' Clover asked, sounding as exasperated as I felt.

'Yep.' I popped the P like so many heroines do. 'How did she find out about today?'

'No idea. Sure you didn't mention it to her?' Clo asked.

'Clo. I haven't spoken to her since I started at Hawthorn. I'm surprised the woman even remembers she *has* a daughter.'

Mum and Andy had made their way over to us, waving and grabbing everybody's attention. Luckily for me, the boys weren't here yet, but it was only a matter of time before they arrived too. There was no way to hide my mum from them.

'Oh, Skylar, darling, I am so happy to see you!' Mum practically shouted, making sure that all those around us could hear her. 'Look at you. You look so fancy. I didn't realise this school was so fancy either.'

'You barely listened when I told you about it, Mum,' I said, my tone flat. In one sentence, the woman who birthed me had shown just how little she paid attention to me.

'I would have remembered if you told me about some-where as grandiose-ly as this. All you told us was you'd be leaving for school and quitting your job at the shop,' she said.

Of course that's all she remembers.

I chose to ignore her use of the word "grandiose-ly". My mum always invented words and threw them into sentences constantly as if they belonged there—an annoying habit of hers.

I wondered how they afforded to keep the roof over their heads seeing as I was gone and couldn't help with the bills. Knowing them, they'd probably just applied for more govern-ment benefits.

'H-how did you know to come?' I asked, looking at them in turn, the feeling of incredulity growing. I could feel my anxiety rearing its ugly head, the sweat rising to the surface of my skin, my nerves climbing, worried that Ollie and Griff were about to enter the hall with their parents and see who raised me. They knew I had a poor excuse of a mother, but knowing something and meeting it were two very different things.

'We got an invite from ya in the post,' Andy said, his beady eyes locking on me, causing a wave of nausea to travel through me.

I hadn't really processed what he did to me the last time I saw him. I came straight to Hawthorn and events at school were more pressing and in my face. But seeing him, hearing him talk, made me want to scream. Or run away and not return until after they'd left the grounds. Until they were far, far away from here.

'That wasn't from me,' I said as I looked Mum in the eye.

I felt confident that I knew who it *was* from, though. It had Odette and her clones written all over it. It hadn't been enough to have people bully me. It hadn't been enough to beat me up. No, they needed to humiliate me in front of the entire school, too.

'It had your name on it,' Mum said, looking at me with a question in her eyes. Maybe she thought I was lying in front of Clover. 'It said there'd be free food and drink here, so obviously we had to come.'

Don't get me wrong, I'm always game for free food and drink. Isn't everybody?

But that was the real reason they'd come. Mum hadn't come to see me or to even see the place her only child was living. No. The two of them had come for the free food and booze.

'Mum. Andy. This is my best friend, Clover,' I said, pointing beside me.

'Hello, darling, aren't you just a dream?' Mum smiled, and I could tell she was putting on her charm. It disarmed people, but I hoped Clo would be clever enough to see through the façade.

'Hey. Nice to meet you, Cora,' Clover said before we shared a look. A look that told me she was bullshitting through her teeth.

One thing I loved about the moment was that Clover didn't suck up.

An hour passed with Clover and me making awkward small talk with Mum and Andy, showing them around the grounds and telling them about what we were learning. Not that they gave much of a shit, but there were still another few hours until the sit-down meal and we needed to pass the time somehow. The two of them went to grab another drink—probably their fifth of the afternoon.

'I haven't seen the boys yet. Have you?' Clover turned to whisper in my ear once they returned, both of them holding a drink in each hand.

I shook my head, not wanting to say anything more in front of Mum. She was the type of woman who loved gossip and any talk of boys would definitely pique her interest, and one thing I really didn't want her to know was about Ollie. I didn't know what was happening between us—or if *anything* was happening between us—but I definitely didn't want her to know about it.

'Shit, there they are,' Clover said as she looked towards the door. It was like a scene in a film, that part where everybody turned to see who had arrived at a party, or like when Mr Darcy arrived at the Meryton Assembly. Ollie was standing next to a stern-looking man with grey hair and grey eyes, wearing a dark blue suit. Handsome in an older guy kind of way. From the similarities between them, it had to be his father.

Then there was a stunning woman with her arm in Leo's, brown hair flowing to her waist, wearing a classic black dress with black court shoes. She oozed power and money. Leo looked pretty dapper too, to be fair, in a grey suit and white shirt that helped highlight the intensity of his blue eyes.

Clover gasped at the sight of them.

On the other side of Leo stood his father—another stern-looking rich man who reminded me of a king surveying his kingdom. His hair was the same colour as Leo's and you could see the family resemblance instantly. Griff stood on the end, looking carefree as usual. Carefree and alone.

Ollie and his father both looked over at me, and together they started walking in our direction. *Just wonderful.*

'Hey,' Ollie said curtly, giving me a quick head nod. 'Dad, this is Skylar Crescent. Sky, this is my father, Henry Brandon.'

'Hello, girls,' Henry said, smiling, but his eyes assessed everything, surveying the entire room. I felt a sharp nudge in my side that definitely came from an elbow. An exaggerated cough followed.

Here we go.

'Ollie. Mr Brandon,' I said, reluctance in my voice. 'This is my mum, Cora, and my stepdad, Andy.'

Everybody shook hands and acted friendly enough, but I could see the level of disgust in Henry's eyes. He even wiped his hands after shaking Andy's—which yeah, fair—but it still made me feel crappy inside.

The conversation resembled a shitshow from the start.

'How do you know my beautiful Skylar?' Mum asked Ollie with a cheeky wink. 'Got her looks from me, didn't she?' She was surveying everybody gathered with us. Probably attempting to decipher the cumulative wealth standing in front of her.

'We're in class together,' Ollie replied, curt, completely ignoring the second part of Mum's sentence.

'How wonderful,' Mum said with enthusiasm. 'Andy, isn't it just super-duper that our Sky has made such *handsome* friends?'

The emphasis on handsome nauseated me.

'Course it is, hot stuff,' Andy replied, leering at Mum.

Could this get any worse?

He grabbed Mum's bum in full view of everyone. Mortified, my face continued turning a deep shade of red from overheating. Of course shit could always get worse with those two around.

The group of us settled into an uncomfortable silence, nobody knowing what to say or do next.

Somebody was clearly looking out for me as a bell rang out through the hall, letting the room know the sit-down part of the meal would commence shortly.

'I guess we'll see you later,' I said, being careful not to look Ollie in the eye. 'It was nice meeting you, Mr Brandon.'

'Please,' Mr Brandon said, brushing my arm. 'Call me Henry.'

I smiled, and everybody else began to say their awkward as fuck goodbyes. After it was over, we went our separate ways to take our seats. Mum made a big song and dance about finding our seats, meandering slowly through the tables and reading each name card out loud.

I take back what I said. There was no saviour looking out

for me. And I knew that, because when we found our seats, they were at the table with Ollie, his dad, Griff, Leo, and his parents.

Go figure.

AS EXPECTED, the meal was awkward as fuck. Barely anybody had spoken after I'd introduced Mum and Leo had introduced his parents, Edward and Lottie. Clover sat there next to me in complete silence, only answering when Lottie had asked her a couple of questions about how her baking was coming along and how her grades were.

The band played throughout, and when we finished the meal, Ms Hawthorn walked out onto the stage. Grumbles went out across the hall, as did a few whispers. I noticed Leo's dad sat up taller and looked interested instantly, but then I remembered he owned this place and was related to the woman standing in the centre, ready to address everybody here.

A projector screen appeared behind her, which could only mean we were going to have to sit through some kind of school bullshit propaganda intended to woo the rich people and entice them to donate even more of their enormous fortunes. How exciting.

'Welcome to Parents' Day, where you are once again able to see how your children and protégés are progressing at this fine institution.' Her grey, beady eyes assessed the room, spending a fraction longer on Clover and me. Or maybe on my mum. Or maybe I was just imagining the whole thing, paranoia getting the better of me. Just because I felt disgusted by her didn't mean everybody else felt the same. A shiver ran down my spine at her words. They sounded so false and pretentious. 'The students of A-Level Media Studies have put together this short film for you. I do hope you enjoy it.'

The lights in the hall dimmed, and the projector screen flickered to life. Images of the school were being shown to a bouncy background beat, then a voiceover started.

'Hawthorn Academy was first established in 1850 by Sir Robert Hawthorn, who hoped the future generations would have the best education money could buy. Still today, this fine establishment does exactly what Robert set out to do.'

Exterior shots of the school played, followed by shots of students sitting in classrooms or out on the field playing team sports.

'Recently, the school has restarted the scholarship fund, in order for those less fortunate to benefit from the connections that can be made here and to obtain the best education.'

My stomach dipped as butterflies started to make a home in there. I wanted nothing more than for that section of the tape to be over quickly. I looked at Clover, who seemed to have the same expression on her face as I did on mine. It was clear from the voice speaking that it had been recorded by Ophelia, which definitely didn't bode well for me.

'The scholarship students fit in well and are a welcome addition to Hawthorn Academy. Although, they do seem to be a little too friendly with the elite business world's future leaders.'

Abruptly, the footage changed.

It changed to a shaky, handheld video recording taken on a mobile phone. Whoever was recording giggled, in that way people did when they were trying to stay incognito and were doing something they knew they shouldn't.

Like the fog on my brain was lifting, I recognised just when the footage was from—and where.

It was from the night of the party in the woods. I could see me and Ollie dancing together on the makeshift dance floor. Then I saw me, on the screen, take Ollie's hand and lead him further into the trees, a soft smile on my face. An even wider one on his.

I knew what came next, and I really thought I might be sick from the butterflies swarming in my stomach, thrashing about and jostling the sides.

How dare they film that? How dare they take a private, intimate moment and taint it? Well, as private a moment could be hidden from a crowd of people. How dare they show that to all of these people?

I was livid in an instant. A hot, burning anger travelled through me, threatening to cause a scream to leave my throat unbidden. But tears were forming in my eyes, near to spilling over at any moment. I sat in silence and watched it unfold along with everybody else, too scared to make a noise. To draw more attention to myself.

Once the content of the footage became clear to everybody in the hall, Ms Hawthorn rushed back to the stage and stopped the tape, the screen returning to white once again. As if it hadn't just shown something so cruel.

Whispers.

The entire hall began to talk in whispers that became louder with every moment. I could hear parents commenting on what they'd just seen. Half of them were angry about the party. The other half were only mad that they'd been made to watch it.

Ollie's eyes met mine from across the table. An angry, yet cold stare that made me pause.

He didn't look sad. He looked furious. I couldn't tell whether it was aimed at me because it happened in the first place, or if it was the fact they'd aired it to the entire school. Not like the two of us discussed it after it happened.

To make matters worse, his father was staring me down with a look of clear disdain. I was a rabbit caught in the headlights. I didn't want to leave the hall and let them see that they'd won. Just because I hadn't seen the girls and their parents today didn't mean they weren't in here somewhere, giggling to themselves with glee. Biding their time. Waiting to see what I'd do. How I'd react.

My mum broke the silence at the table in a way only she could.

'Darling, I wouldn't worry,' she said, a smile playing on her bright lips. 'I used to get up to a lot worse when I was at school. Like mother, like daughter, ay?'

I cringed inside. She even had the audacity to throw a wink in my direction as if that softened any of it.

'Ay.' Andy winked at me too. 'Now everybody knows how much of a slut you are, Sky. Can't hide it anymore, sweetheart.' He leered at me, and all I could picture was his face looming closer to mine, his tongue invading my mouth without permission. That rotten, putrid stench of alcohol clinging to his skin. To mine.

Fuck this. I'm out.

'If you'll excuse me, I must go freshen up,' I announced to everybody and nobody. The table all nodded, and every man but Andy stood when I left. Clover quickly followed me, dashing after me as fast as she could while keeping her decorum. As soon as we made it out of the hall, Clover put her arm around me and steered me to the nearest toilets.

'Those little bitches,' Clover spat, her anger for me etched all over her face. 'I promise you, Skylar, we *will* get them back. Maybe not today, but sometime this year, we will.'

I nodded, still too shocked about the change of events to say anything.

'Although...' Clover trailed off, a cheeky prying look appearing on her face. 'You didn't tell me *that* happened with Ollie.'

I covered my face with my palm. I wasn't embarrassed as such, but I could feel a blush forming, starting on my cheeks and bleeding outward to the rest of my face.

'I know,' I whined. 'To be honest with you, I wasn't even sure it actually happened. After they drugged me, I doubted my own memories. Ollie hadn't said a word afterward about it, so I wondered if I'd just had a super feverish dream as I lay beside him in bed.'

My logic made sense, in my head at least. I didn't want to assume that anything I remembered actually happened, so I'd decided it was best to keep it to myself. But apparently that wasn't possible. Everybody knew the truth thanks to the O girls.

After some deep breaths, Clover and I returned to the hall where the parents were saying their goodbyes. It only occurred to me then that my mum, or Andy, could have said anything while I'd been gone.

I didn't look at Ollie. Or Griff or Leo. I just didn't want to know what they were thinking about me. About the whole *Ollie fingered me, pinned up against a tree* scenario we'd all just watched play out. Not like either of us could deny it when there was footage saying otherwise.

Ms Hawthorn joined the group to say her goodbyes. But her focus was solely on her brother, Edward. Things looked tense between them, but that could be a result of my amateur porn clip. The fact Ollie and I were both sixteen definitely made this even worse. For us *and* the school.

'Miss Crescent,' Ms Hawthorn called out, her voice clear yet hushed. 'I expect to see you in my office first thing Monday morning.' Her eyes narrowed when she looked at me and her lips were pursed together.

'Yes, Ms,' I responded, using my best contrite manner. Couldn't wait for that meeting... *Not.*

'It's been nice to meet you, Skylar. Clover,' Lottie Hawthorn said, giving us both a kind smile that reached her eyes, and I could feel it in my bones that at least one person at the table was genuine.

'Skylar. Clover.' Edward nodded at each of us and left with his wife, Leo following closely along behind them.

'It's been a pleasure,' Henry said, his face telling me it had been the complete opposite of a pleasure, but nobody called him out on it. He and Ollie left together, and although I didn't look at him, I could sense Ollie glanced back at me before he left the hall.

That left me, Clover, and Griff standing with my mum, Andy, and Ms Hawthorn. An odd mix of people who didn't all need to stand together any longer.

'Mum, it's been fun,' I lied, hoping she couldn't hear in my voice just how much I wanted her gone. If she knew I wanted her to leave, she'd stay longer just to spite me. She'd done it in the past, so I knew it was something she'd do. 'Glad you could make it, though.'

'Oh, me too, darling. I'm so glad to have found out my daughter is just as much of a skunk as I am,' she said, slurring her words. Pretty sure she meant to call me a skank, but not like I was going to correct her. The copious amounts of free booze she'd drunk today must be finally catching up with her. I hoped they could get out of here before one of them did something terrible. Or both of them.

'Been lovely to meet you two,' Clover said, also lying through her teeth, the pain in her eyes at her words giving her away. 'Have a safe journey home.' As an afterthought she added, 'You have a lift home, right?'

'Yep. The school sent somebody to pick us up and they're taking us back too,' Andy said. He went to hug me goodbye, but Griff grabbed me out of harm's way and put his hand out for Andy to shake instead.

'It's been real. I'll walk you to your car.'

Honestly, I could kiss him. Instead, I squeezed his shoulder, making it clear I appreciated the way he'd stepped in for me. I'd never told Griff much about my life before Hawthorn, but I reckoned he had an inkling. Especially after today.

He'd been quiet all day, which was unusual for him, taking in his surroundings and listening to the conversations going on around him, but barely joining in.

'I'll meet you two back up at your room.' Griff winked at us, sweeping his arm towards the door, and followed after my mum and Andy. Neither of them walked off in a straight line. *Eurgh.* All I needed now was for them to be sick before reaching the car, and my day of humiliation and shame would be complete.

Luckily for me, roughly an hour later when Griff made it back to our room, he didn't have any puke stories to share with me. I took that as a plus. According to him, they'd got in the car with no real fanfare but had promised to return when next invited.

Believe me, if I have anything to do with it, the two of them will never set foot on school grounds ever again.

Ollie never came to my room to talk to me that night. He

didn't even send me a text. Nice to know he cared about me enough to wonder about me, wonder about how I was coping with what had gone down.

Oh, wait.

He didn't.

Sixteen

'NEW GIRL, you're coming to the swim meet tomorrow, right?' Griff asked.

'I didn't know that there was a swim meet tomorrow?' I asked, confused. 'What the fuck even happens at one of those?'

'A lot of races,' he joked. 'You mean Ollie didn't tell you?' His eyes widened dramatically and his mouth fell open in a comedic way. Prick.

'Not being funny, Griff, but Ollie would have to *talk* to me in order to tell me about it.'

'Ouch. Right. I'm sure he's just busy with his dad. You know he's staying at the Hawthorn residence on the grounds tonight along with Leo's parents.'

'Once again, Griff. He'd have to talk to me for me to know shit.'

'Got it. Anyway, there's a swim meet and your boy is going to kill the competition.'

'By *your boy*, do you mean Ollie or you?' I asked, laughing at his use of words. For starters, Ollie was definitely not *my* boy. But if Griff was talking about himself, then I found that quite sweet in a best friend kind of way. He may have originally started to hang out with us to rile the other two boys up, but I genuinely believed that Griff was just as much our friend as he was theirs.

'Oh, definitely me,' he replied. His cocky grin was charming as all get-out. Not for the first time I wished it was Griff I had a connection with, but all I could see him as was a brother. A big-headed, egotistical, older brother who knew what buttons to push and when.

And I wouldn't have it any other way.

THE CONVERSATION with Griff the night before was how I found myself on Sunday afternoon, sitting in the stands of the swimming pool alongside the other students and parents. Clover begrudgingly sat beside me, but only because Griff and I had begged her to come and keep me company. Apparently, she didn't want to witness Leo's smug grin when he won yet again. *The Sect* were the best on the team and I hated to say it, but I was excited to see just how decent they were.

Even if I still thought Ollie was a dickhead. I'd woken up to a text from him that didn't make me feel much warmer towards him.

DON'T BE MAD. WE'LL TALK LATER. I ACTED LIKE A DICK.

With a roll of my eyes, I responded with a quick **K**. After all, everybody knew what a "K" text meant.

'How long does a swim meet last?' I had no idea what to expect. My old school didn't have a swimming pool, therefore, no swim team.

'Too long,' she replied in a weary tone.

Basically, she was no help at all.

The first few rounds of races were for the younger years, and those races made me realise that swimming wasn't my favourite sport to watch. Not that there were many sports I enjoyed watching, but still. I was the kind of girl who would watch the Olympics, and that was about it. Maybe the odd Wimbledon, because you know, tennis could be pretty exciting to watch, and the entire country got behind it every June. Then promptly forgot about it again by July.

Finally, it was time for Ollie and Griff to compete. I knew that Ollie hid a hot body underneath his uniform, but seeing him like this, his chest in all its glory, was truly a sight to behold. A genuine work of art. He had a six-pack, so defined, that the only image going through my mind was that of him with water dripping down into every crease. Don't get me started on his legs. They were long and pure muscle. Even the tiny shorts they wore weren't enough to deter me. It ensured that my mind was now imagining Ollie's dick. He had that V— you know, the one that led to the main event. Ollie was an Adonis, plain and simple, and I had to wipe away some drool before Clover spotted it. It did piss me off a little that I wasn't the only person witnessing this. There were too many eyes on him, and for a split second, I considered stabbing the eyes out of *The Set* just so they couldn't see him.

Despite my best efforts, I've turned into a basic, petty, horny bitch.

Griff stood beside Ollie, and his body was not one to be sniffed at either. He had wide shoulders and I could see that he was sporting a six-pack *and* an Adonis belt. Even if I saw him as a brother, I could still appreciate that he worked hard on his body. All three of them did, spending a lot of their time training in the pool or in the school gym. It had paid off, that was for damn sure.

I couldn't tell you much of the race itself. I didn't know the length they swam or the stroke or anything like that. All I could tell you was that Ollie won. Every single race he competed in, he won by at least an entire second each time. The crowd cheered and hollered as he brought home yet another medal and another trophy for the school. Griff came second, and he seemed super chuffed with the result. His cheeky façade never faltered, his smile constantly in place. He even winked and dabbed in our direction when collecting his medal. *What a loser.*

The last race of the day was Leo's. According to the whispers around me, *his* was the race to watch. Ollie had been amazing, but Leo was something else entirely. A new species, almost. It also helped that Leo had an impressive body. The whole disinterested thing totally worked for him in a competitive setting, too. He stayed calm before the race, and he flew through that water, leaving the opponents in his wake. He was spectacular and I could totally see him one day competing at the Olympics, or something major like that. Leo was just *that* good.

'Fuck me, Clo. Did you see that?' I asked, astonished.

'Yep,' she replied bluntly. She looked so sour on the outside, but she couldn't fool me. I saw her face while he was racing. She was as tense as everybody else here, and I could totally tell her bum cheeks were clenched just as tight as mine from start to finish. 'He's good.'

'Good? Clover, did we just watch the same thing?' I asked in disbelief at her indifference. I couldn't believe she was being such a dick about it all.

After the race, Ollie and Griff went and showered off the chlorine, then came and joined us.

'Did you see how fly I was?' Griff asked the two of us, his dimples pressing in.

'Fly? Who even are you?' I laughed, shaking my head, knowing that Griff was doing his best to get a rise out of us all and be the comedian like usual.

'I was definitely better,' Ollie said, all smug, and you could tell he really believed in his own hype. Which, yeah, he *was* good, but nowhere near as good as Leo.

'Of course you were, handsome,' Griff said, hugging him. He gave him a big kiss on his cheek. Ollie groaned and wiped it away instantly, but that action made Griff even more determined to land more kisses on Ollie. 'You were legiterally perfect.'

'What the fuck is legiterally?' Clover asked, piping up.

'You know. It's a mix of legit and literally. I made it up,' he said, his face bright.

'No way!' I gasped. Arms came around my waist, hugging my back into a hard chest. Instantly, the smell of Ollie's vanilla and tobacco scent I loved so much filled my senses and I breathed it in. I made a note to find out what it was because I wouldn't mind spritzing my clothes with that smell. He turned me to face him, his blue eyes looking into my soul.

Honestly, this boy gives me whiplash.

'I'm sorry, Sky,' he said, his face blank but sincere. 'I should've tried to speak to you last night.'

'You think?' I said, not wanting to make it too easy for him, but knowing I would let him off. 'You could've tried to talk to me.'

'I know, but I didn't know what to say. And then there's my dad.'

'What about your dad?'

'He's a prick. That's all you need to know.'

'Okay…' I knew he was evading my question, but the glint of apology in his eye distracted me from asking more.

'So do you forgive me?'

'Don't do it again, Ollie. It made me feel cheap and unimportant.'

'Promise,' he said, then placed a soft kiss on my forehead. 'Oh, while I remember. I want you to come to my birthday party next Friday night.'

It wasn't a question. It was a demand, slightly softened with a smile.

'It's your birthday next week?' *Shit*. What on earth would I get him, and why had he only just mentioned it?

'On Halloween,' he said, smirking. 'Costume party in the woods.'

'W-wow. Okay,' I said, trying not to focus too hard on the woods part of the sentence. I looked at Clo. 'Guess we need to put on our thinking caps.'

She nodded but didn't look happy about it. I assumed she knew Ollie's birthday was coming up, so not mentioning it was a bit of a dick move. They must have celebrated last year— even if Clo hadn't been invited, she would've heard shit, right?

'Come on, babe. Let's go watch a film and get some pizza in.' Ollie's arm came around my shoulder, pulling me to him as he walked us away from the pool entrance.

'Let's go.' I smiled as the four of us headed off towards Ollie's room. As we walked past the door to the locker room, I spotted Leo standing there, looking straight in our direction.

Dead eyes staring at us, no light in them.

Seventeen

MONDAY MORNING, I made my way to Ms Hawthorn's office. Butterflies sat heavy in my stomach, and I worried about what she would say to me regarding the whole video debacle. All night my nerves were in overdrive. The others tried to take my mind off it all, but nothing they did helped. It pissed me off that Ollie wasn't being summoned into her office. He was as much a part of that video as me.

Ollie and Griff both offered to come with me, put on a united front, but I decided to come alone. I didn't need them fighting my battles for me—well, not all of them anyway.

I knocked on the large wooden door, the sound reverberating throughout the empty hallway. While I waited, my eyes looked around the hallway, and when they landed on the spot Ollie kissed me in, I snapped my gaze away.

Stop thinking about him.

'Come in,' Ms Hawthorn called from the other side of the door.

I took in a deep lungful of air and pushed the heavy door. Or at least it felt heavier than the last time I opened it. Maybe it was my mind that felt heavy.

'Sit,' she said, curt, her face hard.

The chair cushion squished underneath my weight, the legs gave out a groan, and I looked at Ms Hawthorn across the desk. I maintained eye contact for as long as I could, but her stare intimidated me. My eyes flitted down to the table, where they focused on a wood swirl.

'Miss Crescent, you are on your last warning here at the academy.' Her eyes narrowed. 'I will not have you besmirching this fine establishment.'

'I—' I found myself saying the first thing that came to mind, but not knowing where to go with it, my word tapered off.

'If any reports of further misconduct come my way, I must expel you. Do you understand me?' she asked, and I nodded instantly with a gulp. I couldn't get expelled. I couldn't go back to my previous life.

'O-of course. It won't happen again, Ms Hawthorn.'

'See that it doesn't,' she said, dismissing me, her eyes instantly going back to the paperwork in front of her.

I stood and walked out slowly, trying to close the door softly behind me. I wondered if the other girls were being called into her office today, but I highly doubted it.

If they continued to bully me, the school would expel me. Yep, sounded about right.

Even a week later, I was still feeling a little raw about everything that had happened on Parents' Day. That my mum and Andy had been there to witness my humiliation definitely made it one thousand times worse. Or maybe the humiliation they gave me from being there was worse. Either way, it was all pretty shit.

It was on Sunday night, as Clover and I were sitting in our room in silence, both trying to work on our homework, that Clover turned towards me with a determined look on her face. Things had been tense between us ever since Ollie had invited us to his birthday slash Halloween party.

Clover didn't want to go. And I did.

'Sky, do you really think it's a good idea to go to the Halloween party on Friday?'

I rolled my eyes at her words. We'd been having a variation of the same conversation on and off for what felt like forever. I got her point. The last party in the woods I'd attended I was drugged and recorded. *Not an impressive track record.*

'Honestly, I don't know. But it's Ollie's birthday, and I said I'd be there.'

I smiled, thoughts of Ollie filling my mind. Things were going well between us and I didn't want to snub his birthday party or fuck up the tentative truce we'd come to. Also, everybody knew that Halloween parties were an excuse to dress up as a fantasy, and I had the perfect costume idea for Clover and me.

'Also, not like I can disobey. Ollie invited me and he's a member of *The Sect*, so I can't exactly turn it down without having more mean shit happen to me.' We both knew my excuses were pretty hollow at that point. The girls had backed off after Parents' Day. Believe it or not, they'd got in shit with Ms Hawthorn. It wasn't hard for her to figure out Ophelia's voice on the voiceover, plus the O girls all took media. As far as I knew from what Griff told me, none of them were threatened with expulsion for their actions. Their parents did sign the big checks, after all.

The truth of the matter was I wanted to go to the Halloween party. Yeah, there was a small part of me that knew it could all come crashing down, or that the girls could target me again, but it was a chance I was willing to take. The way Ollie had looked at me this week was real. I could feel it deep down inside of me. And we needed more time alone in a non-classroom setting.

'I get it. I really, *really* do. I've been there, you know. I was in your position once,' Clover said, staring at me intently. I nodded at her, but I was already tuning her out. She meant well, but there were only so many times you could hear your best friend rail on the guy you liked without it pissing you off. 'Last year was really hard for me. I didn't have any friends, and if you think *The Set* is bad this year, they're nothing compared to last year. The two older girls last year made Ophelia and Oralie look like kittens.'

'Right, you mentioned last year before, but, Clo, you've never even told me what happened. Not like they've targeted you this year?'

I had thought about it once or twice. Clover kept hinting at the events of the previous year and how bad school had been for her, but never went into much detail when I asked for more details. Definitely not enough for me to form an opinion. People barely acknowledged her this year, except for when she stuck up for me. I found it hard to believe that their shitty treatment of her stopped overnight. *Something doesn't add up.*

'That's exactly it!' she exclaimed, raising her voice. 'I don't know why it all stopped and I have a terrible feeling about all of this, Skylar. Proper.'

'I know you do. I promise I hear you, Clo. But I can't explain it. I just feel it in my gut. I need to go to this party and I need you there by my side. You're my best friend,' I said, hoping my last sentence would sweeten the deal a little, grabbing her hand in mine.

'I don't want to see Leo,' she rasped, her words filled with so much venom.

I rolled my eyes, hard. It was tiring constantly hearing about Leo and how Clover wanted nothing to do with him. I could see in her eyes, though, that she wasn't giving me the full story. She'd fobbed me off with half-hearted excuses, or she changed the subject to me and Ollie, or even to Griff's jokes, never letting me see the truth. I'd had my suspicions ever since Leo's mum had treated her so kindly. They totally knew one another a lot better than mere acquaintances.

'I know, Clo, and I'm not asking you to.'

'But you are, Sky. Just by wanting to be at the party with Ollie, and Griff, you're asking me to spend time with Leo because at some point you know he'll join us. He'll stand there like the dickhead he is and smirk and judge me with his fucking judging eyes,' said Clo, who, talking of judging eyes, was giving me a very judgemental look.

I couldn't help myself.

I burst into laughter at the way her face had gone as red as her hair. I could feel her anger, but it was also super clear to me that Leo got under her skin because she still had feelings for him.

'Just admit it, Clo. You've got feelings for the guy. Nothing to be ashamed about.'

'That's where you're wrong. Sure, I have feelings for Leo Hawthorn, but you can bet your arse the feelings I have for him are ones born of hatred,' she said vehemently.

I knew that Clo meant her words, I could feel it in the air, but I also knew that she was living in denial. The sexual tension between the two of them was thick and one day they would combust. Something had to give, after all.

'Okay, okay,' I said to placate her. One thing I had learned about having a best friend was that sometimes it was just easier to agree. Easier to have them think you were with them 100 percent even if inside you disagreed with them. 'Course that's what it is.'

'It is, I promise,' she said, a little too indignant, but I didn't push it further. I could tell she was getting close to the end of her patience on the subject—and with me.

'Eurgh, fine! I'll tell you a little. Take this and run with it, 'cause I don't know if I'll talk about it again.'

I nodded straight away, biting my tongue until she stopped talking. I didn't want her to stop before she'd fully opened up.

'Basically, I've known Leo ever since I was really young, but that isn't what's important. What matters is the fact that Leo, Ollie, and sometimes Griff, alongside *The Set*, made my life hell last year. Every single thing I did, they would make it bad. Turn it into something to be ashamed of. They would ruin my food, my exam results, destroy my homework, and constantly write shit about me in the toilets or on the Hive,' she said, looking into my eyes.

I stayed silent, thrilled she was finally talking, and not wanting to do anything to ruin it or throw her off.

'They threw rotten food at me, locked me in the dark caretaker's cupboard, spat at me in class. Literally, they did anything they could to isolate me. I had no friends and nobody to turn to or to keep me sane and tell me that I was worth more than the shit I was getting from them.'

Tears shimmered in her eyes, threatening to fall. Talking about it had brought it all up for her again, and I felt her pain. Felt how much the experience had affected her. The girls had targeted me since the start of the school year, but I had Clover and Griff to help me keep afloat. Their friendship meant that I could keep myself from dwelling on it. I couldn't imagine how I would feel if I was alone. Plus, the start of the school year was less than two months ago.

'That's why I'm finding this U-turn on Ollie's part so hard to understand and come to terms with. Griff too. At least he apologised to me the other night, after Parents' Day. I think the girls showing that footage of you and Ollie really made him see how his actions last year affected me.'

I knew she wanted me to talk, to say something, to agree with her or accept her stance on Ollie and his actions. I wasn't sure what I could say, though. What they'd done to her was beyond shit and shouldn't have happened. But I also couldn't take in everything she said and completely change how I acted around Ollie, Griff, and even Leo because of it.

'I'm glad Griff came to his senses. I get why you feel the way you do, Clo. I promise, I'll be sensible. But c'mon, a Halloween party sounds like exactly what we need right now.'

Clover grumbled, but I thought maybe she sort of agreed with me, even if only slightly.

'Fine. We'll go. But if any funny business takes place, don't say I didn't tell you so!'

'Thank you! You won't regret it,' I squealed, clapping my hands together.

And she didn't. Couldn't say the same about myself, though.

Eighteen

FRIDAY NIGHT ARRIVED and I was terrified.

My friendship with Clover had been tense ever since Monday when we had our mini argument about the party—well, if you could call it an argument. I had to prove that everything was fine. That nothing would go wrong and we'd be laughing tomorrow about what a splendid night we had and just how wrong she'd been about everything. Positive thinking and all that.

Luckily, Clover came around enough to agree to dress in a couple's costume with me. I was giddy just thinking about it. We went for Betty Rubble and Wilma Flintstone. Clover was the perfect Wilma with her red hair and I donned a short black, bobbed wig for the evening that covered my silver hair entirely. It completely changed how I looked and made me feel all mysterious. Like a new person.

The only change we made to the costumes was that we were a super *dead* Betty and Wilma so we covered the dresses and ourselves in fake blood. That cheap stuff you find at party shops that will probably stain our skin and be a bitch to wash off. We both looked super cute but also super sexy—Halloween goal accomplished.

When I caught Clo's eye across our room, I couldn't help thinking about how Leo would react to seeing her dressed like that. She looked like the perfect girl for a caveman like Leo. Even if the two of them were trying to convince everybody that they hated one another, I just couldn't believe it. One day it was going to blow up in everybody's faces and I would happily be the one telling her "I told you so."

Maybe my outfit would spark something between me and Ollie, something more than what had already transpired between us. The kisses and stolen moments we shared had been life-changing. *Okay, a bit dramatic there, Sky.* But they *had* been life-affirming.

Fuck, I'm even making myself *want to vomit.*

CLOVER and I made our way over to the clearing in the woods around eight. We didn't want to get there too early and look desperate, but we also didn't want to arrive too late and have all the premium alcohol be gone. It was always a fine line, or so Clover told me.

'Sky, you still have time to bow out of this, you know. We can go back to our room and nobody will even know we were here,' Clo said as we got closer to the clearing.

'Why would we do that? It's Ollie's birthday, and I won't bail on that.' I shook my head and rolled my eyes at the same time, which was pretty impressive actually if you asked me, but it also probably made me look slightly possessed.

I was a bit bored with Clo's overprotectiveness. I knew she was trying to look out for me, and I totally got why after she told me a little of what happened to her last year, but I couldn't help getting frustrated. Just because you understood some-thing, it didn't mean it couldn't piss you off.

'Plus, it was a direct order from a member of *The Sect*, so not like I can disobey. I don't want to give the dicks here more reason to harass me.'

'And since when have we cared what the other dickheads who go here think?' Clo asked, one eyebrow raised.

'Well...' I didn't want to say anything to upset her, but you know, I also wasn't gonna lie to the girl either. 'Clo, we've always cared. Even if we don't admit it out loud.'

'Bullshit!' she exclaimed, throwing her arms in the air. Catching my eye, we both burst into a fit of giggles. Leaves rustled ahead of us, signalling someone's arrival.

'There you two are!' Griff shouted at us from up ahead. 'I've been waiting for you to get here. Now the party can truly begin.'

He hadn't met us at our room because he'd helped set up with the other members of the "ruling class." He hadn't told us what he was dressing as because according to him, he wanted to *knock our socks off*.

Griff came towards us, dressed as Prince Harry, which made me smile super wide. Of course he was. With his hair, I should have known he would have dressed as Harry. Actually, I was slightly annoyed that I hadn't guessed it.

'Fuck me. You two are looking mighty fine tonight. I must say, my lady luck, that I would love to add to your pearl neck-lace,' he said with a wink. That cheeky grin was ever present on his face. Sometimes, though I'd never admit it to him—imagine the reaction—there were times I wished it were Griff who I liked. But even though he *was* hiding a buff body, I just didn't fancy him. At. All. There was something so carefree about Griff, and his cheekiness always felt infectious, but I'd sold my heart to a beast, and I didn't think I would get it back anytime soon. Unless he was the one to throw it back in my face.

'Oh, ha-ha,' Clover responded, raising her eyebrows at him, almost daring him to repeat what he'd said. 'You are such a filthy bastard, Griff, I swear.'

I couldn't help my guffaw. His filthy jokes often caught me off guard, but I was tickled more than usual.

'You wound me, kind lady,' Griff said, smirking at Clo. 'Or maybe it's the fact that my *pearls* aren't the ones you want. Ay?'

'Oh, piss off,' Clover said, shoving him on the shoulder, causing him to stumble backwards a little. For a split second, his smile slipped, but it was back within moments. She laughed at him, and I knew that none of Griff's words affected her. 'Are you taking us to the party or what?'

'Follow me, ladies. The night has just begun.'

THE PARTY WAS LIVELY by the time we made it deep enough into the woods to where the party was. I spotted Ollie and Leo straight away, both of them with an O girl on each arm. I quickly looked away before Ollie saw me staring. What on earth was he doing with Ophelia of all people hanging on his arm?

Griff didn't leave our side to join them the way I thought he would.

Recently, Griff was choosing us over them a lot, but I didn't want to think about what that may mean. I wanted to believe he was doing it because he liked us both, but there was another part of me that thought he could have been asked to spy on us by Ollie or Leo—or both. Especially after what Clover told me the other night.

Pumpkins, fake cobwebs, and gravestones decorated the wooded area as far as my eye could see, giving the entire place a super creepy feel. There were ghosts and witches hanging from the trees, and the alcohol table over on the right-hand side was covered in skulls and other spooky items. I wasn't sure from where I stood, but it looked as if there were fake eyeballs floating in the large punch bowl placed in the centre of the table. I didn't even want to guess at what was actually in the punch bowl, but it was probably something a lot stronger than all the alcohol I'd had in my life put together. After what happened the last time I came to a party, I was going to make sure I only drank from an unopened bottle. I wanted to remember the night. I didn't want to wake up with no knowledge of what went down.

I looked over at Ollie, who was dressed as Batman. He looked better than any Batman I'd seen before; in actual life and in the movies. The mask fit his face perfectly, really highlighting his blue eyes and full lips. The lanterns lighting the area put everyone into shadows, making the place look sinister and spooky, setting the ultimate Halloween party vibe. A chill shot through me and goosebumps prickled on my entire body, but that could be due to my dress being super short and revealing and the air being super cold.

Leo, dressed as The Joker, stood with Odette by his side, dressed as Harley Quinn. If I didn't hate her, I would totally love their couples costume. It was really well done, and they looked great together. Something I wouldn't mention to Clover.

Shit, I thought as I spotted the large table overflowing with presents, a five-tier cake standing proud beside them. *Fuck*. I didn't get Ollie a present. I had no money, and I wasn't even sure I could get him something he didn't already own. I also wasn't going to be one of those cliché bitches who gave their virginity as a present. I wasn't ready for that, and I hated the whole bullshit idea that virginity was a gift to give in the first place. Gross.

On the edge of the party, Ollie and Leo still stood looking over at us, ignoring the girls at their sides, but not making a move to come over to us.

'What's up with those assholes?' Clover asked, nudging Griff in the side, nodding in the boys' direction.

'Who even knows, girly tots. They've both been acting strange recently,' Griff said, his tone conspiring.

'Strange as in...' I trailed off, waiting for him to pick up the dropped thread.

'Can't explain it.' He shrugged. 'Ollie barely has anything to do with Leo or the girls outside of swimming or classes now. But we're all super tight, so it makes sense that he's talking to him. It's his birthday, after all.'

'Yeah, that's fine, but why the fuck is Ophelia hanging off his arm looking like a tramp?' Clover asked, voicing what was going through my mind. Ophelia, dressed as some kind of slutty nurse, stood next to Ollie, practically pawing at him. Maybe she was a zombie nurse? Honestly, I didn't want to get close enough to find out. I was just happy that she wasn't in a couples costume with Ollie. That wouldn't fly with me.

Even though the two of us weren't a couple or anything, I still felt like there was something brewing between us. Bubbling away in the cauldron, soon to boil over. Something I intended to find out more about later in the evening—if the boy ever came over to talk to me.

Shit, I could go over to him. Be bold. Take the bull by the

horns and all those cliché sayings. Walk over to him and demand his attention. And I planned to go...

After a drink.

'Let's get a drink,' I announced to Clo and Griff, turning to face the two of them.

'Or we could wait here,' Griff said.

'Why?'

''Cause your boy's coming over.'

I turned on the spot. Ollie had untangled himself from Ophelia and was walking over to where the three of us stood.

Guess I wasn't getting that drink first.

Nineteen

'HEY, BEAUTIFUL. YOU LOOK KILLER.'

His words covered me, like honey dripped on my head, travelling down to my blood-soaked toes. His blue eyes locked on mine before trailing up and down my body, taking in every inch of me.

Ollie looked as if he wanted to eat me whole.

'I look dead. So less killer, more like I bumped into a killer,' I joked.

'Well, you're definitely the best dead girl I've had the fortune of meeting,' he said.

'Is there any good fortune in meeting a dead girl?'

'Depends on the occasion,' he bantered back. His top lip rose on one side. 'Right now, I'd say it's a great thing.'

He leaned down and kissed my cheek. The kiss promised more, his lips grazing my skin briefly, leaving a tingling heat in their wake.

'You scrub up well too, Clo,' Ollie said through gritted teeth. Probably not all that genuine, but I could tell he was trying for me, which I appreciated.

'Thanks, dickhead. S'pose you don't look too bad,' Clo replied.

'That must have hurt, Clo,' Griff piped up.

'It really, really did. But I thought I'd try and be kind. You know, it being his birthday and all,' she said, a wide smile on her face, turning to look at Ollie. 'Plus, my girl seems to see something in you, so don't fuck it up.'

'Thanks for that.'

'She's not wrong, dude. I'll be pissed if you fuck it up, too. You've got an angel there,' Griff said, wrapping his arm around my shoulders, squeezing me close.

'Griff, you are such a cutie patootie,' I cooed, reaching up and scratching under his chin like you would a child. 'Remind me to give you a shoulder massage the next time we watch films together.'

'Hey!' Ollie interjected. 'Where's my shoulder massage?'

'You never give me any!' I shrugged. 'Plus, Griff is my boy.'

'I see how it is,' Ollie said and tickled me on my side, causing me to laugh and detach myself from Griff's arm. 'I'll be getting you back sometime soon, New Girl.'

'Well, as lovely as this is to watch, I want to get fucked up,' Clover announced, taking Griff's hand and leading him towards the table with the large punch bowl. Ollie had stopped tickling me and moved to look me in the eye, tucking a piece of the wig's hair behind my ear, away from my face.

'Do you want a drink?'

'Only if it's unopened. Don't want a repeat of last time.'

He nodded. 'Trust me, Sky. That won't be happening again.'

'So you know who did it?' I asked, wondering if he'd been keeping a secret from me. Would it not happen again because he'd told the people responsible to knock it off? Or because he thought he was above it all?

'No…' He shook his head. 'But I made it clear that if any harm comes to you, I'll make whoever is responsible pay.'

I knew he wasn't telling the whole truth. His eyes were flitting around, not focusing on one spot, and when he looked back at me, he was fixated on a spot over my shoulder rather than me.

'Okay…'

'Let me go get us some drinks and then we can dance, yeah?'

I agreed and off he went to the table where Clover and Griff were still standing. Ollie shared some words with them, then made his way back to me, holding two bottles; one was beer and the other was some kind of alcopop. Three guesses as to who was having what.

Drinking when dancing, while difficult, was also a lot of fun. We were laughing and joking around with one another in a way we never had before, and a smile was planted firmly on my face. Ollie had loosened up, and the only explanation I could think of was that he was more drunk than I realised. No matter the reason, I enjoyed seeing a side of him I'd never witnessed before. He seemed more like Griff in a sense. Carefree. As if a weight was lifted off him somehow, and I was so happy that I came here tonight. Clover's warning was a distant memory. It almost seemed stupid that I'd been so apprehensive about tonight.

As we danced, I could feel every ridge, every muscle, and I just wanted to lick him all over.

'You are hot as fuck, Sky,' he whispered in my ear, causing tingles to erupt all over my body. 'This outfit is honestly amazing.'

'It w-was my idea,' I said, quite proud of myself. I wanted to pick something that nobody else would choose. Nothing worse than being dressed the same as all the other basic bitches or the O girls. It was my first time attending a fancy dress party, so I wanted the most original outfit I could think of.

'You chose well,' he said, sending a wolfish smile my way. 'You look amazing. I really wish I could peel this dress off of you.'

'Maybe if you play your cards right, mister, you could,' I whispered, a flush filling my cheeks. Flirting with Ollie was fun, especially as I was the one instigating it. He'd said a lot of shit to me in the past that was borderline flirty and a lot that was borderline *not*. It was rare that we spoke so freely in a back and forth with both of us as active participants.

'It really must be my birthday.'

I laughed and hugged him tight to me, leaning up to instigate a kiss between us. One I felt certain was our best yet.

THE ONLY DOWNSIDE to a party in the woods was the complete lack of toilets. I tried my best to hold it in all evening, but I'd hit that point. Hit that peak and I knew I was about to break the seal and potentially ruin the rest of my evening, but I couldn't help myself. I needed to go.

I walked in the direction of the trees, away from the rest of the crowd, wandering off on my own. I told the others where I was heading, and I was pretty sure they heard me. Clo had nodded at me, at least.

Once I could no longer hear the sounds of the party around me, I found a well-hidden tree, away from everything. I quickly peed, then stood still for a moment, not ready to head straight back to the party. I was having such a good time, but I needed a minute or two alone to process it all. Rifling through my bag to find the packet of tissues I put there—I'd learned from the last time—my fingers brushed against a folded piece of paper.

Hm. Don't remember putting that there.

Knowing me, I could have put it in my bag forever ago. It was super rare I cleaned my bag out, and I always wanted to joke about how it reminded me of Mary Poppins's magic bag, but I'd never had any friends to joke about it with. Huh. Must remember to use that line with Clover sometime.

I giggled to myself. *Man, I'm funny.*

Maybe I was more drunk than I realised. Knew I should have eaten more at dinner, but my nerves had got the best of me.

Anyway, the paper.

I pulled it out of my bag and read it, smiling with each line.

Little One,
Meet me in the Pool House at Midnight.
I want to ring my birthday in with you.
And only you.

I looked at my phone. The time was a quarter to midnight, and I was a good ten minutes away from the pool house, so I knew I needed to hurry to meet him on time. There was no guarantee I'd find the piece of paper he dropped in my bag, so I wondered why he never mentioned it to me. Probably wanted to be all mysterious and romantic or some shit. I supposed if I hadn't found the note, he would've just taken me to the pool house himself.

Stumbling my way through the trees, I headed to the pool house with one thing on my mind: to kiss Ollie at midnight.

I made it to the pool house with a minute or two to spare and quickly made my way inside. Unable to see him in the entrance hall, I walked into the pool room itself. Ollie loved swimming and being beside the water, so it would make sense that he would wait for me there. He'd told me once it was a place he felt at peace.

The way the water in the pool moved, and the way the moonlight hit it through the window, made the room look super cool. There were no words to describe it, but the reflection of the water looked so pretty, so mesmerising. In my drunken state, I thought it was one of the most beautiful things I'd ever seen.

I stopped and stared. Taking in the tranquil feel of the water.

Walking around the edge, I got lost in my own thoughts.

I hope Ollie doesn't expect me to sleep with him tonight.

I hoped I hadn't given him the impression that I was ready for that, even if I had joked with him earlier about peeling my dress off. *Fuck.* Had I fuelled the monster? Unleashed a beast that wanted me to the point he wouldn't listen to what I wanted?

No. Course not. *Stop being so fucking stupid, Sky.*

Maybe one day I would be ready to have sex with Ollie, if things continued to progress the way they currently were.

Lost in my thoughts, I jumped when I heard Ollie enter the room. The door slammed behind him, and the noise reverberated around the large room. Each footstep echoed, the water and the large ceiling causing every sound to amplify, but I didn't turn around. It felt intimate. The tension building between us. A midnight tryst was so romantic—and super fucking sexy.

His breath touched my neck and he took off my wig to

brush his fingers through my hair. The touch was hard, as he pressed down into my scalp, putting pressure there. I tingled all over.

His hands rested on my back at the bottom of my spine. It felt familiar and private. Intimate.

His hands pushed forward, and I flew through the air, entering the pool with a loud splash.

The water rushed up around me, entering my ears, my nose, and my mouth. I thrashed around, trying to make my way back up to the surface, but I couldn't. The fight to stop myself from opening my mouth was taking up most of my energy.

A hand gripped the top of my head. Holding me down. Forcing me under.

Fuck. Water filled my mouth. I tried to get away, but there was no escape.

I couldn't breathe. My vision spotted, darkening around the edges, and a sense of déjà vu hit me.

How have I ended up here?

My mind slipped away.

Maybe a little sleep would be okay.

Twenty

'SHIT.'

A faint voice swore above me. I shivered, and I felt even worse than I did after they drugged me at the party in the woods. What was it with me and Hawthorn parties?

All I could think was that I did *not* want to see Clover soon. She'd undoubtedly tell me I told you so.

'Can you hear me, baby?'

I was certain it was Ollie's voice, but confusion filled me because he never called me baby. My ears were clogged, as if still underwater, and I couldn't reach him from under the weight of it.

Ollie! I called in my head. *Ollie!*

'Baby girl, I really need you to answer me,' he pleaded. 'Or just open your eyes for me.'

I'm trying!

My scream was trapped inside my head, yet I wanted so desperately to reach him. To open my eyes and see what was happening around me. Figure out why I felt so cold; so wet. I knew when I opened my eyes, I would be hit with a light so bright, I could see it through my eyelids.

'Ollie, dude, we need to call an ambulance,' Griff said

urgently. His worry hit me straight in the heart. I didn't want to cause him to worry. I doubled my efforts, trying even harder to open my eyes and reassure him that I was all right.

'I'm with Griff. Stop being such a massive dick and do the right thing,' Clover pleaded, causing a sharp pain to stab through my heart. The two of them had grown to mean so much to me in such a brief space of time. If nothing else came from the scholarship, I would still be so glad I took my place here because of them. Shit, oxygen clearly was leaving my brain. I was starting to get sappy.

I needed to knock that off, fast.

Wake. The. Fuck. Up.

'Call an ambulance and everybody will know our shit,' Ollie growled.

'Maybe he's right,' Leo said. For once, he didn't sound bored. Although, he didn't exactly sound worried either. He sounded interested.

'Not you too, Leo,' Ollie snarled, but then his tone softened. 'Baby, it's me, please open your eyes.'

Almost as if a switch turned on in my brain—or, you know, the fact I needed to take a deep breath—I sat bolt upright. Coughing and spluttering up water, gasping in an attempt to take in deep lungfuls of air. I was right in thinking the light was going to be far too bright.

I was beside the pool, surrounded by Ollie, Leo, Griff, and Clover. Clover's makeup was streaking down her face, the black mascara marks showing her despair. Griff had his arm around her shoulders, looking sombre.

Leo looked like hell. I'd never seen him show much expression outside of boredom, but he looked anything but bored when his gaze locked on mine. His hair was wild, as if he'd been running his fingers through it and pulling it in every direction. It tugged at my heart. Maybe he cared a little more about me than he let on.

Ollie was the last of them I focused on.

If I thought Leo looked like hell, then Ollie looked like he'd been living there for the last year. He'd taken off his Batman mask, his face pale and sickly looking, as if the worry had seeped into his pores. He moved as if he was going to hug me, but I darted back out of his reach. Somebody had tried to drown me, and Ollie was the person who wanted to meet me here in the first place. He was the only reason I was there.

I had to be cautious.

'Get away from her,' Clover bit out. Her face transformed from that of somebody upset to that of somebody who was burning up with anger, an accusatory look in her eyes. 'You did this to her.'

'What?' he shouted so loud that I flinched.

'You! I can't figure out how, Oliver, but I know you're the reason for this.'

'Wow. How did you reach that conclusion?' His tone was as cold as ice, filled with derision.

'Don't talk to her like that,' Griff said.

'Lay off her? Dude, she's implying I had something to do with this!'

'Sky must feel similar because she just moved away from you, bro,' Leo said. He moved closer to me. 'I'll take you to the hospital wing.'

I went into his arms and let him pull me to my feet. For some reason, he was the safer option. The guy who barely spoke to me was the one I sought out for comfort.

'Don't walk away, Sky. Or at least let me take you,' Ollie said, almost begging me, but his eyes didn't match his tone as they flashed with anger.

'No, I'll g-go with Leo,' I said, my body breaking out into shivers.

'And how are you going to explain this?' Ollie asked Leo.

'I'm a Hawthorn. I don't exactly *need* to explain this,' Leo replied in his most haughty tone.

'Oh, using Daddy's name once again. That's rich,' Ollie spat.

'Let them go,' Griff said, still holding Clo, as he looked at Ollie, trying to make him back down before turning to Leo. 'Go on, bro. Go make sure our girl's okay.'

Leo nodded before the two of us ambled away, leaving the other three standing beside the edge of the pool. Ollie and Griff were still growling at one another, but I couldn't hear what they were saying. It sounded like Ollie was professing his innocence.

Shame it seemed to be falling on deaf ears. Including mine.

THE HOSPITAL WING looked no different from when I was there last and I let Leo do the talking with the head nurse. She looked rather worried at having a soaking wet dead Betty Rubble and a harried-looking Joker in the room with her.

The nurse checked me over, and I lay down on the bed she assigned me, as she wanted me to stay overnight so they could monitor me. I got comfortable, prepared to be there until morning, and tried not to think too hard about the whole nearly drowning thing.

'Thanks, Leo,' I mumbled and smiled tentatively at him. 'You didn't have to bring me here.'

'Yeah, Sky, I did,' he replied, looking at me. I waited for more, but it never came.

Instead, he got comfy in the seat next to my bed and stayed silent, slumping down, not intending to move soon. I was trying to understand his motivation, but I couldn't figure it out for the life of me. Other than the odd occasion where I bumped into him in empty hallways, I'd spent little time with Leo. Nothing one-on-one.

It made me feel like a child, too scared to talk, not knowing what to say, and too embarrassed that I would mess up somehow.

An hour passed. We must have fallen into a very light sleep as a commotion somewhere else in the wing startled us both awake. Somebody was shouting and throwing items around.

Great. Ollie, Griff, and Clover must have arrived.

'Skylar! Skylar!' Ollie called. My name got louder the closer he got, and when he flew through the curtain surrounding my bed, he looked frantic, like he'd been trying to get away from Griff and Clover for a lot longer than he'd wanted to be. 'Skylar, I promise I didn't do this to you.'

'Calm down, bro,' Leo said. He stood, raising his hands at Ollie to keep him back and away from me. 'The nurse said to stay calm and not distress Sky too much.'

'Since when have you known what's best for Sky?' Ollie asked. His tone was filled with suspicion, like Leo and I were hiding something from him. 'You two don't even talk to each other!'

'Just leave it, Ollie. Say what you've come here to say and then leave so Skylar can rest.' Leo's words were definite and his tone brooked no argument.

'Skylar, believe me. I wouldn't do that to you,' Ollie said. His eyes bored into mine, causing the opposite effect of the calm he was trying to instil. 'What were you even doing at the pool?'

'You asked me to meet you there,' I said. 'You left me a note in my b-bag.'

'No, baby, I didn't. You must have left your bag somewhere and somebody played a mean trick on you,' he said, attempting to placate me or convince me I was wrong. The same way he did with when I was drugged.

I didn't take it off once, I thought, but didn't voice it out loud. I shook my head at him instead. *A mean trick? Bit of an understatement.*

'Then they must have slipped it into your bag when you weren't paying attention,' he tried again to give a plausible solution.

'It's a bum bag, dude. There's no way somebody could have slipped shit in there without her noticing or at least feeling it,' Leo said, sounding bored again, but this time he wasn't directing it at me.

'I swear to you, Oliver, that I would have n-noticed.'

He was making me feel small, and I didn't like it one bit.

'What did the note say, baby?' he asked.

'To meet you at midnight, to ring in your birthday.' I smiled faintly at him. 'Happy birthday, Ollie.'

He smiled in return and took a couple of deep breaths to calm himself down. I reckoned seeing me in the hospital wing, alive and safe, made him feel slightly better.

That was when Clover and Griff burst through the curtain.

'That nurse woman is such a job's worth,' Griff grumbled. 'Wouldn't let us through as you two douche canoes are already here. Tried to tell her that Sky here would prefer us two, but she wasn't listening to a word of it.'

'I'm happy you're here,' I said as Leo allowed them to get

close enough to hug me. I felt overwhelmed at the amount of love surrounding me. 'I was just telling Ollie and Leo about the note I got.'

'What note?' Clover asked, her eyebrows furrowed, and she looked just as perplexed as everybody else.

'To meet Ollie at the pool at midnight.'

'Okay...' Clo said, tapering off. 'Why didn't you tell any of us you were going there?'

'I found the note when I was going to the toilet. It seemed pointless to walk back to you when I could head straight to the school.' I shrugged. It had made total sense to me a couple of hours ago. In hindsight, it wasn't the best decision I'd ever made, but I'd made it and there was shit all I could do about it.

'Makes sense.' Clo shrugged, gazing off into the distance.

'How did you know I was there?' I'd been wondering about it ever since Ollie was so adamant it wasn't him, because if he didn't send the note, then the pool wouldn't be the first place to look for me.

'We didn't. We were searching the trees for you for a while, but then Leo came over to us and told us to look at the school. The pool house was the closest building from where we exited the trees,' said Clo, her eyes narrowing when she mentioned Leo's involvement. It made sense they searched there first, as the pool house was closest when I exited the trees, too.

'Which is pretty suspicious, Leo,' Ollie said in an accusing tone, turning his glare on Leo.

'Dude, I heard the girls talking about it. They'd spotted Sky walking off alone and were hoping she'd come to harm,' Leo said with a shrug. Ollie might not, but I believed Leo. He sounded sincere to me.

'So proof that they had something to do with it,' snapped Clo.

'Not really, Clover, but nice try,' Leo said, the words clipped. It was strange to hear Clover's name said so formally. So stiff.

'Got any better ideas, twat?' she asked. Her eyes glinted with challenge.

'No. But I know it wasn't the girls. They wouldn't have the strength,' Leo sneered back.

'Funny that. They definitely had the strength when they were beating on Skylar in the bathrooms a few weeks ago,' Clo said, her voice rising with every word she uttered.

The room went silent. Everybody nodded, seeming to agree that the girls' motives seemed shady. Even if they weren't solely responsible, I felt sure they knew more than they were letting on. But something deep inside of me knew that it wasn't one of them in the pool room. I could tell from the foot-steps, from the height of the person standing behind me, that it was a guy. The scent, the strength, there was no way a girl had done this.

'Do you still have the note, Sky?' Griff asked, reaching for my hand and squeezing it tight. I squeezed his back, the warmth filling me, as it travelled up my arm and into my body.

'It's in my bag. Or at least it should be,' I told them. My bag had gone into the water when I did, so I wasn't sure how much the contents had suffered.

Clover grabbed my bag and had a good root through it, finding the note. It wasn't completely untouched by water, but it was still legible. The four of them passed it around, inspecting it thoroughly, trying to figure out where it had come from and who had written it.

The nurse came along, having realised that none of the people who came back here had returned.

'Miss Crescent needs her rest, so you need to be leaving now,' she said, her manner brisk and no-nonsense.

Instantly, Ollie and Leo disputed who was going to stay with me. I stayed quiet because honestly, I wasn't getting in the middle of those two. I also didn't know which one I *wanted* to have with me. It would make sense for me to want Ollie nearby, but there was still a tiny part of me that was cautious of him.

Clover and Griff accepted that they were being kicked out and leaned down to give me an awkward hug simultaneously. It was the most awkward group hug I'd ever been a part of. Actually, it was the *only* group hug I'd ever been a part of.

'See you tomorrow, Sky,' Clo said.

'We'll be here bright and early, New Girl,' whispered Griff.

With a smile, they left together, leaving me with Leo and Ollie.

They both stayed, neither of them accepting defeat. The silence between the three of us was so fucking loud, but nobody broke it.

Eventually, I fell asleep to the sounds of their breathing. Just as I was about to drift off, I heard four words. Quiet, hanging there in the darkness.

'I'm so sorry, Sky.'

But I wasn't sure which one of them said it.

Twenty-One

'WHAT THE FUCK did you just say to her?' My blood boiled. The anger I felt toward him in that moment was ready to be unleashed, a black cloud swarming above us all.

'Nothing important.' Leo leaned back from where he'd been hovering over Sky and looked at me head-on, daring me to ask him to repeat his words. I wanted to wipe that fucking smirk off his face; break his nose and watch the blood gush out.

But I wouldn't do that.

Knowing Leo, he'd enjoy it.

'Want to explain this shit to me?' I gestured between him and where Sky was sleeping, pissed I even had to ask.

'Explain what?' he drawled, looking at me with his disinterested eyes.

In all the years I'd known him, it was rare for excitement to fill his eyes.

'Well, there must be some fucking reason you're still sat here at her side?' My fists clenched, wondering what bullshit he was going to spew in response. The wanker's expression didn't change.

'I care about her,' he said, raising his eyebrow at me.

Care about her my arse, I thought but didn't voice it aloud. Leo didn't care about much. It was one of the reasons we were close and had been since birth—well, that, and the fact we share blood.

'Fuck you,' I spat. 'You've got an agenda here.'

'Good luck trying to get your head around that one, dickhead.' Leo shrugged his shoulders, no longer looking at me but staring intently at Sky in the hospital bed. She appeared so peaceful in sleep, you wouldn't know that her night had gone the way it had.

'Then tell me something. Who did this?' I asked, hoping he'd know more than I did. 'Cause, fuck, I knew nothing here. I hated flying blind. Somebody had attempted to drown Sky, and I didn't have a fucking scooby who had done it.

Hawthorn was *my* school. Nothing happened here without one of us knowing about it. The twats here had no idea just how far our reach truly was, yet we'd heard nothing. Knew nothing about who may have been planning to harm her. *Kill* her.

'No clue, mate,' Leo replied with a half-hearted shrug, still staring at Sky. If I didn't know better, I would think he wanted her, but that couldn't be the case.

There was no scenario where that could ever happen.

She's mine—for now.

'The note, then. Any ideas?' I scratched the underside of my jaw, contemplating who could have given Sky the note. For it to have been slipped into her bag, somebody had to have got close enough to do it, but the question was: who?

At no point had I left her side the whole evening. There had been no opportunity for anybody to get to her. I'd made sure of it.

The Set had it out for her, and I didn't want them getting to her—not at my birthday party, at least.

'God, you're a massive cunt.' Leo's bored drawl took me out of my thoughts.

'Explain that to me,'

'You know how. Don't act like you give a crap about her when we both know that's bullshit.'

'Stop talking,' I demanded. Skylar could wake up at any time, after all, and I didn't need her to hear any of Leo's lies. She'd just started to trust me, and I wanted to keep that trust as long as I could. Already I knew I'd have to grovel for how the evening had gone, and I had fuck all to do with it.

'You afraid?' he growled, his lip curling up at the side.

'Of you?' I scoffed. 'Hardly.'

'Maybe you should be,' he said, his threat clear. I'd never been scared of the fucker in my life and I highly doubted that would change.

'You figure that, how?'

'There's a lot more at work here than we know, clearly. You think the girls did this?'

'I have no fucking clue. Seems too intelligent for them. Especially without a ringleader,' I said, mulling it over. I doubted the girls could pull off a stunt so impressive, definitely not without help.

'Who's saying they don't have one?' he asked, but then laughed. We both knew who called the shots around here, and it wasn't Odette—or any of her cronies.

'Touché.'

Both of us fell silent, our anger dissipating into the air. Neither of us wanted to be mad at the other. *Fuck, in this life there are bigger fish to fry.*

After ten minutes of silence, Leo looked over at me again.

'Do you *like* her?' he asked, nodding his head in Sky's direction.

'Course I like her,' I replied nonchalantly.

'You know what I mean.'

I rubbed my face in frustration. I knew what he meant, but honestly, it wasn't something I'd thought of too hard. Yeah, she was hot as fuck. Yeah, I wanted to rip her to shreds and then put her together again, just to destroy her more. But did I like *her*?

'Fuck knows, mate.'

'I do,' he mumbled.

'Do what?'

'Like her. I know the plans, but she's got spirit.'

'She's got something,' I responded, trying to brush his words off. I didn't need Leo interested in the new girl. Fuck, I didn't need to be interested in the new girl. I wanted nobody interested in her.

'It won't save her,' Leo said ominously.

'Right, *nothing* will save her.'

Glad we both agreed on that point, I slumped further in the hard chair and crossed my arms across my chest, attempting to get comfy enough to sleep. Across the bed, I saw Leo doing the same. Fuck, the chairs were hard as rocks.

'You could leave,' I told him.

'Why would I do that?' he asked, once again raising his eyebrow and tilting his lip up. Fucker.

''Cause you don't need to be here,' I muttered, irritated by his presence.

'Neither do you.'

'She's mine,' I growled.

'For now,' he drawled.

'For now,' I conceded.

Twenty-Two

MY ONE NIGHT in the hospital flew by.

I didn't wake in the night, and by the time I woke, both Ollie and Leo were quiet.

'How are you feeling?' Ollie asked when he saw my eyelids flutter awake, coming closer to my side. 'Do you need anything?'

'I'm okay, thanks,' I whispered, blinking at the harsh lighting.

'I'll be off.' Leo stood from the plastic chair, not looking at either of us, but addressing us both. 'See you later.'

I nodded, and Ollie didn't respond to him, too focused on making sure I was okay. As he fussed around me, trying to call the nurse to get me breakfast and a glass of water, my phone screen lit up on the table next to me.

It was from Leo.

I MEAN IT, STUTTER. CALL ME IF YOU NEED ME.

A smile covered my face, but then a frown came and wiped it away. I was curious about Leo's motives. He always acted so secretive and he clearly didn't want anybody to know that he was texting me. I could understand why he wanted to avoid conflict with Ollie and Clover, but I got the impression they weren't the only reason he wanted to keep our friendship of sorts on the down-low. I hid my phone in my bag so Ollie wouldn't see it over my shoulder.

Once he found the nurse and got me a drink of water, I was more than ready to leave the hospital wing, whether Ollie wanted me to or not. I needed my own bed.

'Can we go?' I jutted out my bottom lip and batted my eyelashes, hoping it would have an effect on him. There were no mirrors in the room, though, and I probably looked like a mess with makeup streaked down my face and my hair clinging to my scalp.

'New Girl, I promise you I didn't do this,' he said. Oddly, I didn't hate it when he called me New Girl anymore. At first, it was a slur of sorts, but ever since he and Griff started to use it affectionately, it felt different.

I tilted my head to look up at him.

'Ollie, please, can we do this later?' I asked, my eyes finding his. 'I'm so tired and I just want to be in my own bed.'

'Let me at least walk you back to your room.'

'Okay.' It was easier to concede to his request than it was to fight him on it. I wasn't lying when I said I didn't have the energy.

Nearly drowning takes a lot out of a girl.

He walked me back to my room, both of us staying silent, and only when we arrived back did he talk. The moment I got the door open, I stepped into my dorm, using my body to cover the entrance so he couldn't slip around me.

'Can I come over later tonight?' he asked, pushing his luck.

Clover, who was hovering by her bed, scoffed at his question, telling me without words she wouldn't stay quiet if he came to our room later on. Not like I had the strength to have the two of them getting into it again, especially when my head felt the way it did. It stabbed like an axe was attempting to split it in two at any moment.

'How about I come over to you tomorrow if I'm feeling better?' I asked, tentative, not wanting to wake the beast I'd glimpsed before.

It was a fair and solid compromise. Plus, it meant we could talk with no distractions, and no Clover talking louder than me, or worse, talking for me.

'Okay,' he conceded reluctantly. His lips brushed against the top of my head and the resulting tingles it gave me travelled down to my toes. A quick moment of pressure, fleeting, and gone just as fast.

'I'll text you. I promise,' I said, closing my dorm door in his face.

I turned around to find Clover standing directly in front of me, blocking the path to my bed. The bed I'd desperately dreamed of all night while trapped in the lumpy and uncomfortable hospital bed. I gritted my teeth as I prepared myself for whatever she felt the compulsion to say next.

'You can't trust him, Skylar,' she blurted out, looking fit to burst.

'Why n-not?'

'Because he sprinted off ahead!' I could tell she'd been holding it in all night, gutted she couldn't get me alone earlier. 'We arrived after he did, by at least five minutes.'

'Okay...' I said, unsure what else to say. I understood where Clo was coming from, and sure, I hadn't realised they didn't all arrive together, but still. We were talking about Ollie. Dark and mysterious Ollie. Didn't mean he was my would-be murderer. 'How long does it take to fall unconscious from drowning?'

'Like I bloody know,' Clo replied, her phone appearing in her hand in an instant. I knew what that meant. Google. Clo loved to Google search everything. For example, the two of us would be watching a film, and I'd innocently ask what other projects an actor starred in, and she'd have a list of their entire filmography in less than one minute flat.

'So?'

'A-ha!' she exclaimed, her eyes shining in triumph. 'Two minutes. It takes two minutes to become unconscious. I *knew* the fucker had the time and the opportunity.'

THE NEXT DAY I was outside Ollie's door, trying to build up enough courage to knock and alert him to my presence. The butterflies in my stomach were causing havoc, and I felt sick. For five minutes I stared at the door with a blank expression, and I could sense the other kids who were passing the hall were staring at me.

On Sundays, students could relax and visit with friends without repercussions from the staff that monitored the halls. Griff had told me that the only reason he and Ollie could visit with us on weeknights was because they were a part of *The Sect*, and therefore above the average school rules. It had its perks, for sure. The pizza delivery being the main one in my eyes.

Man, I love pizza.

I would never understand how people didn't just want to eat it every single day. I would if I could. Easily. Happily.

No more procrastinating, distracting thoughts. Time to lift my hand to the black door in front of me.

I'd never noticed the ominous and foreboding nature of Ollie's door before. Showed how observant I was.

I needed to sum up the courage to hear Ollie out. To listen, and not just assume the worst because all the pieces looked bad. *Really bad.* I didn't feel scared of being alone with him, exactly, but a sense of dread was rising in my gut with every second I put off seeing him. When Ollie lost his temper, he frightened me, enough to create a seed of doubt.

Finally, I knocked on the door in the pattern Clover and I used. If it annoyed him, then tough shit.

I heard him moving around inside of his room straight away, and I barely waited ten seconds before the door opened wide and he pulled me close to him in a tight hug.

'Sky, I was so worried last night,' he said, squeezing me even tighter to him. So tight, I could hear his heart pounding underneath my ear. All around us, I could feel his fear as if it were a tangible thing. 'Please don't do that to me again.'

'I can assure you I don't intend to,' I said, my voice muffled by his taut pecs. I chuckled, as if any of it was my choice in the first place. Oh yes, Ollie, I just loved nearly drowning. *Real highlight of my night.* 'I've had enough happen to me this year to last a lifetime.'

He let me out of his warm embrace but grabbed my hand to pull me further into his room, kicking the door closed behind us. Then, as if he remembered himself, he went back and locked it.

I raised my eyebrows at the action, giving him a stern look. Not sure it translated too well, though, as he was looking at me in the way I imagined the wolf looked at Little Red Riding Hood. Like he couldn't wait to eat her whole.

'Expecting something?'

'Nope,' he said, a genuine smile on his face. 'Just thought

you'd like some privacy. Knowing that dickhead Griff, he'd happily burst in here to check on you. The fact that it would irritate me would be a bonus for him.'

I laughed at the thought of it, but I'd give him that one. Griff would totally try and do something like that. However, unlike Ollie, I knew Griff was keeping Clo company. Leo also knew I was with Ollie because I texted him to tell him. He hadn't responded, but the two blue ticks had appeared, so I knew he'd seen my message.

'So...' I trailed off, looking around at my surroundings. Ollie's room always looked barely lived in, unlike my room. Should I sit on the bed? Or was that too presumptuous?

I didn't want him to assume I'd forgiven him and we could just skip straight back to where we were before everything happened. With sure footsteps, I chose to sit on his gaming chair instead. It gave me enough distance from him and I could breathe without his scent overwhelming my senses. Just being in his room was hard enough.

Once I was comfy, and he'd seated himself on the edge of his bed facing me, I demanded, 'Talk.'

'Where shall I start?'

'I've heard the beginning is a good place. You know, usually,' I smarted.

'Well, aren't you a comedienne? I meant more, what do you wanna know?'

'You wanted to talk to *me*, remember?' I said, acting a bit bitchier than usual, but feeling entitled to it.

'I wanted to prove to you it wasn't me,' he said. The way he looked at me, so contrite, made me want to just believe him with no further grovelling. My heart panged at the sincerity in his tone, but my head told me not to be so stupid. I couldn't put my faith in a contrite look. 'I promise you, I didn't give you that note. I had no fucking idea where you'd gone and I was so worried that somebody had hurt you.'

'Somebody did hurt me.'

'I know'—he winced—'and I'm sorry.'

'Why apologise if you had nothing to do with it?'

What did he have to apologise for?

'I'm sorry that I didn't stick by your side the whole time,' he clarified.

I could tell he meant his words. That he really was pissed at himself for not staying with me the entire night.

'If I had, none of this would've happened.'

'You know, Ollie, when you say shit like that, it makes me think you had something to do with it.'

'Right,' he huffed. 'I knew this would happen! You've let Clover get inside your fucking head.'

'What?' I asked, shocked by the change in his tone, by his eyes glinting with cruelty. 'W-what does that even mean?'

'You heard me, Skylar. Clover has been turning you against me, twisting shit like she always does.' His eyes narrowed in disgust.

'No, Oliver, she hasn't. Am I not allowed to form my own opinions?'

'Of course,' he said, brushing away my words as if that wasn't the real problem here. As if he hadn't meant it in the way I heard it. 'It's just suspicious timing. Even you can see that, surely.'

'Can see what?'

'You *know* what,' he said imploringly. 'You've been attacked, and now Clover's turning you against me. How well do you know her, really?'

'Seriously?' I asked, shocked at his implication. 'For starters, Clover has said nothing! Second, I'd like to think I know her pretty well, thank you very much.' I was on a roll. I took a deep breath. 'How well do I know *you*, really?'

'Explain what you mean. Now!'

'I just don't know where I stand with you. Like. Not at all.'

'Where would you like to stand?' he asked, his tone lighter. Amused.

'W-what?' The way he was looking at me caused a shiver to run down my spine. He was still standing, coming a little closer with each second.

'What do you want from me, Sky?'

I ran my fingers through my hair and looked everywhere in the room but at him. Ollie was somebody I couldn't figure out, and as much as I felt attracted to him and wanted to be with him, I also wanted to run far, far away from him.

The way I felt for him made me feel like a young teenager with their first crush. And in a sense, it was true. Ollie was my first crush and I was still a teenager, with little experience to fall back on.

Should I be bold? Tell him what I wanted, for real, and hope he wanted the same thing?

Fuck it. I was going to take a leaf out of a confident person's book and go for it. I wanted so badly to believe him, to give the attraction growing between us a try, that I threw caution to the wind.

'I want you.'

He blinked, looking thrown back that I'd gone for it. Bet he didn't think I had it in me. Or thought I'd stutter my way through something, as a flush grew on my cheeks.

'I want you,' I repeated, louder this time.

Clearly he'd never expected me to be so open and honest with him. To just come out and say what I wanted, damn the consequences.

'Shit, Sky. That isn't what I thought you were going to say,' he said, looking flustered, a blush on his pale cheeks.

'So…' Ollie said and slowly made his way towards me. I was frozen. Unable to move, trapped by his gaze. 'How about we make this official?'

'Huh?'

'How do you feel about being my girlfriend?' he asked, standing in front of me, and I looked up at him, falling into his blue gaze. I felt like his prey.

'S-sorry, what?'

'Be my girlfriend.'

It wasn't a question.

Twenty-Three

'BE YOUR GIRLFRIEND?' I sputtered, raising my eyebrow at him.

'Yeah. That's what you want, isn't it?'

'Right...' It was what I wanted, but was it what *he* wanted? I wasn't going to agree to be in a relationship with him if he was only doing it to appease me, to make me happy. 'But do you want to be my boyfriend?'

He cocked his head and reached out to grab my hand in his. I let him take it, but stayed silent, waiting for him to say something.

'Why would I ask if I didn't want it?'

'I don't know,' I said with a defeated shrug. 'And technically, you didn't ask.'

'What did I do then?'

'You demanded.'

Ollie scoffed, rubbing his thumb on my hand, in an effort to soothe me. It wasn't working, though.

'Skylar, please, will you be my girlfriend?'

'Well, seeing as you've asked me so nicely,' I said, poking my tongue out at him.

'Is that a yes?'

'Yep. Now stop digging.' I laughed, and he did the same. It was a lighthearted laugh, and it sounded different from the others he usually gave. It felt like praise. Like he was the sun and I was basking in his rays.

'How shall we spend the rest of the day?' he asked, dragging me from the chair so we could lie on his bed.

'Not like that,' I sputtered. Just because he was my *boyfriend*, it didn't mean I was going to give up the goods just like that!

He laughed, bright and airy. 'No, Sky. I just want to be comfortable. Standing up and looking down at you wasn't much fun.'

'Okay,' I conceded. 'But no funny business, Mr Brandon.'

'Whoa,' he said, letting go of my hand to put his flat palms towards me. 'I promise. I just want to cuddle and watch a film, that's all.'

'That's what they all say,' I joked, narrowing my eyes in faux suspicion.

'Skylar,' he whined. 'Why are you making this so difficult?'

'Got to get my kicks where I can,' I said, finally following him and getting on top of the bed with him. 'Let's just watch a movie and order pizza.'

'Isn't that your solution for everything?'

'Yep.' I nodded. 'And I don't see it ever changing, so you better get used to it.'

He laughed, pulling me close to his side. 'Whatever you say, babe.'

'Christmas break is coming up.'

'Right...' I trailed off, adjusting my position on the bed to face him. The two of us were in his room on his bed watching a film in the way we spent most evenings together since becoming an official couple.

We may have only been dating for a short time, but spending time with him was the best part of my days. He made me smile. He made me laugh. He also made me question myself and my life and the way I'd just accepted people treating me badly.

'And I was wondering if you had any plans.'

'For Christmas break?' I thought about it for a second and shook my head. 'Nope. Guess I'll spend it home alone while Mum and Andy do their own thing.'

'Well...' He rubbed his finger up and down my arm, giving me chills. 'Would you like to spend it with me?'

'Just you?'

'No,' he said with a small smile. 'Griff, Clo, and Leo are game for coming too.'

'Clo's agreed to come knowing Leo's gonna be there?' I raised my eyebrow in disbelief.

'Not quite.' Ollie winced. 'When Griff asked her, Leo didn't plan on coming with us, so of course Clo agreed.'

'Then what happened?'

'Leo changed his mind when he heard Clo was coming.'

'Of course he did.' I laughed, imagining the joy on Leo's face when he heard he could torment Clo. 'Why would he pass up an opportunity to piss her off?'

'Right,' Ollie agreed, his smile returning to his face. 'So you'll come?'

'Duh! Not like I want to spend time with Mum and Andy. Thanks for inviting me.'

'No problem,' he said, inching closer on the bed, leaning his head down to mine. His breath fanned the skin on my neck, making my nerves thrum underneath my skin and my pulse skyrocket. He pressed a lingering kiss on my neck, and my breath left me in a short burst. Being on his bed with him always felt a little like tempting fate, and when he kissed me like that, it only worsened.

I met his bright blue eyes and could see the longing in his gaze—his want of me. The corner of his mouth tilted up in a teasing, yet lazy smile. His thumb began to softly stroke the skin on my stomach underneath my shirt that had risen up when I moved onto my side. In every spot his thumb touched, my skin burned, and my stomach was filling with more butterflies the lower his thumb travelled.

'That blush on your face is beautiful,' he whispered. Even his tone lowering was enough to send my thoughts into the stratosphere. 'You're beautiful.'

'Thanks,' I hushed out, holding my breath for whatever was to come next.

He placed another kiss on my neck. Then another. And another.

'Is this okay?' He hummed in between kisses and I nodded, unable to speak. He leaned his forehead against mine and the connection felt good, safe, and a rush of feeling flooded my veins.

I tilted my face forward, pressed my lips against his, and really kissed him in the way I loved. All tongues and lips. Sensuous and serious, I lost myself in the kiss, as my body heated with a longing for him. I couldn't believe he was mine to kiss. To touch.

My hands went to his sides, and I grabbed his hips, pulling him closer to me.

He ran his tongue along my lower lip, and his fingers began

trailing up and down my abdomen, holding me close, while my hands continued to grip his hips.

Fuck, Ollie knew how to kiss.

He grabbed my leg and lifted it to drape it over his hip, pulling my core even closer to his hard dick, the thin material of my underwear and his trousers the only thing keeping us apart.

A shiver ran through my body.

Every time we made out on Ollie's bed, things began to feel more serious between us, and my mind went to the idea of losing my virginity to him.

And I knew I wanted to.

Just not yet.

I wasn't ready to go so far with him, even though I knew it was going to happen. It was inevitable. A forgone conclusion.

Ollie moved his hands to the buttons of my shirt, undoing each one with quick fingers, and I wondered how many shirts he'd undone before to have such a skill with it. Once my shirt was open, he reached around my back and undid my bra clasp one-handed.

I broke our kiss so I could move back from him and get rid of both my shirt and bra, throwing them onto his bedroom floor with abandon.

When I moved back towards him, Ollie took one of my nipples into his mouth, while he massaged the other. A cry left my lips and I was in heaven. His tongue circled me before he took a tentative bite to test my reaction. He knew I loved it, though, so he bit harder the next time.

It was Ollie who broke our connection next, moving so he could take his shirt off, so that our skin could touch. His eyes locked with mine, a hungry look that captured my soul within them, and I licked my lips in anticipation.

'You're fucking beautiful,' he said in a hoarse whisper. 'I could stare at you for days.'

'Right back at ya,' I said, a smile playing on my lips before I pressed my lips on his once more. Our kisses became more frantic, and my fingers went to the button on his trousers, wanting to get him down to his boxers. My skirt had ridden up, and things were escalating fast.

'Ollie,' I moaned against his lips, stopping my hand from travelling into his trousers. 'We need to stop.'

'Why?' he asked, his hands bunching my skirt up around my waist, leaving my lace underwear available to him.

'We should cool down.'

He let out a small sigh but didn't argue with me. He removed his hands from my skirt and wrapped one around my back to pull me closer. My head buried into his bare chest, and I breathed in his scent. A kiss was placed on my head, and both of us lay there, breathing in small pants, willing our heart rates to calm down.

He grabbed a blanket from behind him and put it over our bodies, covering us from the world.

'Do you want to put your shirt back on?' he asked, and I shook my head.

'We can stay like this,' I said. 'Unless it's too distracting for you?'

'Feeling your skin against mine is one of my favourite things, New Girl. I think I can keep my hands to myself...' His smile was wolfish. 'Unless you don't want me to.'

I smiled in return, my breathing back to its normal pace.

'Thanks for being cool about this.' Then I felt I needed to clarify what I meant. 'For being cool about the fact that I'm not ready yet to... you know.'

'No rush, Sky. You'll let me know when you're ready. There's no need to thank me.'

I placed one final kiss on his lips and swooned at how much of a gentleman he was being about it all.

'Now, let's watch a film,' I said.

'Your wish is my command.'

Twenty-Four

CHRISTMAS BREAK CAME AROUND SUPER FAST after that, or at least it felt like it did.

Clover believed *The Set* were responsible for both my drugging and drowning, but Griff and Ollie were adamant that they knew the girls had nothing to do with it.

Apparently, the rulers of the school had their own set of rules that us mere plebeians had no knowledge of, and the girls wouldn't have been able to make such enormous steps without two of the boys agreeing. They'd stressed that they would never agree and clarified that Leo didn't have that kind of power alone.

I'd never mentioned Leo giving me his number to any of them. Well, thrusting his number on me by texting me first. It felt like something I should keep a secret. Something for only me to know, and because I knew this, I didn't think Leo would've set the girls on me. No matter how many times Clover tried to convince me otherwise.

Christmas Day itself was Griff's birthday, which I reckoned had some bearing on the fact that he thought he was God's gift to the world.

Honestly, I was pretty sure he'd even joked to me recently

that he thought of himself as the second coming of Christ. I'd just rolled my eyes at him and laughed.

The four of us were spending the holidays at Griff's parents' estate as they weren't there and the entire mansion would sit empty otherwise. Griff had never mentioned his parents, so maybe it wasn't that unusual that they weren't here to spend Christmas, or his birthday, with him. They hadn't attended Parents' Day either, and nobody had questioned it. It was like one of those unspoken things between everybody.

To be fair, if my mum had the opportunity to leave me alone for my birthday, she most definitely would. What I did know was that Griff was an only child and that without Leo and Ollie, his childhood would have been extremely lonely. It made me realise that Griff's cheeky, cheery personality probably had something to do with his upbringing. He used humour as a coping mechanism for something darker.

My relationship with Ollie had grown so fast, and it still felt super surreal to me that I could call that gorgeous specimen of a human my boyfriend.

Clover was still trying to make me at least question him about the drugging and the drowning, but I wouldn't bite anymore. He was the one who had been there for me after both instances; who had looked after me and ensured that I was okay. He'd never given me an actual sign that it could have involved him. Okay, he'd acted shady and had been hot and cold with me ever since I'd met him, but Clo was trying to imply that was because his ocean blue eyes and his wide smile blinded me. Which yeah, they definitely did. But that wasn't why I trusted him. Not completely. His actions after the fact just didn't add up to him being the person responsible. The way Clover told it, though, I should believe that Ollie held me under the water one minute and then gave me mouth to mouth the next. *Insert eye roll here.*

We'd arrived at Griff's estate a few days ago and I still couldn't believe I was spending Christmas in such an elegant, yet slightly intimidating house. Mansion. Whatever you wanted to call it—it was huge.

Christmas Eve Eve came, and we were all sitting together in the cinema room and a conversation started about what film we should put on next. There was a huge projector screen at the front, and sofas and reclining forest green chairs dotted the rest of the room. A popcorn machine was in a corner, as was a slushy machine, and the wealth those items alone still made me pause. At home I was lucky we owned a toaster.

Clover, Leo, and Griff were sitting on the corner sofa. Ollie's arms were wrapped around me as we sat separate from the others, together on one of the love seats. His arms were warm around my waist, anchoring me to my surroundings. My anxiety around him had definitely improved since we'd become a couple.

'I want to watch *Polar Express*,' Clover announced to everybody in the room.

'No way! That film's for Christmas Eve itself. How about *The Nightmare Before Christmas*?' Leo asked, his tone bored as per usual, but him speaking at all gave away the fact that he was about to get some entertainment.

'That's a Halloween movie!' Clover's voice rose.

'It isn't,' Leo drawled. 'But fine. Let's watch *Die Hard*.'

'That is *definitely* not a Christmas movie!' Clover said, her cheeks flushing a deep shade of red, her face slowly matching her hair. It always surprised me when she couldn't see that Leo did most things just to rile her up.

It had been like this between them ever since we arrived.

Clover and Leo had been at each other's throats the entire time and hadn't been able to agree on anything. Not on snacks, or on the best time was to give presents, or on what to watch. Basically, anything that *could* divide opinion, they disagreed on. I knew it was getting under Clover's skin, but I also knew Leo was getting a major kick out of it if the grin on his face when she wasn't looking was anything to go by.

'It definitely is a Christmas film. The entire film revolves around an office Christmas party. Am I wrong?' Leo asked the room, gesturing at Griff to back him up.

'Sorry, dude, you're on your own for this one.' Griff shrugged his shoulders. 'I'm all for *Santa Clause 2*.'

'I'm with Griff, too,' Ollie piped up, smiling down at me. He knew it was one of my favourites.

'*Polar Express* and *Muppets Christmas Carol* are on tomorrow's agenda. They're definitely Christmas Eve films,' Ollie added, his tone ensuring there would be no argument.

I'd told him this yesterday, so I was glad he'd been listening to me. It made me feel warm and cosy, knowing he hadn't just ignored my ramblings. I *loved* those films, and they were easily my top three. There was just something about the Muppets that made me smile, no matter how down I felt. *I mean, who doesn't find Animal and Miss Piggy hilarious?*

It was nice to feel heard with Ollie. The past Christmases I'd spent with my mum had been pretty dire and we'd never spent time doing what *I* wanted to do. It was always her food, her songs, and her films, which happened to be the awful kind the Christmas Movie Channel showed all season. They were her jam. The ones that were obviously made straight for TV and should have never seen the light of day.

'Sounds like we all agree,' Leo said. Clover looked belligerently at him and he added, 'Well, all of us that matter, anyway.'

I rolled my eyes at their pettiness. I slipped my phone out of my pocket, trying to hide the screen from Ollie's watching gaze. I blind texted Leo.

W**ILL YOU KNOCK IT OFF****?**

I was so sick of the shit between them. I'd hoped that spending time together at the estate in such a small group would improve the frostiness between them. But nope, it had just made it one thousand times worse. *Go figure.*

W**HO SAID I'****M THE ONE THAT NEEDS TO KNOCK SHIT OFF****,**
S**TUTTER****?**

Leo could get under my skin too, don't get me wrong, so I understood how Clover was feeling, but I also found Leo's boredom and overall dick-ish behaviour kind of charming—and being fully honest—really fucking hot.

Not that I'd ever tell him—or anybody else—that.

C****HRISTMAS MORNING WAS**** everything I'd dreamt it would be and more.

I'd told the guys I'd never had a great Christmas experience, and they were all determined to make sure this year would be the best one I'd ever had. There were so many presents placed under the biggest tree I'd ever seen, and we had cheesy music playing the entire morning. Well, most of them were cheesy. Now and then a classic slipped through the cracks, which led to Griff singing 'Good King Wenceslas' at the top of his lungs—and extremely off-key.

It was all a little overwhelming.

I'd opened a fuck ton of cool gifts: multiple designer handbags, plenty of books, clothes, and a brand-new phone. All of which seemed excessive. My current phone was relatively new, and I got one from the school when I started, so I was surprised to see the boys had got me the newest model.

Even Leo had gone all out and got me a real diamond necklace with matching earrings. He'd also handed me a tiny gift box, impeccably wrapped in white paper covered in red berries. Inside, there was a tiny glass bottle with an even smaller rolled up scroll of paper trapped inside. A card sat next to the bottle that read: **Merry Christmas ...**

'It's a tiny telegram in a bottle,' he whispered to me as I examined it, turning the tiny glass bottle over in my fingers. Ollie had left the room, and Clover and Griff were paying more attention to each other than to us two.

'I love it,' I gushed, surprised by the gift. 'I love tiny things.'

We both laughed.

'Not in all things, Stutter, I'm sure.'

I smiled and said, 'No, not in all things. Thank you, Leo.'

'The note inside is real, but don't open it yet. I'll let you know when.'

Inside, my stomach bubbled with nerves. Not knowing what he wrote on the note would be torture for me, and there was no way of knowing how long he'd make me wait, either. I quickly put it back in the box it came in and placed it inside one of the many bags they'd gifted me.

Ollie reentered the room and dropped down beside me before pulling me to him once again, placing a kiss on my forehead. Warmth filled me at his gesture, but I also felt dirty, as if I was keeping a secret from him.

'I'll be back in a moment.' I excused myself from around the tree and went to the kitchen. I needed a moment to myself to just process what was happening. In the past, I was lucky if my mum was home all day on Christmas day, let alone if she gave me a present.

Griff flew in and saw me standing there, almost hyperventilating. He put his arms around me in a massive bear hug and whispered in my ear, 'It's all gravy, Sky.'

'Yeah, I'm fine. I've said happy birthday, right?' I couldn't remember if I'd said it or not. Damn, having your birthday on Christmas day couldn't be fun. The day's about a dead dude, or presents and shit, and you're lucky if people even remember you.

'Yeah, you're good,' he said. Releasing me, Griff opened the cupboard and pulled out mugs to make drinks, most likely an alcoholic one, even though we were all underage and it wasn't even three in the afternoon, but hey, Christmas usually led to rule breaking.

'You don't need to make those for everyone. Let me help,' I told him, wanting to feel useful and to take my mind off the amount of gifts I'd received.

The two of us made the drinks together—peppermint schnapps hot chocolate—and joined everybody again to watch Christmas day TV together.

It was the best day, and by far the best Christmas of my life.

I finally felt like I belonged, like I was part of a group that mattered, that cared about me. And, fuck, it felt good!

Twenty-Five

CHRISTMAS BEING OVER COULD ONLY MEAN one thing: New Year's Eve was upon us. Which meant the New Year's Gala was also encroaching, and I knew I wasn't ready for it.

Not one bit.

Ever since Ollie invited me, I'd been anxious about it and I'd even tried to get out of it a couple of times, but he was having none of it.

'Are you sure I need to go?' I whined. The two of us were on the sofa on Christmas evening after everybody else had gone to bed, snuggling up with the fire crackling away in the large ornate fireplace, and the Christmas tree covering the room in a warm white glow. 'I won't know anybody there.'

'You'll know me, and Griff, and Leo, and Clover. Plus our parents. Isn't that enough?'

'I suppose…' I trailed off, snuggling closer to his chest so I didn't have to look him in the eye. 'Thank you for the dress.'

'I can't wait to see you in it, New Girl. You're gonna be the most beautiful girl at the gala.'

A flush travelled up my neck, covering my face, and burning my ears.

Ollie had arranged for me and Clover to be chauffeur driven to the nearest expensive boutique and have our dresses designed and created bespoke especially for us. He'd had to pay extra for them to be ready on time, and I didn't even want to consider just how much it had cost him.

'I doubt it,' I whispered. 'I just hope you like what I chose.'

'Babe, you could wear a potato sack and I'd love you in it.'

'You're just saying that!' I laughed, poking him in the ribs with my pointer finger, digging in a little more than necessary. 'But thanks.'

'Trust me,' he said, moving to lift my head so our eyes locked together. 'It's going to be a night you'll always remember.'

He placed a kiss on my forehead and I gulped at his implication, wondering if he meant what I thought he meant.

I shook myself from my thoughts and came back to my senses. We were back at school, as the gala itself was being held in the main hall, and I was with Clover in Ollie's room, getting ready for the guys to come get us at seven. According to Ollie, the gala was for a charity the school always supported and that was why it wasn't held at some posh hotel or stately home.

Ever since we became a couple, I found myself getting lost in Ollie's eyes more often than not, and it meant that a lot of the time I forgot what he told me the moment after he said it. *Yes, I'm aware of how disgustingly lovey-dovey that sounds.*

Shoot me.

I looked at myself in the full-length mirror in front of me, running my hands down the material of the dress, trying to ground myself in the moment.

Our final fittings had been a couple of days ago, and I was excited for Ollie to see me for the first time. For the first time in my life, I believed I looked good in something. *Real fucking good.*

The light blue of the dress suited my pale skin tone perfectly, and it also went with my silver-purple hair. I felt like a mix between a fairy-tale princess and an elven queen in a fantasy novel. The second I'd seen myself in it, I'd fallen in love, as it reminded me of Cinderella's classic dress for the ball.

It was an A-line gown with off-the-shoulder half sleeves. Blue flowers trailed from the bust down to the waist, high-lighting the curves of my body, adding to the look of a real-life princess.

Growing up, my self-confidence was low. Part of me was constantly worried that the reason I didn't have friends was because I was unattractive. Almost like my mind had convinced me I was too ugly to be seen with.

Being with Ollie, even for a short time, had changed how I saw myself.

I no longer looked in a mirror and questioned what I saw. I didn't worry that I was too fat, or too curvy, for people to love me. Even if this thing between us didn't last, I'd always be thankful to him for making me feel cherished in a way I'd never experienced before.

I also hoped the way I looked in the dress would lead to Ollie wanting to rip it off me after ringing in the New Year together and we were alone. The timing felt right, and I knew I wanted to lose my virginity to him. We'd been close enough once or twice, but we'd never gone through with it. I hadn't been ready. It was an enormous step and something you couldn't take back after. I had nothing against the girls who just wanted it gone, and I couldn't say that I was saving it for the person I'd be with forever—I wasn't even saving it per se— I just knew I wanted it to be with somebody who cared about me. Somebody who meant something to me, and somebody *I* meant something to back.

Clover entered the room from the bathroom and stopped dead.

'Fuck me, Sky!' she squealed, her eyes widening. 'You look beautiful.'

'I look beautiful? Pur-lease.' I rolled my eyes at her compliment. 'You look stunning, Clover. Really, honestly, truly beautiful.'

She was wearing a long satin jade green gown with a low V-neck and spaghetti straps. The slit went up to her mid-thigh, and when she moved, you got a quick flash of her leg. It looked amazing with her hair colour too. She had debated wearing red to try and break the stigma, but she hadn't found a material she liked enough.

Our eyes shimmered with unshed tears at the sight of each other looking so good, but we quickly laughed and stopped ourselves, not wanting to ruin the makeup we'd spent the better part of two hours on. I didn't want to have to touch it up before we even left the room.

'Ollie is going to cream his pants when he sees you.'

'Ew, Clo, did you have to lower the tone with the word *cream*?' I fake gagged, but really that word genuinely made me want to gag. There was nothing sexy about that term—like at all.

'Fine.' She laughed. 'Seriously, though, Ollie is going to want to rip that dress off you when he gets here.'

'Well, I won't let him before the gala...' I trailed off, a hint of a smile playing on my lips.

Clover looked at me, her mouth agape.

'Whoa, Sky. You think you're ready for that?'

'Yeah, I do. It just feels right, ya know?'

She nodded in response, scepticism rife on her features.

'Did you just know?' I asked her abruptly. Clo wasn't a virgin, and although she hadn't told me much about her first time, I knew she'd talk to me with honesty.

'Mhm,' she said, a thoughtful expression on her face, almost as if she was envisioning the day she'd said yes to her first. 'But I would take it back now if I could.'

'Thanks for the vote of confidence,' I said, sarcasm thick in my tone. 'Even if this isn't the right thing in the long run, Clo, I know it's the right thing for me *now* and that's all I can go on.'

'True, and for your sake, my beautiful bestie, I hope you're right about him,' she said, stopping her sentence when we heard a knock on the door. Our eyes locked, and all of a sudden all my nerves came rushing to me.

'Shit!' I whisper-yelled to Clo, who gave me an evil smirk in return.

Clover yelled, 'Come in.'

They entered, and the surrounding air turned to ice, leaving me slightly lightheaded.

Griff was the first to see us, his eyebrows rising when he took us in fully.

'Wow, you girls clean up nicely!' He hugged me briefly and then moved to hug Clover. Her hug lasted a lot longer than mine, but I was too anxious to see Ollie to comment on it.

It was at that moment that Leo entered the room and saw the two of them hugging. For the briefest of moments, Leo looked lost, but he covered it up within a moment, and when Ollie entered the room, I lost interest in what the others were doing. All I could see was *him*.

Ollie looked the hottest I'd ever seen him look. *Ever*. Which trust me, was tough, seeing as even in our school uniform, I was into it. Into him. Of course I liked his personality, but his looks definitely helped, especially on those occasions when he'd acted like I had a disease you could catch simply by breathing the same air.

He was wearing a black tuxedo jacket with black skinny fit suit trousers and honestly, I was in love. I wiped the corner of my mouth with my hand, just in case some drool had escaped.

'This dress is fucking amazing. I want to rip it off you and taste what's hiding underneath. Do we even need to go to this thing?' Ollie asked. His eyes were heated, staring into mine. I could feel the flame and I honestly just wanted to burn in it.

'You're the one who said we have to go to this thing, so we're definitely going,' I scolded him, but it didn't reach my eyes. Or my smile.

'Fine. But tonight you're mine,' he said, his words filled with delicious promise.

I shivered and goosebumps popped up all over my arms. The night held even more potential than it had a few moments before, and you wouldn't find me complaining.

Maybe I'd enjoy the gala after all.

Twenty-Six

WE ENTERED THE HALL, and my breath left me as I took in our surroundings. It had been transformed into a woodland winter wonderland. The colour white was everywhere, mixed with fake tree trunks in the centre of each table that stemmed upwards and covered the table in a canopy of bright white lights.

The gala was filled with older people dressed in their finest suits and expensive gowns, and I felt completely out of my depth. I hadn't grown up in this world. The fanciest event I'd attended was a wedding reception in a barn a few years ago. And believe me, there had been nothing fancy about it. The groom was drunk before midday and the bride's cleavage spilled out over the top of her dress so much that she nip-slipped every five minutes.

Ollie's dad, Henry, was standing over by Lottie and Edward Hawthorn across the room. They looked exactly how I always imagined rich, powerful people would look at an event, dripping in diamonds and clad in designer suits

'You've got this,' Ollie murmured out of the side of his mouth, squeezing my hand. 'You look amazing.'

I nodded, too nervous to reply, as we made our way over to

the parents, and the greetings and handshakes started up instantly.

I knew Ollie wanted me to enjoy the evening but, mainly, he wanted to show me off as his piece of arm candy to his father, and to all of his father's associates. Part of me was thrilled that he thought I could be considered arm candy, and the other part of me found it insulting that I was amounting to nothing more than my looks. Then again, my confidence in myself was so low that whenever I thought about it, I was back to being thrilled all over again. It had become a vicious cycle, playing out in a never-ending loop in my head.

'Skylar, you look enchanting this evening,' Lottie said with a kind smile, and her eyes made me feel at ease. You would never know that she was as old as she was. Standing next to Leo, she looked like she could be his older sister. 'Clover, darling, you look amazing as always.' She leant down and kissed her cheek, and Clover gave her a tentative smile in return.

'Hey, Mum. Dad,' Leo said and gave his mum a kiss on the cheek and hugged her tight. Edward nodded at Leo and looked happy enough to see him, even if the slight grimace on his face said otherwise.

Edward and Ollie had a much frostier response to one another. They barely made eye contact, and sort of nodded towards each other. After seeing the two of them together on Parents' Day, I'd known there were a few issues between them, but I hadn't expected the iciness currently emanating off them.

'Oliver. Skylar,' he greeted us each with a nod, smiling so wide at me his teeth were on show.

Henry Brandon was an imposing man, standing tall at over six feet and in a black suit that looked more expensive than my entire wardrobe—make that my new wardrobe. He was intimidating, and I wasn't the only person who thought that, because everybody else in attendance seemed to be giving them a wide berth. 'Glad you could join us this evening.'

Ollie rolled his eyes in my peripheral. Without putting much thought into the action, I reached out and took his hand in mine, intertwining our fingers tight together. His lips twitched in response, forming a small smile that lasted for all of a second, but I saw it and it made me feel good inside, like I'd done something right.

'Evening, Dad. How was your Christmas?' Ollie asked tersely.

'Fine, thanks, Son. Spent it at the townhouse. You know how it just hasn't been the same for me since your mum died,' Henry said, looking away from us, trying to school his features back into those of somebody indifferent, but it didn't quite work. I could tell he missed his wife. 'I hope you all behaved yourself on the estate.'

'We did.' Ollie was being curt, not giving his dad much of anything to work with.

I took pity on Henry, who was trying, which was more than I could say about Ollie, and piped up instead, 'We had a lovely time, thank you.'

Within seconds, my hand was icy and empty. I'd obviously said or done the wrong thing, as Ollie not only removed his hand from mine, but he also took a visible step away from me. No matter how many times I believed I was getting somewhere with him, growing closer and understanding his inner work-ings, I was proved wrong. Clearly, I was an idiot who should've known better.

'After dinner, I must introduce you two to some of my colleagues. I've told them how a young, beautiful girl has swept my Oliver off his feet. They said they'll believe it when they see it,' he chortled, as if he'd just told a rather funny joke and not some well-worn remark.

'We look forward to it,' Ollie spoke through gritted teeth and it was obvious to everybody in the circle that he wasn't telling the truth.

'I hope my son got you some wonderful gifts, Skylar.' Henry continued talking as if Ollie wasn't giving him the cold shoulder.

'He did!' I said, smiling at him, making up for the frostiness from my boyfriend. 'I've never been so spoiled in my life.'

'I would say you're extremely lucky, but I can tell it's my son who's extremely lucky to have you.'

The group broke out into awkward laughter, and although my smile stayed on my face, I was unsure how to continue the conversation.

'If you'll excuse me,' Ollie bit out before he turned away from our conversation and walked away at a fast clip without another word, leaving me standing there with Henry, Leo, and his parents. Clover and Griff must have slipped away when the conversation started, and I wished I'd noticed and gone with them.

'He'll be back soon,' Henry said to me in a jovial tone, amused by his son's antics.

Minutes passed in silence. I wanted so badly to be rescued, I didn't even care by who.

'Come with me, Stutter,' Leo said, grabbing my stiff hand in his much larger one. The warmth of his hand surprised me and sent a shockwave of care through my arm.

Leo swept me through the hall, passing people I either recognised as students from school or their parents, out the main doors, and into the next corridor.

Ollie was standing alone further up the hallway, facing

away from us, staring at the wall. His hands were clenched beside him in anger.

He turned around and I gasped at the twisted smile on his face.

Stalking towards us, I cowered a little into Leo's side, apprehensive after seeing his expression. When he left the hall, he was pissed off, but I didn't think he was angry at me.

'Come here,' Ollie commanded with a crook of his finger, and like a silly, submissive heroine, I went towards him willingly, and into his arms without question.

He hugged me against him, his tobacco and vanilla scent filling me with joy, the heat of our bodies causing my nipples to harden, and I squirmed at the flood of want rushing through my body.

The whisper in my ear sent my need for him into overdrive. 'Let's go, Little One.'

Ollie led me away with him, gripping my hand in his, stretching my arm as he moved further down the hall until I had no choice but to follow. Nobody was around, and when I looked back at Leo, he was gone, too. The hallway was deserted and, shielded by the dark, we continued until we were in front of a wooden door that he opened with no hesitation.

'In here,' he commanded, placing his palm on the small of my back, giving me a quick but gentle shove inside.

Once inside, he turned me to face him, and I was once again taken by just how fucking hot he was. Even with a livid expression covering his features. His anger was palpable, coming off of him in waves and entering the small space around us. The closet was tiny, with barely enough room for a few shelves and a mop and bucket.

'What the fuck do you think you're doing, Skylar?' he

growled, and with every word, spittle left his mouth, and I watched it fall in the small space between us.

'I-I,' I said, stuttering again, trying to voice the thoughts that were scrambling around in my head. Common sense was battling it out with an apology. I didn't get time to say more, though, as Ollie violently captured my lips with his, the kiss hard, with no ounce of love and affection in the action. It was a pure need. Pure emotion driving his actions that was *definitely* not love.

'Don't say anything around my dad,' he bit out. 'You're here to stay quiet and look pretty.'

Sorry? My anger rushed forward, and I tried to take control of the kiss.

Locked in a fight of teeth and tongue, both of us tried to gain the upper hand. His hardness was pressing into me, making me want him even more. Every time we got closer to having sex, all I could think about was doing the deed with him, and I'd already decided I wanted to make it happen after the gala.

He pushed the bodice of my dress down, uncovering me, and took a hard nipple into his mouth with a bite. The sensation was otherworldly, and I knew I could come just from the feel of his tongue and teeth alone.

'Fuck,' I moaned as he sucked my nipple into his mouth hard enough I worried he'd leave marks.

With a pop, he let go and looked up at me, covering his mouth with his finger. 'Shh, Little One, or someone will hear.'

He stood back to his full height, trailing his hands down my body until he reached my skirt. The full skirt of the dress made it impossible for him to get anywhere further no matter what angle he tried.

Ollie groaned, part in frustration and the other in need. His trousers didn't present the same problem for my hand, though. I undid the top button and ventured inside to wrap my hand around his hard dick with no problem. There was nothing quite like the warmth of a cock in your hand, the little twitches of excitement, and the small beads of pre-cum sitting on the tip. He thrust into my hand, the two of us completely caught up in the moment, forgetting we were in a caretaker's cupboard with an entire hall of parents and students nearby.

Lost in the sensations. The emotions.

All of it.

A loud, hard knock came on the door.

'Shit,' I cursed, thrown back into the moment.

'Dinner's about to begin. Get out of there.' Leo's gruff voice made its way through the door, sounding pissed.

'Looks like our fun's over, Little One,' Ollie said with a harsh laugh and gave one last sharp pinch on my nipple to tease me before he begrudgingly helped me pull my dress back into place.

'Later,' he promised, the whispered word like a threat.

It made me shiver... but in excitement, never fear.

THE DINNER WAS awkward and stilted between all parties sitting at our table. I was sitting next to Ollie. Griff and Clover were next to me, followed by Leo and his parents, and Henry finished the circle on Ollie's other side. Every so often, a question would be asked and answered, then the table would return to silence.

Henry's gaze seared me as he was looking in our direction, but whenever I looked at him to catch him in the act, he was looking elsewhere or had started up a conversation with Lottie.

With the torture of dinner finally ended, the announcer encouraged everybody to congregate in front of the stage to watch the swing band play.

'Come on, everybody! Don't be shy. The band won't play to an empty dance floor!'

My eyes locked with Clo's, the glint in her eye matching the one I was giving her.

'Shall we?' She was already standing, reaching out her hand to me.

'We shall!' I replied, joining her.

Clover took my hand, pulling me towards the dance floor as the band started to play one of our favourite Frank Sinatra songs. It was nice to just let loose and dance and sing along with her; to pretend like we weren't out of our element here, surrounded by people who made more in a month than our families did in an entire year—or five.

Next, a slow song came on, and I felt somebody come up behind me.

'May I have this dance?' a deep voice asked.

I swirled around to find Henry standing behind me, a sly grin on his face. If I thought Clo was going to save me, I was wrong, because she motioned with her hands that she was going to get a drink and got out of the area in rapid time.

Thanks a lot, jelly tot.

'O-of course,' I replied, seeing no other option but to agree.

Our hands came together, and we moved into the traditional slow dance position. Not being much of a dancer, I hoped Henry was well versed and able to help me through without having me fall flat on my arse. I didn't want to humiliate myself, or Ollie for that matter.

'Skylar, I've been wanting to talk to you alone,' Henry said, as the two of us began to move in unison. *So far, so good.*

I spotted Ollie standing over at the side of the dance floor by the bar, with Leo and Griff by his side, all three of them staring at us. Ollie looked wary, Leo seemed bored, and although Griff was smiling at me, his eyes gave away how he was truly feeling, filled with apprehension.

'How come?' I asked, nervous laughter bubbling out of me. People like Henry Brandon could smell fear. They didn't get where they were without having that sense ingrained in them. He must be having a field day assessing me.

'It's rare Oliver leaves you alone, and there are some things I wanted to ask without him around.' His eyes glistened, a lopsided grin taking over the bottom half of his face.

I nodded, still none the wiser as to why he wanted to talk to me alone. Surely there was nothing he needed to say to me without Ollie around?

'Now's your ch-chance,' I joked. Joking around didn't help the nerves, though. If anything, it made the nausea moving around in my stomach worse. It felt as if my entire body was responding to being close to Henry in a negative way.

'After meeting your delightful mother, I felt rather intrigued to learn more about your father.' I looked at his face, unable to read his expression. 'Oliver didn't have an answer when I mentioned it to him.'

Why would Henry want to know about my dad? There was nothing I could tell him, as I knew *nothing* about him.

'I...' I trailed off, not quite sure what to tell him. After a pause, I decided to go with the truth. 'I d-don't know who he is, sir.'

Henry's eyebrows knitted together, assessing me. I

expected him to comment more about my dad, but all he said was, 'No need to call me *sir*, dear. Call me Henry.'

'Henry,' I whispered, feeling caught in a trap, a web I didn't know how to untangle myself from. 'I'm sorry I don't know more.'

'No need to apologise. Forgive me for intruding.'

His hands moved lower, slowly, heading from my waist to my hips. All of it felt wrong and bile rose in my throat. He was making me uncomfortable the way Andy had, and all I wanted to do in that moment was take a brush to my skin and scrub off every touch that wasn't Ollie's.

'It's fine,' I told him. I pulled myself away from his touch, trying to keep my disgust out of my expression. 'I must go find Ollie before he comes and gives you grief for stealing his girl. Thank you for the d-dance.'

'It was my pleasure entirely. I'll see you soon, Skylar,' he said. His tone ominous; his words a threat.

I located Ollie and Leo near the entrance, so I headed towards the two of them. Moments from reaching them, a body barged into my side, knocking me off-balance. I quickly righted myself, turning to see who had bumped into me.

I should've known without looking.

'Watch where you're going, bitch,' Odette said, her tone scathing. 'I nearly spilled my drink because of you.'

'Sorry,' I apologised quietly. It killed me inside to apologise to her, but I really wanted to just make it to Ollie and Leo, and I knew if I didn't say sorry, I could be stuck with them for far longer than I would like to be. 'I didn't see you there.'

'What Ollie sees in you I'll never know,' she said with scorn, but I didn't miss the flash of envy in her wide eyes.

'Well...' Olivia said, about to add her two cents to the conversation, but Odette jutted her elbow out to shut her up.

She grunted in pain, but knew her place in the hierarchy and didn't say any more.

'You are nothing but trash. You've never belonged here at Hawthorn, but don't worry, everybody will see that for themselves soon,' Odette warned.

With that, the two of them dispersed, leaving me alone once more. Odette's parting words weren't overly encouraging, but with Henry's threat still ringing in my ears, I focused on that more. After all, the girls had already tried to get me kicked out of Hawthorn. Fuck, they'd also potentially orchestrated my drugging and near drowning, too. *Can't a girl catch a break around here?*

Making it back to Ollie's side, the only place I wanted to be for the rest of the evening, he checked me all over to see if I was all in one piece. His eyes simmered with heat as he took me in, checking me out in other ways. All night I'd been taking him in, mostly because I couldn't believe that somebody as gorgeous as him was *my* boyfriend. Fingers crossed he saw tonight ending the way I did.

In bed. Naked. Wrapped up in one another.

Who was I kidding? He was a guy. That was probably how he wished *every* night between us ended.

'Shit. It's already five to midnight. I've got to go,' Leo announced.

I jumped at the sound of his voice. I'd been so preoccupied with looking at Ollie, and him looking at me, that I'd totally forgotten that Leo was still standing with us.

'Where's he off to?' I asked, but Ollie shrugged, then his arms encapsulated me, pulling me up against his hard body in a tight embrace. Heat filled me.

What a way to start a new year.

The room erupted into a countdown.

'Ten!'

I turned to face Ollie. Looking into the depths of his blue eyes, I saw a few different emotions flicker in his gaze, but none of them stayed for long.

'Five!'

A mixture of caring, lust, and anger all played out on his face in quick succession, warring to be the dominant emotion. He settled on a serene look, or as serene a look as I'd ever seen on him, anyway.

'Happy New Year!' The room burst into cheers and glasses clinking. The smacking of lips and the sound of fireworks outside filling the air.

'Happy New Year,' he whispered.

'Happy New Year,' I said in return, a wide smile hurting my cheeks.

Our midnight kiss was like the one I'd dreamt about receiving ever since I was a young girl, wishing I had a boyfriend like the girls in movies. I'd had nobody to share one with before, and I'd spent a lot of my previous New Year's at home alone while Mum and Andy were at the local pub with their friends.

The passion in the kiss wasn't lost on me, and happiness overtook my insides. *This must be what it's like to feel wanted.*

I'd wanted that feeling forever, the feeling of being desired.

The new year held so much promise and I couldn't wait to see what it had in store for me.

Twenty-Seven

THE MOMENT the door of Ollie's suite closed behind us, a chill ran down my spine. I'd been anticipating this moment for quite some time, and it was finally here. Ollie grabbed my waist from behind, then his lips trailed kisses up and down my neck.

The room was lit by moonlight, adding to the magical atmosphere I'd created in my mind, and every now and then the light caught Ollie's eyes, the spark in them beckoning me forward. His hands roamed while I put mine around his neck, pulling his mouth closer for more kisses.

Feverish kisses. Desperate kisses.

Ollie took a step back and ripped his tie off, looking free of the burden the moment it was gone.

Tearing his jacket off with a growl. His eyes burned as they locked with mine.

'I cannot fucking wait to get you out of that dress. You've been torturing me all night.'

'I've done no such thing—'

He cut me off abruptly, slamming into me as he crushed his mouth to mine, his hunger calling to my own in an instant. His body pushed against mine as he devoured me like a starving man, even biting at my lips. He caught my bottom lip and pulled just enough to make me feel at his mercy for a moment.

'Get naked and lie on the bed,' Ollie demanded, pushing me onto the bed with a little too much force, and I stumbled, nearly tripping on the skirt of the gown.

'Help me?' I asked, hoping my nerves would calm the fuck down soon.

He grabbed my hands and pulled me back to my feet. Spinning me around, he slowly unzipped my dress, leaving my back bare and exposed to the air.

To him.

'Finally. Just the way I want you.' Gripping the fabric of the ball gown, Ollie yanked it to the floor, leaving me standing before him in nothing but my light blue lace underwear set. He growled appreciatively.

I turned to face him and stepped out of the material at my feet.

With the way Ollie was looking at me, I thought I'd combust from all the sexual energy surrounding us.

My hands shaking, I removed my bra and slowly slid my bottoms down, watching his eyes as they tracked my every movement. I opened my mouth, unsure what I planned to say, but his hand slapped down over my mouth, eyes burning.

'No talking, New Girl. You're mine tonight, no questions asked.'

I'm sure if I actually told him no, he wouldn't force it, but we both knew we'd been aching to go to town on each other for a while. I may not have loved how he was bossing me around, but I also couldn't deny how hot it was.

'Now get your arse on the bed,' he commanded. A slight shiver ran down my back, but I meekly sat on the bed and watched him without a word, waiting to see what he did next. 'And don't move.'

Again, I contemplated not giving him power over me, but with my hunger growing, the hesitation was easily brushed aside.

Once I was settled with my back on the mattress, I watched Ollie as he pulled off his shirt, hunger rising as I took in his muscular frame. Whatever he had planned, I was certain it would be nothing but enjoyable for me.

The anticipation climbed with every piece of clothing he removed. Nerves filled me, my stomach a sea of thrashing waves. We'd never been so far before, never been so bare to one another.

After what felt like forever, he stood before me naked, a smirk playing on his lips.

His dick was big. Really big. Even though I'd touched it before tonight, I'd never considered its size. I knew every teenage virgin seemed to say it, in every film and book, but I really didn't know how he was going to fit.

Ollie kneeled by my feet, looking over my body, a contemplative look on his face. I stared back, feigning more confidence than I really felt. Nerves knotted in my stomach. Knowing Ollie, he wouldn't be very gentle with me. I was excited by the prospect, but also terrified. What if it hurt?

But I couldn't let myself think that way. I wanted this with him. I wanted to feel him so far inside of me, we became one person. One soul.

Anticipation and terror rose when he pulled my legs apart, allowing him access to my pussy. He didn't immediately attack, though, giving me a moment to process everything that was happening. He kissed and nibbled at my legs first, thankfully allowing me to relax a little by the time he got to the lace knickers, and I started to feel a little less fearful of what he'd do to me.

It took a moment, but with a deep breath, I allowed myself to get washed away by the sensation of his mouth moving from my knee to my hip on one leg and then the other. I slowly relaxed and focused on enjoying myself.

Ollie's hot breath caressed me as his mouth hovered just over me, and I let out a pleased sigh. *What a tease,* I thought when his teeth scraped over my hip. One hand slipped under my back while the other grasped the lace band at the top of my knickers.

It seemed effortless when he pulled them free with his teeth and one hand, lifting me just enough with the other to assist.

God, why does he have to be so hot? So good at this?

It was achingly sweet and frustrating at the same time.

'Come on, New Girl,' Ollie said, his face again hovering above my pussy. 'Don't tell me I was the only one fantasising about this all night. Of kissing you... biting you... teasing you until you scream for me to let you cum. Then slamming into you until your brain short-circuits and your pussy clenches me so hard, I combust.' He sighed playfully, sending hot air brushing over my already aching bundle of nerves.

A sharp squeak of surprise and exhilaration left me when his mouth descended at last, softly brushing over my clit. *Ah, shit.* He definitely had all the power over me. He always did.

My back arched hard when his fingers dug into my hips, pulling me even harder against his mouth, each fingertip sending just enough pain into my body to heighten the experience.

I tasted blood when my teeth cut into my lips to hold back a scream, as I felt the pleasure building, racing toward something I knew would be too intense, like I was a rocket flying directly into the sun.

Somehow, when I did hit that point, there was no pain. It wasn't so overwhelming that it hurt like I thought it would. It was nothing but the purest pleasure I'd ever experienced.

It danced along the edge of being too much, but that somehow made it all the better, like the euphoria of just avoiding something that could kill me.

When I finally came back to myself, Ollie was kissing and biting at my hips, waiting for me to recover while still clearly hungry himself.

'Damn,' I murmured once I remembered what words were. 'That was... Wow.'

Words failed me.

Looking up at me, Ollie smirked and moved his position to hover above me. His hand wandered down my body until I felt a long digit enter me, followed soon after by a second and then a third. My wetness eased his movement and I honestly couldn't think of a time I'd been this wet before.

'Are you sure about this, Sky?' he whispered, his words skating across my skin. The moment became more real the second he uttered my name.

Not *New Girl.*

Sky.

I nodded and sighed in pleasure, his thumb lazily circling my clit. 'Please.'

My voice came out as a whimper, my eyes were at half mast, and I shivered just looking at Ollie's full lips. He kissed me hard, removing his fingers to wrap them around my hips and the head of his cock nudged against my entrance.

Fuck, if he didn't put his dick where we both wanted it soon, I was going to take over.

The moment his cock breached my entrance, I winced.

Shit. The initial sting hurt. My eyes watered, but it wasn't long before the pain eased and I whispered, 'You can keep going.'

With delicious slowness, he slipped inside, inch by inch, and I relished in the tight, stretched feeling of him inside me. It was everything I'd imagined, but also, so much more.

We both let out a small moan once he was completely inside.

He started thrusting slowly at first, but then something broke in him and he began to thrust in earnest, creating sensations I didn't even know I could feel.

'Fuck,' I moaned.

Our breathing escalated together, to the point I started feeling lightheaded, all thoughts escaping me as my world became nothing but Ollie's hands gripping me roughly and the thrusting of his cock as it slid in and out, each hit bringing me closer and closer to another orgasm.

His breath was hot in my ear, one hand on my nipple pinching me hard, the other grasping my wrist and pinning it above my head. No way for me to move it. No way to be free from him.

Not that I wanted to be.

My free hand was in his hair, pulling sections every time he hit that spot inside of me that was elusive to most. I'd never felt this close to somebody before and there were tears in my eyes, both from emotion and the passion between us. It was overwhelming.

'Fuck,' Ollie hissed out through his teeth. Just the sound of his moan caused the sensation of butterflies in my stomach.

'Touch me,' I said desperately to Ollie. I needed him to rub my clit. Now.

He understood instantly, and the second he brushed his thumb over the spot, I came.

I moaned, 'Ollie!'

'Fuck!' Ollie ground out, the words the final push for me to fall into another orgasm, my scream melting into the mattress as I felt like my world shattered around me. His cock somehow swelled larger at the same time, filling me in a whole new way that made the orgasm even more satisfying.

My moan seemed to push Ollie over the edge, as after a few more deep strokes, I felt him spill inside of me.

Spent, Ollie collapsed to the bed beside me, both of us panting. I didn't move from my stomach for a while, exhaustion already creeping in, pulling me to delve into sleep. I already ached a little between my legs, but thankfully it was nothing like the pain I dreaded.

Shit.

We didn't use a condom.

Thank fuck for the school's weird rule about health check-ups and contraception.

Ollie got up and went to his en-suite and returned with a wet towel he then used to clean me. It was strange, but that act felt more intimate to me than the whole *losing my virginity thing* that just happened.

After a moment, Ollie moved to lie beside me, and we were silent for a while. The events of the evening were catching up with us both.

'How are you feeling?' he asked, his voice thick.

'I'm good. That was—fuck, Ollie—that was. Wow,' I sputtered out. I was finding words hard. I felt incoherent. Like my entire body and brain were made of mush, and I'd never be able to form complete sentences again. I wondered if every girl felt like this when they first discovered sex. I made a mental note to ask Clover.

'Told you I wanted to find out how your stutter sounded with my dick deep inside of you. Trust me, baby, it did not disappoint.'

I could only describe the sound that left me next as an embarrassed chuckle. I had sex with Ollie. *Like, what?* Yeah, it had been on the agenda for some time now, and I'd known pretty much from day one that I wanted to have sex with him. But wanting something and having it become reality were two very different things; and they came with two very different emotions.

I fell asleep in Ollie's arms as the little spoon, and I felt safe. Protected. And damn did it feel good.

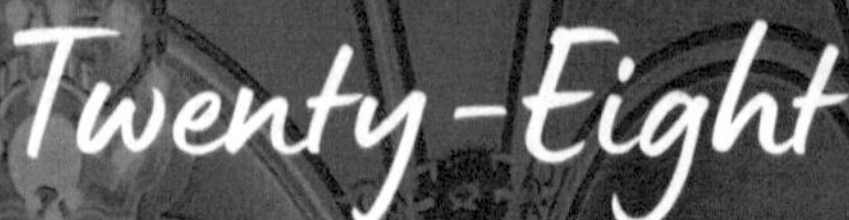

Twenty-Eight

I WOKE up the next morning with a start. On opening my eyes, it took me a second to adjust and remember that I was in Ollie's room, in Ollie's bed, and that he was lying next to me.

To remember that the two of us had sex after returning from the gala, before falling asleep sated and wrapped up in one another's arms.

Still sound asleep, Ollie looked so peaceful. His eyebrows were relaxed and I could honestly say I'd never seen such a serene look on his face. When awake, his mind was constantly working a mile a minute, and he never seemed to switch off and just sit and relax. Seeing him so vulnerable made him seem more human. Like an actual person, with actual emotions—almost.

I got up and went to the toilet, still lost in my thoughts about the night before. I contemplated brushing my hair and sorting out my face, but I decided not to. Ollie had seen me at my worst, meaning there was no need to hide who I really was. It pissed me off that I'd even considered it, because as a rule, I'd never understood that whole concept. If brushing your hair first thing in the morning made a difference to a relationship, you needed to reevaluate.

I got back into bed and Ollie mumbled, 'Morning,' then pulled me back up against his chest and I got comfortable again. I didn't know the time, but the new year already felt promising, even if it had barely begun. We must have fallen back asleep, though, as the next time I opened my eyes, the light coming through the windows made me think it was closer to late afternoon.

Back at home, I didn't have blinds on my windows because my mum had refused to pay for them. Apparently, she and Andy would rather spend the money on something more important—I'd never found out what was more important, but there you go. Because of this, I was pretty good at being able to decipher what time it was just by how the world looked as it came through the windows. Not a helpful skill at all, but a relatively cool one.

'Afternoon,' Ollie mumbled this time before kissing up and down my neck, covering every patch of skin available. 'How are you feeling?'

'I'm good,' I told him. Feeling like I needed to emphasise my words, I wriggled against him. I could feel his dick pressing into my lower back and I smiled. '*Really* good actually.' He pulled back, so I had some space to turn in, and I shuffled myself around to face him.

He was about to say something more when we heard a piercing scream from out in the hall. At first, neither of us moved, but clearly other people who lived in Ollie's wing of the school did, as the commotion outside got louder.

'Skylar,' Griff shouted through the door. I found it a little odd he was calling my name when he was knocking on Ollie's door. Why wouldn't he be calling for him?

Quickly, I threw on one of Ollie's tops and a pair of his tracksuit bottoms that I rolled up at the waist so they didn't instantly fall down. I shuffled my way to the door and opened it to see a frantic-looking Griff, his hair standing up on end as if he'd been pulling at it for hours, staring at me with worry in his eyes.

'What's up?' I asked, keeping my tone light. I looked past him and saw a group of students hovering at the end of the hall, whispering about something with worried expressions. I nudged my head towards the gathering. 'What's going on down there?'

'Come with me,' he said urgently as Ollie came up behind me. 'You too.'

We followed Griff out of the room, but instead of heading into his on the right, he took us into the room on the left. Leo stood in the middle of the room, a bored expression playing on his face, but his foot was tapping in a frustrated rhythm, so maybe he wasn't as bored as he wanted to come across.

'What's going on, dickheads?' Ollie asked, looking at them both with raised brows, sceptical of their motivation.

'Olivia's dead,' Griff said, panicked. He looked sick, like he was one breath away from losing the contents of his stomach entirely.

'Who?' I asked. All three guys swung their gazes to me, and I blushed at the disbelief on their faces. Clearly, I was meant to know who they meant without question.

Olivia. Olivia.

It took me another moment to picture Olivia in my mind.

'Oh!' I gasped, covering my mouth with my hand. 'Olivia.'

The fourth member of *The Set*. To be fair, I'd forgotten she existed for the most part. It was rare I had much to do with her, as it always seemed to be Odette, Ophelia, or Oralie giving me a hard time. Olivia had been a silent companion.

'What?' Ollie barked, his anger a surprise, making me jump beside him. 'How?'

'Somebody killed her,' Leo said, monotone.

'Stabbed,' Griff added. 'She told the girls at the gala she was going back to some guy's house but wouldn't tell them whose house. All she'd say was that they'd be shocked if they knew the truth.'

'How do we know what happened if she went back to some old dude's house?' Ollie asked, sounding bored now that he'd heard more. 'She wasn't even on campus.'

'That's just it, though. They found her on the grounds.' Griff's tone was urgent. 'Her body was lying on the steps of the pool house. They found her first thing, but you know how gossip goes around, so it spread round the school pretty fast.'

Leo stayed silent, standing still in the centre of the room, contemplating everything that was being said. Assessing everyone's reactions. Taking it all in.

'So, why have you got us out of bed?' Ollie asked, pissed. 'You could have told us at dinner.'

'The girl's dead, Oliver!' Griff growled.

'Olivia was holding a lock of Skylar's hair and a piece of her blue dress from last night,' Leo said as he locked his gaze on mine, ignoring the tension building between Ollie and Griff.

'Sorry, w-what?' I sputtered, confused as fuck. Why would she have been holding my hair, or some of my dress? How?

'Yep,' Griff answered me, then looked at Ollie. 'So, that's why we came and got you, wanker.'

'Who found her?' I asked. I had to know. Not that it was okay for whoever found her, but it would be worse if it was a pupil in one of the younger years.

'Ms Hawthorn,' Leo responded in a dull tone.

Wonderful. The woman already acted like she couldn't

stand me. Now that I guessed I'd become a suspect, she would hate me even more.

Fuck, would I be considered a suspect?

'Guys,' I said, looking at them all. 'Will the police think *I* did it?'

The responses from the guys in the room with me weren't positive ones. The winces and unfinished sentences gave away the answer.

I understood. A corpse showing up holding your hair—distinctively coloured hair at that—definitely didn't help my cause.

'So, what shall we do about it?' Ollie looked pissed still. Whether he was aiming it at me or them, I didn't know. Either way, it wasn't any of our faults. He had to know that much.

'No clue, man. That's why we wanted you two here, so we could talk it out.' Griff looked exasperated with Ollie, and I totally got why. He was acting like a total dick. I knew he had different plans of how he'd expected this morning to go—so did I, if I was being honest—but it wasn't like we could help it. You'd think he'd be a little more caring that Olivia was dead. He'd known her for years, after all. Plus, his girlfriend was being implicated in her death. Surely he cared about that?

'Doesn't sound like there's much to talk about. Olivia's dead and Sky's being implicated,' he deadpanned.

Let me just take back my last thought.

'God, you are such a frustrating dick, you know that?' Griff asked, his face slowly turning the shade of a tomato. I'd never seen him so angry before. 'Who would do this to Sky?'

'W-what do you mean? Shouldn't we be asking who would do this to Olivia?'

'Not being funny, New Girl, but literally anybody could have done this to Olivia,' Griff said with a shrug. 'No. Somebody planted your hair and dress on purpose and we need to figure out who.' He gave a questioning look to both Leo and Ollie, one I didn't fully understand.

Great.

More secrets.

Twenty-Nine

SCHOOL STARTED BACK up a week after the gala, and things with Ollie were amazing. Ever since that night, we were inseparable. He'd bribed the dorm monitors into letting me stay in his suite every night, and there was no way I was going to turn that down. I didn't even want to think about how much money had exchanged hands for that to happen, because if I did, I'd feel a bit like he was *paying* to spend time with me. *And that's just icky.*

You know how when you read or heard about girls losing their V-card? They always said some crap about how different they felt or how much sex they wanted to have now that the barrier was gone?

I'm now one of those basic heroines.

All I could think about was *him*. Spending time with him, in the biblical sense, but also just watching films together and enjoying one another's company. My thoughts were even boring me, but I couldn't help it. I was truly happy for the first time in a long time.

After Olivia's body had been found, investigators invaded the school and questioned everybody. They summoned every single student individually to Ms Hawthorn's office, and we all had to relay our whereabouts from that evening. Even those who hadn't attended the gala were being questioned, just in case they were the mysterious person she planned to go home with.

I had no clue what strings Ollie pulled, but they allowed him to sit beside me throughout the interview—seeing as we'd spent the evening together anyway, I supposed it made sense to question us at the same time.

'*Miss Crescent. Master Brandon. I'm Detective Saunders and this is my partner Detective Smith. We've asked you here to answer a couple of questions in regards to the death of Olivia. This is an informal chat, just to learn of your whereabouts,*' *the tall, slim detective said, sitting down in the chair in front of us, next to his short, round co-worker. 'Where were you between the hours of one and four in the morning?*'

'*We were in bed,*' *Ollie replied, bored. 'Where else would we have been?*'

Detective Saunders ignored Ollie and continued his line of questioning.

'*Do you have any idea how Olivia came to hold your dress and hair, Miss Crescent?*'

I gulped, opening and closing my mouth like a fish, unsure how to answer.

'*No, she doesn't.*' *Ollie sat up straighter in his chair, his stare focused on the two detectives sitting in front of us. 'Somebody is framing her.*'

'*And why would somebody have a reason to frame you, Miss Crescent?*' *Detective Smith's narrow glare turned to me, and once again, I was at a loss for words. If I answered truthfully, that Olivia and her friends were the ones bullying me, it would make me look even more suspicious than I already did.*

'*Isn't that your job?*' *Ollie snapped back, not letting the detec-*

tives intimidate him the way they were me. 'To figure out people's motives?'

'We're aware of our job, Master Brandon,' Detective Saunders said with a brittle smile. 'The two of you are free to go, but we'd like you to remain available for future enquiries.'

The way he said it made me laugh inside. As if the two of us had anywhere else to go except school. Not like we were about to do a runner out of the country. I didn't even have a passport.

'It's been a pleasure,' Ollie said, standing from his chair and reaching his hand down to help me out of mine.

I didn't say another word as we silently left the room. Once outside, I took the deep breath my lungs needed—one my body had refused to take when sitting in front of two men who believed I was a cold-hearted killer.

After that, things went back to normal. Or, as normal as they could around Hawthorn.

'So, my dick is obviously the biggest,' Griff said at the exact moment I tuned into the conversation going on around me.

I sputtered, causing my drink to spray out of my mouth. Griff raised an eyebrow at me, the smirk on his face giving away the fact that he was trying to shock and was more than pleased that it worked.

'Oh, give over, Griff. Like I'm even going to say anything to boost your ego, or that dickhead's for that matter.' Clover nudged her head towards Leo and Odette, who were sitting at a table across the room with the other members of *The Set*.

'I'm just saying, my little lady luck, that if you *want* to look, you'll be happy with what you find. More than happy, actually. Fucking ecstatic. Maybe you'll even shed a tear.'

Clover hit him hard on the arm, but I could see that she was trying to hold her laughter in. I didn't hold back, though. There was just something so lovable about that stupid boy, even if I knew he was hiding something from me. If I was being honest with myself, I knew most people were. Especially the ones who used humour as a way to hide from those around them; those closest to them.

'Shut up, prick.' Ollie looked amused, but there was an underlying look of distaste in his expression. I couldn't figure out whether it was aimed at Griff or Clo, though.

'You kill me, Griff,' I said, chuckling. 'Please can we move off the subject of dick size?'

'Miss Skylar, are you sure you don't wanna join in?' he asked, his grin ever present.

I shook my head in response, going back to eating my gourmet meal. 'Join in with what? Not like I can make any comparison notes for you.'

'True, true. But you could just lie and make me feel good, you know, as my best friend,' he said, and I smiled at his words. Having people to call friends made me ecstatic, but at times like this, I wondered why I kept them around.

Oh, who am I kidding?

I tried my hardest not to do anything that would cause them to stop being my friend. I couldn't go back to being a friendless loser—being here had made me fully understand just how empty and miserable my life had been before.

'Pretty sure I'm her best friend, dickweed. Eat your food and shut up,' Clover told him, effectively putting an end to that conversation.

RECENTLY, Ollie had been talking to me about Clover—how he was worried about her. Worried that her words would cause me to question him or his actions sometime in the near future.

'You're being paranoid,' I told him, not even looking up from my textbook. Homework was more important than his worries. I needed to pass everything in order to keep my scholarship. 'Just don't do anything that would make Clo chat shit about you to me, and then we'll be golden.'

'But she might do it anyway.'

'Ollie,' I said, looking up into his wary expression. 'Can we drop it? I get it. You don't trust Clover, and funny enough, she doesn't trust you. So let's just leave it there and move on.'

'But—'

'No buts!' My voice rose as I lost my cool. We were in the library and I knew the librarian liked me, so she'd let me off once, but she wouldn't if I continued shouting. I lowered my voice again. 'I may be quiet, and maybe I don't always stand up for myself the way I should, but I can think for myself. Regardless of how Clover feels towards you, it won't sway my feelings for you.'

'You promise?'

'Yes,' I stressed. 'Now please, talk about literally anything else.'

'I think Leo's gonna ask Odette to be his girlfriend soon.'

'Yeah?' I wondered where that came from, but I did tell him to change the subject to literally anything else. 'I didn't think he actually liked her.'

'What makes you think that?'

'I don't know,' I shrugged. 'I thought he was with her for convenience.'

'Convenience?'

'Sex,' I said, being blunt. Since I'd lost my virginity, I was able to talk about it a lot easier. The word didn't scare me anymore. 'And I always thought it was a way for him to piss Clo off.'

'I've never asked him, to be honest,' Ollie said, frowning. 'But who knows. This is Leo we're talking about.'

'True,' I replied. Leo *was* a mystery. 'Guess we'll never know his motives.'

'Sky...' he trailed off, and I went back to reading the page in front of me. 'Valentine's Day is coming up.'

'Right,' I replied, distracted.

'And I've got a question to ask you.'

'Okay.'

'Sky, will you at least look at me?' His finger prodded under my chin, tilting my head up to look at him again. I smiled, laughing inside at how serious he seemed. 'I want to ask you if you'd like to come to London for the weekend with me?'

'When?'

'Valentine's Day...'

'Oh.' I laughed, nervous. I wanted to go with him, but an entire weekend away from school with Ollie both sounded like a dream and a nightmare. That wasn't what I said, though. Instead, I said, 'I'd love to.'

'Great!' Ollie said, placing a kiss on my forehead. 'This is probably gonna sound a little forward, but I've already booked the hotel and show.'

'Oh,' I said, unease filling my gut. 'You have?'

'It's Valentine's Day weekend,' he said, as if that explained everything, and I supposed it did, if you'd ever had a date or a reason to celebrate that day.

'Will we be allowed to leave school with no issue?'

'Yeah,' he said with a nod. 'We're allowed to leave at the weekend, and we can do overnight stays with permission from our parents. I got my dad to write a letter, and then I was going to falsify one from your mum.'

'Wow. You've got it all worked out, haven't you?'

'I want to spend time with you. Is that a problem?' His tone came out a little stilted, and I knew I'd hit a nerve, whether I'd meant to or not.

'No!' I said, wanting to appease him. 'I'd love to spend time with you away from here, Ollie. I promise.'

'I'm sorry,' he said, blowing out a breath. 'I'm trying to stop acting like a dick, but it's harder than I thought.'

The sheepish smile on his face warmed me. Yeah, he definitely acted like a massive prick a lot of the time, but there was something endearing about it. Maybe I was a stupid bitch who was blinded by first lust, and that was why I let him get away with his behaviour, but I couldn't help myself. The boy looked *good*.

'I forgive you,' I said, gripping his fingers in mine.

Thirty

A COUPLE OF DAYS LATER, Odette and Leo became an official couple, and shit hit the fan.

I'd been given a reprieve from *The Set* and no harm had come to me since Halloween after the whole being held under water situation. But it was a new year. Apparently, I was fair game again.

It made little sense to me that things were getting worse after somebody who supposedly cared about me was dating my bully. Leo had told me multiple times to go to him if I needed help, so I'd thought by him dating Odette for "real" it would have gone the other way and ended the bullying entirely. Clearly that had been wishful thinking on my part.

At the academy, the bathroom toilet walls were covered in graffiti. Apparently, the graffitied walls had existed forever, and no matter how often the school painted over them, they would always just reappear the next day. It was a constant battle between the caretaker and the students.

My name was on every toilet stall wall.

Every time they painted the messages over, they came back worse and more aggressive. The school had given up after the first three repaints and since then, was letting them accumulate.

Skylar Crescent should kill herself.

SC doesn't deserve OB

You have to be a low level of scum to call your daughter Skylar.

There were arrows coming off of the original comments, with more comments underneath. I wanted to be disgusted at how many girls had stooped to this level, but really, I wasn't. It didn't surprise me at all.

Eurgh, she's a skank.

Wish Ophelia would hit her harder.

Whoever attempted to drown her should have done a better job.

Even I could admit that some were funny and so obviously false.

SC has gonorrhoea.

SC is a walking STD.

And my personal favourite:

Sky fingers herself with an electric toothbrush.

Original *and* classy. The best kind of slur.

The messages weren't just all over the bathrooms. Nope. They were all over the Hive too. On every message board and feed. Literally every single place that students had the chance to slag me off, they were doing it. These words were repeated in whispers in every corridor, every class, and at mealtimes. I thought my sort of friendship with Leo meant things would get better, seeing as he was dating the ring-leader, but he hadn't stopped jack shit from happening to me. My hair was pulled, my clothes covered in paint from paint balloons they threw at me, and the essays I had sent off electronically were being altered somehow. They came back from the teacher with a poor grade, the wording completely different from what I'd written and sent in. But I had no proof, and when I tried to tell a teacher about it, they pretended not to hear me.

I tried my best not to let any of it affect me. Tried to keep my head held high and stay above it all. Tried to tell myself they were all just jealous or spiteful—or both.

A majority of the girls grumbled about me using a witch's spell to get both Ollie and Griff under my thumb. *How pathetic.* Like I'd just been sitting in my room with Clover saying spells over a cauldron like some *Macbeth* shit. Petty girls really did say and believe anything to help themselves buy into their own delusions. I had to keep reminding myself of that.

The other thing that was getting me down was my relationship with Clover.

Clover had been acting funky ever since Leo and Odette officially got together, to the point where she wouldn't be anywhere near them, barely spent any time with us, and basically became a hermit that stayed in our room. It was odd behaviour, even for her, and I didn't know what to do to make it better. Not like I could ask Ollie for help as he and Clover barely tolerated each other at the best of times.

I just wasn't sure what to do to make things go back to how they were before. Not like I was going to split up with Ollie to appease Clover. But I also didn't want to lose a friendship—my only female friendship—because of a guy. Hoes before bros and all that.

'Want to watch a film tonight?' Clo asked as the two of us were walking back from dinner, hooking her arm through mine.

'Err...' I wasn't sure what to say but decided to go with the truth. 'I was going to hang out with Ollie tonight.' I cringed, worried she was going to start an argument with me or switch from a playful mood into one made of pure bitchiness.

'Oh. Right.' Her tone had soured. So much so, I could taste it.

'But I can cancel,' I said, feeling guilty, and got out my phone straight away to cancel my plans with Ollie. Yeah, he'd probably be a little pissed at me and blame it on Clo, but I hadn't spent time with Clover, just us two, in a while and I could tell she was missing me. I missed her too, and things were so weird between us, it would do us good to spend time alone. Hopefully, if we spent the evening chilling out, things might go back to being a little more normal.

'Only if you're sure?' she asked. She looked happier, though, like she really wanted me to cancel but wouldn't voice it out loud.

'Course I'm sure. You're my girl,' I told her. When I saw the smile beaming on her face, I knew I'd made the correct decision. 'Let's go watch *a* film and eat some popcorn.'

'Sounds good to me.' She pulled me closer to her side, and I knew that eventually we'd be okay.

'Do you think that's how American schools actually are?' Clo asked me out of nowhere, pausing the film we were watching.

'What do you mean?'

'Like, all cliquey and bitchy?'

'Clo, it's like that here,' I said, laughing at her. But now that she mentioned it, I thought a little deeper. I'd always wondered about American schools and whether they were depicted correctly. 'Not like *The Set* are a bundle of laughs, is it?'

'True. Although I've always wondered where the appeal is,

ya know? Like, why do so many people want to be one of the popular girls? Why do people care so much about Odette's opinion?' Clo asked, her brows furrowed, and her eyes went blank.

'I have no idea. Only thing I can think of is the fact that people are attracted to power. If a person wields power, they're instantly more appealing.' I shrugged, tasting the theory on my tongue.

'Sort of like how Ollie and Leo are sexier because of the power they hold?'

'Yep. Exactly that,' I replied without much thought. It took me a moment to realise that not only had she brought up Leo's name, but she'd also called him sexy. What the fuck was happening? 'Clo, are you feeling all right?'

'I think so...' Her voice went higher at the end, so it came out sounding more like a question than a statement—the epitome of uncertainty.

'You just used the name Leo and the word sexier in the same sentence.'

'I mean, I may hate him... but damn, he's fine,' Clo said, chuckling.

'Yeah, he totally is,' I agreed, laughing along with her, and I could feel the iciness between us slowly melting away. It felt like it had back at the beginning of term, when we'd just met and the guys hadn't got between us yet. 'They're both sexy and they know it.'

'They definitely know it. I think that's one of the many reasons I detest Leo so much. He flaunts his looks to anybody with eyes, I swear. He's a rich bastard too, and that usually has all the girls fighting for his attention. Look at Odette.'

'Odette's not exactly full of brains, though, is she?' I said. I couldn't be certain as she was in the year above and I didn't share any classes with her, but from the conversations I *had* overhead, the girl wasn't the brightest. Couldn't always be helped, though. Sometimes people struggled at school and that was okay. But I could tell Odette didn't care. She believed that she'd bag a Hawthorn and never have to work again—something I'd *legiterally* heard her say.

Oh, for fuck's sake.

I'd started to think like Griff.

I hoped Leo would see sense soon when it came to Odette. Seeing as he was looking out for me, part of me wanted to look out for him in return.

'It irritates me how she's all over him at all times.'

'Why does it bother you?'

Clover looked at me, her eyes narrowed. I still hadn't told her that Leo and I were in contact via texting. It was almost as if I'd kept the secret too long and, if revealed, it would look worse than it was. She'd think I was hiding it from her—which was exactly the case, but still.

'It doesn't. Just don't want to see him used by her,' I said with an uninterested shrug.

'Believe me, I think he's the one doing the using.' Clo pretended to gag and stuck her finger into her open mouth.

'I've walked across those two too often now,' I said without thinking. 'It's not a sight I need again.'

Clover went quiet, probably imagining the image I'd just put into her head.

'Thanks for the visuals, Sky,' she said. I felt a pain in my shoulder and caught sight of Clover's fist as it moved back from the punch it had just delivered. I grunted.

'Bitch,' I muttered.

Clover just grinned at me like a maniac, teeth and all.

'Whore,' she replied, with her smile still firmly in place. I rolled my eyes, and we went back to watching the movie. The only thing breaking the silence was our popcorn eating. It was nice spending time with her like this.

No boys.

No distractions.

Thirty-One

ON A TUESDAY MORNING, History was the first class of the day and it excited me to sit with Ollie. He had swim practice before school, so I was waiting for him at my locker, lost in my own thoughts, when a wet sensation spread from my head downward.

Liquid covered my head.

Freezing liquid.

All I could think was that I hoped it wasn't pee, but that would surely be warm, not ice-cold. The smell gave it away as some kind of ice slush drink that smelled super sweet and was super sticky.

For fuck's sake. I was wearing my last clean uniform. The others were all in for cleaning and Clover wore a different size uniform to me, so it wasn't even like I could go up to our room and steal hers for the day. I didn't even know where the staff did the uniform cleaning, so not like I could venture there and see if mine was clean already—or if they had any spare.

'Shit, Sky,' Griff said, appearing in an instant.

Whoever had put the drink over my head had long since disappeared. I hadn't even got a glimpse of who had done it, but who was I kidding, it could literally have been any student at the school—of any age.

'Listen up!' Griff called out to the hallway and every student in our vicinity stopped and turned to look at him, some with quizzical expressions, others looking bored but knowing they had no choice but to listen to him. 'If I see anybody picking on Skylar, or throwing shit at her, or tripping her up, then you *will* face the consequences. *The Set* may have told you that this shit is okay, but as a member of *The Sect* I will make your lives here hell. Now, go to class!'

Everybody scattered as quickly as possible, bumping into one another in their hurry to get away from Griff's wrath. I'd never seen him look so mad. I expected it of Ollie, and even Leo to an extent, but not happy-go-lucky, cheeky Griff.

'Are you okay?' he asked, taking my appearance in from head to toe.

'Yeah, I'm okay,' I said and gave a tentative smile, 'but I smell like a blue raspberry.'

'Haven't you always wondered what a blue raspberry is? Like, what? How? They're not even real,' he said. His lip curled up at the side, a laugh fighting to leave him, but he seemed determined to keep a straight face.

I laughed at Griff's obvious attempt to cheer me up. Although he was telling the truth. Who decided what a blue raspberry was or what it tasted and smelled like?

While I was caught up in my laughter, Ophelia and Oralie swanned over to us in silence. The smug look on both of their faces told me that even if they weren't the ones who'd poured the drink on my head, they definitely had okayed it.

'Did you have anything to do with this?' Griff harshly whispered to the two of them, trying not to draw any more attention to the four of us. Bless him for trying, but we'd been the centre of attention before the girls had even come along. The girls entering the scene had just made us more interesting to the onlookers.

'Who, us?' asked Ophelia, using that look that all pretty girls thought would get them off the hook. A bite of the lip. A flutter of eyelashes. She moved her head to survey the entire corridor and everybody watching. Her voice was louder than normal, and I knew she wanted people to hear her.

'Yes, you two. Who else would have planned this?' Griff growled, bored of their shit.

'Pretty sure, *Griffin*, there are many people here who would do this to the New Girl. We don't tolerate trash around here. Hawthorn Academy has always been for the elite,' said Ophelia.

Sadly, I knew there was a lot of truth in Ophelia's words. A large number of students would go out of their way wanting to get on *The Set*'s good side and would achieve it by terrorising me.

'I'll be talking to Leo about this,' Griff threatened them, but I wasn't sure what difference it would make. Wasn't like Leo being 'on my side' had helped me much thus far.

I wanted to think that Leo had my back, at least a tiny bit, even if he wasn't able to come right out and say that we were friends. I wanted to get Leo alone to ask him the questions burning through my brain. To find out why he acted like he cared about me via text but was also happy to sleep with the ringleader of my bullies and let her set the entire school on me. It didn't add up, and it wasn't like I could discuss it with anybody else. Nobody knew that Leo and I were in contact with each other.

'Leo's on our side. He can't stand this piece of shit either,' Oralie piped up, shaking her head at Griff.

Now, I was even more confused than normal, and fuck, I hated feeling confused. It was one of my biggest pet hates in life. Anything that made me feel stupid was something I typically avoided.

'Come on, New Girl, let's go get you another uniform,' Griff said over his shoulder as he walked away from the scene. I followed Griff quickly, getting away from the girls, who looked as if they were out for my blood.

Griff knew everything about Hawthorn. Literally, Griff seemed to know every secret and every staff member.

'How come you know everything there is to know here?' I asked, my voice shaking as I tried to keep my focus ahead of me and not behind where I could still feel the glare of the girls' stares.

'It always makes sense to know as much as you can about a place like this.'

Which I guess made sense, even if it was a little cryptic.

Ever since he was eleven, Griff had been a student at the academy, and I could totally imagine the three boys learning all they could in order to survive. Leo's dad owned the place, so maybe he knew the most, but the other two weren't far behind in knowledge about the inner workings of it all.

You didn't get to rule the school without knowing everything about everyone.

According to Ollie and Griff, they even had dirt on the girls, but they hadn't utilised it yet—or so they said. I couldn't see why they had reason to lie, but a large part of my gut didn't trust them.

They were waiting for the girls to do something really dark, which basically meant they needed to succeed in killing me because they'd already drugged and nearly drowned me, and the boys had done fuck all about it. I didn't *want* to doubt them or be that annoying girl who asked too many questions, but something didn't add up.

Actually, something fucking reeked.

Something besides me and the blue raspberry slush I wore.

SOMETHING WAS PLAYING on my mind, and the more I thought about it, the more I couldn't hold it in anymore.

Clover and I were in our room, both studying and getting on with our homework, but I had to tell her the thing sitting on the tip of my tongue.

I still hadn't told her about what happened between Ollie and me after the gala. No matter how much Clo disliked Ollie, I still wanted to share it with her. Best friends didn't always need to like, or agree with, each other's decisions, but they needed to be supportive and understanding, regardless. I just hoped that when I told her, she didn't stab me with her pencil or something drastic.

'Clo,' I called across the room, louder than necessary, but once I knew I was going to tell her, I needed to just spit it out. But when she looked at me, I wanted to pussy out and keep quiet. What if she judged me too hard? My only other option was to talk to Griff about it, and no matter how great he was, I didn't want to talk about sex with him. Maybe Ollie had already told him. After that kiss in the library, Griff knew by the next period, so it would make sense for Griff to know already.

My mind wandered off... Clo harshly called my name to grab my attention.

'Earth to Skylar!'

'Huh?'

'You said my name, then stared off into the distance. You okay?' she asked. I could tell she was worried about my mental state because she'd moved over and sat down next to me on my bed. She knew I wasn't a huge hugger but risked my wrath anyway by entering my personal bubble, wrapping her arm around my shoulder, tucking me closer to her body.

'Right, I did do that,' I mumbled. I took a deep breath, preparing myself to tell her.

The moment she felt me take in the deep breath, something clicked in her mind. I looked at her as her face soured, almost crumbling into itself, and the look of disgust hit me hard in the gut.

'Please,' she begged, shaking her head. She took in a deep breath to match mine. 'Seriously, Sky, please don't tell me you fucked that arsehole?'

'I can safely say I didn't fuck any arsehole.' I went with humour—and deflection. *Sue me.*

'Fuck off, you absolute comedienne.' I could tell she wanted to stay stern, but her face cracked a little. 'You know what I bloody meant.'

'C'mon. I am kinda funny.' I nudged her with my elbow, on purpose digging into her rib a little more than necessary. I was feeling aggressive towards her, so an elbow dig seemed perfectly adequate.

'Yeah, funny-looking for sure,' she said, and I nudged her harder. 'Ow!'

'Stop being a bitch,' I told her.

'Stop trying to tell me shit I don't want to hear then.'

The gigantic sigh I made in response was so loud, I bet everyone on the school grounds heard it.

'Do not sigh at me,' she reprimanded with a wagging

finger. 'I'm trying to look out for you, but, girl, you are not making this easy for me.'

'Should I? You've not made getting to know you easy for me.'

'Touché.'

We both started laughing before we lay down on our backs and got comfortable.

'I know I sound like a massive dick ninety-nine percent of the time, Sky, but I promise you that I'm looking out for you. I know what they're capable of.'

'I get that but just try to be a *little* happier for me.'

'I'll try,' she huffed. 'So, spit it out then.'

'Fine.' I took another deep breath. 'I slept with Ollie.'

'Beside him or…'

I could tell by the naughty glint in Clo's eye that she was trying to make me say the words out loud.

'Fine,' I said, covering my face with my hands, thinking that would make it easier to say the next part. 'I had sex with Ollie after the gala.'

'I knew it!' she exclaimed, almost poking me in the eye with her finger. 'I knew you were acting differently. I mean, it was a toss-up between that or, you know, the whole Olivia being found dead thing.'

'Wow, Clo, didn't know you were so sensitive.'

'Piss off. I know you know what I mean,' she said, and I smiled at her.

It was something we said a lot to one another. To the point that in texts with one another we'd shortened it to IKYKWIM, and both saved it as a shortcut on our keyboards. It was that thing we said that solidified our friendship in my mind.

'I get you. But yeah, Olivia definitely threw me for a loop.'

Then I registered the rest of her sentence. 'What do you mean I've been acting differently?'

'Honestly, I can't explain it. It felt like you were avoiding me, so subconsciously maybe you were without meaning to.'

'I guess I could've been without knowing it...'

'It's all good,' she said, setting me at east. 'I want all the juicy deets.'

'Do you actually?' I asked, sceptical.

'Of course. I may not like the boy, but you're my best friend. Course I wanna know everything!' Getting comfortable, she crossed her legs and leaned forward a little.

'Well, I'm not sure what to say, actually.' I was at a loss, and I felt a tad bit embarrassed just talking openly about it with her. It had been hard enough to spit out I was no longer a virgin. 'It was good.'

'Just good?' Clo looked at me with one raised eyebrow, pity filling her gaze.

'More than good,' I said with a laugh. 'Finding words is hard.'

'That sentence was shocking! You're meant to be the English student out of us.'

'Meant to be? I *am* the English student out of us,' I said. I picked up the closest pillow and threw it at her, but she dodged it. 'I don't know, Clo. It was really, really good. Like, orgasm on the first try, good.'

'Whoa. Now that *is* good!' She actually looked impressed for a moment. Then remembered it was Ollie we were talking about and caught herself. 'I'm surprised he knew how.'

'Oh, ha-ha. Hilarious.'

'You know I am. Seriously, though. No regrets?'

'No regrets.' I shook my head emphatically. 'At. All.'

'I'm glad then,' she said and leaned over to hug me briefly, and I was happy that she hadn't made me feel shitty about my decision. 'Happy for you, girl.'

'Thanks,' I said, unsure if she meant it fully, but I was happy that she'd said it, even if it was pretend. 'The timing felt right.'

'As long as you're okay with it, then shit, it doesn't matter what anybody else thinks. I've got your back.'

For the rest of the evening, the two of us spent our time gossiping about students, teachers, and celebrities. The whole time, though, I wished I'd felt comfortable asking her for more in-depth sex knowledge. It wasn't like Clo wouldn't tell me shit and be honest with me; it was more me not wanting to rub in my relationship with Ollie more than necessary. I knew she wasn't jealous of *him*. Actually, most of the time I thought she was plotting his demise. However, I knew she *was* jealous of Odette, no matter how many times she'd said otherwise. When she thought nobody was looking, she'd glance in Leo and Odette's direction, trying to watch them unnoticed. Leo would turn to look back at her, but he'd always find her looking at anything but them. Being an outsider, I could see it all happening. Even if the two of them thought it was secretive.

I'd given up asking at this point. She clearly wouldn't tell me anything, and I wasn't in that place with Leo where I could ask him deeply personal shit.

Oh, well. If they wanted to keep shit to themselves, then I wasn't getting involved.

Even if I wanted to.

Thirty-Two

VALENTINE'S DAY.

The first one in my life where I actually had a boyfriend. Somebody to spend the day with—well, actually the weekend with. I was beyond excited. I tried to keep my full excitement to myself, though, as I knew Clover was feeling a little sore on the subject. Especially now that Leo and Odette were official. Whenever I brought Leo up in conversation, though, all Clo said was, 'Leave it, Sky. I don't care who *it* fucks, but I do hope his dick falls off.'

Nice to know how she really felt.

But before I could celebrate with Ollie, I had to get through the school day first. Putting on my uniform before heading to breakfast, I made an extra effort with my hair and makeup—more than usual, anyway. I'd never been so happy to attend an upper school that had a uniform. I had anxiety just thinking of the anxiety I would have if I had to pick out my outfit every single morning. I struggled enough as it was picking out clothes to wear at the weekend, or after school.

Clover hadn't got out of bed yet. She hadn't even stirred. Come to think of it, her *many* alarms hadn't gone off. I left it as late as I could before trying to wake her.

'Clo,' I called across the room, but when that seemed to make no difference, I approached her bed and leant down to her. I softly shook her shoulder, hoping not to shock her too much.

'Fuck!' she startled and bolted upright—hitting my nose with her head in the process.

'Fuck!' I exclaimed as I tried to stop my vision from seeing multiple Clovers. My nose was gushing blood in an instant, and I ran to the kitchenette to grab some tissue. Of all the days, I did *not* need Ollie to come get me for breakfast and find me looking like the victim of a crime.

'I am so, so sorry, Sky! Shit! I know how much you've been looking forward to today,' she apologised, breathless.

'It's okay, really. It's not like you meant to do it.' I tried to smile, but it was hard to do while holding the tissue against my nose. I only had the one clean school shirt—something that was starting to become an issue of mine.

At that exact moment there came a hard knock on our door, followed by three quick raps. It was a code Griff had made up so we'd always know when it was him at our door, and Ollie had adopted it. I rolled my eyes, knowing we would have to explain the shit that had just transpired. I knew Ollie only put up with Clover's presence because of my friendship with her, and I seriously didn't want to give him any more reason to dislike her.

I opened the door to find Ollie leaning up against the frame, holding a massive share size bag of crisps and an even larger bag of chocolates. On seeing me, he smiled, but his face faltered when he took in the state I was in.

'What the fuck?' he asked as he launched himself into the room, slamming the door behind him.

I knew he'd closed the door so nobody in the corridor could

look in and spy, but it made me feel wary nonetheless. Clover didn't hurt me on purpose, but knowing Ollie the way I did, he wouldn't see it that way.

Arms surrounded me again, pulling me into a hug I never wanted to end. My mind was moving a mile a minute, so I hadn't realised that Ollie and Clover had continued talking. Actually, they were *shouting*.

'I didn't mean to do it, *Oliver*. Sky was leaning over me to wake me up and she scared the shit out of me. It was a knee-jerk reaction. Nothing more to it.'

I could tell by the look on Clo's face and the shade of red it was turning that it wasn't the first time she'd told him what happened. I knew I needed to get involved and stick up for Clover. It really had been an accident.

'Oh, so this has nothing to do with the fact that today is Valentine's Day and that you didn't set your alarms because you were hoping to skip this day entirely? Nothing to do with last year or Leo?' Ollie's chest vibrated as he spoke, the sensation causing me to try and loosen the hug so I could look at Clover, but he just tightened his grip on me. His fingertips pressed into my skin hard. I winced, sure he was leaving marks on my skin.

'You think you know everything, don't you? People like you make me fucking sick,' she spat, livid that he'd mentioned the L word.

'You just want Sky all to yourself. You know that you have no fucking chance of making any other friends in your pathetic fucking life, so you want to latch on to my girlfriend,' Ollie said, his anger growing with every word. 'I won't let you take her down with you.'

'Take her down with *me*? God,' she scoffed, rolling her eyes.

'You're actually delusional! Tell me you're hearing this shit, Sky?'

I broke free from Ollie's hold and looked at Clover. Her green eyes were filled with unshed tears and I knew the dam could burst at any moment. I also knew she would hate herself if it happened in front of Ollie.

'Babe, I'll meet you outside in two minutes, okay?' I said to Ollie, knowing I needed to get him gone before Clo broke, whether he got pissed at me or not. I didn't want him to think I was choosing Clover over him, but I also needed to let him know that she was my best friend and I wasn't gonna stop caring about her just because she hurt my nose that wasn't even bleeding anymore. It wasn't like she'd broken it or even caused me to need a change of clothes. Accidents happened— Ollie should know that better than anyone.

'Fine,' he spat, 'but you better not take too long, Sky. I won't be waiting out there like a dick forever.'

I sighed, biting my tongue. He was a prick, and I for sure would make my ire known to him later in the evening, but for the moment, I knew it wasn't worth responding to.

'I'll be two minutes, tops,' I said, standing on my tiptoes to kiss his cheek to placate him. He nodded, and after sending another filthy look Clover's way, he put down the bags of food he was still holding and left the room, letting the door slam behind him. The force of the door slamming closed caused a shock wave of sound to emanate throughout the room.

Clover faced me, a look of pity on her face.

'Do you get it now, Sky? Can you see even slightly where I'm coming from?' she asked, her voice small but her words sure.

'I mean...' I trailed off. I could see Clover's point of view, but I also slightly understood where Ollie was coming from, too. Clo had a lot of internal anger for Leo and, by proxy, Ollie. The two of them weren't ever going to be friends, but I hated that I was being lumped in the middle of their feud. 'I get you. Can you also slightly see where he's coming from, though?'

'Sorry,' she said with scorn. 'But are you asking me if I agree that I'm trying to take you down with me?' Her anger was palpable. It tasted all burnt and bitter. 'Why are you so determined to fuck up our friendship and choose his side?'

'There aren't any sides here, Clo. I just want my best friend and my boyfriend to get along. So please, do me a small favour and just be civil for now. It's Valentine's Day. Please,' I pleaded. I'd never had a best friend or a boyfriend, and I just wanted both of them to get along.

'I'll try for now, but I swear to you, Skylar, if I find out he's playing you in any way, shape, or form, I will do everything I can to make you see the truth.'

I nodded. I didn't think he was hiding shit from me, but I could tell Clo thought he was.

'Go. Enjoy your weekend,' she said and hugged me, then made a shooing motion. I left the room quickly, knowing that Ollie was still waiting on the other side of the door for me. I reckoned he was probably five seconds away from busting through the door with impatience.

After the weekend was over, I was going to sit down and weigh up just what Clover had told me. I wanted to believe that I trusted my own judgement, but honestly, I was so out of my league here.

And that was what unsettled me most.

Thirty-Three

THE DAY MOVED FAST and the next thing I knew, we were in London eating at a fancy restaurant I'd never heard of.

Everybody had left me alone at school. It was a pleasant surprise seeing as I'd totally expected some kind of Valentine's Day prank. *The Sect* issued some kind of warning on the Hive to leave me alone, but I was surprised people had listened. I hadn't actually read the warning as I didn't want to read the hateful comments that would accompany it, but Clover had told me the gist of it the night before. It was the first time there'd been a *Sect* sanctioned pause.

I felt bad all day about what had happened between Ollie and Clover that morning, but if I was being honest with myself, it had been brewing for some time, always lurking underneath the surface. No matter how many times he'd tried to prove himself as worthy, she'd found a reason why he must be false.

And I meant what I said to myself. After the weekend, I would think through everything, not letting either of them cloud my opinion.

My mind came back to the restaurant, and I glanced across at Ollie, who was looking down at the plate in front of him.

Every few minutes, I nearly pinched myself, wondering how my life had changed so much in such a short period of time. I didn't know what I'd done in a past life, but clearly something was starting to go right for me.

The two of us had a full, packed schedule for the weekend before returning to school, and it all felt so surreal. We'd checked into the hotel under Leo's name, something to do with the age you had to be to book a room, and I didn't question it. Although I was pretty certain that if they'd thrown enough money around, that wouldn't have mattered at all. One thing I'd learned from these guys and those at the academy was that if you had enough money to waste, people would do literally anything for you. Even if they didn't want to.

I reckoned Ollie actually enjoyed the secretive nature of the arrangement—and really, so did I. It felt sordid, in the very best way.

'Quick question. Why do fancy restaurants have so many pieces of cutlery?' I asked him, staring down at the large plate of food in front of me. I knew that it wasn't a very original question, but seriously, a fork's a fork, right? Like, who really needed that much cutlery for one meal?

'Pretty sure it's another way to make the little people feel little.' Ollie smirked, not realising that he'd lumped me in with the 'little people' he was mocking.

'Right...' I mumbled. I smiled half-heartedly, taking in the surrounding scenery. I was glad I'd been dining in the dining room at Hawthorn for the last few months. Otherwise, I'd have been even more star-struck with how fancy the place looked. Although the restaurant was more sleek and modern—no dark, ornate, wooden panels in sight.

Ollie's cutlery clattered as it landed on his plate. Lips

pursed and eyebrows narrowed, I could tell that something had irritated him. Specifically, that *I* had irritated him.

'What's the matter?' he asked, his eyes hard; the spark that had been there a moment ago fading, about to disappear entirely. 'Tell me.'

'N-nothing,' I said, using the universal code girls used to signify that they were not okay but wanted you to try harder to get a real response.

'I'm not doing this shit, Sky. Tell me. Now.' He slammed his hand down on the table, causing me to jump and the plates and glasses to clink. His rage had come out of nowhere.

'I just don't like being considered a *little* person. It's different for you. You grew up with money.' I shook my head at him, not wanting to get into it here. We'd been having such a great time together. It was our first time out of school with nobody else there, and I wanted to enjoy it to the fullest. Not argue over something silly. Christmas had been good, and we'd spent some time alone, but the others were always down the hall, or at least somewhere close by in the house. 'I didn't have a lot growing up. At all. Fuck, before I got the scholarship here, I worked my butt off trying to keep food on the table.'

'Not like you had to do that, Skylar,' he drawled, his cavalier attitude pissing me off. Dismissing what I said without even fully processing it. 'Cora could have got a job.'

A laugh came out of me, so loud that the people sitting at the tables nearby turned their heads to look in our direction. I hated that he was talking about my mum as if he knew her better than I did. As if she would have gone and got a job if I'd simply told her to. *Yeah, right...*

'Cora does nothing she doesn't have to. Trust me on that.'

'Andy should have found work, then. Been the man of the

house,' he said with a shrug, choosing to ignore my tone and continuing to pursue the conversation. *Silly boy.*

'Sorry, but did you meet the same people that I know? Can you even hear yourself right now?' I asked, disbelieving. I'd stopped eating too, but, unlike Ollie, I'd put my cutlery down gently. Everything I was hearing out of his mouth right now was honest bullshit.

Pure and utter bullshit.

'You could have refused to work. Forced their hands.'

'What and not eat?' I rolled my eyes at his ignorance. 'K.'

I couldn't with him. If I continued talking to him, I'd get mad, and it'd ruin our weekend before it had even begun. I picked up my cutlery and continued eating, ignoring him. The two of us ate in an awkward silence.

Ten of the most uncomfortable minutes of my life passed. Then finally, Ollie looked up from his empty plate.

'Sorry,' he mumbled, so quiet that I only just caught it. I was going to make him sweat a little, though. No way was I just taking his piss-poor sorry at face value.

'Can you hear somebody talking?' I asked the empty space, acting childish but fully aware of it. 'Or was it the wind?'

'Oh, ha-ha, you twat,' he said. He was smiling at me, though, so I knew he didn't actually mean it. 'I'm sorry, okay? What I said was out of order.' He had a sheepish look on his face, and I knew he was replaying his words in his head and hearing them from my perspective. Or at least that was what I assumed he was doing. I mean, that was what he should have been doing.

'I'm going to accept your apology. I mean, it mostly sounded sincere,' I joked, smiling at him close-mouthed while twisting my hair around my finger. It was an attempt at flirting, but I wasn't sure I was doing an outstanding job of it.

Ollie's expression was one of bemusement, as if he wasn't sure whether I was flirting and trying to be sexy, or whether I was just constipated.

I stopped my attempt and then promptly burst into laughter. Fuck me, was there anybody more awkward on their first Valentine's Day date than me? I knew we'd been dating for a while now, but the whole weekend felt serious. Real.

We went back to sitting in silence, but it was a comfortable one. The silence you could enjoy with somebody you shared a bond with.

For dessert, I chose a simple basic bitch option of raspberry sorbet. I'd never really been that into sweet food—chocolate and cake just weren't my thing. When I'd first told Clover, she'd looked at me as if I had three heads. She was incredulous and ever since had forced me to try everything she baked in class in order to convert me. Turned out, there wasn't too much left for me to try and nothing so far had made me fall in love. At one point, she was so offended, I thought it'd come in between our friendship. Even more than my relationship with Ollie had already come between us.

Ollie clearly had no qualms about eating what they called *a proper dessert*. He'd got this real fancy look pie tart thing—at least I *thought* it was a tart. Either way, he seemed to enjoy it.

Good for him.

THE CAR PULLED up at the front of our rather posh hotel and I waited for Ollie to get out first and open my door for me. Every time he did something chivalrous, I swooned inside. He could be a dick, a proper beast, but then he'd melt me by acting like a real prince.

Or maybe I just had *really* low expectations.

I followed him to our room, still high from the show we saw and the evening we'd had. There was something about him that just made me happy whenever I was around him.

Did I question his intentions still?

Sure.

And it may be stupid of me, but I wanted to be his girl-friend, even with the doubts swimming through my mind.

On entering the dark suite, I instantly gravitated towards the large floor-to-ceiling glass windows that looked out onto the London skyline. I loved London at night. Ever since I was young, I'd loved the story of Peter Pan. The boy who never grew up. A story filled with adventure, pirates, mermaids, and fairies. Who the fuck didn't dream of that? I used to fall asleep wondering what it would be like to fly high above London, to look down and see tiny cars the size of ants, people barely a speck, if visible at all. Looking down on it all, rising above the little people—rising above the position life had handed you. *Shit. Now I sound like Ollie.*

He came up behind me on silent feet to wrap his arms around my waist. I transferred my weight back into him, using him as my support, in more ways than one.

'It looks beautiful like this,' I whispered. The darkness surrounding us was in contrast to the brightness of the world outside. I'd never been a city girl. Never wanted to live or work in the city. But damn, I would consider changing my mind if I could look out at such a beautiful view every night. The view was everything to the dreamer inside of me. To the girl who lived with her nose stuck in a book, the Belle of her own story.

'My view's beautiful,' Ollie whispered, leaning down to

brush his mouth against my ear. His breath caused shivers to cover me from head to toe with goosebumps.

Heat rushed through me and my stomach filled with jitters at his words.

Was it a line? Of course.

Did it work? *Of fucking course.*

'Have you ever thought of what it would be like to fly over a view like this?' I asked, my words the only noise in the large, minimalistic room.

'What, like on a plane?' Ollie asked, confusion mingling with his sultry voice. 'I know what that's like.'

'I guess,' I replied quietly, feeling stupid for asking the question. Of course he'd seen the city from above on a plane. He'd lived a much different life than the one I'd known. 'I've never been on one.'

'Never been on a plane?' he asked, the surprise in his tone a little insulting.

'Nope. Mum wasn't big on taking trips when I was growing up. Not ones that would cost a fortune outside of the country, anyway. If you couldn't drive there within five hours, then we didn't go, and even that was a push.'

When I was younger, I'd always been so jealous of the girls at school who would come back after the holidays with a tan and braided hair. It seemed so exotic to seven-year-old me. My mum drove us to Calais once, but only because she could get cheaper cigarettes over the French border than she could at home. We were in France for a grand total of six hours, tops.

'Maybe one day I'll get to take you on one,' Ollie murmured, and when I turned in his arms to look at his face, I caught him deep in thought. His light blue eyes glazed over, like he wasn't in the room with me, but was instead some-where else entirely. He did that often, and at first, it had worried me, wondering where his mind went, but now I let it happen without comment.

He'd come back to me.

He always did.

'Let's go to bed,' Ollie whispered, his eyes glistening with an emotion I couldn't place as he took my small hand in his larger one. We moved towards the largest bed I'd ever seen, the sheets a luxurious cotton that beckoned me in. It was beyond anything I'd experienced before, and as much as I didn't want to, I felt small and unsure.

Gently, Ollie let go of my hand to remove his clothes, one item at a time, as I sat on the edge of the bed, staring up at him in awe. No matter how many times I saw him, I couldn't help looking at him like it was the first time. His broad shoulders, his taut stomach, every single part of him turned me on. Every time I looked at him, I forgot we were the same age because he looked older than me. More experienced and otherworldly.

Excited for his touch, I lay down in anticipation, my dress rising up and resting on my thighs. Before I could get comfortable, Ollie gripped my hand once again and pulled me back to sitting. Naked, he was standing directly in front of me and my eyes rested on his dick. I licked my lips and grazed my bottom lip with my teeth, a small smile curling the corners of my mouth.

I took his hard length in my hand, barely able to wrap it around fully, and it twitched in my grasp. Licking the tip, I tasted his salty pre-cum, instantly wanting more. The moan that left his mouth filled me with warmth, proud I had such an effect on him, as his eyes filled with want when he looked down at me. I opened my mouth, and he slid his cock inside. I felt hesitant at first, but his reactions helped me shed the nerves, a buzzing feeling sitting low in my stomach.

'Fuck,' he said, his voice thick, causing the hairs on my body to stand on end.

I let go completely, his praise spurring me on as I stretched my mouth wider, drawing him in and to the back of my throat, sucking and licking my way up and down his length in a slow, rhythmic motion.

He reached for me, his fingers feathering up my arms until they stopped at my neck. The brush of his thumb on my bottom lip caused a chill to trickle down to my toes and I closed my eyes, the sensations overwhelming me.

'Open your eyes,' Ollie demanded.

I opened them instantly, wanting to see his face. His dark indigo eyes were locked on mine, boring into my soul. My heart beat in an unnatural pattern, getting faster with every inhale. My entire body was growing hotter from his stare.

I need him. Now.

As if he could hear my thoughts, he slid from my mouth with a light popping sound, knocking my confidence, but then he pushed me down onto the bed, holding me there with his strength, his body moulding to mine.

'I need my cum inside you,' he whispered, his tone rasping. He kissed me slow and deep. 'But not here.'

Ollie kissed me again, bruising me as his hand reached between us to travel under my skirt.

My back arched involuntarily off the mattress as his large hand palmed me through my underwear.

'I need to feel you here,' he murmured, giving one last long kiss to my neck as his knuckles ran along my slit. 'So fucking wet.'

I writhed under his touch, whispering, 'P-please,' even though I didn't know what I was asking for.

Without hesitating, Ollie lifted himself off my body,

grasped my legs to align himself, then slowly moved my underwear to the side to allow himself the access he needed.

In one slow movement, he filled me to the hilt. Our bodies trembled with desire and his forehead came down to rest on mine. The action was tender, almost *too* tender.

He stayed there, quiet, for the longest time.

The two of us silent, no words between us, our connection saying all that was necessary. The darkness of the room created an intimate vibe. Nobody could see us.

The intimacy overwhelmed me, the silence deafening. I broke it with a whisper. 'I need more.'

I pulled his lips to mine, and I sucked on his bottom lip, a tease of teeth making little bites.

He pushed up on his arms to take me in, to look me in the eye, and I saw apprehension lying underneath the surface of his. I swallowed, my nerves threatening to stop this beautiful moment.

With his lips slightly parted, his hand trailed down the centre of my chest. His smile tugged on the corner of his lips as he bunched up the material of my dress, as if he needed it gone. Needed to see me bare to him; see where the two of us joined as one. No barrier between us.

Ollie took his time, lazily thrusting into me until we were both breathless and fixated on only each other, racing for the release we both chased.

'Shit.' The muscles in his broad chest seemed to coil tight, his chin dropping as his hand grasped my hips, pulling me to him with urgency. They held me in place, tight, desperate, as if scared I'd fly away from his grasp.

A tortured growl vibrated from his throat.

'Come with me,' he demanded.

The pad of his thumb found my clit, teasing it in slow,

pressured circles and sending me into a frenzy as my body fought for release.

'Oh my God,' I panted, almost at the peak.

My walls suffocated him, clenching and unclenching, as my body tumbled over the edge, over the precipice, and into the best kind of ecstasy, and he came willingly with me.

Our eyes locked. Ollie's blue stare filled with hunger, yet also with wonder.

I smiled softly at him, the only words on the tip of my tongue ones I wouldn't voice out loud. Couldn't voice out loud.

I think I'm falling for you.

Thirty-Four

MONDAY MORNING CAME, and I was still on a major high from my trip with Ollie. We'd had such a wonderful time, and even though I'd told myself I was going to sit down and weigh up Clover's worries once I got back, the weekend made me not want to. After the wonderful time we'd had together, nothing negative was going to compute in my brain for a while. My brain was basically mush when it came to thoughts of Ollie. It was a heart-shaped pile of squidgy matter, and I was a sucker for letting it happen. Since day one, Clover had warned me against the boys and there I was in a relation-ship with one of them.

Spending time together over the weekend without the distraction of school and other people was exactly what our relationship needed. Every day, I fell a little more in love with him. I couldn't stop the train even if I tried—and believe me, I'd tried. Not like I was going to tell him how I felt, though. I didn't want to scare him off, and I knew without a doubt he wasn't ready to hear it. Nobody liked the clingy girl who gushed her feelings too fast.

'Ready to get this shit show on the road?' Clover asked me as we left breakfast, Griff and Ollie trailing along behind us.

They were in deep discussion about something swim team related—honestly, I tried to keep up with them, but I had no clue about any of it.

The four of us were heading to an entire school mandatory assembly. I had seen little of Ms Hawthorn as of late, and no part of me felt upset by that. Every now and again I'd see her in the hallway up ahead, but when that happened, either Griff or Ollie would purposefully lead us in a different direction. Pretty sure they were avoiding her more than I was.

'Any idea what it could be about?' I asked.

'Probably announcing the annual charity fundraiser. Takes place at the end of the Easter term every year,' Clo answered, matter-of-fact.

'Who decides what the fundraiser is?'

'*The Set*. But everybody in the upper two years has to take part in some capacity. Last year it was a silent auction ball that I could hide away during while working in the cloakroom.'

'Fingers crossed for us that we're able to hide away this year,' I said. We locked our arms together, only breaking apart when we reached the hall.

Ollie dropped into the seat next to me on one side and Griff the other. I'd grown quite fond of being in the middle of an Ollie and Griff sandwich. The jealous stares started the moment we sat down—girls of every age giving me the evil eye. *Petty much.*

As usual, the hall was full of chatter until Ms Hawthorn appeared on the stage and then all talking ceased. Just like that. Her mere presence had an effect on everybody and more than once, I'd wondered how she had the school so under her control. Nobody wanted to get on her bad side.

'Quiet now,' Ms Hawthorn said once she'd reached centre stage, even though you could have heard a pin drop in the auditorium and her words were unnecessary. She had always hit me as somebody who took a thrill out of being in control. 'I have gathered you all here today to discuss the end of term charity effort this year.'

I wondered if Ollie knew what it was going to be. Surely if it was decided by *The Set*, the boys would have some clue of what it was. However, when I'd asked, he'd changed the subject.

'This year, boys and girls, we shall put on a charity fashion show for the school charity.'

The room erupted into noise all at once. Instantly, groaning came from the older years, and the younger years cheered and laughed as if this was one of the best outcomes.

I looked behind me to catch Clover's eye. I found her sitting a couple of rows behind me with Leo and Odette next to her. She looked back at me; her face livid, her brows furrowed in anger, and the straight line of her mouth told me just how pissed off she was.

'Settle down, children. Settle down,' Ms Hawthorn spoke softly, but her words cut through the noise regardless. 'The students of the upper years will be organising and modelling in the show. Odette Aston has the list of assigned roles. The Hive will have a copy of the list too, so make sure you are aware of what we expect of you.'

Her gaze found mine, and I swore her facial expression became even more severe, like her grey eyes were looking into my soul, or maybe attempting to poke around in my grey matter somehow.

'That will be all for today. In rows, you are to depart the auditorium quietly and in single file. Make haste to your first period.'

With that last sentence, Ms Hawthorn took a step away

from the microphone and stayed there. As each row slowly left the hall, I saw her assessing everybody. I had a feeling that nothing happened at *her* school without her knowing about it. Meaning she knew about my multiple attacks and hadn't once called me into her office about any of them. Not sure why it was only hitting me as odd now; but fuck me, that was odd. She'd called me in about the video after Parents' Day, but really, that had been a tactic to pacify the parents who had witnessed it and nothing more.

I found myself lost in thought, leaving the room in silence with Griff and Ollie beside me, and it was only when we entered the hallway again and Griff spoke that I came out of my trance.

'Reckon they'll ask me to model underwear?' he joked, wagging his eyebrows comically. 'Everybody needs to see this package, right?'

Ollie and I chuckled at him. *Honestly, this boy.* I could never decide whether he was playing around or if a part of him slightly believed his own hype. He flirted with everybody—and I mean *everybody*. I'd never seen him with anybody outside of our group, either. Even at the parties we'd been to, he'd stuck by Clover's and my sides throughout.

His words settled into my brain, trickling in at a slow pace. I sputtered, 'S-sorry, they could ask us to model underwear?' I could hear the incredulity in my tone, my shock radiating through me in stages. We were sixteen, for fuck's sake. Well, the upper years were aged from sixteen to eighteen, but only people with an early birthday in year thirteen were actually eighteen. Respectable institution, my arse. They constantly sold that vision to the people shedding out the big bucks, but clearly, they were full of shit.

'Potentially. I mean, Odette and her cronies set this up,

remember? They'd love to show off their figures in front of a large crowd,' Griff said, turning to face me.

'How large of a crowd?' I asked, swallowing down my anxiety. The cogs started to turn in Griff's head, as he tried to come up with a suitable answer that would placate me.

'A couple of hundred, I guess? It depends. Last year's silent auction ball had a large audience—you know how much rich people love flaunting their wealth. They were all fighting to outdo one another. The year before, though, was boring and barely any parents attended.'

'What was it?' I asked, curious.

'Honestly, it was so shit, I can't even remember. But I will say, the elite love to appear benevolent. Even if they couldn't give any fucks in actuality,' he said, shrugging.

'Right...' My sentence hung in the air, and I felt none the wiser about any of it.

Clover came and joined us, having finally fought her way out of the hall and through the masses of younger years, all congregating together to discuss the news.

'Girl, you are not gonna like this.' Clover fidgeted, rubbing her hands on her thighs, clearly agitated.

Well, shit. That sounded foreboding.

'Stop with the dramatics. Some of us have places to be,' Ollie said, assessing her. His eyes narrowed—the way you'd look at shit on your shoe.

The two of them still weren't on the best of terms, and to be honest, I was over it. If they wanted to act like bloody children, then I wouldn't stop them.

'Go on, Lady Luck, don't keep us in suspense,' Griff said, playing with Clo's hair, wrapping a strand around his fingers and twirling.

'Right. So, I got waylaid by dickface and ogre number one

as they just wouldn't leave the row and they weren't letting me pass. Odette had her list of roles, ready to bark at anyone who wanted to listen. I found out what's "expected of us".'

I giggled at her choice of words.

'And...?' I tried my best not to roll my eyes at her, but she was dragging it all out a little longer than she needed to. The suspense clearly gave her a thrill.

'And we've been assigned to model in the show!' She ended her sentence with a big flourish, both arms raised above her head before flopping down; all heavy and full of purpose.

'W-we what?' I screeched, causing everybody near us in the hallway to turn and look in our direction. I always seemed to draw attention, and not always in a good way. 'We have to m-model? Model what?'

I started hyperventilating, feeling the onset of a mini panic attack, and obviously it was at that moment that Odette and Leo finally left the hall and became witnesses to my meltdown. *The Set* had done this shit to me on purpose. The smug look on Odette's face told me as much.

'Whatever the coordinators decide you'll look best in,' Odette said as she gave me a snotty look from head to toe. 'But let's be honest, New Girl, I highly doubt they'll find anything that will look good on your boxy frame.'

Yep. I resemble a box because I'm not stick thin with my ribs showing. Nice one, Odette.

I didn't say what I was thinking, though. Nope. All I uttered was, 'Oh.'

Nice one, Sky.

'Let's go,' Leo said as he pulled Odette away from us, walking her down the corridor, his grip firm on her arm as they went. When our group started up their conversation again, I looked down the corridor to see Leo looking back at me. He winked, his lips raised into a smirk before the two of them disappeared into a classroom.

'...you won't even help us. Typical. Don't you think he should, Sky?' Clover asked me and I looked back at the group to see Clover staring at me. Griff was looking over my shoulder to where Leo had just been, his features forming a quizzical look, and Ollie was looking rather proud of himself.

'Huh?' I asked, confused about what Clo wanted me to have an answer to. I'd clearly missed something while Leo held my attention and winked at me.

'Ollie should intervene with *The Set* and put us on cloak-room duty.'

'Err...'

Did I think that? I knew that was what Clover wanted me to think—to agree with her wholeheartedly and hope that we could get out of this shit pile we'd somehow landed in. But I wasn't so sure. The tradition *was* for the girls to organise the charity effort, and I wasn't going to make myself even more hated by trying to mess with tradition.

Rich people took that shit seriously.

Fuck, my mum took tradition seriously, and she lived in a house paid for by benefits—benefits I felt pretty certain they'd swindled, or outright lied, to obtain. Got to love Cora.

Plus, *The Set* wanted me to model for a reason, and I wasn't the kind of person to back down when challenged.

'Oh, for fuck's sake, Skylar. You really are turning into a pathetic, desperate whore, you realise that?' Clover said, derision filling her face. Her features twisted, her whole face contorting in a grotesque manner, and my stomach bottomed out. She'd never looked at me with such scorn in the entire time I'd known her.

She stomped away and all I could do was stand there in shock; frozen in place like an ice statue.

She'd also never spoken to me that way before. Never called me names or made me feel irrelevant. Unimportant.

If I was in a cartoon, my jaw would have dropped to the floor like an anvil, exaggerated and comedic.

But this was real life. And no part of what just happened was comedic.

So, I did what any respectable girl would do in my situation: I cried.

Ollie and Griff both stood still, uncomfortable and unsure of the best action to take. A split moment later, Griff hurried away to catch up with Clover, and Ollie hugged me tight to his hard, warm body.

I instantly felt a little better, but then I remembered that Griff had flounced after Clo, and my stomach sank once more.

'She had no right to say that to you,' Ollie whispered in my ear as he moved us into an alcove so we were away from the foot traffic surrounding us. 'And I don't think that you're pathetic or desperate and you are definitely not a whore.' His eyes hardened on the last word, filled with anger at Clover.

He lifted my chin up, tilting my face so he could see me fully, and I gave him a small, tentative smile. Even though he sort of had to say that, being my boyfriend and all, it still made me happy that he did.

Was I slightly pissed at Griff for ditching me to go after Clo? Yes.

According to her, they'd bullied her last year, and she was here on scholarship too, so it wasn't like she'd been friends with them before I came here.

Okay, so maybe I was more than slightly pissed off. I

thought Griff and I were close. Obviously, I'd been blind to the truth.

'Try to forget about her, babe. She's just jealous and bitter and not worth it,' Ollie told me in a calming tone. His hands started rubbing up and down my arms in a soothing, circular motion. It grounded me and although the tears didn't stop, they slowed down. I nodded, mostly to make him feel as if I agreed.

I didn't know if I did, though. I didn't know *how* I was feeling.

'Do you want me to talk to Odette?' he asked, lifting my chin to look into my eyes. 'Because I will if *you* want me to. Clover, of all people, won't force me into it, but I'd do it for you, babe. Believe me, she was trying to save her own arse and not yours like she said.'

I thought about my decision for a minute or two. The two of us were still standing in the alcove, the rest of the hall quiet as pupils moved to their first class of the day.

'Babe, we're going to be late for class,' I told him, but not making any effort to move from his hug. I took a deep, calming breath and said, 'I don't want you to talk to Odette.'

He hugged me tighter, squeezing me to the point that I felt my lungs cry in protest.

'You sure?' he asked as he swept a strand of hair from in front of my face and tucked it behind my ear. Every time he did that, I melted a little more inside.

'Yeah. We don't need to antagonise them more and I can model in the fashion show. How hard can it be?'

Famous last words?

Duh.

Thirty-Five

IT FELT strange not to be on talking terms with Clover. Our room was silent whenever we were both there, and no matter how hard Griff wanted to resolve the issues between us, nothing he'd tried so far had worked.

In my eyes, Clover needed to apologise for what she'd said. It was uncalled for and even if she believed it to be true, I was still fucking insulted she'd put the words out into the universe. She could have continued to think it and I'd have been none the wiser.

'C'mon, Sky, you two need to talk,' Griff implored me as we listened to Mr Sommers drone on about Bentham and Utilitarianism. Okay, I wasn't listening at all. I was in my head thinking about everything and nothing at the same time. My mind stuck in that place where I weighed up my feelings about my friendships and relationships—but also about what pizza toppings I preferred. 'Clo wants to talk to you. I know she does.'

'Not gonna lie to you, Griff, but I'd rather hear that from her. Not once has she tried to talk to me, and we share a fucking room. She's had enough opportunities in the last week.'

I doubted Griff had intended to piss me off, but trust me,

he'd succeeded.

The fact she was trying to use Griff as a go between was such a shitty thing to do. It wasn't fair for him to be in the middle, but also, part of me felt like he'd taken her side anyway and had put himself in the centre of it all. Yeah, he was talking to me while in class, but outside of class, he spent every minute with her.

Shit, they weren't even sitting with Ollie and me at dinner or anything.

'She's worried. She knows she fucked up, New Girl. You've just got to give her the chance to say sorry,' Griff said, sounding worried himself.

'I didn't know she needed me to come to her for an apology,' I snapped, irritated that he couldn't see where I was coming from. 'If she's as sorry as you say, then she could have told me already.'

'I've told her that, but she's worried you hate her.'

'Of course I don't hate her. But I do feel like she's been thinking shit about me behind my back for a while. She meant what she said at the time she said it. She called me a whore, Griff.'

'Yeah, at first, I reckon she meant it. But I know she doesn't *actually* think that of you.'

'Oh, has she told you that then during one of your super secret couple's nights?'

Griff blushed, a sheepish expression on his face, as he faltered in his response.

'It's not like that.' His meadow eyes felt as if they were penetrating my soul, reaching deep inside of me, trying to make things right between us. 'She doesn't feel comfortable around Ollie right now. She's worried he's going to retaliate on your behalf.'

'Eurgh, I am sick of her always trying to paint Ollie as the bad guy. He's done nothing to her all year. She believes you've turned over a new fucking leaf, so why can't he have too?' I raised my voice, causing the other students in the class to turn and look at us. The teacher shook his head at us but continued chatting about ethics. Even if he didn't really talk about it, Griff *was* a part of *The Sect* and that gave him sway, even if he never abused that power.

'I did actually say sorry to her,' he mumbled. Maybe he thought being quiet would make me less mad at the fact that he was obviously criticising Ollie, and probably Leo, too. 'Look, Sky, I don't want to fall out with you, but just know that Clover's coming from a good place. A true place. Ollie hasn't always acted this way...' Griff trailed off, not saying any more, which made me even more curious to get to the bottom of what he meant.

'In what sense?' I asked, hoping he'd give me a little more to go on.

But he didn't. He merely said, 'Just be careful, babycakes. You don't have the full picture.'

'Give me the full picture then,' I demanded, frustrated that he was being so cryptic with me.

He shrugged. 'I would, but it's really not my place, babydoll.'

Honestly, his words and attitude disgusted me.

Babycakes? Babydoll? Is he for real?

'You can be a right wanker. You know that?'

'True, but I'm a wanker with your best interests at heart. Remember that,' he said, his whole demeanour condescending.

I continued to ignore him for the rest of the lesson, as I

hoped my silence would lead to him revealing something to me.

He didn't.

So when the bell rang, I left the classroom as fast as I could, ignoring him calling my name behind me.

On my way to my next lesson, I stopped in an alcove to root through my schoolbag, willing myself to calm down. Griff had raised my temper and I knew I couldn't go to a lesson with the O girls in a foul mood. Who knew what I'd do?

As I moved my hand through my bag, I felt a note sticking out of the top of my history textbook. I pulled it out to figure out what it was and found a simple, handwritten note in Ollie's distinctive scrawl that read:

Meet me outside after third period.

I read it and wondered when he'd put it in there. Was it a repeat of Halloween and a total trap? Maybe, but that note had been typed to disguise the sender.

Or maybe it was Ollie's idea of romance?

Either way, I'd go stand outside after third to find out, and I could always text him if he didn't show.

Heading into English with a spring in my step, I smiled.

How exciting relationship stuff could be.

THE MOMENT my third lesson ended, I rushed outside straight away, barely stopping to take a breath. I wanted to give myself enough time to spot Ollie before lunch. If the note wasn't from today, then I'd know within ten minutes.

'Skylar.' My name sounded like dirt coming out of Odette's mouth. Ever since Olivia had been found with a lock of my hair, I'd worried the girls would escalate, but if anything, they seemed to back off a little. Like they were scared of me, of what I could do to them if they crossed me.

'I'm waiting for Ollie,' I said. Maybe if they knew he was coming soon, they'd bugger off and leave me alone.

'Oh,' Ophelia said, confused, pointing off in the distance. 'I thought I saw him by the tree line a moment ago.'

Right, like I was going to fall for that one. They probably just wanted to get me alone over by the trees. Barely any teachers would be over there, making it a prime spot. They must have been biding their time, waiting for the perfect moment to get me back for harming their friend.

'Thanks. I'll wait for him here,' I said as I got out my phone to text Ollie and find out whether that note was from today. I could also text Leo if shit got out of hand too. I tapped out a quick message while the girls stood and stared at me, their hatred shining on their faces, leaking out into the atmosphere.

HEY, BABY, DID YOU WANT ME TO MEET YOU NOW?

It wasn't long until I got a reply from him.

YEAH, I'LL BE THERE SOON. JUST SETTING UP.

I wondered what he meant by setting up. It being lunch time, maybe he'd sorted some kind of picnic out. That'd be quite cute—sexy and romantic, too. I'd always wanted somebody to care about me and make me cute sandwiches and shit.

'He'll be here in a m-moment,' I told them. Not sure why I felt the need to fill them in, but apparently I wanted to prove something to them. And yeah, I wanted to rub it in a little. Okay. A lot. After all, Ollie had picked *me*. Not one of them, with their over-bleached hair and their obviously enhanced features. But plain old curvy me.

I was frustrated with myself too, though. I'd been doing so well at controlling my stutter and not letting it control me, and then *The Set* came along and fucked it up. My anxiety still lived underneath the surface, lurking in the dark, but I had found it easier to breathe recently.

'Eurgh, I thought you'd got rid of that fucking horrible stutter,' said Oralie, fake shivering. 'You could have been one of us, New Girl, if you weren't such a poor fucking freak.'

I made a big deal of rolling my eyes. Even their insults weren't hitting the mark the way they usually did. Maybe it was my newfound confidence guiding me. Or maybe I'd realised that they were just insecure rich bitches who had no real power over me.

'If you'll excuse me,' I sassed, walking away from them with a sway of the hips, leaving them standing with their mouths wide-open. Pretty sure they were just as shocked as I was.

I'd walked away from them, for maybe the first time, and, damn, did it feel good!

Come meet me by the tree line.

I followed Ollie's command and went to the edge of the trees to wait for him.

'Hey, beautiful.' Ollie came up behind me and scared the ever-loving shit out of me. I jumped as he grabbed my waist to steady me. 'Fancy a picnic?'

I smiled, turning around so I could see his face. His eyes

were the lightest of blues today, like a really clear ocean, or maybe more like a sky on a cloudless day. A super rare sight, but one I welcomed.

'I'd love one. Please tell me you have cheese sandwiches?' I asked, almost whining at him to give me good news. A picnic without cheese sandwiches was a crime.

'Course I do. They're your favourites,' he said simply, like there hadn't been another option for him. My heart thumped an extra beat, my stomach fluttering at his thought and care.

'Let's be honest, they should be *everybody's* favourites. Honestly, there are monsters out there who don't even like cheese. That's some serious effed up shit.'

'But, babe, there are people who like cheese and then there's you.'

Taking my hand, Ollie walked me a little way into the woods to where he'd arranged a picnic blanket and a basket. The blanket was one of those quintessential red check picnic blankets that I swore you saw in every film and TV show and it made me smile. *How cute.*

'Oh, ha-ha. Hilarious,' I said, loving the fact that I felt like I could be myself around him these days. 'I like cheese. Is that a crime?'

'No. But it should be a crime *just* how much you love it.'

'I can't help it if I'm a turophile,' I told him. I'd learned the word for a cheese lover recently, and I thought it sounded like something else entirely, but once learned, a new word must be inserted into every conversation. 'Actually, I found an article the other day about a guy who puts cheese on top of his milk cereal AND on his ice cream.' The look of disgust on Ollie's face was a picture. I wasn't joking—and, of course, the guy was British.

'The day you put cheese on ice cream, babe, is the day I

leave you.'

'That's totally fair,' I said with a laugh, accepting his statement as fact.

I got comfortable on the blanket while Ollie sorted out the food and drinks. I couldn't decide what he was hoping to get out of this, but he was winning some definite brownie points, that was for sure.

The food tasted delicious. Alongside cheese sandwiches, Ollie had made the kitchen prepare some of my favourite snacks. It was these sort of things that made me fully realise he must *actually* listen to me. Or notice what foods I loved and always ate more of. I'd never had this level of attention on me and my habits before. If I wasn't already falling in love with him, then I would've after my fourth cheese sandwich triangle.

'Thank you,' I said, finishing my bite with relish. I leaned over to him and gave him a quick kiss on the lips. It was brief but filled with my gratitude. The boy had hit me in the heart.

'It was my pleasure,' he said, a young and wholesome smile on his face. 'I have another surprise for you.'

'You do?' I asked, my lips forming into a matching smile.

'Yep. I'm just gonna go grab it. Don't move from this spot,' he commanded. He stood and left our secluded area at a fast pace. He was out of my eyeline in no time.

I laughed at his retreating back. Where would I even go?

Ten minutes passed, and I worried he wasn't coming back.

A rustle of leaves behind me made me pause.

'Ollie, is that you?' I called out. I hadn't seen anybody else since we entered the woods, and I didn't think it was Ollie as the sound was coming from a totally different direction to the one he'd sprinted off in.

Wonderful.

A dull pain shot through my skull.

What. The. Fuck.

I tried to catch my bearings before the next blow came, but it came too quick. Pain rippled across my shoulder, making its way down my entire right arm.

My cry pierced the air, and bird wings flapped away.

I glimpsed over-bleached blonde hair in my peripheral. Of course it was a member of *The Set* hurting me. Or maybe all three of them. They were watching me when I entered the woods to meet Ollie after all. Purposefully staying close by in case a situation presented itself.

Where the fuck had Ollie gone to?

'Let's teach this little bitch a lesson,' Odette said, then giggling followed from the others.

'Yeah, New Girl,' Ophelia spat. 'This is for Olivia.'

The kicks and punches continued and my vision faded, the pain vibrating through my entire body. *Man, it hurts like a motherfucker.*

Even after the blows ended, all I could feel was pain everywhere.

'Sky? Sky? Are you okay?' a voice called out to me. Footsteps got closer and although I couldn't see him, I knew it was Griff. I couldn't mistake that voice. When I tried to call out to him, no noise came out of me except for a harsh, rasping breath.

His footsteps came closer, then a 'Shit, Sky,' slipped out of his lips, which meant he'd found me.

I wanted to cry in happiness that he was there and that I didn't need to crawl through the woods in my current state.

Although, that wouldn't have happened if Ollie had come back.

Fuck. *None* of it would have happened if Ollie had come back.

The real question was, why didn't he?

Thirty-Six

ONCE AGAIN, I found myself in the hospital wing. I'd spent so much time there since joining Hawthorn, I may as well put my name above a bed and make it permanently mine. Griff sat in the chair beside my bed, cheeks flushed with emotion. After he'd found me and helped me back to the school, he hadn't left my side. He really could be super sweet and caring—the perfect gentleman.

'This is getting fucking ridiculous. I'll be having words with Ollie and Leo later,' he grumbled. He got out his phone and started furiously typing. 'Can't you and Clover beat them up at some point?'

'Erm...' I trailed off, wondering if I could actually throw a punch at Odette.

Don't get me wrong, I'd thought about it. The repercussions didn't seem worth it, though, as we could both lose our scholarships. Plus, Clover was in her last year here and had plans to go to a great university. I couldn't ruin that for her.

Not like we were on talking terms either, so it wasn't like I could ask her.

'Not really,' I said, my tone sure. 'She's not talking to me, anyway.'

'Well, it's not like Ollie and I can. We can make them outcasts, yeah, but we can't physically harm them,' he said. The look on his face told me that fact pissed him off. I also didn't believe they could make them true outcasts, either, otherwise they'd have tried harder already. 'And you and Clo will be fine. I promise.'

I ignored his comment about Clo. Earlier that day he'd been singing a completely different tune, and I didn't want to reignite our argument when I felt so ill.

'I want to hurt her,' I said. 'Believe me, I would love to see Ophelia with a broken nose because I punched her so hard. But I just feel like I'm above that, right?'

'Yes!' Griff said enthusiastically. 'You are above them, New Girl, completely.'

'Thanks, Griff,' I said, smiling at him. He always knew the perfect thing to say that would make me feel better.

'Sky.' Griff's voice got quieter, and he stopped me from grabbing my phone off the counter to text Ollie. 'I need to talk to you.'

'Okay...' I leaned back, getting more comfortable in the bed. 'What about?'

'About my parents,' he whispered, sheepish. Worried, too. 'So, I don't know what you know about them?'

'Not much,' I said with a shrug. 'Nobody will tell me anything.'

'Right.' The chair cushion groaned as he fidgeted. 'So, my mum's name was Eliza Hawthorn and my dad was Damien Cooper. They died when I was five in a car crash. I was in the car too, but I don't remember any of it.'

Shit. He'd completely thrown me off, as I hadn't expected him to tell me that. I'd spent Christmas at his parents' estate and nobody had ever mentioned that they weren't alive.

Parents' Day too it was just sort of implied they couldn't be there. Now I felt like a right bitch—I'd grumbled to Griff so many times about my mum and Andy.

'After it happened, I went and lived with Leo. His dad, Edward, is my uncle, 'cause he's my mum's older brother. The other option was to live with my mum's twin, Millie. Ollie's mum.'

Slightly struggling to keep up, I nodded, trying to wrap my head around it all. I knew that the three boys were close and had known each other since they were kids, but I didn't realise they were all related and were cousins with a Hawthorn link.

'So you're related to Ms Hawthorn too?' I asked. Why that was the first question that came to my mind, I had no clue. Maybe it was because I didn't want to say anything else too deep, or say something that would put my foot in it.

'Yep, she's my aunt, but having a different surname means Ollie and I can keep more of a low pro. I forget that you haven't known us all since birth. Most of the kids here have parents that are in the same circle as us, and they all know who we're related to.'

'Wow. Maybe I would've known too if one of you had told me.' How had I known them all as long as I had and not known any of it? I knew the boys were keeping secrets from me, Clover too, but I'd put them to the back of my mind and rationalised that they'd tell me when the time was right.

'Yeah, wow.' He chuckled. He looked lighter, if that were possible. Like finally getting the truth off his chest and letting me in more had made him feel better. 'You okay?'

'Not gonna lie, Griff, I hadn't even registered what your surname was until just now, but honestly, I'm good.' I chuckled too. 'Seriously, though, are you okay?'

'I'm good, New Girl.' The playful smile returned to his face.

We were both silent for a moment. 'I really think my mum would have loved you.'

'You reckon?'

'Yeah.' Griff shrugged. 'She was beautiful. Her smile could light up a room.' His eyes were glossed over and I knew his mind had travelled elsewhere. 'You remind me of her.'

'I do?' I asked, surprised.

'Mum was strong. Let nothing faze her. Just like you.'

'I don't think that's entirely true,' I mumbled. 'I definitely let shit faze me.'

'Maybe on the inside, New Girl, but it rarely shows on the outside.'

'Why are you always so nice to me? Even on day one, you weren't horrible to me.'

'Honestly, I'm not sure why I wasn't. They'd instructed me to give you a hard time. New girl in the school, on scholarship, nobody was sure whether you could hack it here.'

'Have I proved that I can hack it now?'

'Girl, you proved you could hack it after that first party in the woods.'

'That feels so long ago. But here I am, still finding myself in here.' I gestured around to the rest of the empty hospital wing.

Griff reached out and took my hand in his, squeezing it tight. The gesture made me feel loved, and as if the two of us shared a secret of sorts. Like I'd made a friend who liked me for me. Not because he wanted in my pants. Not because he had some misguided sense that he needed to protect me. But because he wanted to be my friend and keep me safe. It felt good.

'I'm glad. Not that you're in the hospital wing again, obviously. But the fact that you're here. At Hawthorn still. I worry that one day, you won't want to be friends with me anymore.'

His eyes were more green than blue today, and they stared straight into mine. He leaned closer to me and squeezed my hand again. 'Promise me that no matter what else happens this year, we'll still be friends at the end of it?'

I could feel his nerves as he asked. Not sure if the nerves were because he was worried about my answer or just from the fact he'd voiced an insecurity like that out loud. Usually, he came across so carefree. I wondered what was running through his mind and why whatever it was made him feel the need to ask in the first place. And yeah, it was suspicious as fuck.

'I promise,' I answered instantly, no qualms about making the promise, even though I felt unsure of his reasons. I opened my arms wide for a hug and Griff instantly leaned into them. It was one of those tight hugs, where you could hear your ribs groaning in revolt. Believe me, mine were screaming.

I spotted Ollie over Griff's shoulder and I lifted my lips into an unsure smile, slowly leaning out of the hug I'd just started. Griff noticed that my attention was elsewhere and glanced behind him.

'Hey, dude,' Griff said through gritted teeth, anger rippling off of him. 'Wondered when you'd get here to be with your girl.'

'I would have got here faster, but apparently *my girl* and my best friend were too busy getting cosy to let me know where they were.'

Huh? Griff had been writing furious texts the whole time we'd been here, and I'd assumed they'd been to Ollie—but clearly not.

'S-sorry. I thought you knew where we were.' My voice rose at the end, so it came out more like a question. I really thought he knew we were here. Surely he must have known that the girls had got to me again? And if he'd returned to the spot he left me in, surely he could tell from the state of the area that something had happened?

'No. I did not,' he growled. His eyes, like his words, were hard and I could see the anger there. The anger he was directing at me, like any of it was my fault.

I wanted to say, *Oh yeah, Ollie, sorry I didn't tell you where I was while three girls were ganging up on me.*

I rolled my eyes at his shitty attitude.

'Got something to say, sweetheart?' he drawled.

'Oh, I don't know, dickhead. Maybe you should ask her if she's okay?' Griff stood, puffing up his chest, taking a step closer into Ollie's space.

I was pissed. He hadn't asked if I was okay, even after he'd glanced briefly at the bruises forming on my face, but other than that, he hadn't even tried to come closer and touch me.

'Stop it. Both of you,' I shouted loud enough that the two of them stopped sizing one another up and turned to look at me. 'Maybe you should go.'

My eyes were staring intently into Ollie's. As much as I wanted him there to comfort me, it didn't seem like he'd be doing that soon and honestly, *fuck that.* I deserved to have somebody by my side who wanted to be there and cared that I was hurting. Griff had been nothing but nice since he'd found me, and Ollie's presence was ruining the camaraderie we'd established. The cloud of happiness Griff had created had burst.

'You seriously want me to leave and have this fuckwad stay here?' Ollie asked me, one eyebrow raised.

'Y-yes.' I held firm, our eyes boring into one another. 'Go.'

'Fuck this,' Ollie growled.

The curtain around my bed fluttered as he stormed out, the door of the wing slamming not long afterward.

I sighed.

I had wanted him to fight me on it. To grovel, ask to stay. Fuck, even just ask me how I was. But he hadn't. He hadn't fought at all, and it was the worst he'd made me feel in the entire time I'd known him.

I left the hospital wing the next day, and it was Ollie who met me in the morning to take me back to my room.

'Where's Griff?' I asked, having expected him to come get me.

'I asked him if I could come get you,' Ollie said, shifting his weight from leg to leg. 'I need to apologise for how I acted yesterday.'

'You do, yeah,' I said, not letting him off. He'd acted foolish and we both knew it. 'You acted like a right knob.'

'I know. I'm sorry, babe.' He opened his arms and I stepped into them, wrapping mine around his waist, pulling him close. I breathed in his tobacco and vanilla scent, letting it fill my senses and ground me. 'I didn't know how to feel after you got hurt and I lashed out.'

I took a step back so I could see Ollie's face when I asked my next question.

'I've got to ask, Ollie,' I said, doing my best to keep calm and collected. 'Why did you leave me alone?'

'I'd forgotten to bring my gift for you,' he replied instantly, an eyebrow raised, cautious of me and my next sentence. 'So I went to get it.'

'What was it?'

'Your favourite dessert,' he said. It made sense that he'd arranged my favourite dessert for the end of the picnic. My stomach grumbled at the thought of salted caramel cheesecake. 'But when I got back and you weren't there, I may have thrown it in anger.'

'Thanks... I guess?'

'I'll get the kitchen staff to make it for you another day.' He tried to tug me back into his arms, but I resisted. 'What's up?'

'Did you know?' I asked, assessing his gaze, watching his eyes for any flicker of a lie. 'That the girls were going to come hurt me?'

'What?' he roared, snapping his hand back towards him, no longer trying to pull me closer. 'How could you think that of me?'

'I mean...' I was looking for the right words to say—words that wouldn't make him more mad. 'It's a little suspicious, don't you think?'

'What is?'

'That the very moment you left me there, alone, the girls showed up and attacked me.'

'What exactly are you implying, Skylar? Stop beating around the bush and spit it out.' His anger was palpable, and I knew I'd pissed him off, but it didn't matter. I needed to ask. I needed to know the truth—good or bad.

'I'm asking you if you set it up with them. I'm asking whether or not you knew something like that was going to happen.'

'I promise you,' he said, reaching out to grab my hands in his, 'that I didn't know they were going to do that to you. For fuck's sake, Sky. Part of me is irritated that you think that of me, but I know I've not always been the best to you, so I get it, and I'm going to let it go. Life's too short and I like you, you know? I hate seeing you hurt. It kills me to know you're in pain and I can't do anything to stop it.'

The sincerity in his eyes gutted me and made me feel crap for not trusting him. Of course the girls seized the opportunity they saw—literally. They saw me enter the woods, and they must've been close by when Ollie left me alone.

'I'm sorry,' I said, opening his arms up so I could hug his tense body. After I squeezed his ribs, he relented and reciprocated the hug. 'I was just being paranoid.'

'We're good, New Girl.' He placed a kiss on the top of my head, and I sighed with happiness and relief. 'Now let's get out of here.'

'Let's.'

Thirty-Seven

I HAD FELT that ever since Griff had opened up to me, we'd grown even closer. I understood him so much more, and I understood why he covered a lot of his genuine emotions with humour. Yes, he'd annoyed me, but ultimately I knew we'd make up. He was one of my favourite people in this shithole.

One person who wasn't that happy about how close I'd become with Griff was Ollie. Well, 'wasn't that happy' was an enormous understatement.

He was pissed. *Really* pissed.

'If you'd stop spending time with Griff, then maybe we could actually spend some time together?' he grumbled.

'We do spend time together.'

'Yeah, we do, but rarely just the two of us.'

'I don't think you're being fair,' I told him. 'It's not like Clover or Griff crash our time alone often. Fuck, babe, Clo isn't even talking to me still.'

'What did Griff talk to you about?' he asked, accusation thick in his voice.

'When?'

'In the hospital wing. After the woods.'

'Nothing. Nothing of importance to you, anyway. He was telling me about his parents.'

'Sure you're not lying?' He looked so paranoid, and I didn't know why. Something had agitated him. 'Are you keeping shit from me?'

I laughed out loud, literally, in his face. We were sitting next to one another at a table in the library as we shared a free period, both of us trying to work on our English homework. Or at least I was. Ollie had been giving me sex eyes, and I knew he wanted to resolve this tension between us. He didn't seem to understand, though, that he'd caused this tension in the first place. I was matching his energy, not the other way around.

'Why would I lie to you? There's literally nothing to lie about...' Although that wasn't exactly true. I was keeping some of it from him, only because I didn't want to share too much. It was for Griff to talk about, not me. It wasn't my business to talk about *his* business.

'I'm sorry. Just seems like you'd rather spend time with him,' he said, pouting a little, his bottom lip jutting out and looking totally biteable.

'That's not it at all. I want to spend time with both of you and I *do* spend time with both of you.'

'Well, I want to spend time with you alone,' he said. I couldn't be certain, but I thought I glimpsed Ollie's eyes roll in my peripheral.

'Okay? All you have to do is ask or, you know, communicate with me. If I'd known you were feeling insecure, I would have spoken to Griff about it.' I shrugged.

Not having had a boyfriend before, this was all new to me and so stupid. I said nothing about Ollie still spending time with Leo, and I *never* mentioned the fact that he spent time with Odette and Ophelia because of Leo. Those girls were the reason for everything that had happened to me, or so we assumed, yet he acted okay with them when I wasn't around. Come to think of it, that was way worse and even more disrespectful towards me than my friendship with Griff could ever be towards him.

'I'm not insecure,' he spat out, his anger growing, and for the first time, I felt a little scared of him. 'I shouldn't have to beg my girlfriend to spend time with me. You should want to without being asked, Sky.'

'Of course I want to,' I mumbled. I rolled my eyes, probably for the millionth time during the conversation. 'How about tonight we hang out in your room? Just us two.'

I waggled my eyebrows, hoping to make him laugh. Who was I kidding? Ollie rarely laughed out loud. I hoped he'd give me at least a slight smile, though. Fuck, I'd settle for a lip twitch at this rate.

His face didn't move, which made me feel even more stupid. But he did respond with a curt, 'Sure.'

Not overly convincing, but I'd take it. I needed him to be okay with me. I didn't want yet another person I cared about to decide that I wasn't worth knowing. My friendship with Clover being on the rocks had really hurt me. I thought we were closer than that, but she wasn't talking to me still, and when we would both be in our room at the same time, she'd ignore me.

The tension was unbearable.

And I hoped it would be over soon.

OLLIE'S ROOM, ever since New Year's Eve, had become a place I took comfort in. Maybe it was because of the whole losing my

V-card thing, but part of it was the fact that I felt closer to Ollie here. Like I could see inside of a tiny portion of his brain and understand him better.

The room was neat and minimalistic. Barely any furniture occupied the room, other than the bed and the sofa. No photos or posters adorned the walls. No personality at all. But really, though, when I thought about it, the room showed his personality perfectly.

The two of us were snuggled together under the duvet in Ollie's massive bed, the credits having just started on one of my favourite action films. Ollie had let me pick the film—he was clearly trying his best to get on my good side.

'Griff told me that Clover wants to apologise,' I blurted out, without thinking about the words themselves. It'd been playing on my mind ever since Griff spoke to me in ethics, but after the attack and our conversation in the hospital wing, it had slipped my mind, but now that it had re-entered, I couldn't think of much else. Ollie groaned the second it left my mouth, moving away from me in the bed slightly to turn and look at me.

'Course she does,' he said sardonically. 'What she did was out of order and she knows it.'

'Right. But should I forgive her?' I asked, unsure whether I even wanted to hear his opinion but needing to know, anyway. Griff was biased whenever I spoke to him about it, and it wasn't like I could ring up Leo and get him to weigh in with his opinion.

'Depends on what she says really, doesn't it?'

'Guess so...'

I reached out to him, hoping to pull him tighter to me again, but he resisted, annoyed at me, but I wasn't sure why. Either he didn't want me to forgive Clover or he was just aggravated that I'd brought it up on our night alone as a couple.

'Look, you clearly want to accept her apology. I can tell that she's been at the front of your mind ever since she said what she said.' Ollie sat up, the cover falling down to his waist, and I got slightly distracted by how good he looked in his bright white school shirt that fit him just right. 'Go running back to her.'

I followed suit and sat up too. 'What's that supposed to mean?'

'It means, little Sky, that you obviously don't give a shit that she was a total cunt to you. You're going to go give her a rim job the second she says sorry. No need to lie and act otherwise.'

'I'm not going to go "give her a rim job" as you've so delicately put it,' I spat, pissed he'd even said that. Having a best friend and wanting them to be happy didn't mean that you were licking their arse. 'But I am going to hear her out. Everyone can say shit in the heat of the moment that they later regret. I'm sure you've done it.'

'Course, but she called you a pathetic, desperate whore. Not exactly something that springs to mind without having thought a little about it first.'

'Rub it in, why don't you,' I said with a wince, the words hurting just as much as they had the first time they were hurled at me.

'I'm just saying. Have some respect for yourself.'

'What did you just say?' My blood boiled in my veins as I fought the urge to hit him. Who did he think he was, telling me I should have respect for myself? What a fucking wanker. I couldn't be near him any longer.

I climbed over him and got out of the bed. Fuck staying here with him. What on earth was happening around here?

'There's no need for you to leave.' Ollie looked at me and I could see the anger on his face, his lip twitching in irritation. 'You're going to let her ruin shit between us? *Again?*'

'Right now, Ollie, you're the one ruining shit between us. I'm gonna go before one of us says something we regret.'

I made my way to the door, opened it with a force I didn't know I possessed, and slammed it behind me. So blinded by my anger, I didn't spot Clover standing in front of me until the very last second. I halted, centimetres away from a full-blown collision.

'Hey,' she mumbled, looking embarrassed I'd caught her standing outside of Ollie's door, her eyes shifting from side to side.

'Hey,' I replied, stopping and taking a deep breath.

'Can we talk?' she asked, shuffling her weight from foot to foot, looking as uncomfortable as I felt inside.

'Sure,' I replied, irritation still in my tone, wanting to get this talk over with. My emotions were all over the place, and I wasn't sure if I trusted my own instincts right now. Fresh from an argument with Ollie probably wasn't the best time to talk to Clo about her hurtful words. 'Let's go back to our room.'

I didn't want to have to talk to her out in the open. Also, I didn't want Ollie to come out of his room and find the two of us standing there together. That would *not* go down well.

We made our way across campus in silence. Neither of us wanted to break the moment, the truce we'd come to while walking.

In no time, thank fuck, we made it back to our room. Clover entered first, and I went in behind her, filled with anxiety. I knew she wanted to apologise, but I also worried that she was planning to give me some "home truths" or some other type of advice that I did not want to hear right now.

'So...' I said as I perched down on the edge of my bed. Across the room, Clover did the same on her bed. Our room was so small, we were still close enough to see each other clearly.

'So...' Clo repeated and I giggled. This was silly. *We* were silly. We were best friends, which meant we were above this shit, or at least we should've been. We shouldn't have let it get to the point where we weren't on speaking terms and were avoiding one another in the halls. 'I am so sorry, Sky. I never should have said what I did, and for the record, I don't think you're a whore. Or desperate or pathetic either. I was mad, and I let my anger out on you.'

Our eyes locked across the room and a tentative smile played on my lips. Her apology was sincere—or so I believed—and really, I just wanted my best friend back. It wasn't fun walking the corridors without somebody to gossip and giggle with.

'Can you forgive me?' she asked, wiping a tear from underneath her eye, looking at me imploringly. 'I've been a right twat.'

I laughed, agreeing with her.

'Guess I could find it in my desperate and pathetic heart to forgive you.'

She laughed at me, and I could tell we were going to be fine. We were like a pot that boiled over and had simmered back down again.

'Promise you forgive me?' Clo pleaded, her eyes watery once again.

'Honestly, Clo, there's not much really for me to forgive. You said something you regret and you've said sorry. Let's just move on and act like it never happened.' I shrugged, not wanting to drag it out too much. And even though I didn't say it out loud, I was still going to be a little wary going forward, just in case it happened again.

'You're the best! I promise I won't let you down,' she said, crossing her legs on the edge of her bed to get comfortable. 'Now, tell me why you stormed out of Ollie's room.'

I rolled my eyes, remembering my argument with Ollie. 'Well...'

And I spent the rest of the evening doing just that. The two of us discussed why boys were such dickheads sometimes and how they didn't even realise it half the time.

It definitely made me feel better.

Thirty-Eight

OLLIE and I still hadn't made up a week later. At first, my anger had blinded me and I hadn't wanted to speak to him at all. He'd texted me a couple of times, but I'd ignored them, too mad to reply. But as time passed, the sadder I got about it all. Every couple had their first fight, but nobody had told me it hurt so bad.

History class was a bit awkward, and Ollie had even moved from the desk next to mine at the back to sit up front next to some girl who looked way too happy about it. Wasn't sure what she was so thrilled about. As far as I was aware, we were still a couple and she had no chance.

As soon as he'd done that, it solidified to me he was being petty and that we should have some space away from each other. Everything had gone super quick after we'd first slept together and taking a step back was probably for the best in the long run. Even if it made my heart physically hurt.

My phone buzzed in my blazer pocket and I removed it and looked when Clover wasn't looking in my direction. She'd taken a rather dim view—putting it politely—of Ollie's actions and was getting annoyed that he was still texting me.

CHECKING IN. YOU OKAY, STUTTER?

I smiled at the text from Leo. Ever since the events of Halloween night, I'd received a similar text once a week, and it made me think about him in a new way. It was super nice of him and totally went against his whole bored vibe. We rarely spoke in person, as he spent all of his time with Odette and *The Set* were still attempting to make my life miserable, but I also didn't feel like he was ignoring me either. The most recent tactic of the students was to put rotting food in my schoolbag and attempt to trip me up in the corridor. Luckily, I always found my balance at the last moment and hadn't gone down face first—yet.

'So, do you think we'll be able to get out of the fashion show?' Clover asked once we sat down for breakfast. 'I mean. Ms Hawthorn's not actually going to penalise us, is she?'

'Honestly, I doubt we can get out of it. I reckon she'd punish us and enjoy doing it,' I replied. The woman had looked like she meant business when she'd announced it during assembly, and the fact it was for charity and to make the school look good meant that we probably had to join in. 'The woman is a bit of a dictator.'

'True. The Hawthorns have always been sketchy motherfuckers.'

'What do you have against the Hawthorns?' I asked for probably the millionth time.

'Hm?' Clover feigned ignorance. She ate her food, making her mouth so full that she didn't have to respond straight away.

'You know what I mean. You always use every opportunity you can to slate them, but I don't really understand why. Lottie always seems so happy to see you.'

'Hmm. I don't want to talk about it right now, but one day I will.'

'Is that a promise?' I asked, sceptical as all get-out.

'Nope. Just maybe.' We both chuckled, but mine was fake as fuck. It irritated me, or should I say, she was irritating me. I felt like I gave a lot in our friendship and Clo never reciprocated. It didn't help that we'd only recently made up. 'I really don't want to take part in the charity show. I'm worried it'll be like last year.'

'Last year?' I asked, casting my mind back to what she'd told me about it. 'I thought you worked in the cloakroom away from it all?'

'Okay, so don't be mad at me, but I may have lied about what happened at last year's charity thing.'

'Okay...'

'I didn't really work in the cloakroom,' she said. The revelation slightly irritated me, but I kept calm. My face clearly didn't give me away, as she continued without commenting on my sour expression. 'I was one of the girls on stage who announced the winners of the silent auction part of the evening.'

'So what happened?' I asked.

'Well, it was fucking horrible, and they pulled a *Carrie* on me.'

I'd just taken a sip of my coffee and spat it out onto the table in front of me. 'Sorry, what did you just say?'

'They pulled a *Carrie*. When I announced the winner of the weekend getaway to New York, they poured red paint all over my head and they ruined the expensive designer dress I was wearing.'

'You've never mentioned it,' I replied, petulant.

'Course I haven't. It was fucking embarrassing.'

'You could have told me, though. They've done some pretty shitty things to me this year. Would've been nice to know that you understood.' How had she managed to stay silent about it, even when she knew I was going through something similar?

'I know. I knew you'd understand, too,' she said. Her spoon stopped halfway to her mouth. 'I was just ashamed.'

'What's there to be ashamed of?' I asked, baffled at why she'd feel that way around me. We were best friends, and that meant never feeling ashamed around one another.

'I wanted to come across as somebody who had their shit together. You were the one person here who knew nothing of the past. I kind of wanted it to stay that way.'

'What do you mean?'

'Being new here, you knew nothing, and all I wanted was to be your friend.'

'We *are* friends, Clo,' I stressed.

'Yeah, now we are, but I didn't know that to begin with.'

'In the future, you can talk to me about it. If you ever want to.'

'Thanks,' she said with a wide smile, and I hoped she felt better for telling me the truth. It irked me that nobody had told me about it—not just Clo, but the guys as well.

Clover and I didn't speak for the rest of breakfast, and I couldn't say it was a comfortable silence. We were both lost in our own thoughts, thinking of what we'd said and our feelings about it. I was slightly pissed at her, to be honest. She'd had so many chances to tell me exactly what had happened last year and that she related to what I was experiencing. It made me question our entire friendship and whether it was as solid as I'd believed it to be.

Questioning shit sucks.

WITHOUT OLLIE by my side at all times, I'd been keeping a low profile during school hours. I didn't need somebody to attack me or cover me from head to toe in slush again. The library had recently become a refuge of sorts, and I spent the majority of my free periods there. Mostly because it was easier—and away from the other students. Nobody wanted to be caught dead in the library, after all.

'Sky, I need to talk to you.' Clover came flying towards the table I was occupying, avoiding a trolley of books at the last moment. 'Urgently.'

'Okay...?' Puzzled, I put down my pen and stopped what I was doing.

'In private,' she whispered. I looked around, confused about why Clo had specified privacy when we were the only two people in the back of the library.

'Can we not talk about it here?' I asked with a groan, not wanting to move.

'No. Let's go,' Clover said as she packed up all my things in a hurry, putting them into my bag for me, not giving me a chance to stop her.

Within moments, we were leaving the library, and I found myself speed walking behind her back to our dorm room. She was a woman on a mission.

Rushing inside, Clover almost threw me down onto my bed and took the space beside me. I turned to face her, crossed my legs, and got comfortable. I could sense whatever she wanted to say was gonna be good.

'Sky, there's no simple way for me to say this.'

I rolled my eyes at the dramatics. 'Just tell me. It's obviously important enough to take me away from studying—and from people.'

'Look. I overheard the girls talking and I really think you need to hear what they were saying.'

'Go on.'

'They were talking about what Ollie's got planned.'

'Right...?' I didn't fully understand her point.

'Sky. It's bad shit. Like, he's the reason for everything that's happened to you this year, bad shit.' She made eye contact with me, I could feel her imploring me to believe her. To believe that what she'd been telling me about Ollie all along was true. She'd made her feelings clear about him all year, and for her, what she'd heard was only confirmation that she was right.

'Not trying to be a dick here, but what does that even mean?' I tried to stay calm. Tried to keep my tone casual. Tried not to let my anger show.

'It means that everything that has happened to you this year at the hand of *The Set* or the other students was at Ollie's say so. He's been pulling the strings this whole time.' She grabbed my hand and gave it a tight squeeze.

'A little far-fetched, don't you think?' I asked, laughing, but the look on Clo's face told me she wasn't joking around. She truly believed it all. 'How do you know the girls didn't just say it for your benefit?'

'Sky, they didn't know I could hear them. They thought they were alone.'

'Where were you?' I sounded suspicious, but fuck. I was.

'In the food classroom cupboard getting more supplies. They came in and only checked to see if the classroom was clear, not the cupboard.' Her words were coming out super fast. Soon I'd need subtitles to keep up. 'Odette was telling Ophelia and Oralie how Ollie had come to her during second period to tell her the plan for the fashion show.'

'And pray tell, what exactly is the plan for the fashion show?' Using my best posh British accent, I attempted to make a joke out of the situation.

Clover did *not* appreciate it.

'This isn't a fucking joke, Skylar. I'm trying to save you from being *Carrie*'d too. Not exactly like you can exact your revenge with telekinesis, is it?'

She had a point. They *had* blindsided me on Parents' Day, and we never figured out who took the footage they'd shown, even though my gut told me it was Odette without a doubt.

'No, but think back to Parents' Day and what the girls showed everyone. Ollie didn't film that.'

'One of the girls or Leo must have filmed it for him.' She nodded at me, like it made total sense in her head. 'I was with Griff that whole night, so that rules him out at least.'

I should fucking hope that I can rule Griff out. He really had become one of my closest friends—ever. I didn't want to believe he could have done that to me.

'But we've always known that it was one of the girls. What I mean is, *why* would Ollie orchestrate that? Why would he want that kind of footage made public?' I asked, fine-tuning my question.

'If his end goal is to hurt you, then I'm sure he wouldn't care.'

'Clo. What they showed that day was child pornography! Do you really think he'd risk that just to hurt me?'

Her response was so quiet, I almost didn't hear her words and it was only because I was looking so closely at her face that I saw her lips move. 'I do.'

Wonderful.

'What reason does he even have to hurt me?' I moved on my bed, no longer able to sit still while I listened.

'The girls kept mentioning something about your family and how you deserve this,' Clo said, leaning forward, her voice a fraction higher than a whisper. She was probably worried somebody was listening through the door, but I didn't want to ask her, because I felt certain I would laugh at her answer.

'My f-family?' I stuttered, unsure what my family would have to do with anybody that attended the academy. My family had never been rich. At all. Then it hit me like a lightning bolt. 'Reckon this has something to do with my dad?'

'Thought you didn't know who he was,' Clo snapped.

'Well, I don't,' I said with a shrug. 'But doesn't mean somebody else doesn't know.'

'Yeah, that's probably it.' She didn't look convinced. 'I don't know, though, Sky, I feel like this year is going to be worse than what happened to me last year. I really wish you'd listen to me. *The Set* plans to reveal the truth about everything at the fashion show, whatever that means.'

If I knew Clover the way I thought I did, she wouldn't drop her suspicions anytime soon. Trust me to get a best friend, and a boyfriend, and have them both hate one another. Of course that was how it was. It would be too easy for them to just get along.

'Well, did you hear anything specific?'

'How much more fucking specific did you want them to get?'

'I don't know. Just seems odd to me they didn't mention any actual part of the plan. Like they *wanted* you to overhear them.' I shrugged. If they'd known Clo was listening, they could have said shit on purpose, knowing she'd run straight to me and repeat what she'd heard. They did talk about it in the cooking classroom, the one place where Clo was always known to be.

'Or they didn't say any part of the plan because they were being cautious, not wanting anybody to learn of their plans.'

Okay, so Clo had a point too. Either scenario could be the correct one, and there was no way to know for sure.

'Just be on your guard, yeah?' Clo asked, raising an eyebrow at me. Her green eyes were shining with worry for me, and I hated that we were still on such awkward footing with each other even after I'd forgiven her. I nodded, and she added, 'You sure you don't want to ask Ollie to see if you can swap roles with somebody else? If their plan revolves around you being on stage, then you can at least make it a little harder for them by working backstage or something.'

'I'm sure,' I said, my tone hard. 'I'm not exactly on talking terms with Ollie right now, and even if I was, if I asked him to change my role, they'd know I was running scared and I don't want to give those bitches the satisfaction. We're modelling in the show, Clo. Deal with it.'

'Fine. But I don't have to like it.'

Fuck, I didn't like it either, but I meant what I said. I wouldn't bow down in fear. Not to *The Set*. Not to anybody.

Thirty-Nine

THE TEXT from Ollie came through at the end of last period, and I wanted to reply straight away, but at the same time I wanted him to sit and stew for a little longer. I had let him stew for a while, though, and if I was being honest with myself, I wasn't mad with him anymore. Mostly I'd wanted him to realise how silly he was being about my friendship with Griff. He must have realised that Clo and I were friends again, and that I'd accepted her apology for what she did.

Another text came through, and it melted my already thawing heart.

After giving it a moment's thought, I messaged back that I'd meet him at his room after I'd been to my own room to drop my stuff off and get changed out of my uniform. Wearing a stiff blazer and tight skirt all day wasn't the comfiest after a six-hour school day.

I changed into a baggy top and some leggings, not wanting

to dress up for Ollie, especially not when he needed to grovel—big time.

Clover came rushing through the door covered in flour, looking harried.

'Where are you off to?' she asked when she saw I'd already changed out of my uniform.

'Going to Ollie's room,' I told her, pulling my jumper over my head so my words came out muffled.

'Oh,' she said. I turned to face her, and she looked confused, like she couldn't understand why I'd be going there. 'You gonna forgive him?'

'I mean, it depends on what he says, but I'm no longer mad at him if that's what you're asking.'

'Honestly, I don't know what I'm asking. Are you going to at least ask him about what I overheard the girls saying?'

'Of course! He's been a dick, and I'm not gonna let him rail-road me.' I forced a smile. 'I'm going now, so I'll see you later tonight.'

'I won't wait up,' she said, resigned.

I closed the door on her strained facial expression and tried to put the tension between us to the back of my mind. Something was brewing between us, and I knew that eventually we'd come to blows. Knowing that and accepting it were two completely different things.

OLLIE LIVED in a different building block to us, so I made my way across campus to his as quickly as possible. Walking alone around here always gave me the heebies. You never knew who could be hiding around the corners. Or in plain view.

I knocked on the door, and it opened instantly, warmth surrounding me within seconds. Vanilla and tobacco had recently become my favourite scents. It surrounded me every-where now, and my brain automatically linked it to Ollie.

Ollie stood on the other side of the door, looking nervous.

'Hey,' he mumbled and moved aside to let me in.

'Hey.' I smiled. Seeing Ollie unsure was unusual, but it was what I needed to see. If I'd arrived and he looked all cocksure, it would've put me off him.

I went and sat on the two-seater sofa he had in his suite and he came and sat beside me. It was different from the last time I came to his room, unsure of myself, not knowing where to sit. I crossed my legs underneath me and turned to face him. For the first time since knowing him, I could see genuine worry in his features. He studied me, scrutinising my face, and I hoped my smile would let him know I wasn't here to fight again.

'Thanks for coming. I wasn't sure you would,' he said. I felt the warmth of his hand on my knee, and as he talked, it moved in a familiar circular motion, creating a swirling pattern.

'That's okay,' I said and continued before he could cut me off. 'But before you say what you want to say, I've got some-thing I want to ask you about first.'

'Okay,' he said, blinking at me. 'What's up?'

'You probably know that I accepted Clo's apology,' I started, and he nodded. 'Well, the other day she overheard something the O girls were talking about that she thought I should know.'

'Okay...'

'They were in the food classroom and they didn't realise Clo was in the cupboard. They were talking about the fashion show, and about *your* plan for it.'

'My plan? For what?'

I shrugged. 'Well, that's just it. Clo didn't overhear any of the actual plan, but they said it had to do with what you wanted them to do to me.'

'I know that Clo won't believe this, but I really hope you do,' he said, imploring me with his eyes. 'I have no plans when it comes to you and the fashion show, other than watching you kill it on the catwalk.'

'So why were the girls talking about that?'

'I've got no clue.' He shrugged. 'Maybe they knew Clo was listening in.'

'That's what I said!' I blurted out, then realised I was meant to be suspicious of him, not agreeing with him. 'So, you promise you've got no clue what they were talking about?'

'I promise, babe.'

My eyes were locked on his, and I couldn't see anything in his gaze that made me distrust him or think he was lying.

'I believe you,' I told him. 'Now go on. Say what you want to say.'

'I'm sorry for being a dick. I should've never snapped at you for your friendship with Griff and I also shouldn't have got annoyed because you wanted to forgive Clo for what she said in anger. I've done things in anger too.' He took a deep breath. 'I'm also sorry for being so petty over the last couple of weeks.

My face must give away my disbelief because as soon as he saw it, he said, 'No need to look so shocked, babe.'

'I-I'm surprised you came straight out and said it, that's all.'

'You are, huh?'

'Yeah, I dunno. Thought you might try to talk circles around me or something,' I said, shrugging. Not like he hadn't done it before.

'Why would I do that?'

'You can be a little forceful,' I told him tentatively.

'Oh yeah?' he said in a calm tone, but his nostrils flared, like he was making an extra effort to come across as composed. 'Forceful how?'

'You sort of railroad me a lot.' I shrugged again, finding it hard to think of exact examples when his eyes were boring into mine the way his were at that moment. And yeah, I'd told Clo earlier that I wouldn't let him railroad me during our conversation, but I'd never said that it hadn't happened before. 'I can't pinpoint an example right now.'

'Well, I'm sorry for that too,' he said, letting out a long exhale. Slowly, his hand moved from my knee to take my hand in his. 'I don't want to be like my dad.'

'Huh?' I asked. Not sure how we'd found ourselves on the topic of Henry, but I'd roll with it.

'My dad has always railroaded everybody around him. He did it to Millie when I was younger, and he does it to me now. Or at least he tries to.'

'Millie?' I asked.

Ollie surveyed my face, scrutinising me. 'My mother.'

It surprised me to hear him mention his mum. In all the time I'd known him, he'd never actively talked about her.

'Oh.' The shock must have shown on my face as he was still looking at me with questions in his eyes. 'Do you want to talk about her?'

'What about her?'

'Well, you've never mentioned her...' I was tiptoeing around him, worried I'd say something to piss him off and close himself off before we'd even begun. 'What was she like?'

'Obviously she was beautiful. Rich. Full of grace and poise.' He nodded, as if all of this was a given and hadn't really needed voicing out loud. 'She and her twin Eliza were the youngest of the four Hawthorn children and were very close.'

'Eliza was Griff's mum?' I asked, recalling what Griff had told me in the hospital wing.

'Yeah. The two of them were thick as thieves, always keeping secrets from everybody else. It drove their husbands mad, and then when Eliza died, my mum couldn't cope. She went completely off the rails and everybody worried about her.' I lost Ollie to his thoughts, and I could see the torment in his eyes. 'I remember little as I was only five when it happened, but I've heard a lot from the staff that helped raise me and from my dad when he's in a loving mood.'

I stayed silent, not wanting to interrupt his flow with an inane interjection. He didn't need me to speak. He moved our position, so he had his arms around me as I was sitting in between his legs, no longer able to see his face. His voice vibrated through his chest into my back.

'I remember how my dad would treat her, though. He couldn't understand her grief. Wanted her to keep up the impression of a *stiff upper lip*. Henry made her feel small, and I've never wanted to make somebody else feel that way.'

I nodded. Having met Henry Brandon, I could fully believe what he was saying. The man had seemed no-nonsense to me —and creepy as fuck.

'When I was ten, only five years later, Mum decided that she couldn't survive anymore. Didn't want to live in a realm without her twin.' Ollie sniffed behind me, holding back tears. I knew Ollie, and he would never cry in front of me—fuck, I doubted he'd cry in front of anybody. 'She committed suicide. Took a lethal cocktail of pills and alcohol and went to be with her dear Eliza. Left me with *him* without much more than a goodbye.'

I wasn't sure what to say. I knew his mum had died, but I didn't know the circumstances surrounding it were so sad. Unsure what to say next, I paused. I personally hated it when somebody said that they were sorry for your loss. It always seemed so disingenuous to me. Not like they'd known them.

So I said what I would want to hear if I was in that position.

'I bet she's so proud of you, Ollie. I can already tell that you're ten times the man Henry is and fuck, she knows it too.'

'You think so?' he asked, his voice low, and I wondered if anybody had ever told him that before.

'I do. None of it is your fault. Remember that.'

'Right...' he trailed off, distracted.

I could tell by his tone that he didn't believe me, but I knew he wouldn't. I sensed that there was a lot more to it—to him—than what he was showing me on the surface.

I could be patient, show him that I wouldn't be going anywhere, no matter what he thought about himself. Or how much he believed he was like his father.

Forty

MOTHER'S DAY had always been a Sunday that I didn't really care for. Not like I wanted to spend an entire day celebrating my mum, and my nan had died when I was younger. I knew nothing about the guy who helped make me, so I had no clue whether he had a mum alive out there somewhere.

Hawthorn opened up the school grounds on Mother's Day and invited the mums to come and spend the day with their offspring. They set up an Afternoon Tea type thing; the highlight of a proper British afternoon. Meaning Mum would receive an invitation to come here and, after the last time, I knew she was going to come. Free food and booze? Sign her up. She wouldn't turn down that kind of free shit. Especially if the school sent a car for her like last time.

'Clo, is your mum coming today?' I asked, fiddling with the tiny buttons on my floral tea dress as I tried to fasten them.

'God, I hope not,' she responded so fast, I knew she meant it. She'd still never really opened up about her parents, and I knew she hadn't seen them since the beginning of the school year. They were in contact over Christmas via text, but that was the only time she'd mentioned messaging them. Still one more occasion than my mum had texted me, though, so swings and roundabouts and all that.

'Would it be so bad?' I asked.

'Definitely. Lottie Hawthorn's going to be here,' Clover said, as if that explained everything.

'Again, is that a bad thing?' I asked, not really getting it. Leo's mum would be there, so what?

'Yeah,' she muttered. Clo didn't elaborate and I just couldn't be fucked trying to get more out of her. Was her evasion of my questions normal for female friendships? I wished I knew. Not like I could ask Griff because I doubted he'd be able to help much—even if he did love to act like one of the girls.

'Okay... Cool.' I stopped talking to her and continued getting ready. The boys got me some great clothes for Christmas, so my wardrobe had improved so much since I'd first started here. No more stained items with holes in that were obviously cheap or secondhand. I knew beyond doubt that Mum would comment on it, probably out of jealousy. She'd always wished she could afford designer clothing and the newest trends. I didn't even want to think about just what she'd be wearing today. If I knew her as well as I thought I did, there would be animal print on her outfit somewhere.

Great. Can't wait.

Mum wafted into the school in a cloud of knock-off perfume and hairspray. Honestly, I thought she was auditioning for the West End production with the way her blonde hair was coiffed into a rather large bouffant. You couldn't make it up. Of course it was *my* mum looking like she belonged in some bad soap opera from the nineties and not anybody else's.

'Oh, darrrr-ling, don't you look bee-u-tiful,' she said the moment she saw me. Seriously, the woman had no low volume setting. Her voice carried and the entire hall heard her greeting. Shame filled me every time she spoke, and I hated that about myself, but it was an involuntary reaction. 'Your outfit is divine!'

'Thanks, Mum. Happy Mother's Day,' I said, keeping my voice down, not wanting to draw any more attention towards us. Fuck, people already called me a charity case and constantly reminded me that I was there on scholarship. Then Mum came along and made it even more obvious that we were *not* in the same league as the others.

I was also right about her outfit. Mum was wearing a short denim miniskirt, cheap—and very fake—UGG boots and a tight vest top which, you guessed it, was zebra print. But not just a black and white zebra print, nope, it was black and silver glitter zebra print. I shuddered just looking at it. Blatantly a market stall purchase, or maybe it was from one of those shops that sold every item in one size at one price.

'So, what kinda spread they putting on today? I made sure not to eat breakfast, you know, to make the most of being here,' she told me in a conspiratorial manner.

Sometimes you just had to roll your eyes. Especially on those occasions where you were about to either laugh or cry. Really, I should be glad she hadn't shown up drunk. Small mercies and all that.

'Where's that ginger friend of yours?' she asked, her face focused on mine intently.

Ground. Swallow me.

'If you mean Clover, she's back in our room.'

'Shame, I really like her,' said Mum, nodding, clearly remembering the last time she was here. 'She was nice. Glad you've made friends, sweetie. It surprised Andy and me. We didn't think you'd make *any* friends, what with you being so boring and all.'

'Gee, Mum, thanks for that,' I said, thick with sarcasm, but I could tell by the look on her face it didn't register because she believed she was helping me by being honest.

'No problem, darling.' She patted me on the shoulder, nodding at me.

'Afternoon.' A deep voice joined us and before I could turn around, Ollie slung his arm around my shoulders and squeezed me close. I hadn't asked him what he planned to do today, but I thought maybe he'd be spending it with Griff. After all, neither of them was getting a visit today and as much as I grumbled about my mum, at least she could be here. 'Nice to see you again, Cora.'

'Oh, hello, Oliver,' Mum said. I swore she actually tittered at him. 'You are just as handsome as I remember. Still putting up with my moody daughter, I see.'

'Actually, we're in an official relationship now,' he said and smiled at Mum, and as far as I could tell, he wasn't judging her too hard—yet. 'Skylar doesn't act *too* moody with me.'

'Aren't you a lucky one then? I'll let you in on a little secret.' She leaned closer to him, almost putting her lips into his ear. 'Sky's always been difficult. Ever since she was a little girl. Used to write all kinds of things in her diary.'

If I thought shit was embarrassing before, it had nothing on that moment. Her loud arrival and god-awful outfit had clearly been the tip of the iceberg. She'd always had a thing for the Titanic, after all.

'Well, thanks for that, Mum.'

'Oliver should know just who he's dating.' She shrugged, looking around the room, people watching most likely. I loved to watch people too, but my mum was judging everyone. Laughable really, seeing as they were all definitely judging her more. Fuck, *I* was judging her, and we were related.

'I think he knows,' I said. Ollie and I smiled at one another, a stiff smile on his face, his upper lip almost a straight line.

'I'll let you and your mum enjoy the day and I'll see you later, baby.' Ollie gave me a brief kiss on the cheek and I couldn't decide whether I was glad he wouldn't see the shit show that was my mum or if I was mad that he wasn't saving me from being alone with her.

'I'll see you later. I'll text you when Mum goes.'

He nodded, gave my mum a kiss on the cheek too, and then left the two of us alone. The blush on Mum's face from the kiss almost made me laugh. She looked beside herself with joy. Who knew if it was because I had a nice boyfriend or that a handsome young boy had kissed her. I decided to not even ask.

'I honestly don't know how you pulled that one, Sky.' Mum raised her eyebrows, and her forehead wrinkled, and I knew she didn't know what Ollie saw in me. Whoever said mums were a confidence booster had obviously never met mine. 'He's gorgeous, and you're so drab and plain, honey.'

'Loving this time together, Mum,' I said, my tone dry. 'Let's go get a drink.'

'You know me, Skylar. No need to tell me twice!' she replied, chortling to herself.

There was a bar set up in the main hall again, and the dark-haired bartender visibly winced when he saw us heading in his direction. Nice to see that Cora had made a lasting impression.

'Two gin and lemonades,' Mum said. Using her knuckles, she rapped on the bar, as if that worked in place of a *please*. It didn't. Also, she was ordering both drinks for herself, without a care in the world as to how that looked to other people. Guess she was going to spend the day double parked.

'Diet Coke, please,' I said, beaming at the barman, trying to make my please cover both of our orders.

'Sure thing,' he replied smoothly, no longer wincing. The pitying look in his eyes was worse, and the expression on his face was almost enough to make me wish the ground would devour me whole and spit out my bones. *Fuck, it can keep my bones, too.* I already didn't want to be here with Mum today, but if she got drunk, the day would only decline further.

'Once you've got your drinks, we'll go outside? Think they've set up some stalls out there.' I gestured out the large windows, to where we could see people hovering out by some makeshift stalls. Maybe there'd be a raffle shelling off old body washes and the likes. Mum loved those.

'Ooooh, I would love to see what stalls a fancy-schmancy school like this deems acceptable for a day like today.' Mum got out her mobile and began to pay more attention to that than to me, probably messaging Andy. Back when I lived at home, I'd found her behaviour irritating, but now, I was kind of glad that her focus was off me for a while. 'What time is this Afternoon Tea, then?'

'In a couple of hours, so we've got time,' I said, the *unfortunately* implied but not uttered. No matter how hard things were between me and Mum over the years, I was still too scared to voice them out loud.

'So we can have a few more drinks here first. We're in no rush,' she said, her gaze fixed elsewhere, looking at the stained glass window, the sun shining through and turning the room into various hues of colours.

'The weather's good right now, though, Mum. Never know

when rain could strike. We're on top of the hill, remember?' Plus, I didn't want her to have more time to drink.

'A little rain won't hurt us. Well, it might hurt my hair a little,' she guffawed. Loud. Even the people far away on the other side of the room from us looked over with disgusted looks on their botoxed faces. Being honest, it surprised me that any of the mums here could show emotion at all. 'I spent quite some time back combing this beauty.'

Mum started smoothing her hair with her hands, looking too proud of herself. I swore the woman saw something different in the mirror than what everybody else saw.

Hang on. Was I being a snob all because I was wearing a dress more expensive than my mum's rent?

I thought about it for less than a second.

Nope, that had nothing to do with it. Guess I'd always looked down on her for some reason or another. Even when I was standing next to her wearing secondhand clothes, I still looked down on her.

'It looks great, Mum,' I said soothingly. Sometimes it was easier to placate somebody, rather than tell them the truth. 'Top looks good too.' I nearly choked on my lie.

'Do you like it? Leslie got it for me at the market the other weekend,' she said, twirling around with her arms wide, so I could appreciate it from every angle.

Nailed it.

'It's definitely something.'

Forty-One

THREE HOURS later and Mum was three sheets to the wind. I'd known it was going to happen, but I'd hoped it wouldn't anyway. We'd made it outside to look at the stalls, thankfully, and the sun was really shining, which was super rare for a Sunday in March.

'Skylar, darling, is that you?' Lottie Hawthorn seemingly appeared from nowhere and swept me into a big hug. Her Chanel perfume entered my nostrils, warm and deep, and it was exactly how I'd always imagined an older, rich lady would smell. 'You look wonderful!'

'Thank you, Lottie. You remember my mum, Cora?' I asked, sweeping my arm to indicate the woman standing next to me. Not that she needed it. Mum stood out like a sore thumb.

'Yes... Cora, hello.' With a grimace, she nodded daintily at Mum. 'How have you two been? Leo mentioned you had a great Christmas together. I was going to talk to you about it at the gala, but I got distracted.' Lottie swept her arm and motioned Leo over, who had been standing a little distance away.

Coming over to stand beside her, his blond hair glistened extra bright in the sunlight as it shined through the clouds. His blue eyes sparkled at me, like we shared a secret. Which we did. He texted me from time to time checking in, and I'd started to think of him as a friend.

'I'm good, thank you. Leo's telling the truth. Christmas was wonderful,' I replied to Lottie. I smiled at Leo, surprised they'd approached us, especially after seeing my mum wobbling while standing still. A skill mastered by the very best of the drinkers. 'How have you been?'

'I've been well, thank you. So happy I could come here today and see my baby boy.' She rubbed underneath Leo's chin and he blushed, a light pink colour entering his cheeks, looking embarrassed at the affection his mum was showing him. 'Just hoping I don't run into Winifred,' Lottie added in a conspiratorial tone. Seemed mums both rich and poor loved to share confidences—or for a better word, gossip.

Mum and I both looked at each other in confusion. Who the fuck was Winifred? Leo noticed the confusion on both our faces, and he clarified, 'Ms Hawthorn.'

'Ohhhhhh.' Mum and I both said at the same time. I'd honestly never wondered *what* Ms Hawthorn's first name was. Forgot she'd even have one, to be honest.

'How comes?' Mum asked, slurring the end of the sentence.

'Oh, Winifred thinks we should talk because she happens to be my sister-in-law. I've tried to make it clear over the years that just because we're related by law doesn't mean that we're friends,' she said, adding a light laugh at the end to soften the harshness of her words.

'Mum...' Leo said to her in a curt tone. 'You're just likeable. Course she wants to be your friend,' he added, clearly saving himself, because Lottie smiled warmly at him in return.

'Thanks, sweetheart. Would you two like to join us for

Afternoon Tea?' Lottie asked, the smile still embedded on her face.

Honestly, I wasn't sure whether we should agree. I thought that, if anything, Leo and Lottie would sit with Odette and her mother, but I realised I hadn't seen either of them. I hadn't seen Leo with Odette in the last week, actually.

'We would love to, wouldn't we, Sky?' Mum answered before I'd even fully formulated my thoughts, emphasising the word *love*.

'Of course,' I said through gritted teeth, not wanting to sound ungrateful but dreading it all nonetheless.

THINGS WERE GOING OKAY.

Well, as okay as they could with Mum ordering Irish coffees instead of going for the traditional English Breakfast tea. The catering staff had filled the platter in the centre of the table with mini sandwich triangles and mini cakes. I'd put a couple on my plate, not wanting to look greedy, but Mum didn't have that worry. She'd instantly piled her plate high, to the point where at least two-thirds of the platter sat on her plate alone.

'So, Skylar, what does your father do?' Lottie asked, attempting to restart the conversation.

'Mum, Skylar's dad isn't around,' Leo said in a hushed tone, giving her a narrowed glare, trying to prevent embarrassment for both me and his mum.

'Oh, I'm so sorry, Skylar, I didn't realise.' Lottie looked flustered, her cheeks the same shade of pink as Leo's had been earlier. I wanted to make it better but had no idea how to. Not like it was her fault. It was an innocent question.

'Don't apologise to her, love. Sky is better off without her father around,' Mum said after a beat. It was probably the most my mum had ever said on the subject of my *father*. She barely mentioned him to me, even when super drunk, and I'd never been able to get much out of anybody who may know more. Her words slowly became more slurred and incoherent. 'You see, Jacob Cooper was a total dick. But damn, he was a hot one.'

'C-cooper?' I only knew one Cooper, Griff, and I thought about how odd it was that my surname could have been the same as his. Instead, I got stuck with Crescent. Sixteen years old and it was the first time I'd ever heard the name of my sperm donor.

'Jacob Cooper?' Lottie and Leo asked simultaneously. Lottie's face was a mixture of confusion and shock. Leo's face was a mix of somebody trying to feign boredom and somebody acting hard to seem as if the news had shocked them, but I could tell it didn't shock him at all. His jaw tightened, the muscles in his cheeks flexing, like he'd known already.

'I said that, didn't I?' Mum asked, laughing at their expressions. 'He was from around here. You know him?'

'Yeah. Or at least I used to know somebody by that name.' Lottie looked like she didn't want to say much more than that. 'Way back when.'

'What a coinky-dink. Well, I've not heard anything from him since Sky was born. He split not long after he found out about her,' Mum said, hitching her thumb in my direction. This was what she'd always told me when I'd asked growing up, so at least that hadn't been a lie.

'Maybe it's for the best, Cora, that you haven't heard from

him,' Lottie said, her tone darker than I'd ever heard it. Her words sounded ominous and the closed off look on Lottie's face also made me think there was a whole lot more to the story.

'Oh, I know, Lottie darling, I definitely have found the best in Andy. He's my knight in shining armour,' said Mum, winking at Lottie as she did so. Almost as if the two of them were best friends and in one another's confidence.

And yep. My mum classed the man who kissed me without consent as her knight in shining armour. *Lucky me.*

'He sounds charming,' Leo piped up, trying to take the heat off the subject of my dad. 'Andy seemed like a great guy when you were both here for Parents' Day.' Honestly, if I didn't know Leo, I would have believed his act to be genuine. His eyes were wide with interest and a smile was playing around his mouth. The boy could charm anybody—and I mean anybody. But was he the charmer or the snake?

Mum smiled at Leo's appraisal of Andy, and I could see the cogs forming a sentence. Who knew what would come out of Mum's mouth next.

'Skylar. Why are you with Ollie when you know this perfect specimen?'

Jesus. Could my mum go a day without saying something super cringeworthy? Just one day. Was that too much to ask?

'Mum,' I snapped.

'Ollie's pretty great too, Cora,' Leo said, coming to my rescue by listing a couple of Ollie's great attributes. He finished by saying, 'He really cares about Sky.'

'That's good, of course. But you would also be great for her,' said Mum, the slurring slipping into every other word, and I knew I needed to get Mum out of there before she said anything more.

'Come on, Mum. Andy's probably wanting you to come home soon,' I said, wrapping an arm around her shoulder. I was actually surprised she'd stayed as long as she had without mentioning going home to him. It was super rare that the two of them spent time apart—especially a whole day apart.

'True, darling. It's been so nice to see you two. Lottie, we must do this again.'

I chuckled in my head, slightly confused why my mum was treating it like Lottie herself had invited her here. I nodded along, sure if I agreed with her, then she'd leave quicker. Here's to hoping, anyway.

'I'm sure our paths will cross again.' Lottie smiled, no teeth this time, and nodded at my mum. 'Come on, Leo, let's give these two some space to say goodbye. Can't wait to see you soon, Skylar.'

'Good to see you, Cora. I'll text you, Sky,' Leo said, nodding at me in a secret message of sorts that I didn't understand. I raised an eyebrow at Leo, but he glanced away, ignoring my attempt at eye contact.

We all waved at one another and they left the table. I watched them go, wishing I could talk to Lottie or Leo some more about Jacob Cooper. The thought of my dad had never overly fascinated me—I'd never wanted to learn anything about him, for that matter. Clearly, he ran in classier circles than my mum and I could admit that having a name made me slightly more interested.

I walked Mum outside, and we waited for the car to pull up. I felt more than happy to stand and wait in silence, but apparently she had other ideas.

'Sky, Jacob Cooper is a wanker. You should be glad that I never told you more about him.'

'How did you meet him?' I asked, curious, wondering how much she'd say.

'I was staying at a hotel that had a gala that evening. Bumped into this penguin suit wearing man who had gorgeous blue eyes and black shiny hair.'

'Sounds romantic.'

'It was something,' Mum grumbled under her breath.

The car pulled up and Mum went to get inside. She gave me a brief hug, something she always did, but I'd never hugged her back. Not because it was Mum, but because I didn't like to hug *anybody*.

'See you soon, Mum,' I said, hoping it wouldn't be too soon.

Hey, I'm done with Mum. Where shall I meet you?

I texted Ollie the moment I saw the car meandering down the hill. I was hoping Ollie just wanted to have a chill night in with some pizza or something. I really wasn't feeling up to talking loads or doing much. While staring at my phone, a text came through from Leo that made me smile wider than I had all day.

Thanks for today, Stutter. Somehow, I enjoyed it. We can talk about Jacob Cooper soon. Alone.

I hoped he'd stick to his word and tell me more about him, but Leo and I were never alone. One thing I felt certain about was that the news of my father hadn't surprised him one bit.

Meaning Leo probably knew a lot more than I'd given him credit for.

Fuck.

Forty-Two

CLOVER'S eighteenth birthday came around pretty fast after Mother's Day, and I was super excited for her to see the present I'd arranged for her. It was hard to get her something with no access to money. Ollie had offered to let me use his card, but I didn't want him to think I was with him because he was rich. I'd heard the way the girls at school spoke about the boys as if they were their meal ticket to a better life and it made me sick. I wasn't going to be one of those girls, especially as I didn't come from wealth. I'd look like even more of a gold digger than the one they'd already accused me of being.

It had pained me to do, but I'd messaged my mum, asking her to send me my nan's recipe book. When my nan was alive, she'd loved to bake and had always enlisted me to help her. I'd never really fallen in love with it the way she'd hoped, but she had passed down her recipes to me when she died. I obviously wasn't going to give Clo the original copies as they were in Nan's handwriting and the only thing of hers I owned, but I was going to give her a scrapbook with copies of them in.

I'd also included pictures of us from the gala, Christmas, and some random fun selfies we'd taken while trying out silly filters. I really hoped she'd like it as I'd been working on it in Ollie's room in secret and it had taken me quite a few hours to put together. It had taken so long because I had made sure, multiple times, I'd copied every recipe and ingredient exactly how my nan had written it. Clo was family to me now, and I wanted to pass on my family's food to her.

We were spending her birthday as just the four of us. Griff had ordered Clo's favourite food, and we were going to watch her favourite films. It was a Thursday night, so our options were pretty limited and we'd all agreed that a gathering in the woods was not the way to go, even if she was hitting a huge milestone.

After classes had ended, I'd rushed back up to our room, trying to get there before her. I wanted to put up some banners and balloons and decorate a bit. I'd never had the chance to do something so grand for somebody before, and I was so excited to see her reaction. Bitch better appreciate all the effort I'd put into making the day a great one for her.

The evening went perfectly, and the four of us had a good time. Ollie even managed to keep his dislike of Clover on the down low, which I was happy about.

Clover had loved her present, and I was so glad I'd thought of it.

'*Sky, this must have taken you forever!*' she gushed, a wide, beaming smile on her face. '*Thank you so much. I'll cherish this shit, I swear.*'

The guys left around ten, and the moment they did, I jumped into action.

'Right, I'm going for a shower.'

'Ite, babes. Try not to use too much hot water!'

'You're the birthday girl, so you can totally shower first if you want,' I told her, feeling generous today. I hated showers really, so I always needed to psych myself up for them, but I'd let her go first if she wanted to.

'It's cool, just don't take too long.'

It took me ten minutes tops, but when I re-entered our room, Clover was looking at me with a narrowed gaze and her mouth was pursed together into a point.

'Something you want to tell me?' she asked, venom in her voice.

'S-sorry, what?' I asked, confused. I had no idea what could have upset her in such a short timeframe.

'You left your phone out here,' Clo said, her voice so quiet, I had to strain to hear her.

'Right...?'

I usually did when I showered. With a bathroom the size of a toothpick, I worried I'd get it wet and damage it beyond repair. I'd never had a nice phone before and didn't want to fuck it up; it had been a Christmas present from Ollie after all.

'You got a message.' She held my phone out to me.

I froze by my bed, towel still wrapped around me, and wondered what she was going to say next.

'Oh, thanks,' I said as I took my phone from her outreached arm. When I looked down, I saw that it was unlocked and it was opened to my message thread with Leo. Had Clo been going through my texts?

'Is this about my dad?' I asked, remembering the last text from Leo was one where he'd told me we'd talk about Jacob Cooper alone some time soon. 'Mum told me his name on Mother's Day and both Lottie and Leo seemed to recognise the name.'

'Huh?' Her lip curled up at the corner in a sneer. 'When were you with Lottie and Leo?'

Shit, I remembered why I'd "forgotten" to tell her. I hadn't wanted to explain spending time with the Hawthorns. Clover always tried to avoid them whenever we were in the same place.

'Oh, didn't I mention it?' I asked, hoping she'd take the bait, but all she did was look blankly at me, staring through my bullshit. 'They joined us for Afternoon Tea.'

'You definitely didn't mention it. Since when were you and Leo close enough to spend time together?' Clo's incredulous tone irritated me.

'My bad, I thought I did.' I shrugged it off. *God, I am such a liar.* 'Well, Lottie's always been nice to me, and she wanted to join us. Leo didn't exactly get a say.'

'So, your dad?' Clover gazed at me, trying to suss out why I'd failed to mention such big news. 'Who is he?'

'Somebody named Jacob Cooper. You heard of him?'

Clover shook her head. 'I don't think so. It sounds familiar, though.'

'Right? I thought that too, but then I realised it's probably just because Griff's surname is Cooper too.'

'That's probably it,' she said, but her gaze hadn't returned to normal. She was still pissed at me for something. 'But I wasn't going to ask you about your dad.'

'What's up, then?' I asked, glancing down at my phone and looking properly. There was a new message from Leo that I hadn't spotted. When she told me I'd got a message, she didn't say who it was from.

HOPE RED HAS A GOOD BIRTHDAY. HOW IS SHE? LET ME KNOW IF YOU NEED ME, STUTTER.

'Been spying on me for Leo, have you?' she asked, her tone scathing, and I wasn't sure how to respond. I hadn't been spying on her for Leo, but I'd answered questions he had about her. She'd never given me a good enough reason not to, and neither had he.

'It's not like that,' I told her.

'You sure? 'Cause that's exactly what it looks like.'

'Positive. He just checks in every now and again,' I said, not feeling comfortable enough to tell her any more than that. I wasn't exactly in the mood to be kind to her after she'd gone through my phone and broken my privacy. Knowing her, she'd argue it was because she cared about me.

'And you're so stupid, Sky, that you don't even see how shady that is.'

God, I was getting bored with her calling me stupid—or whatever name she'd decided on that day. It may be her birthday, but I wasn't going to let everything slide.

'Shady how? It's the complete opposite of shady.' I took a deep breath, trying to rein my temper in. 'If you know something the boys are hiding, then maybe you should tell me what *you've* been hiding? And don't bullshit me and say nothing!'

Clo's eyes began to fill with tears, and I could see the frustration leaking from her. I'd let her off from answering me so many times.

'It hurts me to talk about it all,' she said, her tone breathy and pained. 'I'm not ready.'

'Fine!' I huffed. 'But the boys have never hidden shit from me the way you have.'

'Oh, continue telling yourself that. The boys are up to something and if you don't want to believe me, then that's on you.' Clover shook her head at me, the sad look on her face sliding away as rage took its place. 'Did you even ask Ollie about what I overheard?'

'I—'

'Actually, don't answer that,' she said. 'Because whatever he said was bullshit. You know what? There's nothing I can do to help you anymore. You're intent on ignoring me and I honestly can't be fucked with it.'

'With it? Or with *me*?' I asked, knowing what she really meant.

'Any of it, Sky. I'm done. I hope they do fuck with you at the fashion show. You deserve it,' she spat spitefully.

With that, she stomped into the bathroom, leaving me standing there in my towel, wet and cold, holding back tears. Unlike the last time she spat shit at me, I knew there wasn't a simple way for us to get back to how we were. She'd pushed me too far. It was different from her snapping at me about being a whore, which was something that still smarted but easy to forgive. Somebody snooping through my phone and severing my trust was different and a lot more serious.

For fuck's sake. Once again, the boys had come between us, causing a chasm that felt too wide for either of us to breach.

Though, I never thought it would be Leo who would cause our rift.

Forty-Three

THE NIGHT of the fashion show arrived, and you could cut the tension with a blunt knife. Everybody had been on edge, but not for the same reasons.

Clover, although barely talking to me, was still adamant that shit was going down tonight. Even though she'd said only a few sentences to me, they'd all had to do with Ollie and what she'd overheard Odette, Oralie, and Ophelia whispering about. I wasn't sure at this point who would be more surprised if shit didn't go down; her or me.

Griff had also been acting distant with me ever since Clo's birthday, choosing once again to side with her. I couldn't find it in me to argue with him, but the entire situation made me sad. I thought we were stronger than that.

Ollie acted on edge, mostly due to the fact that he was worried I actually believed Clover. I'd told him so many times I trusted him and that if what Clover overheard had any truth to it, then he should let me know before it went too far. Not sometime later down the line when I'd found out the truth, but he was adamant that wasn't going to happen.

'Clover's just jealous and bitter, babe,' he said every time I brought it up. And as much as it pained me to say it—or think it—I could see his point. She had been acting a little jealous, but I also needed to weigh up our friendship. We were best friends. Why would she lie? And what would she gain by lying?

Somehow, Ollie had got out of modelling in the show, even though when I thought back on Clo telling me we were going to model, she never explicitly said Ollie would be too. He and Oralie were arranging the music and backgrounds, and I wished I were working alongside him. Instead, I would model six different looks, with five people who weren't my biggest fans: Griff, Clo, Ophelia, Leo, and Odette. It was a crazy world seeing as Leo was the one I felt closest to in that mix. Showed how quickly things could turn to shit in friendships.

An hour until show time and I was in the makeshift dressing room they had given me that was really just one of the French classrooms with a slight makeover. Ollie and I were looking at what they expected me to wear, confused expressions stamped on our features as we flicked through the hangers on the rack.

'You're gonna look great, babe,' he said, giving my arm a quick squeeze to reassure me.

'Thanks for trying to spark my confidence, baby, but I really don't feel like I will. Odette was in charge of who wore what, so I've definitely been given the worst looks out of the six of us. Honestly, the sleepwear makes me look like I'm ready for sleeping... On the streets.'

Odette had not been playing around when she chose my clothes. Even Clover looked a million pounds in her six outfits, and then there was me, wearing clothes from a high street brand while they were all wearing couture. I'd stayed quiet about it, though, because really, it could be a LOT worse. If the clothes were a part of the "messing with me" Clo spoke about, then I could deal. Bad clothes wouldn't be the end of the world.

'Maybe so, but I know you're going to be the hottest one on that stage.' He kissed my cheek softly, then promptly went back to looking at his phone. 'I would.'

A cheeky smile overtook his face, and it made me feel warm inside. We hadn't said it to one another yet or anything like that, but I knew I was in love with him and I hoped he felt the same way, but I hadn't been brave enough to voice it, just in case he didn't. How fucking embarrassing would that be?

'Well, maybe not after you've seen me in the sportswear outfit,' I joked, but part of me wasn't joking. He very well may see me in a different way after he saw the camel toe the leggings gave me. 'What time do you need to head backstage?'

'Guess I should head there now.' He stood, gave me a long kiss on the lips, and gathered his things together. 'Good luck, babe. You'll do great.'

'Th-thanks. Now get out of here before we get distracted.' That kiss had made me want more, made me want his lips to press firmly into mine while his hands roamed south, and mine raked through his dark hair, but it was *not* the time for that to happen.

'I wouldn't mind watching you change into the first outfit,' he said, raising his eyebrows up and down at me in a way that burst the lust bubble. It just didn't do it for me. I laughed and shoved his shoulder in a playful push.

'Get out of here. You'll meet me here as soon as the show is over, yeah?'

'Of course,' he said, then gave me one last lingering kiss before leaving me there alone.

There were six rounds of outfits: swimwear, sleepwear, office wear, sportswear, and formal wear. The one I was most looking forward to was formal wear. A, because my dress was beautiful, and it was the one piece of clothing that didn't look cheap. I think they'd been donated to the school by wealthy benefactors, so Odette hadn't been able to sabotage me. And B, it would mean that the show was over and I'd survived.

I changed into the swimwear and felt sad that I didn't have Clover by my side to get ready with and laugh with to get rid of the nerves. We could have joked about all of it together, united. It annoyed me she was still using Leo's text against me. It wasn't as if I'd asked him to send it, and honestly, the message from Leo wasn't even that exciting. All he'd done was ask how Red's birthday was and if she was okay, which was hardly something to burn him at the stake for.

I felt lonely getting ready, though, especially without Ollie around. Before I started at Hawthorn, feeling lonely was something I was used to, even to an extent something I *enjoyed,* but since the start of the school year I'd stopped feeling alone. I hated that I was back in a space mentally where I was reverting to my old frame of mind.

I just need to get through this show, and then everything will be okay again.

NOBODY HAD EVER MENTIONED to me just how nerve-racking modelling clothes could be. Not that I knew anybody who would have been able to tell me about it, but still, every time I went out on stage, I was close to bricking it. It took everything in me not to trip and fall flat in front of the crowd. One thing that was good was how nice the crowd was—and supportive.

Everywhere I looked while on stage, all I saw were kind

eyes staring back at me. There had to be at least five hundred people here, a mix of students and parents, all watching us closely, and it sent my nerves into overdrive.

I'd never felt so scrutinised. It must be how a bug under a microscope felt.

I'd made it through the first five parts of the show with no major mishaps. I'd stayed upright, worn all the clothes the way Odette had told me to, and I hadn't vomited or passed out, so I was counting the night as a win. I'd been the third in the line-up for every look, so at least I wasn't last, and by the time I got to the end of the catwalk, there was somebody else coming down it to steal the attention. My final dress of the show was the most intricate, and it took me some time to get into it and style my hair.

It was a beautiful, yellow satin two-piece. The top was in the Bardot style and was flattering for my cleavage as it had a sweetheart neckline, and because the sleeves were off the shoulders—my signature look—I didn't look as wide as I normally did. The skirt was a flattering A-line skirt with pockets, reaching the floor, and the whole look made me feel like a princess. It reminded me of a modern-day version of Belle's ball gown.

Somehow, I put my hair up in a low, loose chignon, and when I looked in the mirror, I was surprised at the sight of me. The entire look was perfect. I wished Ollie were here to see me, but I knew he'd get a kick out of taking it off me once the show was done.

One of the other students working the show popped their head into the classroom and said, 'Skylar, you're up.'

'Let's get this shit over with,' I said to myself as I followed the guy to the stage. Just one more turn of the catwalk and I was free—not just of the fashion show but of school. It was Easter break and the majority of kids were heading home. Griff had hinted about going to his parents' estate again, but that was before my tiff with him and Clo, so I wasn't sure if the invitation still stood.

The moment I walked up the steps, the air felt different. I couldn't put my finger on what had changed in the brief time it took me to change, but something clearly had.

I looked up to find Odette coming down the steps from the catwalk, and instantly I knew shit was off. The plan had been for Odette to finish the show; to be the last one down the catwalk like she had with every other look.

'Don't trip, New Girl,' she whispered in my ear as she passed, her cool arm brushing up against mine.

Music pumped through the speakers, and I heard my cue. I had no time to change course before a hand on my lower back pushed me up the steps towards the stage.

I tried to keep my head facing forward. Tried not to look at all the heads in the crowd and think about all the eyes glued to me.

I got to the end of the catwalk, and that was when shit changed.

The music cut out abruptly, leaving me standing there not knowing what to do next. A voiceover began to play, and Odette's nasally voice filled the auditorium, reminiscent of the Parents' Day video.

Fuck. Maybe I should have listened to Clover.

I turned to the back of the stage, as a video started to play on the projector screen they'd set up to show background images during the show.

'Hello, everyone,' the voice said, addressing the room. 'I

hope you've been enjoying our fashion show this evening and plan to give money to our charity. I know you've all got deep pockets, and the school appreciates your generosity.'

I went to walk back towards the steps, but the voice stopped me.

'Stay right there, Skylar. I think you'll find this next part more interesting.'

That doesn't sound good.

'I'm here to tell you tonight about *our* favourite charity case. Miss Skylar Crescent. Skylar is a scholarship student here at Hawthorn Academy and has had quite the eventful year. I'm sure you all remember Parents' Day.' She laughed, and I saw some heads nodding in the distance, the bright lights stopping me from seeing too much, but I could still see enough to feel the kind eyes turning to judgemental ones. 'Let's have a look at some of her other highlights from the year, shall we?'

The video began to show a reel of everything that had happened to me over the course of the year. Me getting covered in blue raspberry slush in the corridor; me being tripped up and pushed around. Rotting food falling from my locker, how I'd looked after being found beaten in the toilets, and Griff ushering me into the school after finding me at the picnic.

They had literally recorded every single thing that had happened to me and were playing it for everybody to see. And all I could do was stand there and watch it unfold in silence.

'As you can see, Skylar has had a hard time this year. Even her best friends have turned against her.'

The scene changed to footage taken from inside mine and Clover's bedroom. *What the fuck?* How long had there been a camera in there? And who had put it there? My mind instantly went to thinking about what else that camera could have seen, but then the images on the screen once again stole my focus.

The footage playing was of Clover and Griff sitting next to one another on Clo's bed. The date stamped the video as the day she'd called me a whore, so it must be what happened after Griff followed her.

Their heads got closer, the two of them as close as they could be. Then, watching through a dream-like haze, I saw the moment Griff and Clover kissed on the screen.

Betrayal trickled down my body, starting at my head and reaching my fingertips and toes. An ice queen forming, frozen to the spot.

At no point had either of them told me about this. Fuck, they'd never even hinted at it! They'd carried on like nothing much had happened in the time we weren't on talking terms.

I looked around and caught Leo's eye. He was standing by the screen, his expression blank, but I could tell he was unimpressed. The question was whether he was unimpressed with me, or because of the kiss?

'Forgive me,' Odette tittered, sounding unapologetic. 'Let me formally introduce the poor, pathetic case of a human still standing at the end of the stage. Everybody, this here is the daughter of Jacob Cooper, who I believe those amongst this circle knew well.'

Instantaneously, the crowd gasped.

A secret had been outed, and I had no idea why it was such shocking news. I knew that Lottie and Leo had recognised the name, but Leo never had got around to talking to me about it. I'd forgotten to ask him after what had happened with Clover.

The images still flickered on the screen, footage still rolling of every kiss Ollie and I had shared since the start of it all. All the times they'd picked on or harassed me.

The night I'd lost my virginity played next, and although grainy and difficult to decipher, I knew exactly what was being shown on the screen. How dare they? How fucking dare they take that away from me, too?

The only footage that wasn't shown was from the night somebody had tried to drown me. If they had, then we'd know exactly who it was, and I knew the girls didn't want that to become public knowledge if they had something to do with it.

I shivered, the hairs on my arms standing on end. I needed to leave. I couldn't stand here any longer listening to such shit.

'Poor breeding.' Odette's voice filled the room again, and I promised myself there and then, I would make her suffer. I'd been a doormat for too long. I had to stand up for myself and come next term, I was going to become her worst nightmare.

I rushed to the back of the stage, to where the screen was showing footage of my mum and Andy from Parents' Day necking back drinks and acting like the pissheads everybody had already guessed they were.

Shame filled me.

Everybody here knew everything.

Even something I didn't know.

Why did it even fucking matter who my dad was?

Catching Griff's sad and confused look as I climbed down from the stage, I wondered what he was thinking. I could tell he wanted to say something to me, but really, what could he say that would make everything all okay? I felt humiliated once again. *Is everything in my life a lie?*

I should have seen shit coming. Should have listened to Clover when she told me the girls had something planned. But then I remembered how Clo had been lying to me for weeks, too.

I wanted to cry, but I didn't want them to see me crumble. I didn't want to give them the satisfaction of breaking in front of them all. *Fucking rich kids.*

They were all as bad as each other.
So I did the next best thing.
I ran.

Forty-Four

I RAN from the auditorium as fast as I could. I wanted to put as much space between me and those people. I felt cheap. Dirty. Like the charity case they'd constantly told me I was. I kept tripping on the dress I was wearing, the length too long for a quick getaway. Fuck me, no wonder Cinderella lost her shitty glass slipper during her escape.

Heavy footsteps came from behind me, getting closer with every second. For every two steps I took, I swore they were only taking one, which meant they were going to reach me soon. I couldn't let that happen.

I left the main building and ran to the pool house. I definitely wouldn't have headed there if I wasn't in fight-or-flight mode. Not after some unknown person had attempted to drown me there after the Halloween party. But I needed to be alone, and that building was the one place I thought nobody would find me.

After entering the building, I ran up the stairs and made my way to the connecting corridor that led to the hospital wing. I stopped. I heard angry voices coming from that direction, and they were getting louder. I pivoted on the spot and made my way back down the stairs.

I entered the pool room itself and nearly jumped out of my skin when I came face to face with Ollie.

He was standing at the other end of the pool, staring at me silently. His face hard in anger in a way I'd only seen once or twice.

'Hey. I'm sorry I ran away. I just c-couldn't stay there,' I stuttered my way through my sentence, embarrassed I was finding it hard to talk to him. Which was ridiculous? It was Ollie. The guy I'd lost my virginity to and had had all those meaningful moments and conversations with. Although, when I looked up, it didn't feel as if the same Ollie stood in front of me.

All I wanted was to run to him and fall into his arms, but I stopped myself.

'You deserved what they did.' His tone was ice-cold. I shook my head, his words not making any sense to me. 'You've deserved all of it.'

'S-sorry?'

Where was the Ollie I'd woken up next to that morning? The one who had made Easter break plans with me and kissed me like he would never get enough of me?

'Sky, did you really believe any of this year was real?' he scoffed. 'Every single thing that *The Set* has done to you has been on my command. I asked them to do whatever they could to turn the entire student body against you.'

'But I d-don't understand...' I trailed off. None of it added up. I was so sure that Clover must have misheard everything, that she had just heard the girls' conversation out of context. Ollie had even promised me that he wasn't a part of their plan.

I felt so stupid. I had fallen out with my best friend over Ollie and it turned out that I should have believed her all along. I'd acted like every idiotic heroine I hated.

'That's because you're too stupid to understand anything, Skylar. The fact that you couldn't see the truth right in front of your eyes tells me as much.' Ollie seemed to be enjoying this. I could tell by the smirk on his face. 'The amount of times we've all been laughing at you behind your back and you never even knew.'

Don't cry. I repeated the mantra in my head, knowing if he saw my tears, something would snap between us. Something I wasn't sure we could ever come back from. Maybe I was stupid like he said because nothing made sense. Had I really just been that blind to the truth?

Clover had tried to warn me. Even Griff had made some cryptic comments that I hadn't looked into enough. Things had been going so well with Ollie that I hadn't wanted to rock the boat. Make a nuisance of myself. The only one who had said fuck all was Leo. Nice to know he never meant any of those texts.

I knew things had taken a turn for the worse when I looked into Ollie's eyes and could see the true depth of his hate.

His eyes, normally a startling bright blue, were now a dark indigo filled with anger and loathing. I could see the exact moment the mist descended.

I shivered.

I wasn't sure what else to do, and I didn't know where I could run to.

Trapped.

The worst part was the fact I'd been blind to my situation and had walked willingly to my fate. I was the reason I was there. There was nobody else to blame. I hated myself for it, maybe even more than I hated him at that moment.

I couldn't help but ask, 'W-why are you doing this?'

I had to know. I was certain something must have

happened in the last few hours to have caused the change in him. No part of me could accept that it had been coming for longer... the alternative was just too much to think about.

'You don't belong here, Sky.' He smirked at me. 'You never did.'

I crumbled. I could feel the tears pricking my eyes, and I was trying my hardest to stop them from falling.

I should have known better. I should have never fallen for the beast, and I most definitely should have never thought of myself as the beauty in my tale.

I flew out of the room. I couldn't stand to see that look in Ollie's eyes a moment longer. The one that made me feel an inch tall. That made me feel like the charity scholarship case. Since September, he'd been adamant that he didn't see me that way. More fool me.

I ran around the corner and made my way quickly up the staircase, heading towards the corridor to the hospital wing. Fuck the voices I'd heard.

I made my way along the corridor and turned a corner to head further into the building. It was then that I saw a shadowy, tall figure standing ahead of me in the dark hallway. None of the lights were on as the school was meant to be empty for the holidays. Everybody was over in the auditorium dealing with the fallout from the fashion show. I paused. I needed a moment to try to quiet my breathing—to make myself invisible.

That was when I saw it.

The body lying on the floor at the feet of the figure. I couldn't make out who it was from here, but it definitely looked like a girl. A girl wearing a dress similar to the one Odette had worn as she'd brushed past me.

I tiptoed closer.

The figure still hadn't seen me, too focused on the limp body at their feet to notice me creeping up on them. A body that wasn't moving or making any sound. They were still. My mind tried not to connect the dots as to what a still body meant.

The closer I got, I just knew that the body—the girl—*was* Odette. The dress she had been so smug about earlier torn and covered in dirt. Her face was trapped in a scared expression, her mouth slightly open and her eyes wide—stuck forever-more. Blood covered her stomach, a knife handle visible sticking out in the centre. Bile rose up my throat as I tried to get my breathing under control.

I tried to take a step back, but I somehow caught my footing on the bottom of my skirt, and I gasped at the twist of my ankle. I tried to keep my balance so I wouldn't find myself sprawled at the stranger's feet.

It was the gasp that did it.

The figure turned.

I glimpsed their face, their hair, their eyes—I couldn't breathe. *What the?*

None of what I saw made sense.

It was as if my mind couldn't compute what my eyes were seeing. My vision blurred around the edges and I fought the blackout I knew was coming; the black spots in my vision were already forming, closing in on me. My breathing shallowed, my heart beating so slow, yet so loud, I thought that the person in front of me could hear it as loud as I could.

The figure approached. I tried to turn again, but my legs had turned to jelly, my ankle giving out beneath me. I couldn't move, no matter how much I wanted to. The moonlight coming through the windows caught the glint of a knife.

A knife that was heading in my direction.
A knife getting closer with each step of the figure.
Then pain.
Nothing but pain.
Then nothing at all.

Epilogue

I SMILED as I watched her walk away. Well, more like she ran away.

My plan couldn't have gone better. I'd achieved what I had set out to do.

To ruin her.

To make her feel worthless.

I knew I'd touched a nerve, and I felt pure happiness shoot through me at the thought of her leaving this place and crumbling. I'd wanted to wait until the end of the school year, but things had snowballed of late. The situation started to run away from me and I knew I had to act.

Who knew girls could be such bitches when given free rein?

I didn't feel any guilt, but I knew when to say when. If I'd let it continue, she would have ended up dead. And I didn't want that—not yet, anyway.

I hoped she would never return to Hawthorn Academy. She didn't deserve to be here. With Easter coming up, we had time away from this cursed place and I was hoping she'd make the right decision. The *only* decision. To leave. And never look back.

If she showed her face again, I would make her regret it. It would make the first half of the year feel like a holiday.

After all, things can always get worse.

To be continued in *Disease*

Skylar's time at Hawthorn Academy has only just begun!

Want more hawthorn academy while you wait?

Head to my website
www.katielowrieauthor.com/disorderbonusmaterial
for some extra goodies!
Including Valentine's Day from Ollie's POV.

Acknowledgements

When I decided I wanted to re-write this book, I was in a particularly hard place.

Life wasn't going great and I needed a distraction.

This list is a lot shorter than the original acknowledgements that accompanied this book, and I've found that as you write more, people you know in person care less.

I'm glad these people and my readers are the opposite.

Thank you Bills for always supporting me, no matter what decision I make.

Els, as always, I appreciate you and everything you bring to my life.

Fi, Jess, Jess, and Tay, ily.

Lou, thanks for being the best beta and loving this story!

Thank you to the readers! Skylar's journey is far from over.

About Katie Lowrie

Katie Lowrie is a twenty something year old Brit who loves to read and write.

A list in no particular order of her greatest loves:
- Henry VIII and the Tudor era
- Her baby cat, Cress
- Musicals
- Disney
- Cheese

She loves to stalk people online (in a good way) and understands if you do too.

instagram.com/katielowrieauthor
goodreads.com/katielowrieauthor
facebook.com/katielowrieauthor
bookbub.com/authors/katie-lowrie

Also by Katie Lowrie

Hawthorn Academy Series:

Disorder

Disease (2023)

Disturbed (2023)

Rebels of Hollowdale High:

Haven at Hollowdale High

Hero of Hollowdale High

Heirs of Hollowdale High (November 2022)

Hated at Hollowdale High (2023)

Re-Imagined Series:

Key of Cunning (**Dark** Billionaire Romance)

The Sleep Eternal (**Dark** Mafia Romance) *(2023)*

Under the pen name K. Lowrie:

Model (mis)Behaviour

Acting Out *(October 2022)*